The
Forest
Beyond the
Earth

A post-apocalyptic novel
By Matthew S. Cox

Matthew S. Cox

The Forest Beyond the Earth

Table of Contents

Yellowgreens 4

Off With Their Heads 12

Thunderbird 18

Shooting 32

The Mother Shrine 38

Monster in the Woods 43

Quiet Time 48

FN-FAL 61

Breaking the Rule 67

Spirit's Whisper 73

No Haven's Guard 78

Trail's End 83

Little Thief 88

The Forest Comes Alive 99

Expedition 106

TV Dinner 112

The Ancients' World 121

Escape 129

The Boy 136

Supplies 143

Zen 147

Work 154

City of Ghosts 162

The Many Havens 178

The Purpose of Bars 197

Negotiations 201

Black Magic 207
High Ground 211
War 223
Abandoned 237
Buggy 242
Forest Wisp 252
A Home of Silence 258
The Tree Walkers 265
Mirror 268
Head Sickness 273
Mother 280
Epilogue: A New Haven 284
Acknowledgements 288
About the Author 289
Links 289
Other books by Matthew S. Cox 290

Yellowgreens
~1~

Sheltered among the great moss-dappled trunks, Wisp peered out from her hiding place at the forest of monsters, barely breathing, lest the Tree Walkers hear her.

She glanced back over her shoulder at Dad, twenty feet away and closer to the cabin. Distracted by fiddling with his rifle, he hadn't noticed her wander off toward the little yellow flowers. Being so far away from him tightened a knot in her belly, but she pushed fear aside. Hunger had far more of a hold on her, and besides... the sun filtered down through the pines, strong and warm. Tree Walkers didn't come out in the day.

Or so she hoped.

Wisp eased her toes into the soil, on guard for sharp rocks, stinging insects, or other dangers. The leather scraps of her skirt brushed at her legs with each tentative step. Dad recently made it to replace the same tattered dress she'd worn for the past two years. The frayed garment had grown so tight the fabric was ready to come apart if she breathed in too deep. He'd also given her a shirt he'd found on one of his scavenging trips, but she'd been less thrilled it with due to its bright pink color. It made her stand out. Not to mention, it had been torn so short it left her stomach bare. This outfit wouldn't do well in the colder months, though Dad seldom let her out of the cabin then anyway, so perhaps it wouldn't matter. While he didn't *make* the pink mess, he did fix it for her. The former T-shirt had belonged to a grownup, but he'd added a crisscross of leather cord at the neck to cinch it tighter.

Despite the horrid color of her shirt, at least she could move around and not worry about destroying her clothing.

She squatted low to the ground, her thighs peeking out from two slits in the front of her skirt. A flap of thicker leather hung down between her legs, almost touching the soil as she brushed her hand back and forth looking for signs of edible insects or plants. Straight blonde hair fell around her, also nearly in contact with the ground. Close to home, they'd harvested everything of value already. To find food, they would have to venture deeper into the woods and risk the Tree Walkers finding them.

The thought brought a shiver.

"Wisp?" called Dad, worry in his voice. "Where are you going?"

Suppressing a gasp of fear, she twisted around to peer back at him. Before she could say a word, a distant *snap* echoed behind her in the woods. She crouched even lower and whirled back to stare in that direction, fingers and toes digging into the dirt, ready to run like hell for the cabin door.

Dad jogged up behind her. "What are you doing so far off? You know you're not supposed to wander away from me like that."

She lifted one hand to point at the distant forest floor full of tiny yellow flowers. "I found yellowgreens."

"You shouldn't scare me like that." He took a knee and placed his arm around her back, the rifle in his right hand still pointed at the forest. "You forget the Tree Walkers."

Wisp continued to watch where the noise came from. "But it's day now. They cannot move when the sun is on them."

"We have not yet seen them do so, but you shouldn't believe something true simply because you have not witnessed it. Our not seeing them in the daylight doesn't prove they fear the sun—only that we have never seen them."

"I'm sorry." She leaned against him, hands clutched at her chin, shivering at the fear the Tree Walkers might've got her for breaking one of the rules: stay close to Dad, always.

He squeezed her and kissed the top of her head. "Shh. It's all right. Much better for you to make a big mistake and tell me about it than make a small one and keep silent. Mistakes will happen and that's okay. It's only bad to hide them."

Wisp fought back the sniffles while nodding.

"Come, now." He brushed a finger at her cheek to catch a fleeing tear. "You're getting a little big to cry at the mere *thought* of Tree Walkers anymore."

"But they're going to take me… I don't want to be taken." She shivered.

Dad tickled at the base of her ribs. "You won't be. I will protect you."

Trembling became squirming and giggling. He grinned at her. Wisp shifted from squatting to kneeling, and plucked bits of leaves and a few roasted grasshopper parts from his beard. He made a childish face and fussed at her hair, though she couldn't tell if he did it to be silly or found anything to clean away. His shirt, the same dark-blue one he'd always worn, had developed a new hole. Hairs poking out matched the black atop his head, including some of the silver. Wisp made a sour face and slipped a hand up under her shirt, offering a silent prayer to Mother that something would go wrong with her body so she'd never have so much hair on her chest when she became a grownup. It looked *so* itchy.

"Hmm. I think you're right." Dad glanced around once his amusement at her laughter subsided. "We've picked the woods clean around here."

She stood back to her full height and crept forward, placing her feet around rocks and roots. Small low-lying branches sprang back as she passed, clattering against the metal armor over Dad's shins. The reinforcement he'd stitched onto his jeans didn't match from leg to leg. She liked the colors on his left side more: white-and-green metal with mountains and the word 'Colorado' below bigger letters: 5B8 – BRK. An ugly shade of yellow adorned the plate on his other leg. Red paint had worn off the bigger numbers, but still made the words 'New Mexico USA' harsh on her eyes. Every time she looked at it, the lettering seemed to float off the metal and wobble.

Another *snap* came from the left, too far away to see anything, but Wisp knew better. The Tree Walkers could make themselves look no different from the underbrush, creeping closer and closer invisibly—until an explosion of roots and vines rose up and took her.

Again, she froze and fell into a squat.

Dad raised his rifle to his shoulder, peering through its scope in that direction. "Don't see anything. Probably a badger or maybe a boar piglet."

The patch of yellow puffs caught her attention. She pointed at a swath of dandelions growing around a large area of greenery with tiny white flower clusters, before darting over and raking her fingers at the ground, digging.

"Yellowgreens!" she cheered, stomach growling.

"Do you remember this one?" Dad trapped the flower cluster of a different nearby plant between two fingers and pulled it toward her.

She nodded. "Yes. That's pennycress."

"Can we eat it?"

"Yep." She grinned. "There's so much. We shouldn't harvest it all or it'll go bad before we can finish it."

After gathering a mess of dandelions and pennycress, she clutched dinner to her chest and followed Dad back to the cabin. Upon seeing home, a surge of relief and excitement came over her. Every trip into the woods brought with it the worry of Tree Walkers finding her, but she didn't fear them so much when she had her Haven nearby. Today, she'd walked almost a hundred steps away from the cabin, a frightening first—but also exciting.

Dad had built this cabin many years ago, before she could remember. The right third, unlike the rest, consisted of a rounded, metal box he called a 'trailer.' The outer wall even had a broken wheel on it, almost as if it could've gone rolling around. That part contained Dad's room, though another one of his rules forbid her from going inside. The rest of the cabin he had built from wooden boards and panels of scrap metal, attaching it to the trailer as best he could.

Wisp waited by the entrance while he fiddled with the opener that made the lock work. When he pulled the door aside and held it for her, she ducked under his arm into the cabin's main room, which took up most of the interior space. A purplish-pink blanket covered her Haven, which stood in the left far corner, next to the shelves full of her books. On the left side, a door led to the shrine where Mother remained ever vigilant, protecting them both. Opposite that, three narrow metal stairs hung below Dad's door, left of his worktable and the machine that put bullets together. A table with two chairs sat next to the front wall to the right of the entryway, and a cinderblock fireplace waited for her at the middle of the rear wall straight ahead.

She hurried over to the collection of plates and pans, unloading her harvest on a rectangular table with six-inch legs. From her tenth birthday, she'd taken over most of the cooking. Having prepared their meals for about two years, she set to the task with confidence. Usually, she sat on the floor to work, so Dad had made a short-legged table for her.

He eased himself into a rotting cushioned chair by his worktable. The ancient relic only had two functional wheels of five, and creaked every time it moved. He checked over his rifle while Wisp scooted over to kneel in front of the fireplace, arranging kindling before grabbing a dark stick he referred to as a 'ferro rod.' He'd once called it something much longer, but she didn't remember. Whenever she struck it against a rock (or better yet, a file), a rain of hot sparks fell from the end. With a little puffing and waving, she coaxed embers into flames. She sat back on her heels and nursed the fire until it built enough to add a larger log.

Dad arranged the disassembled pieces of his rifle on the worktable before standing to reach at the shelf above it, rummaging past his canisters of magic fire dust to grab the one full of cleaning supplies. He insisted on oiling and wiping down the rifle every two days, even though he hadn't fired it in a while. She glanced at the door to his room while prodding the kindling with a metal poker. In there, he had 'dangerous' stuff she'd been warned never to go near. Yet she feared it wouldn't be able to keep the Tree Walkers away for good. Wisp feared them more than anything, since they also frightened Dad.

After washing the soil off the greens, she tossed a couple of oyster mushrooms from a storage bin onto the cutting board. The enormous knife she used to cut them had been made for people to kill each other with—Dad found it long before she was born—but anything could be washed. As best she could tell, it hadn't been stuck into a person for at least as long as she'd been alive, maybe never. The same knife kept Dad's hair from going past his shoulders and his beard from getting too long. She used it on her own hair whenever she started sitting on it by accident, but she liked letting it stay long. Mother had quite long hair, and Dad always told her how much he loved it, so Wisp wanted to be like her.

One by one, she sliced the mushrooms into bite-sized hunks and dropped them in a shallow bowl-shaped pan before using the knife to scrape some congealed boar fat from an old coffee can. She tapped the knife on the pan edge until the blot of grease fell in. Soon, the room filled with the fragrance of pork. Every so often, Dad would go off for a day or two on a hunting trip and bring back a boar. Whenever that happened, they'd have a few days of good food. Sometimes, he'd find a deer and they'd eat well for a week.

Dreaming of the wonderful, tasty meat while chopping the washed yellowgreens and pennycress, she smiled. It bothered her a little having to stay home in her Haven while he went off to hunt, but she loved the meals his trips provided. And, she could at least pass the time reading. Sometimes, she could even hear the distant *bang* when he got the kill.

Handful by handful, she added the greens to the already-cooking mushrooms until the pan looked in danger of overflowing. The first time he'd shown her how to cook, she'd been certain they would make too much food, but greens shrank in the pan. Thinking of meat made her add another oyster mushroom. They'd soak up the flavor of the grease and she could easily pretend she ate ham.

Ooh!

An idea hit her.

She scrambled to the pantry shelf and opened a jar of beetles, some of which remained alive. A handful went into the pan to add a little more nutrition, and she spent the next few minutes corralling them with the knife so they didn't climb away. Dad fiddled with the bullet machine, grumbling. He sounded more annoyed than angry, so she didn't worry much.

Eventually, the last of the live beetles went still and stopped attempting to escape the heat. Grease sizzled and spat, causing her to scoot back an inch or two. Her new shirt didn't protect her belly from flying drops of ouch like the old dress did. Not that she disliked what he'd given her—after all, Dad did give it to her—but, she missed the simplicity of a dress. One piece, easy to slip in and out of, and it kept grease spatter from burning her a little more. The new skirt hung more heavily around her hips than the dress—a strange feeling to get used to. Undoing its two belts annoyed her enough to where she usually didn't even bother taking it off when she had to let the bad water out. Still, she wished Dad would find her a new dress. Something light and *not* pink. The Tree Walkers would see her easily among the woods in her current shirt—unless she found a growth of amaranth to hide in or something.

"Where did you find these clothes?" asked Wisp.

"I made it," said Dad.

"I mean the pink stuff. You made the heavy part." She pinched the fabric of the shirt and tugged it at him. "This is from before."

He chuckled. "You're right. We can find things here and there, but none of it is close to home, and most of it is in bad shape."

"Can I go next time?" She glanced left at her Haven, covered in the bright blanket. She could hide in it and no one would know she existed.

"Well… it's dangerous out there, Wisp."

"It's so dangerous. How are there still people?" She pushed food around the pan with the knife, barely containing her drool at the nicely browned beetles. *Almost done.*

He swiveled on his chair to face her, hands on his knees. The leather armor he wore over his shirt resembled her skirt's heavier pieces, suggesting he'd likely made it from leftovers. Unlike her skirt, years of fangs, thorns, and knives had left his vest scuffed and scratched. "Things weren't always like this. When my grandparents were children, the world had been different."

She grasped the pan's stubby wooden handle, thrusting it forward in sharp jabs to make the contents jump up the edge and fall back inward, stirring it about without needing to use the knife. "Big places with lots and lots of people all together."

"You're right. But, one day, there got to be too many people for the planet to tolerate. The people could not be nice to each other and fought over everything. This made the great Fire Dragons angry; so angry they burned the people to ashes."

She'd heard this story already, but she liked listening to Dad's voice. Whenever she read a book, she'd hear him speaking it in her head. Wisp said the same thing she usually did around this point, though no longer with the quivering voice of a terrified six-year-old. "I'm scared of the Fire Dragons. What if they come back?"

Dad smiled, sensing she played along rather than needed to hear it. "The Fire Dragons were foolish. *People* made them, so by destroying most of the people and all of the ancient magic, they destroyed themselves. Now, there are no more Fire Dragons."

"Angry is bad." She pulled the pan off the fire and used the knife to section the greenish-brown result onto a pair of plastic plates in two equal portions.

"Yes." Dad took his plate, plus a spoon from the shelf. "Especially in the world we've made for ourselves. I mean people, not you and me. Getting angry will make you do dumb things, and can kill you. Think." He tapped the spoon to his head. "Plan." He stuck the spoon into the food. "Act." He ate.

Wisp giggled, almost spitting her half-chewed mouthful of beetle-and-greens. She'd gotten it just about perfect. The bugs came out crunchy on the outside and tender within. Dad had once compared them to 'shrimp,' but she had no idea what he meant. At least one of her books had a character eating shrimp, but didn't much describe what it tasted like. Of course, all of the stories came from before the Fire Dragons burned everything. She didn't think the world still had anyone who made books. Some of them told tales of long, long ago, of made-up worlds that sounded quite a bit like the one she knew, only with different magic. At least, she'd never seen anyone throw fire out of their hand before.

After they ate, she rinsed off the plates and pan, then set everything back on the shelf. With the weather warm for summer, she let the fire die out and curled up on Dad's lap after he relocated to his big chair in the corner. He opened his enormous book of plants, with plenty of pictures, and continued teaching her about them.

Soon after the sun went down, a pronounced *crack* of wood came from the forest nearby.

She froze, staring at the dark window near the fireplace, her muscles tensing. *Tree Walkers are coming!*

"Time to sleep," said Dad in a stern, worried tone.

With a brief nod, Wisp leapt off his lap and rushed across the room. She pulled the blanket up to expose the bars of her Haven before crawling inside onto the soft red padding he called sleep bags. Terrified the Tree Walkers would burst into the room at any second, she pivoted around and pulled the door closed with a *clank,* then scooted back to the innermost corner, curling into a ball.

They can't get me in here. They can't get me in here.

Dad took the Haven's opener from under a can on a high shelf to the right of the fireplace. He walked over, crouched to one knee, and made the door so the Tree Walkers couldn't get to her. At the *click* of the lock, she stopped trembling and managed a weak smile. Dad reached in past the bars and patted her on the cheek.

"It's all right, Wisp. You're safe. I love you, baby. And so does your mother."

She cradled his hand against her cheek with both of hers, smiling. "I love you too, Dad."

"Sleep now."

Wisp nodded and curled up on her side atop the plush softness beneath her. Dad smiled lovingly for a moment before tugging the blanket back down over the bars so nothing bad could see her.

Confident that nothing could hurt her, she closed her eyes.

Off With Their Heads
~2~

Wisp awoke in a pink-purple haze, the dim light of early morning seeping through the blanket. It took a moment for her head to clear and a strong sense of discomfort to register. She grunted and squirmed. The bad water wanted *out*.

"Dad?"

A moment of silence passed. Wisp pushed herself up to sit and grasped the bars of her Haven's door. The coarse metal rods, as thick as Dad's thumbs, had a crisscross pattern of raised lines and were, for the most part, straight. She pushed and pulled at the door, rattling it. Nothing short of the opener could break the protection keeping the Tree Walkers from taking her.

"Dad?" called Wisp, louder. "I gotta let out bad water."

After a short while of listening to silence, she groaned from the building pressure in her bladder and grabbed herself to stop it from coming out on its own. With her other hand, she tugged the blanket up and tucked it overhead so she could see out into the cabin. The door to

Dad's room remained closed, but he always kept it closed, so that didn't mean much. She peered left and up at the high shelf where the opener hid beneath a dented coffee can all the way on the other side of the cabin past the fireplace.

Wisp stuck her arm out between the bars, reaching for the can, trying to do that magic she read about in one book where the character could make objects fly into his hand. Despite her strongest concentration, the can didn't move.

"Ugh." She grumbled and shook the Haven's door harder. "Dad!"

Again, she glared at the can way up high. Would he be upset with her if she left the Haven when he wasn't around? That had always been his number-one rule for her safety. Only the Haven could protect her from the Tree Walkers if he wasn't there for her. Of course, she had no way to get to the opener, and no way to get herself out of the Haven, so thinking about breaking that rule only wasted time.

She peered up at the bars overhead, faintly remembering a time when she could stand up inside. Now, even sitting, she didn't have a lot of room between her and the overhead bars. The Haven had been getting progressively smaller. It had more room from side to side on the long end, but she still wound up with her feet sticking out past the bars if she tried to lay flat. Of course, she never did. The Tree Walkers could attack anything outside the Haven, and she did *not* want to wake up without feet. Whenever Dad slept (or went off hunting), the Walkers could come right into the cabin without fear.

Her need to release the bad water crashed headfirst into the fear of getting in trouble/being taken. She cringed, biting her lip and whining out her nose. *I'm gonna mess the floor.* If she did that, the bad water would soak into the soft padding between her and the bottom bars, and then her Haven would stink forever. She whined, determined to hold it.

"Ngh!" shouted Dad, sounding somewhat distant—no doubt in the outhouse. He let out a few more loud grunts and groans.

Wisp grinned to herself, amused by how Dad almost always said 'ngh' when he made *ngh*. Her amusement faded fast, and she unconsciously pulled and pushed at the door, protesting the lock. For a brief moment, she hated being confined to the Haven, but as soon as she thought that, she recoiled in guilt. Dad had built the Haven from his need to protect her and stop the Tree Walkers from taking her away in the night—his love made into a physical object. The magic he put in it kept her safe.

Eyes closed, she held back the bad water with every ounce of willpower and both hands, rocking gently from side to side to distract herself.

The clatter of the outhouse door opening got her bouncing with anticipation. Soft crunching footsteps went around the outside of the cabin, past Dad's room, to the front. She peered at the entrance, still bouncing, and let out a squeak of happiness when he pulled it open and walked in.

"Dad! Need to let out the bad water."

He gave her a quick apologetic look before hurrying to the shelf and plucking the opener from beneath the can. As soon as he unlocked the Haven, she pushed the door open, crawled out, and scrambled upright. Dad followed her close behind all the way around the house to the little shack of cinder blocks not far away. It gave off such an awful smell, she briefly considered waiting for the air to clear, but couldn't hold it any more.

Wisp groaned at the foulness. "You made a big *ngh*. It stinks!"

She turned her head—not that it helped—and took a huge breath before climbing inside. Dad eased the outhouse door closed and stood guard outside. Wisp pulled her skirt out of the way and sat on the ancient plastic ring.

The horror in the air blurred her eyes, but she still wound up laughing to herself at him for shouting *ngh*. He didn't yell 'bad water' when he did that. She didn't usually say '*ngh*' when she had to do it, however, sometimes (after too many seeds and berries) she did. Usually, she tried to stay as quiet as possible so the Tree Walkers didn't hear her. Dad once told her that if they heard a child's voice, they'd swarm like flies to a pile of *ngh*. Better to be quiet than taken.

Exactly what they'd do to her if they took her away, she had no idea. Dad never mentioned it, but he didn't have to. Watching him cry said more than any words could convey.

Once she finished letting all the bad water out, she stood and did a little shimmy to get the skirt to fall back where it belonged. Dad stepped forward when the door bumped him in the back, smiled at her, and proceeded to walk off toward the cabin.

Wisp strolled along at his side, staring down at the ground out of habit. Ever since she stepped on a wasp at seven, she always watched where she put her feet. She'd asked Dad about making her boots or sandals or something, but he'd never quite gotten around to it. In the cold weather, he didn't let her go outside at all, so her attempt to argue about warmth hadn't gotten her anywhere. The lush padding along the bottom of the Haven plus a blanket kept her plenty warm enough.

She eyed his hand, swinging back and forth beside her. "Dad? Why don't you hold my hand anymore when we go to the outhouse?"

"Well… when you were small, the Tree Walkers could've flown by and grabbed you before I had a chance to do anything to protect you. Now, you're a little too big for them to carry off so fast." He smiled, then reached over to clasp her hand in a gentle, but firm grip. "But if you want me to."

Wisp grinned, and flung herself into a brief, but tight hug.

He kept holding her hand as they walked around the cabin. Once inside, Dad headed over to the worktable and unfurled some old maps to study. Wisp rummaged the pantry bins, selecting some root tubers to slice up for breakfast, along with a jar of grasshoppers she'd caught a day or so ago. She entertained a brief craving for earthworm, missing the chewiness, but that would have to wait until the next time it rained and she could gather enough to be worth cooking.

After pouring the grasshoppers out into a wooden bowl, she picked one up and twisted its head off, gently pulling until a strand of entrails emerged from the body, dangling like a booger from the removed head. She tossed the guts into the fireplace, de-winged the grasshopper, and dropped the body/legs in the cooking pan.

One by one, she plucked the heads from the grasshoppers, gingerly tugging until the snotty bits came out. It made her think of something she'd read, and when she popped the sixth grasshopper, she said, "Off with his head!"

"What's that?" asked Dad.

"It's from a book." She plucked another one. "Off with his head!" After tossing the body into the pan and the severed head into the fire, she smiled at Dad. "There's this queen, and she's all angry and stuff and keeps saying that."

Dad pointed a little light-maker at her. "Well, don't get angry at breakfast."

"I'm not." She laughed, twisted the head off another grasshopper, and muttered, "I'm late. I'm late. A very important date."

He chuckled and resumed studying the maps.

Awhile later, she finished beheading a small army of grasshoppers and wiped off her hands. The shelf of jars that held the taste powders made her frown. Most of the bottles, especially the reddish-brown one she loved, had almost run out. Still, no point having them without using any, so she dusted the grasshoppers with a pinch or five of the good stuff.

"Dad. We're almost run out of taste powder."

"Yeah. That stuff is hard to find. Most of it's from the old world, before the Fire Dragons. I'm amazed it still even works."

She stirred yellowgreens into the grasshopper mix, and added a tiny bit of boar grease. That, too, ran low. "We need another boar, too. Maybe I can go with you this time?"

"Maybe."

Wisp grinned to herself, too shocked at his not saying 'no' right away to come up with a reply. A *snap* came from the fireplace along with a flaming grasshopper head sailing out onto the floor. She leapt up and stomped on it before the dry floorboards lit fire. At a small jab of pain, she fell seated again, and pulled her foot up to examine her sole. A tiny black dot marked her skin, but it wiped off—ash, not a burn.

When the food smelled done, she portioned it out to plates and carried one over to Dad, leaning up alongside him to look at the big white paper with red and blue lines going all over the place.

"Thank you, sweetie." He kissed her on top of the head and took the plate she offered.

"Where are you going?"

"I'm looking for a likely spot to scavenge. Maybe somewhere I haven't gone before."

She shoveled two grasshoppers and a slice of tuber into her mouth at once, nodding.

Dad leaned to the side, looking her up and down. "Well, Wisp, you're twelve now, close as I can figure. Maybe it *is* time to start giving you a taste of the 'out there.' Would you rather wait in your Haven, or come with?"

"Umm." She ground her toes into the floor, casting an uneasy look back at her safe place where nothing could hurt her.

Whenever Dad went hunting or scavenging, he'd always insist she stay in it. Sometimes, he'd be gone all day. Other times, she'd spend two or three days in a row safe inside the bars. If not for the bookshelf, she'd hate being alone and bored for so long. Finally getting the chance to see the forest more than a one-minute walk away set off an explosion of excitement inside her. Fear dampened it somewhat, as the Haven still beckoned her into its loving embrace, but she whipped her head back to grin at him.

"I wanna go. If it's okay."

Dad set the plate down on the map and put his hands on her shoulders, staring her in the eye. "You will need to listen and do whatever I say, without question or hesitation."

"Yes, Dad." She nodded. "I will."

"And stay close. Don't go rushing off."

She shook her head. "I won't... go running off."

He smiled. "All right. Let's finish eating first, huh?"

Wisp hopped up to sit on the workbench, swinging her feet back and forth while shoveling food past her giant grin.

ThUnderbird

~3~

W isp stood in the middle of the cabin, arms slightly raised to either side as Dad walked around her rubbing his chin. She lifted and lowered her toes, twisting her head to watch him. He stopped, tapped his foot for a moment, then disappeared into his room, the metal door banging shut behind him.

When he returned, he took a knee in front of her and held a slab of leather up to her right thigh, the top about touching the hem of her skirt. He fidgeted at it for a few seconds before smiling. Wisp waited while he tinkered at the worktable for a little while, then carried the leather thing back over, now with a bunch of thin black strands hanging from it. Again, he pressed it to her thigh.

"Hold it."

She put a hand on it, examining a narrow pouch on the outside.

"These will clip in place. It's probably going to feel strange at first, but you'll get used to it. They need to be tight enough to hold it on, but not so tight your leg feels funny."

"Okay."

Dad pulled the thin nylon straps around her leg and clipped plastic parts together with a sharp, but quiet *snap*. He repeated it for the lower set, but neither one had any real grip on her leg. It took him a bit of fiddling with another section where the straps twisted around metal clips, but he snugged both loops smaller and smaller until they squeezed into her skin. He tried to get his fingertip under one, couldn't do it, then loosened it a little bit.

"Does that hurt?"

"No."

"Let go, see if it stays there."

She removed her hand, and the leather object remained stuck to her leg. Dad nodded, crossed the room to the shelf long enough to retrieve a knife similar to the cooking-and-hair-cutting one, but somewhat smaller. He slipped it into the leather sheath and closed a small loop over the handle to keep it in place.

"Jump up and down a bit. Try to make it fall."

Wisp examined the knife hanging on her leg, unable to figure out if she liked or disliked the sensation of having something tied to her thigh. Eventually, she decided she had no opinion either way. She bounced on her toes a few times, then jumped a couple inches off the ground and came down hard on her heels. The sheath slipped straight down her leg to the floor.

Dad chuckled and brushed a finger at a faint mark where the strap had been. "Well, I suppose that's good for now. It'll get a bit easier on you once you have some shape."

"Huh?" She peered up at him.

"You still have kid legs." He made a double-chopping motion in the air. "Like asparagus stalks. No shape."

She raspberried him.

"One moment." He grasped her leg behind the knee to lift her foot out of the knife sheath straps. A few minutes of tinkering at the worktable later, he carried it back over and clipped it around on her again. He'd added another strap that went up to loop around her skirt's belt. "There. Now I can even loosen the other ones."

She bounced and jumped, but the knife stayed put.

Dad grinned. "Perfect. An asparagus sheath."

She raspberried him again.

"Right. So. Knife." He tapped the handle. "That's in case something happens and you get in trouble, okay?"

Wisp nodded, pulling her hair out of her eyes. "I understand."

"Oh, one thing you *can* help out with…" He retrieved another nylon belt from a shelf with two green pouches on it. "Here."

She clipped it on and held it up while he adjusted it down to her size. Once it sat properly, he handed her a pair of plastic bottles, both the same drab green.

"Oh. Water!" She grinned and put the canteens in the holders on her belt. "We're going for a long trip?"

"Not too long, but we'll be walking most of the day. We should bring some water in case we can't find any."

Dad grabbed his rifle and led the way outside.

She followed beside him, a half-step back on the right, to the small stream a minute or so away from the cabin. There, they both drank before filling canteens. Wisp crouched shin deep in the chilly flow, keeping her attention to the south while holding the canteen under the water's surface.

Tree Walkers always came from the south.

Dad stood guard, eyes on the forest around them while she filled her second canteen, then the two on his belt. She replaced the canteens in his belt pouches, closed the Velcro flaps, and patted them twice. He took her hand and helped her step up out of the water.

That he headed north comforted her to some degree since it meant moving *away* from the Tree Walkers. However, those creatures could be anywhere and everywhere in the woods. At any moment, a patch of greenery could spring to life and come rushing at them, as it had done hundreds of times in her dreams. She pushed herself to walk faster, keeping close to him in case one of the monsters tried to grab her. Her attention to ground hazards suffered for it, but aside from an occasional uncomfortable pebble or hard root making her stumble, she didn't stick a foot into anything dangerous.

It had rained quite a bit the previous day, leaving the air thick with the fragrance of moss and wet wood. Trees surrounded them, some small, some huge, many dappled with patches of pale green lichen. The forest had become so thick she couldn't tell which way led home anymore. In every direction, greenery stretched off in a seemingly endless spread of life. She couldn't remember ever walking so deep into the woods that she couldn't turn around and see the cabin.

Dad said the forest took the Earth away from people after the Fire Dragons burned them all.

Nervousness made the flavor of grasshopper burble up into the back of her throat perhaps an hour into the journey. She'd never been so far away from the cabin, so at risk of being taken by the Tree Walkers. Of course, she also had not been twelve years old the last time Dad decided to go off on a trip, either. She simultaneously felt like a frightened child and a small adult proud of her increased freedom.

Dad walked with purpose but not hurry, his rifle angled sideways and downward to the left. She wanted him to hold her hand, but accepted he could not as it would get in his way if he needed to shoot a monster.

A few hours into the trip, he slowed to a stop, looked around, and let out a relieved exhale. "Gotta let out the bad water."

"Okay."

Dad took two steps to the left and stood with his back to her. She decided to take advantage of the pause as well and squatted, pulling her skirt out of the way. Soon, they resumed the trek, sipping from canteens while walking.

"Where are we going?" asked Wisp.

"There used to be a small settlement a ways north of us. Scavengers have probably been and gone already, but I'm hoping they didn't take everything. There's gotta be something of use left there."

"What's a settlement?"

He let go of the rifle long enough to pat her on the head. "It's a place where people used to build houses all close together. Must've been a defense tactic. I guess even the ancients had tribes. People banded together for protection. Much easier to defend themselves when they put their cabins all together."

"Oh, like a city?" Wisp peered up at him. "There's cities in some of the books. I think 'towns' are like the same thing, but smaller. I wonder what it's like to have so many people around. I think it's kinda scary."

"People change, sweetie. Before the dragons came, they weren't quite as mean to each other as they are now. Back then, you didn't have to worry so much that any person you ran into would try to hurt you and take all your stuff... or take you."

"Take *me*?" She blinked. "Like the Tree Walkers?"

"Not exactly. You remember me telling you about marauders?"

She nodded. "Bad people, but not monsters like the Tree Walkers."

"Right. They roam in packs, and sometimes they steal people, too."

"What for?"

"They force them to work. Sometimes they make them fight each other as a sport. A few of their groups even use people for meat."

She gagged. "Yuck! Well, no one's going to take *me* for meat."

"Nope. You're way too skinny. They'd throw you back and keep fishing."

Wisp poked him in the side and raspberried him. "Am not! I don't taste good."

"Did you taste yourself?" He glanced back at her.

"No. I just don't want to taste good. I'll smear red berry all over me so I look like the firepillars. Red means don't eat."

"Right. Maybe that'll work." He winked at her.

The ground pitched into a hill, at one point growing so steep she had to grab handfuls of dirt to make the climb. Vines with thousands of tiny prickling thorns scraped at her legs. Dad waited at the top, staring at something in the distance. She pulled herself up enough to see over the ridge, her nose even with ground level, and gaped in awe at a huge metal object covered in runner vines and plants. It had the overall shape of a tube, much bigger than the cabin, and many times longer. Squarish panels resembling windows ran down the length over an angled flat section on the side that had gouged into the ground. The huge beast had a tall, vertical fin opposite a pointy end with more windows. All sorts of junk littered the ground in the area.

"What is that?" she whispered.

"A thunderbird," said Dad. "A machine from long ago."

"Like your bullet maker?" She pulled herself past the ridge and stood.

Dad crept toward the wreck. "Only in that they are both machines. This one is far more complicated. I don't even begin to understand how it worked."

"Complicated. It's difficult?" She tiptoed after him.

"I mean it's got a *lot* of parts. It's beyond me to understand how something like this could work. I think they used to fly."

"Wow… but it looks so heavy." She pointed at the angled part on the side. "Is that a wing? How did it flap?"

He shrugged. "Magic that has been lost to us. All I know is they used to carry people over great distances, high in the clouds where the Tree Walkers couldn't reach them."

Wisp stepped around a tangled mess of metal and placed one foot on the wing above where it dug into the earth. The dull-grey metal warmed the bottom of her foot, but not painfully so. She leaned her weight forward, arms waving to the sides, and walked up to the long, tubular body.

"Be careful," said Dad.

She squatted beside the curved wall and put her face over the window, shielding her eyes with both hands. Two small fog spots from her nostrils appeared on the plastic. Inside, a few of the seats held desiccated remains, mostly skeletons wearing tattered bits of clothing in styles she'd never imagined. The skeleton nearest her had a dark shirt over his ribs with the word Nike on it.

"It's a shrine! They've all gone to the Other Place," called Wisp, before lowering her voice. "I'm sorry for disturbing you. I'll go away now."

She crawled on all fours down the wing and leapt to the ground. "What's nikkey?"

"What?" asked Dad.

"A man by the hole had it on his shirt. N-i-k-e. Nikkey."

"No idea. Could be his name. Some of the marauders do that... write their names on their chest armor."

She grinned, peering down at her chest where the faded image of a cartoonish bunny rabbit skull stared off into space. "Like my shirt, but it's not words."

"I think that was meant to be cute."

Wisp took a few steps to the side before plunking herself down on a square cushion that resembled the bottom part of a chair. Fortunately, it turned out to be soft. "What's cute?"

He glanced over at her and cracked up. "You."

Her eyebrows shifted together. "What?"

Dad stepped toward her. "Well, it means something or someone that, when you look at them, you feel happy enough to want to..." He scooped her up into a hug. "Squeeze them."

Wisp squealed with laughter.

He spun her around once before setting her down. "Hmm. You know, there might be something useful in here if we can find a way in."

"Isn't it a shrine?"

"No. Those people went to the Other Place from right here. A shrine is something made to show how much you love someone, even after they go there."

, "Oh."

They circled around the other side, where more of the underbelly showed. There, the entire side of the thunderbird had been charred black. Most of the trees nearby had either died or had huge swaths of bare wood showing where the bark had disappeared. Plenty of underbrush covered the ground, but the soil beneath the growth showed a definite blackening compared to the rest of the forest. The windows on this side had melted to openings.

This wing jutted up into the sky, about twice as long as the one she'd climbed, but looked as though it should've been much longer. Twisted metal strips dangled from the end a short distance past where an enormous round pod full of blades hung. As soon as she gazed into it, an overwhelming fear that it would suck her in and shred her to little strips of bacon came out of nowhere. She grabbed onto Dad.

"What's wrong?"

"It's bad. It wants to hurt me."

"It doesn't *want* anything. It's a machine. Or… it *was* a machine. It's scrap metal now."

She glanced at the windows. "Are they watching us?"

"Could be," said Dad.

He kept walking around to the tail end, where a small ramp opened into a vast, empty space. If anything had been in there, someone had already taken everything.

"How did they all go to the Other Place at the same time?"

Dad took her hand and led her off into the woods, leaving the thunderbird behind. "It fell out of the sky and hit the ground so hard, they all went to the Other Place."

"Oh." She looked up at him. "Did a Fire Dragon kill the thunderbird?"

"It's possible, but I think if that happened it would be in much smaller pieces."

She giggled, but felt bad about it.

They walked on, continuing well past noon. With each passing hour, her constant dread of seeing Tree Walkers lessened. Traveling away from the south, plus having gotten so far from home without seeing one, reassured her. Of course, it could be that the daytime kept them sleeping. Worry of sunset got her squeezing his hand.

"What?" he asked.

"Are we going to be home before it gets dark?"

He brushed his thumb back and forth across her hand. "Yes. We're almost there."

"To the city?"

"I changed my mind. The city's farther off than I thought it would be, and I don't want to risk taking you on such a long trip. We're going to a place where I hid some stuff."

"Okay."

She resumed staring at the ground to avoid painful encounters with rocks, roots, or bugs. A mulch of dead leaves with the occasional tract of moss made the ground as soft as the bottom of her Haven. Wisp looked up at a sudden leftward tug from Dad.

"We're close."

Dad followed a light brown path of soft sand that resembled a stream with no water in it. A few minutes later, he veered to the right and headed up a shallow hill, atop which sat a strange mound of vegetation. It had the same brick-like shape as her Haven, but far larger—bigger even than the cabin. She gazed at the fluttery bits in various shades of green, never having seen any plants before even close to that.

"What kind of bush is that?"

"It's not real." He stopped by one of the narrow ends, stuck his fingers into the foliage, and pulled it aside like a curtain to reveal a metal door. "It's plastic."

She grasped a dull green strip. Slick and flimsy, it certainly did not have the texture of a leaf. "Plastic leaves? Why?"

"To hide this place from marauders."

"What is it?"

"Our stuff."

He pulled an opener out of his pocket, slid it into a hole, and turned it. The door gave way with a loud creaking groan of rusting hinges. Dad stepped over a metal flange, ducking to enter a door-shaped hatch. She scrunched up her nose at the strange chemical smell, but followed him in. Her foot came down on a smooth, cold surface. The bizarre sensation of walking on such a surface startled a gasp out of her.

She stared down at a floor that appeared made of stone, but perfectly flat. "Dad, what is this?" She patted her foot around, making a clapping noise.

"Concrete," said Dad.

Wisp squatted and ran her hand back and forth across the floor. "It's cold. Is it supposed to be cold? It stinks in here, but not as bad as when you make *ngh*. *Nothing* is that bad."

Dad's laughter echoed out of the dark.

"You're smelling rubber and a bit of ethanol."

She stood and took a few steps forward until the glow from Dad's light-maker washed over the face of a huge black monster with eyes almost as big as her face, and a tall, snarling mouth. Screaming, she leapt backwards and crashed against a metal wall, causing a resounding *boom*. The unexpected noise made her shriek again and spin around.

"What?" shouted Dad. He ran to her.

"Monster!" She pointed at the creature while hiding behind him.

He pivoted and pointed his light-maker at the horrible face. When he started to laugh, she went from petrified to furious.

"Sweetie, that's not a monster. It's a Jeep."

"A Jeep?" She narrowed her eyes. "Stop laughing at me."

"It's an old car. No gas. Doesn't work anymore. It's a machine like that thunderbird."

"It's so dark in here. I thought I saw a face. Stop laughing at me."

Snickering, Dad moved over to a set of shelves and picked among cardboard boxes.

"Is the Jeep yours?"

"Well, I suppose it is, but it's not useful anymore, except maybe to get out of the rain."

She edged around the evil face and stared in awe at a huge black ring covered in dust and nubs, as tall as her chest. Scratches, scuffs, and dents covered both sides of the old vehicle. Rusty metal plates dotted it as well, added to cover holes or perhaps as armor. Another matching ring jutted out from the back end of the Jeep. The machine appeared to have four of them, one at each corner, like feet. She climbed up to stand on a narrow ledge running along the side and peered in at comfortable-looking chairs. Both had dark stains on the beige fabric.

"Is that blood on the chairs inside?"

Clanks and clatters came from the shelves behind her. "Your mother and I were attacked before we got here. Yes. That's blood, but our wounds were not as bad as it looks."

She stepped down from the running board. Thinking that Mother had used this 'Jeep' thing made it feel like a shrine, too. "Is that why she went to the Other Place?"

Dad remained quiet for a few minutes. When he spoke, his voice nearly cracked with grief. "No... at least, I don't think so. We were here for years before she... had to go there."

Wisp padded up behind him and wrapped her arms around. "I miss Mother."

He froze, again silent for a moment. "I do, too."

"I'm glad she can watch and protect us."

Dad pressed his hand over hers, clasped at his chest. "She's always with us."

The somber mood lasted a while before he resumed digging among the boxes. She released her hold and hovered nearby, folding her arms as the cold of the place seeped into her bones.

"Why did you leave your things here but home is so far away?"

"Aha!" Dad grabbed a large white plastic jug and shook it, making a sound as though it contained sand. "Found it. Umm. Well, we stayed here at first, but it's just an old bunker. Even in the summer, it's cold inside, and it has no windows... Your mother wanted a nicer place to live. So we decided to leave our valuable things here and went off to find a better spot."

She glanced at the entrance, wondering how that big machine ever made it through a hole that small. "How'd you squeeze the Jeep in the door?"

Again, he laughed. "There's two doors. One's much bigger." He pointed around the 'wall,' explaining how it split open down the middle and swung open. "There's a little door inside the big doors."

Wisp wandered around the room, eyeing shelves of cardboard boxes, plastic jugs, and unidentifiable metal parts. "How did all this stuff fit in the Jeep?"

"Most of it didn't. A lot of this was here when we found the place. Found this here." He patted his rifle. "And the bullet machine." Dad held up the white jug. "And the magic fire dust."

She laughed.

He stuffed the jug in his backpack as well as a pair of plastic bags full of shiny metal bits. "Damn, last box of primers. I should probably start hunting with a bow or something. Save the bullets for emergencies."

"You can pick up an arrow and shoot it again." Wisp shook her head. "Can't do that with bullets."

He waved for her to come closer. "Come on. Time to go home. And you're right. But arrows also don't always kill the monsters in one shot."

Wisp hurried to the exit and climbed through the hole in the bigger door, brushing the camouflage netting out of her way. She ran a short distance away and jumped into a patch of sunlight to get feeling back in her toes.

Dad climbed out, giving her a startled/angry stare for a moment. Right as she expected him to yell for her getting too far away, he shook his head and muttered to himself. She stood still, feet together in the sunlight patch, and basked in the warmth. Once he had the door locked and the fake bush back in place to hide it, he hurried over.

"Sorry. I was cold. My toes went to the Other Place."

He patted her on the head and ran a hand down to her shoulder. "It's all right. We're far enough away from the Tree Walkers here, but don't make a habit of it."

Relief spread over her that he hadn't gotten angry. "Yes, Dad."

He hefted his rifle, spun in place while examining the forest, and decided on a direction. Wisp followed with a huge grin, thrilled to be going home again and overjoyed to have been allowed to be with him on one of his trips. Of course, walking so much made her legs tired, but the vastness of the Endless Forest kept her awestruck enough not to care.

Not long after the late-afternoon shadows began to creep across the ground, Dad pointed at a spread of greenery. "What are those?"

Wisp glided ahead of him, nearer to a plant with small trumpet-shaped pink flowers, a reddish stem, and thin green leaves. She sniffed at it, getting a mixture of pine and lemon. "Umm. Whack runt?"

Dad smiled. "You're almost right… did you mean wax currant?"

"Oops. Yeah."

"Can we eat it?"

"No, but the flowers will turn into berries in like a month or two, and we can eat those."

He grinned. "You *are* listening."

Wisp ran back to his side, proud of herself.

They walked among the woods for a little while more until Dad pointed at another shrub with leaves somewhat like pine needles.

"Juniper," said Wisp, barely looking at it. "Can't eat it and the berries are poison."

He ruffled her hair.

Moments later, he gestured at a bush with stark pale blue berries.

"Creeper Gone Grape. Can eat the berries, but they taste bad."

"Oregon grape," said Dad.

She repeated it.

Dad nudged her around to his left side and walked with an arm around her back, one handing his rifle. "Your mother would be proud of you."

"She *is* proud of me." Wisp looked up at him, confused.

He wiped at his eyes, smiling. "Yes. Of course. I meant she *is* proud of you."

Feeling proud of herself, she walked at his side, gazing around at the plants while reciting their names and identifying the ones they could eat.

Heavy crunching in the woods off to the left a few minutes later made her dart back around him. She crouched low and scampered up behind a tree, clinging to the trunk. Dad lowered himself to one knee, bringing the rifle up in that direction. Wisp held her breath to be as quiet as possible. Every wavering bush started to become a Tree Walker in her mind.

A smear of dark moved in the distance. She honed in on it with widening eyes. The trees hadn't started to come to life to grab her—a black bear wandered along, tracking right to left at an uncomfortable distance: not close enough to be terrifying, but not far enough to be reassuring.

Dad lowered his rifle and inched backward toward her.

"Food?" she whispered.

"No. We're too far from home. He's way too big for me to carry. We'd never get him to the cabin. I'm only going to shoot him if he comes after us."

She nodded.

While the bear meandered off to the left, they headed the other way, which worked out as they'd already been going in that direction. Not quite an hour later, Wisp's heart ceased pounding in her chest. The bear hadn't noticed them, and since it hadn't come bounding out of the weeds by now, it probably wouldn't.

Dad stopped and raised a hand.

She froze, listening. In seconds, the burble of running water became apparent. "Stream?"

A proud smile spread over his face. "Correct. Where?"

Wisp turned her head side to side in a slow sweep, considering how the sound changed. She pointed to the right and a little forward. "There."

"Good. Thirsty?"

"Yeah."

Wisp walked in the lead, Dad a step or two behind her. Thigh-high ferns and bushes slowed her down, but within a few minutes, she emerged onto bare dirt at the edge of a fast-moving stream littered with head-sized rocks. Though the water spanned wider than the length of the cabin, it didn't look too deep.

"Good for swimming?" asked Dad.

"No. The current is moving too fast. It's not too deep, but I'm small and the water would sweep me away."

He patted her on the back. "Very good. You can step in the edge a bit to drink, but don't go in deeper than your knees."

She squatted at the edge and scooped handfuls of water to her mouth. Dad did the same, but nudged her with an elbow before pointing at a flash of silver a little downstream.

"Fish." She grinned, stomach growling. "But your line's at home."

"There's more than one way to snag a fish." Dad winked, and headed back to the trees.

She followed, curious, watching as he picked among the woods until he located a long shaft about an inch around and a little longer than his height. He pulled out a knife and cut off a bent gnarl before slicing the knife back and forth across the end to make an X-shaped gouge. She sat cross-legged on the ground beside him, keenly interested as he continued to work the knife into the fallen branch. In a few minutes, he'd wedged the blade in deep enough to split the end into four separate tines, each of which he sharpened.

"Fish are tricky to hit underwater." Dad cut a nugget of wood off the gnarl, and wedged it in between the four pointy bits to spread them apart. "A four-pointed spear makes it much easier to hit them."

She nodded.

He took some twine from his pack and tied the nugget in place. Wisp trailed behind him on the way back to the stream. "It's important to be quiet, and patient. Fish have good hearing and they startle easily."

She sat on the bank, arms around her legs with her chin on her knees, observing Dad as he made his way out to stand on a big rock a few feet from shore. He crouched, the spear poised high. Minutes passed in exciting silence. Worried that the noises in her stomach would scare the fish away, she pressed her hands into her belly.

Eventually, Dad jammed the spear into the river and pulled back a flapping fish a little over a foot in length. Still on his rocky perch, he swiveled and extended the spear toward her. She leapt to her feet and wrapped her arms around the struggling fish, yanking it away from the pointy wood. He went back to scanning the river, presumably to catch another fish. Wisp spotted a flattish rock on the shore not too far away, and decided to use it as a table to scale and gut the fish with the knife she'd been carrying on her leg all day long.

She'd about finished with it by the time Dad walked over with his spear, another fish hanging dead on the end. Wisp took it without a word, and proceeded to clean it as well while he put together a fire. Once she had both fish skewered on thinner sticks and hung over the flames, she tossed the guts in the water for other fish to eat.

They reclined on the bank, enjoying a pleasant breeze and the warmth of an early-evening sun. Every so often, a fish leapt out of the water, oblivious to the fate of its brothers over the fire. Wisp spotted a bird and pointed.

"Hawk," said Dad. "Means good luck."

"I think Mother can see him, too."

Dad's smile faltered for a few seconds. He coughed and picked at his eye. "Yes, I'm sure she can, but you make her happy more than anything."

For as long as she could remember, Dad often told her about how Mother had wanted to have a daughter with all her heart, but sadly, she'd fallen ill soon after Wisp's arrival.

"She was so happy to have you." Dad sat up and wiped his eyes. "Even when she got sick, holding you made her smile."

Wisp frowned. "I don't remember her."

"Oh, you wouldn't. You were only a baby then. You, umm... weren't even walking yet when she went to the Other Place."

Her lip quivered. Sniffling, she scooted over to lean against him. "I hate that she had to go."

"I do too, sweetie." He rubbed a hand up and down her back. "More than I hate anything."

"More than you hate the Tree Walkers?"

He nodded. "I don't hate them. What I feel for them is fear and worry, because they would take you from me."

"Why?" She idly scratched at her foot, resting her cheek on her knee.

"Because they do." He turned the fish over. "Monsters don't really have a 'why.' They just do things because they're monsters."

"Oh." She wiped away the tears shed for Mother, and frowned. "Well, I hate them. For making you scared."

They sat in silence for a little while before he took the fish off the fire and offered her one. "Hungry?"

"Ooh!" She grabbed it, blowing on the crispy browned skin to cool it enough to bite. She loved fish as she loved deer and boar meat, since a bite could fill her mouth. Not like insects, which she had to eat three or four at once. "Yes!"

As happy as she'd ever been, Wisp reclined in the grass beside Dad, ankles crossed, and feasted upon her fish-on-a-stick.

Shooting

~4~

Upon noticing the daylight weakening, Dad sprang to his feet and kicked dirt over the smoldering remains of the fire. He scarfed down his fish far faster than Wisp could manage, grabbed the spear, and set off at a brisk stride without waiting for her to finish eating. She hurried after him, munching while walking. The sun's rapid retreat behind the hills in the west made it clear they'd never reach the cabin before night set in. She hovered close behind Dad, gazing at the shadows deepening between the trees with each passing minute. Worry twisted the pleasant fullness in her belly into sick.

Dad didn't show any outward signs of alarm, so she allowed herself to remain more or less calm. The woods around her gave off a general sense of familiarity, which meant they couldn't be too far away from home. Not being in the Haven at night—or at least inside the cabin—frightened her more than the grizzly.

For minutes, she crept along behind Dad, the soft squish of his boots upon the ground seeming loud enough to beg the Tree Walkers to come after them. Wisp startled at the occasional twig cracking under his feet or soft *thump* of a moving animal, whipping her head back and forth in search of anything moving.

Moonlight painted the landscape in a deep blue shade. The woods more than fifty yards in any direction had become a dense murk of nothingness. Wherever leaves fluttered in the moonlight, she cringed away, from the lurking Tree Walkers she expected. Wisp clung to Dad's arm with both hands, her pale fingers all but glowing against his deep brown tan.

"It's all right," said Dad in a near whisper. "We don't have far to go."

She nodded. It hit her that acting like a little kid might cause him to leave her in the Haven next time he went out to hunt. Except for *right now*, the journey had been amazing and fun. Wisp straightened her posture and let go of his arm, attempting to appear brave. At least in the dark, he couldn't see her wide eyes and shivering hands.

A rippling cascade of snapping echoed out of the forest, like a bear crushing an entire bundle of twigs at once.

Or a Tree Walker rising up from the ground.

She held back a startled yelp that echoed in her brain and snagged the pistol from the holster on Dad's belt, clutching it in both hands. Within a second of her pointing it at the woods where the sound came from, Dad grasped her by the wrists and pushed the weapon down.

Wisp shifted her eyes to him, asking 'why' with a stare.

"You cannot kill the Tree Walkers with a bullet," whispered Dad. "A gun will only make them angry… and the loudness will tell them where you are."

"I understand." She fidgeted her grip on the pistol. "It might not be one of them. What makes that noise?"

Dad let go of her and grabbed the front of his rifle, training it generally in that direction. "Sounded like a big person stepping on branches. Down."

Wisp sank into a squat, staring at the forest. Her mind played evil games by making her think every shadow held a creature of living vines coming to take her away from Dad. *Mother, please protect us.*

Another crunch came from ahead and a little farther to the left. She shifted her facing toward it, but didn't raise the pistol. Dad took a knee beside her, a little in front to shield her from arrows.

A chill wafted by on the early evening breeze. Leaves rustled overhead. Cricket song surrounded them and the rapid skittering of a squirrel zipped by overhead.

Her toes dug deep into the rain-damp soil. The pistol wobbled in her hands. She swallowed hard, trying to be brave, trying to show courage so Dad would take her on a hunt again. He would do anything to protect her, and he didn't like seeing her frightened. If he thought going out scared her too much, he'd keep her safe in the Haven. She thought back to how nice it had been relaxing beside the stream, watching birds and eating fish with Dad. If every day could be like that, she'd be the happiest girl in the world.

Her trembling stopped. She narrowed her eyes and lifted the gun, ready to shoot a monster.

Dad panned his rifle back and forth, scanning the woods. Minutes passed in silence before the soft crunching of a person's footsteps became apparent. She shifted left, facing toward the noise. Motion caught her eye.

A tall man strode across the woods not far away. The shadowy figure entered a patch of moonlight, revealing dusty, brown leather armor on top of black fabric, as well as a white mask over his face with eyeholes. Faint rattling emanated from a quiver of arrows at his belt, and the handle of a large blade jutted up from behind his back. He clutched a bow in his left hand, arm relaxed at his side, no arrow nocked.

He hasn't seen us.

Dad released his left hand from the front of the rifle to cover Wisp's mouth for a second, a sign to stay perfectly quiet.

She didn't even nod, holding as still as Mother.

The man marched on, passing within twenty feet of where they crouched. At one point, he appeared to look right at them, but didn't react. Likely, in the dark, he hadn't been able to see them among the foliage—despite her pink shirt. Wisp narrowed her eyes. The next time they went out on a hunt, she'd leave the shirt home. Though, the fabric *did* mute the blue moonlight glow of her exceptionally pale skin. Perhaps she'd keep the shirt after all—or smear dark mud all over herself. Maybe she'd ask Dad to make her an armor top like he had. The skirt's rich dark brown worked well for hiding.

Wisp lifted the pistol, aiming at the figure crossing by. She didn't move her finger to the trigger, holding it firm along the side of the weapon. Once the man passed the point where he'd begun to walk away from them rather than closer, she relaxed.

Dad waited two minutes before nodding to the right and standing.

She got up.

He held out his hand, and she placed the pistol in it without hesitating. A smile flickered across his lips, piercing the serious glower he still aimed into the woods. After stuffing the gun back in his hip holster, he took her hand and resumed walking.

Wisp's head filled with memories.

Nine-year-old Wisp smeared her hands down the front of her faded dress, no longer able to tell if it had been pink, orange, or somewhere in between. She smiled up at Dad before holding her hands out.

He eased the pistol into her grip. She did the best she could trying to hold it the same way he showed her, but he still adjusted the position of her fingers and arms. Today was special. He would let her fire some real bullets at a couple of metal cans he'd hung from twine near the cabin.

"What's the first rule?" asked Dad.

Wisp closed her left eye and peered over the handgun at the biggest can. "Don't shoot if I can run away."

"Correct. Second rule?"

"Don't touch the trigger until I want to shoot."

"Third?"

"Don't point a gun at anything I don't wanna destroy."

He crouched behind her, his hand under the gun, nudging her arms upward as he talked about how to position the gunsights on her target. "When you're ready to shoot, move your finger onto the trigger. Squeeze it gently, almost like you want the gun to surprise you when it goes off." He held up his hand and clutched it into a fist a few times, hard. "If you clench too much, you'll miss."

She focused on the can. "I see it. Can I shoot it?"

He checked her over, looked around the woods, and smiled. "Is there anyone behind your target you don't want to hurt?"

"No. Just trees."

"Okay. One shot."

Wisp moved her finger onto the trigger, trying to keep the can lined up with the little red dots on the gunsights. She increased pressure little by little until a loud *bang* startled a scream out of her. The gun kicked back harder than she expected, almost jumping out of her hands. Dad had been ready for it though, and his arm hovering over hers prevented the gun from bonking her in the face.

"Sorry," she whispered.

"I did the same thing my first time." He pointed. "You hit it though."

Wisp grinned. Mother would be so proud of her!

She smiled at the way Dad had been proud of her that day. He'd let her fire four more shots, and she'd hit three for five. After the first shot, she knew how the gun would feel, and controlled the kick well enough not to lose the weapon. It had been almost three years since she'd used a gun, but she still remembered the feel of it. If she had to destroy a monster, she could do it.

A few minutes of silent walking later, they emerged from the trees into the clearing around the cabin. She veered for the outhouse. Dad waited outside while she got rid of the bad water, not that two people could've fit in the little cinder block shack anyway. When she'd been really small, almost too long ago to remember, he'd gone in with her so she didn't fall down into the hole. She could probably still squeeze through it, but not without a lot of effort and certainly *not* by accident. And who would ever *want* to fall into a giant pit full of *ngh?*

She finished and eased the door open. Dad took her hand and walked her around the cabin to the front door. He needed his light-maker to find the right opener, and as soon as he unlocked the door, she rushed inside.

Dad entered behind her, closed the door, and locked it again.

"Why did we run from that man?"

He slung his backpack off and set it on the worktable. "He didn't see us and we were not in danger."

Wisp padded up behind him. "Why didn't we talk?"

"Those people are dangerous. He's a marauder. Only they wear armor like that. If he saw us, we would've had to shoot him because he would have attacked us."

"Marauders," said Wisp, slow and deliberate as if trying out how the word felt on her tongue.

"They are bad people. They take, they hurt, and they won't be nice to you because you're not grown up yet."

She stared down. "Yes, Dad."

"Don't forget how loud guns are." He set the rifle on the worktable before turning toward her and resting his hands on her shoulders. "Marauders are never alone. We *saw* one, which means there had to be at least three, maybe even more. You might destroy one monster, but if it has friends, they'll all know where to find you. Always run if you can. Only shoot if you have no other choice."

She stared down at her toes. "Why are people mean to each other?"

"I don't know, sweetie."

"Are marauders as bad as the Tree Walkers?"

"No. Nothing is." He slid his hands off her shoulders to her back, pulling her into a tight embrace. He sniffled, sounding on the verge of sobs. "I don't want to lose you or have anything hurt you."

Wisp wrapped her arms around him, unsettled by Dad crying. He usually only did that when talking about Mother. That he'd gotten so worked up over *her* being in danger filled her with a warm, radiant love. She squeezed him with all her strength, grateful to have him to care so much. Face mushed into his chest, she stared at the front door, dreading what might be out there waiting to hurt her.

"Are you ready for bed?" asked Dad.

"Yes."

She stepped back out of the hug and removed the canteen belt. After setting it on the shelf, she walked over to her Haven. Ever since the light began to weaken, she'd longed to have the bars between her and Tree Walkers and couldn't wait to feel safe enough to truly rest. Wisp fiddled with the plastic clamps until she figured out how to remove the knife from her leg. It probably wouldn't be smart to sleep with that on. She set it on the bookshelf and crawled into the Haven.

Dad eased the door closed and inserted the key. "Goodnight, sweetie."

At the *click* of the lock, she let out a deep breath of relief. The Tree Walkers couldn't get her now, no matter what they did. She put her face against the bars. "Night, Dad."

He leaned down so she could kiss him on the cheek, then turned her head for him to return the smooch. Dad headed off to the outhouse. Smiling, Wisp curled up on the plush red fabric, snuggled her head into her pillow, and closed her eyes.

Safe in her Haven, she had not a care in the world.

The Mother Shrine
~5~

An hour of foraging the next morning yielded a lovely breakfast of grubs, some of which had been bigger than Dad's fingers. Wisp impaled them on thin sharpened sticks she'd made long ago for grub roasting, and toasted them over the fire.

She stretched and roamed around the cabin for a little while after, debating another walk into the woods to find some mushrooms. It would be better if Dad could find a boar or something, even if she had to wait home while he did so. However, between them being gone all day yesterday plus the morning grub hunt, Dad appeared quite intent on putting time on the bullet machine.

Rather than disturb him, Wisp decided to visit Mother.

The cabin's main room had three doors. One led outside, the metal door went to Dad's room, and the door opposite Dad's room led to Mother's shrine. It had been a few days since she spoke with her, so it sounded like a perfect idea.

She padded over and knocked twice on the thin door made of planks nailed together. "Hello, Mother. May I enter?"

No sound of protest came from within, so she pushed the door open and got a breath of air so heavy with the scent of pinesap the taste settled on her tongue. An undertone of another fragrance, musty and unpleasant, simmered at the edge of notice beneath it. The small chamber, barely a quarter the size of the other room, contained two small tables each with a single drawer, standing on either side of a large wooden chair. White plastic panels covered both windows, dimming the light, but still allowing enough to reveal a slender figure in the chair.

Mother sat as still as ever, her hands clutching the ends of the armrests, talon-like nails yellow and cracked. Long, dusty dark brown hair framed a face as grey as the dress she wore, lips peeled open enough to bare her teeth, giving her an expression like she'd stepped in something cold and slimy. Her right eye opened more than her left, both black, empty sockets. Stain trails ran down her cheeks from long-ago shed tears of darkness.

Coffee cans littered the ground by the chair, containing pinesap, and other magical substances Dad said allowed her to see out from the Other Place. Years of dead flowers formed a ring around the chair, tokens of love she'd placed there on special days going back as far as she could remember.

"Hello, Mother," said Wisp.

She clasped her hands in front of herself, bowed her head, and shuffled forward, moving her feet an inch at a time until she stood by Mother's withered right hand. After a reverent moment of silence, she knelt and rested her head on Mother's arm, the coarse fabric scratchy against her ear.

"Dad taught me about how to make a fishing spear yesterday. He caught fish with it for supper, and we went on a walk. He let me go with him!" She reached up and placed her hand upon Mother's, careful not to damage the dry, crusty skin. "I'm twelve now, but you knew that since I visited you on my birthday last month. I like the summer. It's warm. I'm glad my birthday's right before the summer starts."

Mother didn't reply.

"I am sad that you had to go to the Other Place and can't be with us. Is it nice there? What is it like? Do you see other people or can you only watch us here in the forest?"

Mother said nothing.

Wisp caressed Mother's hand with her fingertips while telling her all about the walk with Dad, finding the crashed thunderbird, and the hidden cold room. "I saw your Jeep. Dad says it's broken now and isn't useful anymore, but I was scared of it at first because it looked like an angry monster face. Dad laughed at me. The blood on the seats made me sad. I'm sorry you got hurt. Dad said you got better though. This cabin is much nicer than that place. I'm glad you asked him to go here."

Mother continued to gaze into nowhere.

"I hope I'm being a good daughter. Dad said you'd tell me if I'm bad."

Only silence came from Mother.

Wisp beamed, proud of herself. "Thank you!" She lifted her head away from the dried out arm, stood, and leaned close to give her as much of a hug as she dared, lest she hurt the brittle shrine. "I love you, Mother. Thank you for watching over me and Dad."

A sniffle startled her.

It took her a second to realize it came from Dad, standing in the doorway behind her. Tears streamed down his cheeks, glistening over his frizzy, black beard. Wisp smiled at him before turning back to Mother and picking up the gauzy bundle of cloth in her lap. She held the tiny dress up to the feeble light from the white plastic covering the windows. After dusting it off, she refolded the toddler-sized garment in a neat square and set it back on Mother's lap.

Floorboards shifted under her feet as Dad walked up behind her. While she stood with her hands clasped in front of her, head bowed at Mother, he put a hand on her shoulder. Wisp looked down at the footprints she'd made in the dust. Dried out and browned flower petals scattered across the wood in front of her toes.

I need to get her some new flowers. She brushed at the tiny dress.

"That used to be yours," said Dad. "It's the very first thing you had to wear. Mother likes to keep it close, so she feels like you are with her all the time."

"I don't remember it." She struggled to think, but couldn't picture ever being small enough to fit into the sacred garment. "Are babies that big? Where do they come from? What did I have before that?"

Dad grinned. "Nothing. As soon as you were old enough to learn how to use the outhouse, Mother made you that dress."

She peered up at him. "I had to learn how to use the outhouse? What did I do before?"

He wiped the last of the tears from his face, and chuckled. "Babies just… well… let go wherever."

Wisp laughed. "They *ngh* everywhere?"

"Oh yeah. You used to start playing with it if we didn't get to you fast enough to clean it up."

She cringed, horrified. "We probably shouldn't be talking about *ngh* in Mother's shrine."

"Mother doesn't mind. Some day you might understand. When you have a child, everything they do is wonderful. Even when they make *ngh* on the floor."

Wisp narrowed her eyes in disbelief. "*Ngh* is not wonderful." Her mood fell somber, and she again rested her hand atop Mother's. "Tell me about her? What was she like before she went to the Other Place?"

"When we met, she was, oh, about two or three years older than you are now." Dad stepped closer and stroked Mother's hair. "I love her hair."

Twelve, thirteen, fourteen, fifteen... "Mother was fifteen when you found her?"

"About that, yes. I was a little older, almost nineteen. We knew right away we were meant to be together. It didn't take her long to start talking about how much she wanted a daughter, more than anything. But, our people had decided she should be with someone else, a choice made before she had become even old enough to walk. Your mother did not have any love for him, so she begged me to go into exile with her."

That he had given up his home, everything he had known, for Mother got her sniffling. "Did it hurt when she went to the Other Place?"

Dad pulled his hand away from Mother's hair and covered his mouth, holding back a sob. "I... don't think so. If she was in pain, she never said anything. I don't know what happened more than a sickness took her. At first, I was afraid she'd eaten a dangerous mushroom, but I didn't get sick or even feel strange, and we'd shared all our food." He sank to his knees and took Mother's hand in both of his. "Nothing I did helped. I couldn't protect her. She knew she was going to the Other Place, and found peace with it. Knowing she had you made her happy."

Wisp knelt beside him, tears welling up in her eyes as she put an arm around his back. "Don't cry. Mother is still with us. She's watching from the Other Place, keeping us safe. Maybe once she got there, she made the sickness leave you alone."

Dad lapsed into heavy sobs, muttering apologies and rambling incoherently for a few minutes.

She rubbed his back, hugging and muttering, "It's okay," and "Mother loves you," every now and then. He set Mother's hand back on the armrest, patted it, and turned to embrace Wisp, pulling her into his lap as he rolled off his knees to sit on the floor.

Dad, her fearless protector, clutched her like a small child holding a doll, weeping openly until the shoulder of her shirt had soaked through. "She's watching us."

"Yes," said Wisp, her voice a mere breath on the wind. "She's still here."

He squeezed her close, rocking side to side. Wisp clung to him until he got himself under control a few minutes later. Dad leaned back enough to make eye contact, smiling at her. "We are lucky to have a daughter like you."

She reached up and wiped his face. "Mother's flowers are all brown. Can we go collect some new ones?"

"Of course." He took a couple deep breaths, and the strong, fearless Dad returned. "She will like that."

Wisp grinned and gave her a quick kiss on the cheek. "I'll be back with some new flowers for you."

Mother said nothing.

Monster in the Woods
~6~

The repetitious *squeak-clank-squeak* from the bullet press faded out of Wisp's awareness after a few hours.

She sat cross-legged inside her Haven, leaning against the bars closest to the cabin's back wall, the pillow tucked behind her head, book perched in front of her. The door remained open, since Dad was awake. If any Tree Walkers found them, he'd be able to protect her. She'd been reading since they finished supper. The story had been hard to follow, so she'd been cycling through various positions trying to get comfortable enough to keep going with it. Most of the stuff about 'computers' made no sense at all, and even Dad couldn't help her understand. Somehow, this woman in the story could do things with them that made powerful men get angry and want her dead.

…Katrina bolted from the elevator, ducking gunfire from two security men as she rushed across the lobby…

"Dad?" She marked the spot on the page with a finger.

"Hmm?" The squeaking paused.

"What's a lobby?"

"Uhh. Something about politics I think."

"What's politics?"

"Oh, wait. I think a lobby is like a big, fancy room." He snapped his fingers a few times. "Like the front room in a huge cabin, the one where the door to the outside is."

"Okay."

She resumed reading.

… bullets ricocheted off the marble floor behind her, zipping past her legs …

"Dad?"

Again, the squeaking paused. "Hmm?"

"What's riko-chet-ted?"

He spun around on his stool and tilted his head at her. "What?"

"A word. 'The bullets riko-chet-ted off the marble floor.'"

"Oh, I think that book spelled it wrong. It's ricka-shay. If you shoot a gun at something that's hard, the bullet will bounce off and keep going in a different direction."

"Really?" She stared at him.

He illustrated a bullet flying into a solid surface and bouncing away at an angle with his hands. "It's kinda like that, but it's almost impossible to guess where it'll go."

"Wow." She pictured a woman running and people shooting the ground behind her. "I understand. Thanks."

"You're welcome. Learning is always a good thing." He swiveled back to the bullet press.

Squeak-clank-squeak.

Wisp turned a page, squirming so the pillow sat a little better at the back of her neck.

…Katrina raced around the building into the alley, where Rodolfo waited with the limousine…

Again she poked the paper to mark her spot and looked up. "Dad?"

He swiveled to stare at her, one eyebrow twitching. She'd seen him make that face a few times… usually when something he worked on frustrated him.

"Sorry." She flashed an apologetic grimace and resumed reading.

Dad let a long breath out his nose. "It's all right. Go ahead."

"What's la mouse-e-nay?"

"Not a damn clue. That's either spelled weird or you're not saying it right."

"Limo… O… o-seen?"

Dad stroked his beard, thinking. "Maybe limousine?"

She peered through the bars at him and shrugged. "I guess."

"It's a big kind of car that a lot of people can get into all at once and go somewhere."

"Oh, like a SUV." She nodded. "Thanks."

"What's a suvve?"

She flipped back a couple pages and hunted for where she'd seen it. Once she found the spot, she crawled out of her Haven, stood, and walked over to him. "Here. It sounds like a big Jeep that a bunch of people can get in."

He looked at the page above her pointing finger. "That's SUV. See how all the letters are big? That means it's not like other words around it. You just say the individual letters, not pronounce it like a word, 'suvve.' It's ess-you-vee. Words like that with all the letters big are like a code."

"Strange..." She traced her finger around it on the page and muttered, "S-U-V. What's the difference with a limousine?"

"A limousine is more like a car, but long. The SUV is like the Jeep. Big tires."

"Tires?"

Dad rubbed the bridge of his nose. "You remember the Jeep?"

She nodded.

"Those big black round things?"

She nodded.

"Those are tires."

"Don't cars have tires, too?" She tilted her head.

"Yes, but they're not as big."

One of the books had a picture of a car on the front. She ran across the room, leaning over the Haven to pluck it from the bookshelf before bringing it back to show Dad.

"That's a car. Okay. A limousine... take that car and stretch it out like twice as long."

She nodded. "Who's strong enough to do that?"

"I don't mean actually stretch. A limo just looks like that."

"Oh." Wisp stuck her tongue out and rolled her eyes at herself. "Dumb. Sorry."

"A SUV is taller, and not as long. Some of them can even drive off roads."

She tilted her head around while the thoughts swam within. "If we got a car, it should be an SUV since there's no roads left."

"There's no SUVs left either, sweetie."

Wisp shrugged. "Oh."

"Besides. We don't need to go anywhere that far that we'd need a SUV, a car, *or* a limousine. We're happy staying right here at home."

She giggled. "Yeah."

Dad rotated back to face the bullet machine. She hovered close, watching him pour a little bit of the magic fire dust into a brass case, seat it in the machine, and turn a hand crank until a rod came down and pushed a bullet in. The repetitious task proved, at least for a few minutes, more interesting than the book she struggled to understand.

"What's a computer?"

"It's a kind of machine from before." Dad wheeled down the crank. "Electronic stuff."

"Oh. If it's not alive, how can it get a virus?"

"Where'd you get that from?" asked Dad.

"The book. This girl is making the computers have viruses so they do what she wants them to."

He laughed. "That book is silly. Machines can't get sick."

"Yeah." She flipped it closed and sighed. "I think I'm going to read a different one."

A faint buzzing came out of the distance, increasing in volume. At first, she started looking around for the bug, but the noise kept getting louder, filling her head with images of a bitey-bug the size of a black bear.

"Dad! What is that?"

The buzzing pulsed higher-pitched and fell low, back and forth a few times at random. Fearing a tremendous insect about to crash through the wall, she screamed and ran to the Haven. Dad rushed after her, pushing the door closed and locking it.

"Stay hidden. Stay quiet."

Wisp looked up at him, but the words her brain struggled to find evaporated at the look of fear in his eyes. She'd never seen him that frightened before. She barely managed to nod.

He reached in and patted her cheek. "I love you, sweetie."

"What *is* it?" She grabbed his hand. "Dad, what's that noise?"

"Dangerous. Stay as quiet as you can."

He withdrew his arm from the Haven and pulled the blanket down to cover her.

His footsteps drifted away across the room. Wisp curled up against the innermost corner, hiding her face behind her knees. *Mother, please protect us from the giant bug! Make it go away!*

The buzzing lessened to a low, constant rumble. Dad's rifle clattered. Footsteps crossed the room faster. Squeaky hinges announced the front door opening. She jumped when it slammed closed with a loud *whack* of wood-on-wood.

46

Wisp curled her toes into the soft bedding and wrapped her arms around her legs, pulling them tight to her chest. Her hair cascaded down over her shins as she bowed her head to her knees.

The Haven will protect me. If it can stop Tree Walkers, it can stop giant bugs. She grabbed one of the bars on the door, pushing at it to make sure he'd locked it. When it refused to swing open, she breathed a sigh of relief, and again curled up with her chin atop her knees.

Mother, please keep Dad safe.

oUiet Time

~7~

Wisp escaped a dream of running through endless forest. She jolted awake, curled up on her side, safe and warm in her Haven. The nightmare of the Tree Walkers, a churning wall of vegetation and grasping vines chasing her, had plagued her as long as she could remember.

She lay still, not opening her eyes, letting her mind steep in the truth that she did not have monsters nipping at her heels. A haze of still, warm air hung within the blanket-covered Haven. Trickles of sweat dribbled across her back, and the glow of mid-morning sun upon closed eyelids tinted her vision red.

Lingering fear and confusion from her sudden leap to consciousness kept her silent and still for a while until reality seeped into her mind, shooing away the dread of her old nightmare. She'd had that dream ever since she'd been tiny, always the same thing: trapped in the forest alone at night, trying to get away from a rushing wall of vegetation and grasping vines—the Tree Walkers.

As she grew older, the dream happened less often, but every time she fell asleep while scared, it happened again. She didn't bother sitting up—or even rolling onto her back—trying to sort out what had happened last night, if indeed anything had. Giant insects couldn't be real? Surely, if such creatures roamed the Earth, she'd have seen one long ago. Of course they couldn't be real.

I dreamed it. There's no such thing as huge bitey-bugs.

She struggled to open her eyes, but a thick layer of crumblies had glued her eyelids shut. Wisp reached up with one hand and wiped the gritty annoyance away, and kept pawing at her face until she ceased brushing granules off her cheeks. She peered out at the oversaturated pinkish orange of her little chamber. Bands of shadow from the Haven's bars wrapped over her right thigh, which peeked out from the split in her skirt. She fixated on a trickle of sweat gliding down her leg to where her knee touched the thick padding.

"Oh. I slept too late. It's almost midday." She took a few breaths, trying to wake from the heavy fog of oversleeping. "Dad?"

Wisp listened to the silence for a little while before the memory of last night—Dad rushing her into the Haven, looking terrified—hit her in a flood. He'd grabbed his rifle and run out to protect her from the giant buzzing insect.

"Dad!" shouted Wisp.

Forgetting herself, she shoved upright on her knees to call for Dad again, but her head smacked into one of the overhead bars. She grabbed her skull in both hands and fell back over sideways, making random mewls of pain. Once the hurt faded enough for her to attempt moving again, she rubbed her scalp and pulled her hand back to check for blood. Fortunately, she hadn't cut herself.

"Ow." She cradled her head where she'd cracked it into the metal. "Dad needs to make the Haven bigger."

She thought back to being six or so when she could still stand up inside it. At some point, she could kneel up tall, but now, she had to sit. With her rear end on the padding, only a few inches of space remained overhead. The Haven had protected her from the Tree Walkers every night as long as she could remember, and during the day whenever Dad went away on trips. She adored the safety, but a little more room would be nice.

"Dad?" asked Wisp, then yelled, "Dad?"

When no reply came, she grasped the bars of the Haven's door and rattled it. Still, Dad didn't yell from the outhouse asking her to wait a moment, nor did he come over to let her out. She sat cross-legged, wearing a sour face and picking a thumbnail at one of the bars. Sweat continued to roll down her back and over her belly.

Wisp stuck her hands out past the bars and gathered the blanket upward. Cool air blew over her, and she fanned herself while taking a few deep breaths. A bit of tugging and pushing got the blanket wadded up on the top of the Haven, leaving all the sides exposed and air moving freely.

She raised her arms and stuck her feet out past the bars at the end, stretching until she collapsed in a slouch. The shelves behind her, between the Haven and the wall, held over a hundred books, most of which she'd at least tried to read already. Dad once told her the ones she didn't like would be better when she'd gotten older. She'd accused the ones on the bottom shelf of being too boring and making no sense, until he mentioned she'd been trying to read old school textbooks like a story. That, of course, required an explanation of school.

It's like how I'm teaching you to read and everything, only instead of one dad and one daughter, its one adult and a whole bunch of children.

Eyes closed, she savored the memory of his voice in her thoughts. Her mind drifted off, trying to imagine what it would be like to have other people to talk to. Or children for that matter. Except for the marauder the other day, she couldn't remember the last time she'd seen someone other than Dad and Mother—or if she ever had. She'd read of other people, but had no frame of reference for what anything the words described really looked like.

With a sigh, she looked back toward the end of the Haven facing the cabin's front wall. Her water jug, still only half-full, sat beside a pair of metal coffee cans. She crawled over and pressed her face up to the bars, wondering if Dad had left her food while he'd gone off on a hunting trip, but both appeared empty.

Dad didn't leave food, so he won't be away long.

She leaned back to sit, idly tapping her big toes together while making random silly noises. A while later, she glanced at the bookshelf, but didn't feel much like reading due to worry. He always told her before he went off on a trip, never simply disappeared. Wisp spent a few more minutes tugging and rattling at the Haven's door and calling out for Dad, but he didn't answer or show himself.

Again, she crawled to the end of the Haven, this time peering over her water bottle at the door to the Mother Shrine a few feet away.

"Mother, please tell Dad to come home. He needs to open the Haven. I have to let the bad water out."

Mother didn't say anything.

Usually, that made Wisp happy. Dad once told her that people in the Other Place have to work so hard to send their voice back to the forest that she would only ever speak if Wisp had been a bad girl. So far, Mother had never said a word. Grinning to herself for being a good daughter, Wisp sat with her legs bent to the side and ran her fingers down her hair, thinking about how Dad would often say how pretty it was. Mother had long, straight hair, too, only dark brown instead of bright blonde.

Wisp called out for Dad on and off for another few minutes, until the need to let out the bad water verged on painful. She grabbed the bars, shook the door, and screamed, "Dad! Let me out!"

Her voice echoed in the silence. She froze, gripped by a sudden fear she'd been bad. Never had she raised her voice like that. Near to trembling, she turned her head to peer at the entrance to the Mother Shrine. Her imagination pierced the old, brown wood, picturing Mother's wrinkled face staring back at her. Dread stopped her from breathing for a few seconds, wondering how the voice would sound. If Wisp ever did bad, would Mother speak like a person or would her words scratch at the air, creaky and dry like her body?

Mother said nothing.

"Whew…" She slumped, leaning her head against the bars. *I understand. I'm not yelling* at *Dad. I'm yelling* for *Dad.* "Dad! Where are you? I gotta let the water out!"

She pulled at the soft bedding, trying to move it out of the way before she had an accident. Beneath the inches-thick padding lay more bars, and floorboards marked with blotchy dark stains. She picked a finger at a discolored patch, remembering what Dad said about babies just making *ngh* wherever they happened to be at the time. It didn't smell at all, so if the stain meant she'd made *ngh* in the Haven, it had to have been a really long time ago.

"Dad!" shouted Wisp, shaking the door. "Please!"

She glanced back and forth between the door to his room and the front door. No sign of Dad appeared. Her need to let the bad water out worsened; any second now, it would happen whether she wanted to or not. Eyes locked on the cabin's front door, she struggled at the bars, but the Haven's square door refused to do anything but rattle.

Desperate, Wisp reached out past her water bottle and grabbed the largest of the empty coffee cans, one with a rotting black-and-yellow label. A modified bar by the bottom corner nearest the bookshelf created a wider opening specifically for that can. Anywhere else, it wouldn't fit between them. This can, she used for bad water and sometimes *ngh* when she had to spend long periods in the Haven because Dad had gone off somewhere. At least he didn't make her clean it after; that, he always did for her. The can offered a much smaller target than the outhouse seat, but she managed to avoid creating a mess. Once she finished, she continued hanging on the bars over her head for balance, too overwhelmed with relief to move for a little while.

Eventually, she eased herself down to sit, and, careful not to spill any, set the can outside the Haven as far as she could stretch her arm, but not so far she couldn't retrieve it the next time she had to let out bad water. Deflated, Wisp sat cross-legged with her chin in her hands, confused, and worried—even a bit annoyed at being locked in.

I'm not little-little anymore. I can go with him!

She waited for some time, long enough that the few errant droplets on the wood evaporated, then smoothed her bedding back in place so it filled the entire bottom of the Haven. The lush padding she'd slept on for years was so thick and soft she couldn't feel the bars beneath it. Wisp lay back with her fingers laced behind her head and her legs tucked close, feet flat on the cushion, knees pointing straight up. She stared up at the pink-orange blanket overhead, trying to understand why Dad would leave her in the Haven all day. He hadn't said anything about a trip, nor did he set out any dried fish or deer meat as he usually did.

The chirp of birds outside and the gentle rustle of wind in the treetops kept her company for a long while. Every so often, she yelled, "Dad?" but he didn't answer. Wisp rolled onto her side and clutched the bars by her face, 'hugging' them because they reminded her of how much Dad loved her and wanted to keep her safe from the Tree Walkers. Even if he couldn't be here, the Haven would protect her.

Wisp stretched her legs, placing her feet on the bars at the end. After a moment, she found herself pushing on them, wanting to get out and stand up. A sense of being confined crept into her thoughts. She cringed at herself, ashamed that she could somehow be annoyed at her Haven. Dad made it out of love, to keep her safe.

"I'm sorry," she muttered to Mother.

She held still for a tense moment, but relaxed when Mother didn't scold her for thinking bad thoughts about the Haven.

Daydreams took her back to a time when Dad left her home alone for two days. She'd been eight years old then, but he'd spent at least half a day explaining about the trip and that she'd have to stay in the Haven while he was gone so the Tree Walkers didn't get her. Wisp remembered crying so bad she couldn't see straight when he told her, not wanting to be away from him that long, but he had to go for food. He'd left her with a sack of dried salted fish filets, three jugs of water, and of course, the big can to use as an outhouse. Back then, she could almost pace around inside the Haven while stooped, even stretch and such… but now?

Getting bigger stank.

Wisp idly kicked at the bars, resenting that she had to stay inside. Just the other day, Dad trusted her to go on a walk for the first time. *I'm twelve! I'm not a little kid anymore.* She sat up and grabbed the bars of the door, rattling it hard. *I'm old enough to go with him!* Had he noticed how frightened she'd become when the marauder got close? Of course, she'd thought a Tree Walker was coming for her, not a man with leather armor. That had to be it. Dad saw her act like a scared little girl and decided she couldn't go out again.

She sulked, ashamed of herself for getting frightened so easily. Minutes crawled by. She frowned, picking dirt from under her toenails, and decided to kill some time with the file, as her nails had gotten a little long. Wisp's cheek mushed against her knee as she worked, sawing the file back and forth. By the time she finished both feet and all ten fingers, Dad still hadn't come home.

"He's gone hunting… That's right. I asked for a boar."

After taking a few sips of plastic-flavored water from the bottle, she reached out between the bars and snagged a book off the shelf. *He didn't leave me any food, so he won't be gone too long.* Wisp settled back against the inner wall, pillow behind her head, and began reading *Watership Down*.

The made-up world filled her head, taking her out of the Haven where she spent hours in a world only slightly less scary than the one she lived in.

Eventually, a snarl from her stomach distracted her from the pages, and made her aware of a growing discomfort in her bladder. She blinked at the thickness of the paper in her left hand, surprised at how far along she'd gotten in the story. The daylight coming in the window by the high shelf appeared to be weakening.

"Oh, no… it's almost dark! Dad!" Wisp tossed the novel aside and shifted around to face the Haven's door. She paused a second, glaring back at the book while grumbling at herself for losing her place. "Dad! I don't have any food! Where are you?"

She shook the door, clattering the bars, but the metal refused to yield. The shelf of jars holding what little food remained in the cabin sat a short distance away against the back wall of the room, but as much as the Haven protected her from the Tree Walkers, it kept her away from the food—or anywhere else. Trembling started as her mind scrambled to come up with an explanation. Dad didn't leave her any supplies. He hadn't told her about going anywhere. A giant insect had buzzed the cabin last night, and Dad went to make sure it didn't hurt her.

What if something *bad* happened to him?

Wisp curled up in a ball, hiding her face behind a curtain of hair. If Dad went to the Other Place while she stayed safe inside the Haven, no one would open it for her. She'd never be able to get out and find food. Soon, she'd wind up in the Other Place, too. But, if he'd made the Haven out of his love for her, wouldn't it disappear if he journeyed to be with Mother?

"No. Love is forever." She squeezed the bars, gazing up at the shelf where the opener sat beneath a can. Again, the bad thoughts came. She wanted to leave the Haven. She didn't want to go to the Other Place yet, and certainly not by way of starving. That, she'd read about in more than one book, and it did *not* sound fun. A man trapped on a desert island with nothing to eat had a little more room to run around in, but their situations did not sound too different.

Idly tracing her hand back and forth over her growling stomach, she stared longingly at the jars of bugs and greens. For the first time in her life, her Haven almost scared her.

"Mother? Can you open the Haven, please?" She tapped her toes, waiting. "Well, no… she'll only talk from the Other Place if I'm bad. I doubt she can touch things." *I should probably try to get out.*

Worry about Dad being upset if she somehow got out of the Haven kept her still and silent for the better part of the next hour. Flat on her back, she eventually gave in to fear and began shouting, "Hello?" or "Dad?" every few seconds. Right around the time her throat became sore, she decided to stop—and felt foolish. In twelve years, she'd never seen another person until the marauder. Who, exactly, did she expect would hear her shouting?

Frustrated, she double-kicked the door.

The Haven shook. It almost seemed as though the whole thing moved. She glanced around the enclosure, examining all the places where the bars touched each other and turned blue-black. Dad had created the Haven from individual rods, using magic to make them stick together, the same magic that the Tree Walkers couldn't break. But, more and more, the fear that something bad had happened to him got her restless. Too many things felt wrong about this: he hadn't said anything about going away, didn't leave her food, and he'd gone out right after they heard a giant bitey-bug flying around.

She grasped the bars in both hands, peering up at the shelf where the opener sat beneath a can. Dare she do something? *Could* she do anything but wait for him to return and hope she didn't starve? From as long ago as she could remember, Dad had made her learn the rules:

"Never go outside the cabin without Dad.

"Never get more than two steps away from Dad.

"When Dad's not here or asleep, I have to stay in the Haven.

"Never shout or yell, because the monsters will hear me."

Wisp needed the Haven to protect her if he wasn't here, or else the Tree Walkers would swoop in and take her away forever. She shivered at the thought, but a sliver of doubt crept in. For years, she'd been terrified of that happening, but the more she thought about it, the stranger it sounded.

How could the Tree Walkers know I'm not in the Haven?

She extended her right leg out past the bars and set her foot on the floor. That should fool them. If the Tree Walkers could sense her being vulnerable, exposing herself (even one foot) should make them appear. She'd only have to pull it in the second anything happened, and she'd be safe.

"I've got a foot out," said Wisp, staring at the front door. She waved her leg around, spread her toes, and stomped on the floor. "See? I'm out of the Haven? Come get me."

Five minutes later, she extended her other leg past the bars. She waited, barely breathing, watching the front door for any indication the living forest would come to take her. The only sign of life came from distant birds chirping. She patted her feet on the floor back and forth to sound like she walked around.

Still, no Tree Walkers came rushing in.

"Oh, I'm being silly." She sighed. "It's still day out. I have time."

Again, she stared up at the shelf. Even if the Haven sat directly beneath it, she'd never be able to reach. Disappointed, sad, and a little afraid of starving, she bowed her head. Wisp sank to the side and curled up, asking Mother over and over to bring Dad home fast while her stomach growled. She thought of how happy she'd been only yesterday beside the stream, eating fish. Worry for him brought tears, but they soon gave way to her wanting fish.

She lifted her head to frown at the four-pointed spear leaning on the wall by the fireplace. It wouldn't do her much good while she remained stuck inside the Haven. But she couldn't really go outside alone anyway, so…

"Let me out!" shouted Wisp, pulling on the overhead bars and kicking the door until she worked up a light sweat. "Dad!" Defeated, she sagged forward and burst into tears. Dad had never been this mean to her before. "What did I do? Was I bad? Mother didn't say anything."

Sniffling, she raked her hair away from her face and tucked it behind her ears. Her tears stopped at a random thought. That didn't make any sense either. If Dad had become angry with her, he would have said something. He had never shut her inside the Haven as punishment. Also, Dad never became angry. He knew the Fire Dragons destroyed themselves with anger, so he remained calm. Even the time he hit himself in the hand with an ax, he'd acted no differently than if he'd spilled water.

Worry for him swelled in her gut, pushing hunger aside.

"Something's wrong. He wouldn't go away without telling me, or leaving food."

Wisp looked around at the cabin. The opener sat on a shelf she couldn't quite reach, even if she'd been out of the Haven on tiptoe. She pulled up the bedding and pressed a hand to the floor. An idea formed in her mind, and she rolled up the sleepy bag into a bundle, exposing most of the Haven's bars beneath her. She squatted with her feet on the wood between bars, then lifted her back to press against the roof while straining to straighten her legs.

The Haven shifted a little, but she couldn't lift it. Exhausted, she sank into a squat and gasped for breath while picking a finger at the place the opener went. A metal bar thicker than her thumb slid out of the lock mechanism into a hole to keep the door secure. When Dad turned the opener, the bar pulled back so the door could move.

Against everything she believed, Wisp couldn't help but worry that the Haven could harm her. If Dad didn't return to let her out, she would go to the Other Place from not eating. More, if Dad *couldn't* return, she was in a lot of trouble—and not the misbehaving kind.

She turned to put her back at the door and braced her feet on the wood between the bars again. Her fingers curled around a horizontal bar a few inches up from the floor. While pushing with her legs, she tried to lift only one side of the Haven instead of the entire thing. She grunted, shoving with everything she had. Her feet shot out from under her, but the effort had shifted the Haven a few inches away from the bookshelf.

Clinging to a glimmer of hope, she grinned. "Mother, am I doing bad?"

She waited a few minutes, but Mother did not reply.

Confident she'd decided on the right thing to do, she turned around to study her situation yet again. Her face pressed to the bars, she looked at the high shelf, Dad's worktable, the food shelf, the fireplace, the door to Dad's room. There had to be some way for her to get the opener down, even trapped so low to the floor.

"I need to make my arms longer."

Wisp fixated on the fishing spear. Leaned against the wall, it almost touched the ceiling. That would reach the opener… She spun around to put her back against the side of the Haven again. With a series of kicks, she rammed her body against the bars, lifting, shoving, and grunting. An inch or three at a time, she dragged the ponderous metal box across the cabin, leaving long squiggly scratches in the wooden floor. After she'd dragged the Haven four feet from where it belonged, she collapsed, out of breath.

She hoped Dad wouldn't be upset about the scratches, but since Mother hadn't yelled at her, she trusted he would understand. If she did anything bad, if she became a bad daughter, Mother would tell her so. Dad would not want her to go to the Other Place because she couldn't get to any food.

Once her strength returned, she resumed bumping the Haven across the cabin. Every minute or so, Wisp peered back over her shoulder past the bars at the approaching wall. Eventually, she dragged the Haven far enough that she could reach out and grab the fishing spear. She let off a cheer of victory and set the spear across the top of the Haven. After a few minutes to catch her breath again, she resumed struggling, scooting past the fireplace to a spot under the high shelf. The task became harder since she devoted one hand to holding the spear tight to the bars overhead. If it got away and rolled to the other side of the room, it would take hours to go get it.

Wisp rammed herself against the bars over and over, pushing at the floor with her feet. When she got the Haven close enough to the high shelf to think of trying, she didn't even wait to give her body a chance to rest. She pivoted around to kneel, stuck her arms out past the bars, and raised the spear up toward the can that concealed the opener.

If I knock it over, the opener's going to stay there. It's under the can. Gotta slide it. Careful… Careful…

Gingerly, she touched the end of the spear to the side of the can and pushed it left. Bit by bit, the can slid as she tapped. Barely breathing, she nudged the can closer and closer to the left edge for an agonizing few minutes until the opener slipped out from beneath it and fell. The small bit of metal struck the floor with a high-pitched metallic *ping*. The can followed, clattering off the top of the Haven and rolling all the way across the cabin to the front door.

Wisp lowered the spear to the floor sideways and stretched her arm out toward the opener.

When she realized several inches separated her fingertips from the key, she screamed, "No!"

Before anger and terror could bite into her brain, she flipped over on all fours and stuck a leg out as far as she could. The gap between the bars pinched her thigh, making the task quite uncomfortable, but she tolerated it long enough to get her big toe on the opener and nudge it closer. She gasped and grunted while fighting to get her leg back inside; the bars didn't want to let go of her. After slipping loose, she spent a moment rubbing the sore spot before trying again to reach out with her arm. That time, she seized the opener and pulled it inside.

Wisp clutched the tiny bit of metal to her chest, shivering with guilt. She'd never been allowed to touch it before. Once, she'd asked why Dad had to keep it on such a high shelf so far away from her; couldn't she keep it hidden under the pillow so she could let herself out of the Haven?

That would put you in danger, sweetie, said Dad in her mind. *The Tree Walkers can make you do things. They will look into your eyes, and you'll be unable to resist. They'll make you give them the key and then, they will take you!*

Having the opener in her possession frightened her almost as much as asking the Tree Walkers to come get her. She remained frozen for a few minutes, but no Tree Walkers burst in the front door. Soon, the need to let out the bad water and her ravenous hunger overpowered even her fear of the forest monsters.

Wisp scooted up to the door on her knees and stuck her hand out. She fumbled the opener around at the front of the mechanism, hunting for a small hole she couldn't see. When it finally slid in with a *click*, she let off a squeal of delight and turned it. The Haven door swung open, creaking, and clanged against the bars. She scrambled out on all fours, leapt her feet, and loped to the front door. Hours stuck sitting or curled up kept her stiff and wobbly all the way to the outhouse.

It didn't hit her until she sat down on the plastic ring that she'd been *outside* without Dad anywhere close by. After she finished letting the bad water out, she stared at the outhouse door, too frightened to open it. Somehow, she'd made it without the Tree Walkers grabbing her. Would she be so lucky going back to the cabin? Weakening daylight heightened her fear. She fidgeted, swinging her legs, thumping her heels against the front of the seat. If she didn't want to spend all night in a space even smaller than her Haven, she'd need to risk it soon. Once it got dark, she'd be too scared to try.

Wisp eased her weight onto her feet, crept forward a few inches, and stood on tiptoe to peer out the small hole in the door. The woods remained quiet. Wavering leaves made the fading sunlight dance upon the forest floor. Nothing bigger than birds moved anywhere in sight. The rear-facing wall of Dad's bedroom had a pair of white tanks mounted beneath the window on a metal shelf. Wisp didn't want to go near them, since she remembered him saying they were for *pro* pain—not just normal pain. At least they had become empty long before he ever found this place, but still, she did not want to be anywhere close to a machine designed to hold suffering.

She shoved the door open and sprinted around the cabin, the soft *thump-thump-thump* of her feet on the forest floor so loud she expected Tree Walkers to rise up from the ground at any second. Once inside, she slammed and locked the front door, then leaned back against it out of breath.

A trail of lighter brown squiggles traced the Haven's path from the corner it had always been in to the wall left of the fireplace, and a beyond that to the right where it presently sat beneath the high shelf.

Wisp decided to clean up the house first, and spent about ten minutes struggling to drag the Haven back into place. Moving it while not stuck inside it was *much* easier, since she could pick up one end, drag it a little, then repeat the process from the other side. It only took her a few minutes to haul it back into the corner by her bookshelf. Her gaze fell on the bad water can, and she whimpered.

I gotta go outside again.

Biting her lip, she decided it best to get the chore done before the sun went down. It would smell bad if she let it sit too long. Whining out her nose from worry, she fast-walked around the house with the bad water can held at arms' length, and dumped it down the hole in the outhouse seat. With the danger of spilling gone, she ran back inside and locked the front door.

That done, she rearranged the blanket over the Haven as it belonged before attacking the food shelf. She tossed some chanterelle mushrooms in a pan with yellowgreens from a jar. They'd withered a little, but not so much she didn't trust them. The last tuber in the bin, she cut into slices and threw in as well before scraping boar grease out of the can and adding it for flavor. Since Dad wouldn't be eating, she didn't touch any of the taste powders. Best to save the good stuff for when he could share it.

Every few minutes, she cast a furtive glance at the door to the Mother Shrine, but no voice—creaky or otherwise—issued forth to scold her for being bad. She'd broken one of Dad's bigger rules, being out of the Haven when he wasn't awake and nearby. Her worry focus shifted to the front door while nudging leaves, mushrooms, and tuber bits around the bowl-shaped pan. Grease spat and sizzled. Bacon-scented wood smoke filled the air and trailed off up the fireplace chimney. Though she loved that smell, it didn't make her feel better.

Hopefully, the Tree Walkers would give her enough time to eat before they came to take her.

FN-FAL

~8~

Wisp transferred her meal from pan to plate, and scurried with it into the Haven, though she did not close the door. Hunger got her picking at her too-hot dinner before it had cooled, but she kept eating nonetheless. The overwhelming quiet of the cabin unsettled her. She tried not to scrape her fork over the plate because she feared it would be loud enough to attract Tree Walkers.

She ate too fast to taste much, most of the time staring at the front door. Dad had never done anything like this before. Whenever he went away, he'd always tell her about it and spend a while holding her and making sure she understood how much he loved her.

The more she thought, the more she came to the conclusion that something bad had happened to him. She didn't want to believe the giant bitey-bug had gotten him, but for all he had done to protect her these past twelve years, she owed it to him to help.

Decision made, she scarfed down the last few pieces of her dinner and crawled out of the Haven. She'd made more than she would've eaten normally, but not quite as much as she would have to feed two people. Despite the larger portion, she didn't feel stuffed, and contemplated eating more since she had gone all day without food.

No. I have to be smart. Make it last.

Her worry for Dad got her to set the dirty plate down without washing it and creep over to the door. She grasped the handle, but doubled back to pick up the fishing spear. Wisp took a few steps toward the door while carrying a stick almost twice her height in length, but stopped. She set it back down and darted to her bookshelf where she'd put the knife. After clipping the knife onto her right leg, she again headed to the door, and again, stopped as soon as she grasped the handle.

Wisp looked back over her left shoulder at Dad's worktable. His small gun still hung in its nylon holster from a peg. Last night, he'd run out the door so fast he didn't even take it with him, only the rifle.

She padded over to stare at it. "I should…"

After transferring the knife to her left leg, she adjusted the holster's belt down from Dad-sized to snug around her waist. The pistol sat heavy on her right hip, but its weight came with a sense of security. Except for a Tree Walker, if a bad person or bear got too close, she could handle it. The spear would be too awkward to use for defense, and probably wouldn't hurt a person much at all. That, she'd save for fishing. Besides, Dad showed her how to use a knife. A wooden block outside bore scars from many hours of practice. Of course, unlike a hunk of wood, a monster would probably scream if stabbed—and hit her back.

Always try to run first.

Wisp nodded to herself. Best to do as Dad instructed and avoid monsters whenever possible. In the made-up worlds inside her books, people could go to places called hospitals if they got hurt. In reality, Dad told her that sometimes even a deep scratch could send someone to the Other Place. She stared down at her feet, trying to scrape up the courage to go outside.

"Am I being bad?"

She waited a few seconds before looking at the door to the Mother Shrine.

No answer broke the silence.

Somewhat reassured by that, she edged up to the door and opened it. The early evening sun would probably give off light for another hour. Wisp hovered with one foot outside the cabin, listening to the birds and the rustle of leaves. Nothing bigger than a sparrow appeared to be anywhere close. She swallowed, took a breath, and made herself walk a few paces out into the clearing.

"Dad?" asked Wisp.

A bird leapt from a branch nearby. She pivoted toward the sound, her eyes tracking the small, black creature gliding off into the woods. Step by step, she proceeded to walk in a circle around the cabin, searching for any sign of Dad. Around and around she went in an expanding spiral, getting farther and farther away from home with every full circle. Mostly, she studied the ground, both to make sure she didn't stick her feet in anything painful, but also for signs of blood, footprints, or anything out of the ordinary.

The whole time she walked, her gut wound in knots. Dad always got agitated if she wandered more than 'lunge and grab' range away from him. Now she'd gone quite far from the cabin alone. Fear of the Tree Walkers and the worry Dad would be disappointed in her worked together to make her sick. Twice, she almost threw up from being nervous, but held her jaw shut. She couldn't waste food.

When the setting sun oranged the sky, a glint of reflection off to the side flashed among the weeds about a hundred yards up a hill behind the cabin. Going to investigate it would pull her a scary distance away from safety, but it might be important. Also, if she walked away, she'd never find that glinting spot again. She clenched her hands in fists and decided to go after the glowing thing on the ground. A mostly straight path away from the cabin brought her up a long stretch of shallow hill. She took note of yellowgreens, bolete mushrooms, and a dead log possibly containing grubs on the way. Never had she foraged alone, without Dad standing watch. Collecting food couldn't wait for him to return, especially if she had to help Dad. If she became weak from not eating, she wouldn't be able to do anything for him.

Wisp marched up to the spot where the glow had been, but didn't see anything lit up. She slowed to a creep and panned her gaze back and forth, searching the forest floor. Another glint, not too far ahead, flickered beneath the underbrush. She hurried over to find Dad's rifle abandoned on the ground. Not far from where it lay, two long strips of bare dirt cut a path in the greenery, leading way off into the forest.

She crouched by the rifle, tracing her fingers down the side, remembering what he'd named it. "Fabric national three-oh-eight."

Dad made sure she knew about guns. He'd also let her shoot the rifle, teaching her about the scope and iron sights. The weapon had a small long-distance scope on a hinge that could flip up top to use for far-away monsters, or fold off to the side when she didn't need it, for close monsters. She'd been almost ten when he decided she'd gotten big enough to give it a try. The first time she pulled the trigger, she wound up flat on her back with her legs in the air, crying because her shoulder hurt.

Thinking about how he'd laughed got her crying over missing him. A tear splattered on the side of the rifle, creating a tiny puddle of reflected sky. Finding the weapon lying there scared her as much as if she'd seen a Tree Walker. Dad would *never* just drop it. If he had to put it somewhere to be sneaky, he'd have hidden it—not tossed it on the ground.

The scope remained folded down, so she knew he hadn't seen any monsters far away. But if he'd been expecting a huge bitey-bug, he wouldn't have needed to use the crosshairs. She picked the rifle up with a soft grunt and rested it across her lap before removing the magazine to count bullets. All twenty remained, a few shiny, but most dull. One had even turned green.

Wisp tugged back on the lever, exposing the tail end of a live round inside the rifle, ready to fire. Saddened, she let it snap closed, then put the magazine back in before standing and slinging the rifle across her back on its strap. "He didn't shoot at anything."

Gaze on the ground, Wisp maneuvered around the area, careful not to step on any tracks or signs she could use to figure out what happened. Footprints she thought to be Dad's went in a relatively straight line until a deep, sideways boot print suggested he'd swiveled, aiming to the left. Another set of footprints came up behind him. She pictured a man on the left being a distraction while another snuck up and grabbed Dad.

She gasped.

"They took him!"

But… Tree Walkers didn't leave footprints. They *were* the forest. Magic and wood and vines and leaves and roots all bundled together with a deep hunger to steal children.

"Tree Walkers didn't do this." Wisp eyed the ground. "Men and some giant monster."

She approached the strange double tracks, somewhat like footprints, but much deeper and continuous, as though the men had been dragging a pair of large stones across the ground. The tracks had a curved shape, deeper in the middle and shallower at the edges, with a repeating pattern of dots slightly smaller than her fist.

"What monster has feet like this?" She stood to her full height and tried to see the end of the tracks, but couldn't. They went too far, weaving around the trees.

Minutes passed in silent thought while she gazed down the length of the strange trail.

Wisp pulled the rifle off her back, holding it like Dad always did, sideways across her chest, with the barrel pointing slightly downward.

"Don't touch the trigger until you want to stop a monster," muttered Wisp.

She walked a few steps forward, following the tracks.

"Don't point it at me," said Wisp, quoting Dad.

A squirrel dashed by not far ahead, but she couldn't aim fast enough to get off a shot.

"Don't let any part of yourself go in front of the tip."

She lifted it to firing position, snugging the butt against her shoulder, cheek against the side. The smell of oil and metal filled her nose. For no particular reason, she aimed at a tree. It didn't take long for the rifle's weight to make her arms shake. She lowered it back to the sideways position, cradling it more than holding it in a posture ready to shoot.

"Dad?" she called, advancing a few steps. "Dad?"

Other than managing to startle a few more birds out of trees, her voice did nothing.

It will be dark soon.

Thoughts of being grabbed like Dad sprang at her from the shadows, as did the fear of Tree Walkers. A rustle in the weeds came from the right. She held in the urge to gasp, keeping silent, and hoisted the rifle to her shoulder, aiming into the deepening shadows of late evening. The longer she stared at the dark spaces between trees, the more frightened she became. Too petrified to look away or flee, she stood in place, snapping her rifle toward any motion. One minute became four; still she couldn't make her legs obey her. Wanting to run, but paralyzed in fear, she emitted a soft whine from her nose.

A small cluster of branches leaned out from behind a tree. Another patch of leaves a few feet to the right seemed to slide forward, growing from a flat low-lying mass of vegetation to a taller, thinner blob. Two more masses wavered about even farther away, reaching toward her with snapping vines despite being over a hundred yards off.

Tree Walkers!

Wisp sprinted back the way she'd come, somehow managing not to scream. Twilight forest blurred by on all sides, exactly as it always did in her nightmare. She couldn't bring herself to look behind her at the rising wall of roots and vines she knew would be rushing closer. Every time she had the dream, she made that mistake. Whenever she looked back, she'd be so scared by how close the Tree Walkers got, she'd do something stupid like trip or run smack dab into a tree and fall on her butt.

If she looked back, they would get her, and not in a nightmare—for real.

Heart pounding in her ears, she pumped her legs as fast as she could run, not caring what she stepped on. The cabin had gotten frighteningly small in the distance, but she hadn't gotten so far away she'd lost sight of it. Racing downhill, she ducked low-hanging vines, jumped the dead log, and zigzagged around bigger trees that hadn't yet decided to come after her.

Her more direct route home encountered a great gouge in the hillside. Too panicky to think, she hurled herself into a leap, fearing going around it would slow her down too much. She fell a short distance before landing in a somersault, keeping the rifle tucked tight to her chest. Fear propelled her straight out of the roll back onto her feet, and she kept running hard.

The pistol bumped against her leg; the knife rattled in its sheath, and the air burned in her lungs. A tremendous roar of snapping branches and crackling twigs would rush up behind her any second, but she still refused to look back.

Wisp reached the clearing around the cabin and bolted for the front door so fast she nearly slipped and fell when rounding the corner of Dad's room. She darted in the front door, slammed it, locked it, and rushed over to her Haven. Hands shaking, she lay the rifle across the top, pulled up the blanket, and crawled in. Not until she'd spun around, slammed the door, and locked herself in, did she spare a second to breathe. She snugged the blanket down to hide and scooted as far back in the corner as she could get, clutching the opener in both hands at her chin while staring at the pink-orange blanket in the direction of the door. Still, the roar of an onrushing wave of vegetation flooded her mind.

"You can't get me in here. You can't get me in here."

She tucked the opener under her pillow and sat on it. Dad might've been missing, but the Haven's bars felt like he hugged her from far away.

"You can't get me in here," she whispered. "You can't get me in here."

No loud smashing noises came from the room beyond the blanket. The Tree Walkers hadn't bothered coming in since they knew she'd taken refuge in the Haven. After a few minutes to let her mind cling to the hope she'd be safe, she curled up in her bedding to sleep for the night, but couldn't close her eyes.

"They can't get me in here," she muttered.

Breaking the Rule
~9~

*C*latter.

Wisp startled awake at the bang of a door. "Dad?"

She pushed up on the blanket so she could see out into the room, but the cabin remained empty. Confused, she sat in silence for a little while until a gust made the front door jostle about.

Her heart sank.

"Just the wind," she whispered.

Light coming in the window to the left of the fireplace, above her Haven, suggested early morning and nice weather. It hadn't yet become too warm to enjoy being in her safe place. She yawned and started to stretch in the confined space, but stopped, feeling a touch silly.

Wisp pulled the opener out from beneath her pillow and fumbled to insert it in the keyhole on the outside since she couldn't see what her hands did. Her head had never been small enough to fit between the bars. Once she got the door open, she stashed the opener under the pillow again and crawled out into the room. There, she stood and stretched, yawning a few more times.

"Dad?"

No response came to her knocking on the metal door to his room.

"Dad, I know I'm not allowed inside, but is it okay if I look just this once to make sure you're not hurt?"

When only silence answered, she peered back at the door to the Mother Shrine.

"If I go in because I am worried about him, does that make me bad?"

Mother said nothing.

Relieved, Wisp walked up the three metal steps hanging in front of the room's other tire, and turned the knob. Breath held, she pulled the door open.

She stuck her head in past the doorjamb, afraid to do more than that. A large bed on the right, something like a huge version of her pile of sleepy bags, was empty. At its foot end sat a giant trunk, about the size of her Haven. Cabinets lined the opposite wall, all closed. Bookshelves surrounded a tiny desk on the left side of the room, but she couldn't make out what any of them said from the doorway. A trio of tall, narrow metal tanks stood in the far corner with rubber hose draped over them. Drab green metal boxes clustered under the desk, another stack off to the side. Clearly, Dad had not returned to his room.

"Sorry," she said to no one in particular, and backed out before shutting the door.

Nothing in there *looked* scary, dangerous, or worthy of her being banned from the room, but Dad's rules said she couldn't go in there. She would've broken the rule if he'd been in there and needed help, but with the room empty, she didn't want to get in trouble.

Wisp took the rifle from where she'd left it atop the Haven, slung it over her back on the strap, and went outside. She made use of the outhouse before continuing past it up the hill to the stream where Dad had built a metal enclosure with a flip-up lid and mesh grating walls that extended into the water. The frigid creek would keep the meat from going bad for quite some time, while the enclosure prevented scavenging animals from stealing anything, or the current from sweeping it away. Whenever he took down a boar or deer, he'd salt the extra meat, put it in plastic bags, and store it in the cold.

With a grunt, she heaved the lid up with both hands and stared at one bag of venison hanging on a cord from a hook on the wall.

"No!" she wailed, then slouched, disappointed. "I thought we had more."

She frowned, but fished the last packet out of the water anyway. It had been there a while now, and probably wouldn't last much longer.

On a whim, she headed back toward the hill where she'd spotted the strange tracks, confident the Tree Walkers would remain in hiding for the daylight hours. After collecting a handful of bolete mushrooms along with some yellowgreens, she hurried back down the hill to the cabin.

Once inside, she plopped on the floor and cooked her breakfast. It had been days since she'd had any meat, and the smell of it after a few minutes in the pan got her salivating. While prodding the venison around the pan amid a mixture of mushrooms and greens, she kept fidgeting with unease for breaking another of Dad's rules. She'd never been so disobedient before, yet here she sat, defying him by being out of the Haven alone.

"He'd let me go outside if he needed help, wouldn't he?"

With her meal ready, she slipped into the Haven to eat, but again left the door open. His rule required her to be *in* the Haven, but it didn't necessarily say anything about it being locked. Besides, she felt safer in there anyway. She'd almost forgotten how good deer tasted, and had to work hard not to eat the entire piece in seconds, chewing each bite until the meat broke apart into mush and stopped tasting like anything. Taking her time with it also made the relatively small portion seem bigger.

Once she'd finished her meal, she crawled from the Haven and washed the pan and plate before lugging the big jug out to the creek to refill their primary water supply. She thought about refilling her water bottle as well, but she'd only need that if she had to stay in the Haven and couldn't get out. Until Dad returned, she didn't have to worry about that. As much work as it took her to get the opener, she would not lock herself in the Haven and toss the opener away to trap herself.

Well, maybe she would if the Tree Walkers came in the door, so they couldn't take over her mind and make her give it to them. But, if she threw it, they could just pick it up.

"Argh," she muttered. "I'd have to like eat it or something."

She paced around the cabin for a while, trying to come up with something to do. Staying here alone did not feel like a great idea. Leaving Dad to whatever grabbed him would make her feel too guilty. What would he want her to do?

Lost, she approached the door to the Mother shrine and knocked. "Mother? Can I talk?"

The usual wait of ten seconds passed without a denial.

Hopeful, Wisp opened the door and stepped into the gloomy chamber. So soon after eating, the mixture of pinesap and the underlying bad smell caused her stomach to protest. Mother sat as she always had, but at least the ring of flowers had a few spots of white and bright green now. She hoped it cheered her up.

"Hello, Mother."

She padded up to the chair by the right armrest, head bowed, hands clasped. Since no voice told her to go away, she exhaled in relief and lifted her head to look Mother in the eye sockets. A bit of food bubbled up in the back of her throat at the weird smell in here, but Wisp swallowed it, trying not to grimace too much, lest she offend Mother.

"Dad didn't come home for two days. I don't know what to do."

Wisp stood there, waiting, but Mother said nothing. So, she knelt and rested her cheek against the dried-out arm and took hold of the desiccated hand, lacing her fingers with Mother's. "Please tell me what to do. I know Dad said you would only talk if I was a bad girl, but I'm scared. I think something bad happened to him. A strange monster with people riding it took him. I didn't see blood, so I don't think it ate him. It's not a huge bitey-bug. It's something else, and I don't know what to do."

Mother didn't speak.

She gazed downcast at Mother's grey foot and claw-like toenails. Years ago, she'd asked to file them, but Dad said no, explaining that it could hurt her. Plus, he'd added, in the Other Place, spirits needed claws. Mother had a pretty ankle bracelet with beads of red, blue, and clear glass. Wisp traced a finger around her own ankle, thinking about wearing something like that, too. She'd asked Dad about it once, but he said it came from a faraway place, too dangerous a journey for something as unnecessary as a bit of jewelry. She hadn't dared ask to wear Mother's. Especially not with it being part of a shrine.

"I don't know what to do," said Wisp, staring at the floor. She told Mother about her walk, finding the rifle, the footprints, and the strange tracks that disappeared into the Endless Forest.

Mother continued to stare off into a place only a spirit's eyes could see.

While the silence reassured her that she hadn't done anything wrong, Wisp had been hoping Mother would guide her in the right direction. Since that hadn't happened, she stood, backed up to the door, and bowed.

"Goodbye, Mother. I'll be outside if you need me."

She eased the door shut before sighing at the room. Pacing and thinking ate an hour with nothing to show for it. Having no better ideas, Wisp grabbed the fishing spear and headed outside to the stream, where she waded into the calm water to a little over her knees. A handful of tiny fish took notice of her and began nibbling on her toes, heels, and legs. She giggled at the sensation, but ignored them since they didn't hurt, nor were any of them close to being large enough to consider eating.

Eventually, a reasonably sized fish came by. She stabbed at it, but missed, and the fish vanished into a streak of silver, zooming out of sight. Sighing, she resumed her wait. When another fish came by some time later, and she missed it too, she suspected something strange went on. Using a rock on the creek bed as a test target, she extended the spear at it, and noticed her aim wound up being off by a couple inches. For some reason, everything below the surface of the water appeared offset from where it actually was. Her legs lost feeling after a while from the cold, so she climbed up to sit on a rock and spent an hour and some odd minutes practicing her aim on stones. Not wanting to break or dull the points Dad carved, she stabbed with the blunt end.

Once she felt confident in her ability to judge the true position of objects in the water, she shifted her weight onto her feet and squatted upon the big, round stone, spear held high. Some minutes later when a fish came gliding by, she jabbed her weapon into the water and sank two of the four points into its side. The sizable fish thrashed about, but she leaned all her weight into the spear, pressing her future dinner into the creek bed. Flashing silver scales soon disappeared amid a cloud of muck, but the wooden shaft kept bucking and twisting.

Wisp waited for it to go still, and hauled the dead fish out of the water. The weight of her catch bent the long spear shaft when she held it up, so she figured she'd get a least two meals out of it. This meant she'd have to use the cold place to preserve it. She carried the fish back to the cabin on the tip of the spear. Once home, she cleaned and gutted it, dumping the head and insides into an empty coffee can. She'd watched Dad filet them often enough to not do *too* bad a job at it, and hacked off two big slabs of fish meat. Upon seeing that, she reconsidered its yield from two meals to four. It would probably keep well one day at least, so she'd have some tonight, and more for breakfast and supper tomorrow.

She placed two slabs in plastic bags with a handful of salt, a third slab in without salt (for tomorrow breakfast), and left one piece in the pan. The three extras, she carried out to the creek and hung them in the food storage box. She climbed up on top of it after closing the lid, peering off into the woods along the strange tracks. Not that she expected to see Dad walking home, but she had to fight off a sense of guilt for not going after him. Too many things, he'd never explained to her—like where he got salt from, or where he went to scavenge stuff like her new shirt. She peered down at her bare stomach, picking at a fray where the fabric ended. More than likely, it had ripped long before she'd ever been born. Sad thoughts of who might've worn the shirt before her melted into sadder thoughts about Dad.

What would he want me to do? Stay here or go find him?

Head swimming with confusion, she trudged back inside, locked the door, and read for a few hours before cooking her fish. Smelling it made her think of the day she'd gone for her first trip. Dad's absence grew painful, and she wound up eating and crying. Every bite reminded her of not having Dad nearby, bringing more and more guilt. How could she eat while she didn't know what happened to him and did nothing to help? She forced herself to finish it, trusting Dad would want her to eat so she didn't become sick.

After her meal, she rinsed off the plate and pan, then spent an hour or so pacing around the room until the sun went down. Dazed by guilt and worry, she automatically crawled into the Haven and locked herself in. Wisp tucked the opener under the pillow and curled up before realizing she still had the gun on her hip and the knife on her left thigh. Neither one caused discomfort, so she decided to ignore them.

When the room outside became too black to see anything, she reached up and tugged the blanket down over the bars to hide. She considered what to do if the Tree Walkers showed up. Would they know she had the opener close by and command her to give it to them or would she be able to talk false to them? Could they even talk?

"Dad, please be okay," she whispered.

The Haven had always made her feel safe and protected, like Dad's love made solid. But no matter how tough the bars were, they couldn't protect her from loneliness, or lack of food, or bad people with bows and arrows.

Staying here without Dad, even with a Haven to hide in, had become a scary thought.

What else can I do? This is home.

Every time she tried to fall asleep while frightened, she had the Tree walker nightmare. Wisp snuggled into the pillow and closed her eyes, wondering what sort of dream she'd have from falling asleep sad.

Spirit's Whisper

~10~

Uncomfortable warmth dragged Wisp away from a dream of following Mother through a sunlit grove. Though the grey-skinned apparition hadn't spoken a word, a powerful need to follow her had taken hold.

She'd stayed up far too late, but not by choice. Worries and fears circled her thoughts like wolves, harrying and nipping at her for hours. Based on the humid ick in the air, it had to be midday or close to it. At least she found herself still in the Haven, unharmed—untaken by Tree Walkers.

Wisp yawned and pushed herself up on all fours, yawned again, and grabbed the opener. In her half-awake daze, she fumbled and dropped it outside while trying to get it into the keyhole. Fortunately, it didn't land so far away she couldn't reach it. She unlocked the door, crawled out, and sat on the floor for a few minutes enjoying the cooler air.

Dad's room remained empty. Again, she only risked peeking her head in to see if he'd returned home in the middle of the night. Disappointed and worried, she trudged outside to the outhouse, then up to the creek to grab the pouch of unsalted fish from the water.

Her routine kicked in, and without much thought, she cooked. A bit of fish plus its juices dribbled onto her foot while she ate, so she pulled her leg up and licked the spot, not wanting to waste any food. She smacked her lips at the faint dirt flavor, and noted the clean spot an inch behind her big toe. It had been about a month since Dad prepared a bath for her, but she usually only had them once every three or so. Warming the water used up a lot of wood. The metal basin sat outside behind the cabin over the fire pit, which always made her feel like a giant tuber being put in a soup whenever she took a bath.

"Bleh." She spat a few times to the side, regretting tongue-to-foot contact.

She rinsed the plate and pan off, set them on the shelf, and wound up staring at the door to Dad's room. Out of nowhere, a sense of inspiration and courage came on. She grabbed the rifle and stormed out the door, heading back up the hill to where the monster got Dad.

Upon reaching the spot, she crouched in the foliage nearby on one knee. After clicking the scope up into position, she peered through it down the length of the rutty tracks. The rifle let her visually follow the trail for a long distance, but failed to reveal any trace of Dad or the monster that took him away.

Tickling drew her attention to her foot, at a red-and-black caterpillar crawling over her toes. *Firepillar!* She went still, fearful the long hairs on its back would sting her. One thing she *did* know, red or bright colors meant danger. When the annoying thing decided to stop and sun itself on her instep, she gingerly leaned to the side to grab a twig, which she used to nudge the tiny beastie into motion. It undulated, a rippling sheen moving across its hairs, and made its way back onto the dirt. Wisp examined her surroundings before moving, so she didn't step on another one. Some bugs like that had poison all over them, and stepping on them could hurt a lot. She didn't know if it would be worse than an angry black wasp, but having her foot blow up to the size of Dad's fist for a couple days wasn't something she wanted to go through ever again.

The wasp sting had left a small scar on the underside of her second toe, but after a few weeks, her foot had shrunk back to normal. She hurried away from the caterpillar area and followed the ruts for a little while, occasionally stopping to use the scope to look ahead. It soon became obvious that any attempt to follow this monster wouldn't be something she could do in a single day and remain able to go home at night.

How much trouble will I get in for leaving home?

She bit her lip and walked backward a few steps. If Dad had simply gone hunting, she'd already be in a heap of trouble for being outside the Haven. If he caught her outside the *cabin* too, he'd probably punish her. As much as she could remember, he'd only punished her once, a long time ago. She might've been only five at the time, and she faintly remembered that she'd decided not to go to sleep when told and ran away when he'd tried to put her in the Haven, racing around and around the cabin, making him chase her. To punish her, he went a whole week without reading her stories before sleep. He'd gotten cross with her one other time when she'd been ten. She'd walked outside to use the outhouse without telling him. He hadn't punished her for it, but he did threaten to make her sleep outside the Haven for one night if she *wanted* the Tree Walkers to get her. She'd been so terrified at the thought, she'd begged him with tears in her eyes to lock her in at night.

Two years after the fact, she doubted he would have really done that and only wanted to scare her. Not since his biggest rule said she *always* had to be inside the Haven at night. He loved her too much to risk letting the Tree Walkers get her.

And… that's why she had to help him. Even if it meant breaking all his rules.

However, she had to be sure.

Wisp jogged back toward the cabin, drifting into the woods away from the tracks at the temptation of a huge burdock. She hadn't eaten that in a while, and though the leaves had a bitter flavor, she could cook them right. Boiling with a water change took the ick right out of them and made them yummy.

Carrying an armload of burdock leaves, she hurried back to the cabin, the rifle bumping her in the back the whole way. She ran to the nearby creek to fill a pot, and set water to boil before once more approaching the door to the Mother Shrine.

She knocked twice, soft. "Hello, Mother."

No reply came from inside.

Eyes on the floor, she pushed the door open and stepped in. Whenever the days had a lot of warmth, like today, the unhappy smell in the room got worse. It swirled with the pinesap, strong to the point she couldn't tell which fragrance overpowered the other. She covered her mouth and coughed.

"Please help me, Mother." Wisp shuffled over and knelt in front of the chair. "I want to go help Dad, but I don't know if he would be upset with me for leaving the cabin."

Mother said nothing.

Wisp leaned forward and wrapped her arms around Mother's legs, her forehead pressed to bony knees. "Please, Mother. Tell me what to do." She clung to the shrine, calling out with her deepest inner sense, begging Mother to reach out to her from the Other Place. The burble of boiling water eventually broke the silence. "Excuse me, Mother. I'll be right back. The water's ready."

Wisp released her embrace and scooted back before standing and walking past the door into the main room. She dropped the burdock leaves in the water and poked at them with the cooking knife for a little while before feeling satisfied that they'd begun cooking.

Upon returning to the shrine, she looked left and right at the white plastic sheets covering the windows.

"Oh… maybe you can't see outside."

Dad had attached thick rectangles of plastic to wooden frames, and hung them over the windows on both sides. Wisp approached the window on the right, the back face of the cabin, and tugged at it until she noticed the hooks holding the shade up. She had never asked Dad why he put them over the windows, but figured he wanted to protect Mother from strong sunlight. Unfortunately, because of them, Mother couldn't see outside to understand what had happened to Dad. Maybe if she opened the window all the way, she could see the tracks from the Other Place and know what to tell her.

Up on tiptoe, she grabbed the frame and lifted it off the hooks. A momentary puff of wind pushed her back a half step and blew all the dust from Mother's hair. Wisp set the frame down, leaning it against the wall by the window, and returned to kneel in front of the shrine.

"There. Now you can see. Out behind the house, up the hill. A hundred steps or so away. The monster's tracks, where Dad dropped his rifle."

Mother didn't say anything.

Wisp gazed up at her from the floor, watching her long, brown hair drift in the occasional breeze the unblocked window let in.

Maybe it takes time?

"I need to finish cooking. I'll be right back."

Wisp stood and walked back out to the fire. She tossed a slab of fish in the pan and set it over the flames before carrying the burdock pot outside and straining the boiling water off into the dirt. She refilled the pot from the jug and put it back in the fireplace. It didn't take long for the fish to cook, so it had to wait while the second boil on the burdock finished.

She sat right by the fireplace and her little table with the six-inch legs to eat, not bothering to crawl back into the Haven.

Full, she rinsed off the dishes and walked back to the shrine.

At the door, she froze stock still, staring at Mother.

Her left arm had swung out to the side, pointing at the window. All the flowers that had been in a ring around the chair lay scattered off away from the opening. Wisp froze in awe, gazing into the empty eye sockets of the dried-out woman, slumped somewhat to the side. Some great blast of energy had to have come through from the Other Place to do that, probably when she made her body move.

"Mother?"

A strong breeze blew in the window, again tossing Mother's hair about and stirring up a whorl of dust at the back of the room. Mother's left arm wobbled, emphatically pointing at the window.

Wisp sucked a hard breath in her nose, filling her lungs with confidence and determination. "I understand, Mother. I must go find him."

Mother didn't say anything.

"Should I put the window back? Or do you like it open?"

For a little while, Mother did nothing, but before Wisp gave up on waiting, the dry body sagged more to the left and her pointing arm fell slack.

"Yes, Mother," said Wisp. "Right away."

She ran to the window, grabbed the frame, and secured the thick plastic back in place, making the room once again dim and sacred. Wisp helped Mother sit up straight and balanced her arms on the armrests. She hummed merrily to herself while collecting all the scraps of flower petals, stems, and leaves back into a circle around the chair.

Mother's head lolled to the right with a soft *crunch.*

"Gah!" Wisp gasped, momentarily terrified at seeing a shrine move. "I'm sorry! I'll go right now!"

She scrambled to her feet and rushed out into the cabin, looking around while her heart pounded. Mother came close to being angry with her for wasting time collecting flowers while Dad needed her. *So dumb! Why did I do that!* She grabbed the rifle from atop the Haven and spun to face the door.

"I'm coming, Dad."

No Haven's GUard
~11~

Mother's encouragement had chased away the last of her doubts.

Wisp no longer believed she would get in trouble, but that didn't mean she'd gotten over her fears. Still, with Mother keeping an eye on her from the Other Side, she had to trust that she'd be okay. She got halfway to the door before she stopped and peered down at the rifle in her hands.

"I'm going to need more than this."

She set the rifle on the worktable for the moment, and grabbed Dad's small backpack from the wall. This trip could be long, so she decided to take important things. One of the ferro rods to start cook fires, a file to strike it on, some kindling, twine, the jar of yarrow powder in case she cut herself, her favorite bowl-shaped pan, and one deeper pot, plus a small blanket. Next, she took two more magazines for the rifle off Dad's shelf (all he had) and added them to the bag, as well as three for the pistol. Catching herself, she doubled back to the supply shelf and stuffed a small coil of rope in the backpack, since Dad thought no one should ever leave home without a bundle of rope. Exactly *why*, she didn't know, but better not to tempt bad luck. While there, she spotted the two-canteen belt she'd worn for the trip, and decided to put it on too.

A 'grab and wiggle' check of the pistol confirmed it snug on her hip. The knife hung secure against her left thigh. Wisp slipped her arms into the backpack straps and snugged it tight. Dad always carried it on one shoulder, but she wasn't quite big enough for that. Last, she picked up the rifle and crossed the room back to the shrine.

Mother remained as she had been, sitting straight, her head lolled to one side.

"I'm going to be far from your shrine, but I know you will protect me from the Tree Walkers, since you told me to go find Dad."

Mother didn't say a word.

She shivered at the brief mental image of Mother's head shifting. Despite loving Mother, watching a shrine *move* had been highly disturbing. She scurried away from the room before getting in any more trouble, and jogged outside. Since Dad had the opener for the front door, she couldn't lock the cabin without being in it, so she had to hope no one found it before she came home. Then again, in twelve years, she had seen only one other person besides Dad, and that marauder had been pretty far away from here.

Still charged with the scare of watching Mother's head move, Wisp hurried up the hill toward the strange tracks, stopping at the creek long enough to fill the canteens and drink her fill. One good thing, being deep and obvious, the ruts hadn't faded much in the few days since Dad disappeared. She decided to walk in the track since the inclined edges let her feel her way along while keeping her eyes on the forest for danger. The ruts also offered a clear path of soft dirt to walk on without many rocks to hurt her feet.

Minutes stretched into hours. When she got thirsty, she veered off into the woods to search for a stream, deciding to save the canteens in case she wandered far away from running water. Within minutes, her ears led her to a tiny brook. After a quick check around for danger, she crouched at the edge and scooped handfuls of water. Once she drank her fill, she rested a little while before getting up and once again following the tracks.

Whatever beast made them had to drag itself along the ground like a huge slug, considering the marks formed a continuous line, unlike footprints. The trails vanished in places, picking back up soon after. A little poking with her toe confirmed her belief that the ground had been too hard in those spots for the creature's feet to mark it. Comparing her shallow footprints to the inches-deep ruts the monster left behind made her think it weighed a lot.

I really don't want to let it see me. But, it's probably really slow, so I could outrun it.

By late afternoon, she caught sight of a spattering of dark red against the green at eye level. She slowed to a stop by a four-foot tall plant with leaves shaped like notched arrowheads and clusters of tiny white flowers. Some of the leaves had dark red spots or lines smeared on them.

"Ninebark. Not edible," said Wisp, as if Dad stood behind her. "The roots can be boiled to make a pain poultice."

She spit on her finger and rubbed it over the dark spot, which liquefied into blood. It didn't appear to be a large amount, but the way it spattered reminded her of what water looked like on the floor when she swung her hands to dry them. A bleeding person probably ran by really fast.

"I bet Dad shot the monster and tracked it. Maybe he got lost."

She sighed and stared down at Dad's rifle in her hands. *He didn't shoot it. All the bullets are still here.*

"Okay, he mashed it in the nose."

Her lip quivered and tears gathered at the corners of her eyes. It couldn't be Dad's blood on those leaves. It *had* to be the monster's, or the people who rode it. Thinking that a monster carried Dad off frightened her in a way the Tree Walkers never had. She'd spotted them sometimes, but they'd been well off in the forest, and always at night, surrounded by thick shadows. What the Tree Walkers would do to her had always been a question of imagination, since Dad never gave her any direct answer to that question. However, his going missing provided a concrete, real problem. Bears took fish into the woods and she didn't think those fish lasted long after that.

Worry built and built until she found herself standing there crying. It took her a minute to get herself under control and sniffle back the sobs to calm.

"No… Mother told me to go. She wouldn't have if Dad didn't need help." She hefted the rifle up so she could wipe her tears on her forearms. "I will find him."

Wisp adjusted the backpack's weight, then fussed at the canteens above her butt. Tired of holding the heavy rifle, she slung it over her right shoulder and gripped the strap in one hand, her left arm swinging free at her side. She groaned under her load, but trudged onward. If she needed the rifle fast, she'd be in trouble, but her arms had had enough. Even if she ran out of bullets, the huge gun weighed so much she could whack a monster over the head with it and probably *still* send it to the Other Place.

Step by step, hour after hour, she walked along the mysterious rut. Here and there, she spotted signs of blood on the understory plants, but always to the right of the tracks. Fatigue set in, and she spent a while staring down at her toes sinking into the dirt with each step. Her shoulders hurt from the backpack straps and she'd become quite hungry.

She entered the forest away from the clear path in which the tracks lay. Wavering leaves from the low-lying growth tickled her legs as she stalked among the trees, looking for a decent spot to sleep for the night. Within a few minutes, she discovered a sheltered area surrounded by tall plants on a nice patch of elevated ground that appeared unlikely to suffer a washout if a sudden heavy rain started. At a guess, she figured she had an hour and a half of daylight left. A wave of fear hit her, but no matter what she *wanted*, she couldn't possibly get home before it got dark at this point. She'd walked too far away. She could only help Dad if she remained alive, so she decided to use the last bits of sun for self-care.

The rifle weighed so much she unloaded it first, letting out a groan of relief after leaning it against a tree trunk. Another grateful breath followed her unburdening herself of the backpack. Wisp left the canteens behind as well, keeping only the pistol and knife. Without all the stuff on her back, a second wave of energy hit her that made it seem possible to walk for another ten hours, but she dare not travel in the dark. She foraged until she located a spread of purslane. The area had some mushrooms as well, but they all had gills. Since she didn't recognize them, she heeded Dad's warning to avoid gilled mushrooms.

"If you don't know what it is, don't eat plants with milky sap, spines, tiny hairs, or thorns. Avoid plants with seeds in pods, or that taste bitter." She scrunched up her nose. Dad had told her never to eat any plant that smelled like almonds, but she had no idea what an almond was, or smelled like. "Or anything with three-bladed leaves."

A few minutes' more hunting yielded some wild raspberries.

Neither the purslane nor the raspberries required cooking, which simplified things. She returned to her campsite with her dinner, set it on the backpack, and walked off into the woods, downhill, to find a spot to release the bad water. While watching the rivulet make its way off along the ground, she thought about how on their trip to the Jeep place, Dad hadn't squatted when he let out the bad water. Maybe because he wore those 'jeans' as he called them. But she didn't understand how he could get the bad water to go straight out in front like that. Even if she wore jeans (assuming such a thing existed small enough for her) she'd wind up making a huge, disgusting mess if she tried that.

Wisp sighed and wandered back to her stuff. She had far worse things to worry about than whatever magic Dad used to control his water.

She sat, munching on fistfuls of purslane and raspberries as the last vestiges of daylight gave way to the moon. Without the blanket-shrouded Haven, the night, even in summer, took on an uncomfortable chill. Wisp dug the blanket out of her pack and curled up under it, using the lumpy backpack as a pillow. She snugged the fabric to her chin, only her face exposed to the world.

Every *snap* or soft *thud* made her jump and stare in the direction it came from.

Her hands mushed into her chin; her whole body trembled. Without the Haven, the Tree Walkers could get her. She had nowhere to go. Mother's annoyance had so rattled her that she hadn't even thought about what she'd do at night when she ran out the door. Here she sat, with only a thin blanket between her and danger.

The blanket wouldn't protect her.

Dad said the guns wouldn't hurt the Tree Walkers.

Would the knife? She thought about it. Of course, roots and vines... a bullet would sail right through the tangle without doing much. The knife could slash and break. Wisp pulled her knife from its sheath and clutched it in two hands under the blanket. She refused to let the Tree Walkers take her without a fight.

Wisp shrank in on herself, peering over her blanket-covered knees at the darkness, begging morning to hurry up and get there. At every tiny noise, she twitched. Her mind played tricks, making each shadow turn into an approaching Tree Walker. She dare not scream, or even breathe too loud. Remembering Dad's instruction to make her shape as not-person as possible when trying to hide, she lay flatter.

Mother, please protect me.

She closed her eyes and tried to believe that since she had been commanded to go find Dad, Mother would extend the protection of the Haven to her wherever she went.

She wouldn't have sent me out after Dad if I'd get caught by the Tree Walkers. Right?

Shivering, but not from the cold, she hunkered down and prayed to Mother.

Trail's End
~12~

A heavy *snap* startled Wisp awake.

She jumped, dropping the knife in her lap and flailing at the blanket.

Five feet away, a huge buck froze stone still.

Wisp locked stares with it, her barely-awake brain unable to understand what kind of monster looked back at her.

When it clicked that something huge and alive had spotted her, she screamed.

The deer whirled about and took off into the woods, crashing through the understory and tearing branches off taller shrubs.

Gasping for breath, Wisp pressed herself against the tree, a hand to her chest, not moving until the rapid thumping of a running deer no longer reached her ears. She rubbed her hands over her face, yawned, then rolled onto her side, moaning at being stiff and sore.

"Ugh… just a deer."

Tempting as meat could be, she decided against tracking it down since it had run away so fast, and she couldn't possibly use all the meat nor even manage to get it home. *I'll only shoot a deer or boar if I'm starving. It's wrong to waste it.* If she *did* reach that point though, she planned to camp by the remains until she either ate them all or the meat rotted beyond being edible.

As soon as Wisp stood, a certain urgency struck her. She again walked away from her campsite, gathered a bunch of broad leaves, and found a spot to make *ngh*. There, she used the knife to dig a hole. Minutes later, with the evidence buried, she grabbed more purslane and raspberries for a hasty breakfast, and slugged down water from her canteen.

After pulling all her gear back on, she made her way again to the tracks and continued following them (hopefully) to Dad. She sipped from the canteen on and off over the next few hours, snagging more purslane and some creeping Oregon grapes to munch on the way. The bitterness made her cringe with each bite, but she could grab easy handfuls of them and they'd keep her fed.

The sun crept by overhead, worrying her with how much time passed and still no sign of Dad. About an hour past midday, walking grew easier, like she traveled along a slight downhill slope. The angle of the trees around her confirmed it. She followed the tracks as they swerved to the right around a dense cluster of pines. The trail looped back to the left on the other side, snaking past a boulder before veering off to the right again and disappearing entirely about thirty feet away where the ground became hard and rocky.

"No…" She looked around, but couldn't find any more tracks. "The monster didn't disappear. Did it fly away?" Her eyes widened. A heavy beast that could fly meant only one thing—dragon. "Eep!"

She ran to hide in the boulder's shadow, staring up past the trees at the clouds. Over the course of several minutes, she spotted nothing bigger than a hawk gliding overhead. And though she *felt* like a mouse, the bird had no interest in her. With each passing minute, the idea of dragons drifted from terrifying to unlikely to dumb. A dragon couldn't be here since they'd all destroyed themselves when they lit the world on fire.

How did people make dragons? She scrunched up her nose. *Magic?*

Flailing her arms, Wisp tried and failed to stand against the weight of all her gear. She grabbed the boulder and pulled herself upright. *Mother wouldn't tell me to go if I couldn't do anything. I'm giving up too easy.*

She walked to the place where the tracks stopped, and crouched. The ground, peppered with rocks, appeared too hard for whatever monster made the trail to disturb it. It had to go this way, but left no tracks in the dense, rocky soil. Wisp spun in place, staring out at the forest in all directions, but found no sign of any continuing trail. She shrugged the rifle off her shoulder and tried with the scope, but other than a black bear and two cubs way off to the northwest, she saw nothing but trees.

"There has to be more tracks *somewhere*."

Wary of danger, she carried the rifle despite its weight, and proceeded to walk out in an expanding spiral pattern from the end of the trail, scanning the ground for more tracks, blood splats, or some sign of which way the monster had taken Dad. She wasted over an hour before getting frustrated to the point of growling and drawing her foot back to kick a tree in a fit of rage.

She stopped herself before breaking a toe, and stood in place silently seething with shaking, clenched fists. "It's not fair! Why did you take Dad away?! I don't want to be alone."

The echo of her voice faded in a few seconds, and she felt silly for shouting, which only made her angrier. Mother had trusted her to do this, and she'd done it wrong. She failed as a tracker, and she'd never see Dad again.

The dragons destroyed themselves.

At Dad's voice in her mind, the anger building inside her burst into a great upwelling of sorrow. She shuddered, mouth open, silent tears running down her face.

But Mother still didn't speak to her.

Before the explosion of sobbing started, she closed her mouth and collected herself. If she'd been bad, surely, Mother would've yelled, or told her to come home. *Mother sent me. I can find Dad.*

She hurried back to the boulder, which came up to her shoulders, and climbed on top of it. Looking down the length of the trail back the way she'd come, then to the left where it disappeared gave her a sense of direction. The monster that took Dad had been heading generally to the east. Not seeing any tracks here didn't prove she'd *never* find any.

After taking note of a few distinctive trees and another huge rock in the distance that lined up with the trail, she climbed down and resumed walking. Without a rut to walk in, she moved at a more cautious pace, splitting her attention between the ground, her immediate surroundings, and distant landmarks.

The downward incline of the terrain increased. An hour past the boulder, she reached the edge of a drop off with a hill so steep it qualified as a cliff, studded with green vines and protruding roots. Gazing at a potential fall many times the height of her cabin caused an unpleasant sensation like a spirit had stuck its hand inside her to tickle the bottom of her stomach.

The Forest Beyond the Earth

I bet the monster probably started flying here. If it jumped or tripped, it would've made a big hole at the bottom.

Wisp turned her back to the slope, crouched, and lowered herself over the edge before making her way down at a careful pace, hunting for roots to grab or step on so she didn't slip and go tumbling. Wherever she encountered soft dirt, she stabbed her feet into the ground like knives, clutching soil between her toes.

At the bottom, she dusted herself off and turned her gaze out over relatively flat ground with thinner trees and less underbrush. Since no obvious signs of which way to go presented themselves, she decided to rest there for a little while, staring off into the forest. Eventually, guilt overpowered tired, and she resumed walking while gazing upward at the sky. The sun gave her an approximate idea of east, so she followed it, walking in as straight a line as she could manage until the sky dimmed with evening.

Within a few minutes of her making the decision to stop for the night, she caught sight of a large, sleeping monster up ahead.

Silent, she dropped to one knee, taking cover behind a huge pine. She lifted the rifle to her shoulder and put her eye to the scope while aiming at the form lurking in the weeds. The front grille of a long-dead car filled the crosshairs.

"I'm being dumb." Wisp sighed and pushed herself back up to stand. "It's not a monster. It's a hunk of metal."

Curious, she approached the car, keeping her rifle poised in case something less friendly than a rusting vehicle lived nearby. This car didn't have the huge tires like the Jeep, only bare metal wheels. It seemed hardly possible for it to have ever moved on those. Some parts of the body had turned brown with rust while others remained dark green. Cracks crisscrossed the big window in front, but none of the glass had broken completely. She approached and tugged at the handle. The door pulled out a little, but stuck. A harder yank got it open, releasing a musty, damp stink.

She cringed, but after the initial blast, decided Mother's shrine had a stronger (and worse) smell. Small beetles and other insects crawled around the bottom, a few on the seats, which bore a lush spread of mold.

Wisp frowned. She'd considered sheltering inside it, but Dad once said something about breathing near mold being bad. She slammed the door (shattering the window into a rain of tiny sparkling bits) and walked for a little while more until she found a spot where clover and chicory grew in abundance. The forest appeared the same in all directions, with no particularly great shelter or high ground available.

With a shrug, she set the backpack down by a tree and proceeded to collect a meal's worth of chicory and clover. Dad once said something significant about clovers with four leaves, but she didn't spot any, nor could she remembered what made them special. While gathering plants, she happened upon a huge, rotten log. That got her stomach growling, so after she carried the greens over to the backpack, she ran to the log and smacked it with the butt end of the rifle until a piece came off.

After breaking off a couple sections of rotting wood, she found what she'd hoped for: grubs. She collected a handful of the squirming critters and carried them back to her temporary nest. They tried to crawl off while she dug the deeper pot from the backpack, but none were fast enough to avoid being caught again.

She hunted down a branch, which she split into sharpened skewers with the knife. Next, she cleared away a spot for a fire. The area offered little in the way of non-live wood, so she took some pieces of the rotten log and used kindling from her pack. A few scratches of the ferro rod over the file got a fire going. She sat close, nursing the beginning wisps of smoke by waving air over it until the flames grew strong enough to handle the larger hunks of rotting wood. While she waited for the fire to grow, she stuck the grubs on the sticks, forcing their tubular bodies out straight, and whittled a crude rack to hold the skewers over the fire: two Y-shaped branches she jabbed into the dirt on either side of the flames.

By the time the sun went down, Wisp enjoyed a nice meal of fire-roasted grub with chicory and clover, which she ate raw. Sitting and eating let the fatigue of walking all day sneak up on her. Having barely slept her first night away from home, she struggled to stay awake long enough to eat. The once-scary noises of the forest failed to reach her mind. Her eyelids sank closed, popped open, and sank closed again. Chewing became a confounding task.

Wisp barely noticed the half-eaten fourth roasted grub fall onto her chest as she passed out.

Little Thief
~13~

A tickle at her chin woke her early the next morning.

She'd fallen flat on the ground, arms and legs splayed to the side. Something not terribly heavy perched on top of her chest. Wisp angled her head upward—and locked eyes with a raccoon munching on her grub.

"Hey!" she yelled.

The raccoon chittered at her and darted off with the grub in its mouth. She scrambled to her feet and chased, but the small fuzzy blur disappeared among the greenery after less than a minute.

"Grr!" She stomped, snarled, and growled again.

After plodding back to her campsite, she growled a third time. Two empty skewers remained on the rack, proof she'd fallen asleep before she could eat them… and the raccoon had probably feasted upon them first before being brave enough to steal the half-grub that had been laying on top of her.

Wisp made a hasty meal of the remaining clover she'd gathered, drank about a quarter of a canteen's worth of water in one long series of gulps, and gasped for breath. Still trusting Mother's help, she repacked her stuff, deciding to keep the Y struts in case she found more grubs, and set off toward the rising sun.

A little over two hours into her walk, she stepped in bear *ngh,* and almost tripped over a root while scrambling to get away from the pile. Balancing on her left leg, she examined the brown smear mushed between her toes and over most of her sole, snarling again before scraping her foot on the ground as well as a nearby swath of greenery. She swung the rifle off her shoulder and carried it, giving serious thought to having bear for dinner that day—if she could find one.

At least it didn't stink quite as bad as Dad's.

"Am I going the wrong way, Mother?" asked Wisp.

Between the raccoon stealing her food and stepping in nasty, it sure felt like someone or something tried to send her a message. Dad had been pretty clear when he said Mother would *speak* if she ever thought her a bad girl. But, did that mean she had to be nearby? Could someone in the Other Place talk to people regardless of far they'd gone from a shrine?

Close to midday, she encountered another steep hill, this one upward and not too big, perhaps only twice her height. Wisp pushed past the weeds and plant growth, climbing up to a strange metal barrier. The odd fence only stood as tall as her hips, though it had many posts in the ground, suggesting it could withstand a lot of force. The purpose of such a squat barrier baffled her, since even a girl her size could get over it with ease. It ran along the edge of a flat rock-like surface that stretched into a long ribbon. Small weeds sprouted up from thousands of cracks in the surface, crisscrossing the stone path far as she could see before it vanished among the trees. Some of her books had mentioned 'roads,' and this place did resemble the pictures on a cover or two. She pulled herself up and over the barrier, testing the hard ground with a few toes before putting weight on it.

The dark stone warmed her foot, but didn't burn.

Wisp gradually leaned onto that leg until she decided the road would hold her without breaking, then pulled her other leg over the barrier. Based on the sun's position, she thought the path traveled north-to-south, but the thick trees made getting a good idea of direction iffy. For a minute or three, she spun in circles, staring around in all directions. Eventually, she decided to go straight across the road and deeper into the forest.

A similar metal barrier abutted the other side, though the forest floor was even with the surface there, so she didn't have a hill to climb. She placed her foot atop the barrier and vaulted over with ease.

Following Mother's directions, she marched onward. Hours passed with little distraction other than distant birds tweeting or the occasional cry of a hawk. Eventually, the rifle became too heavy to carry, so she shouldered it and let her arms dangle limp at her sides. How Dad could hold it all day, she had no idea. When they'd gone to the Jeep place, he'd had it in his hands for the entire walk, putting it down only by the stream while they ate.

She stopped once to let out bad water, and lucked into another cluster of raspberries an hour or so past midday. She ate so many she expected her *ngh* would be splattery, but she didn't care. Any food she didn't have to cook helped. Building a fire took time away from finding Dad. The occasional peek up at the sun plus a large helping of Mother's pull kept her going in the direction she thought those tracks went.

Late in the afternoon, bubbling on the left tempted her off course in hopes of finding water. The delicate churning sound led her to a shallow stream full of smooth rocks only a few minutes away. She sat on a big stone at the edge, letting her feet dangle in the icy water to wash away the bear *ngh*. Careful to put the canteens in upstream from her feet, she refilled them and drank until her head hurt from the cold. Once she couldn't bear another sip, she spent a little while rubbing the nasty off the bottom of her foot. Despite no longer seeing any muck there, she still scrubbed as if to erase the memory of it.

Her brief rest over, she got up and headed back into the woods. After almost three days of constant walking, being stuck inside her Haven while Dad went off to hunt no longer sounded like a bad idea, even if she didn't have the opener. Though confinement frustrated her, it took a whole lot less work to sit around reading.

She trudged on, shifting the rifle back and forth from wearing it on her shoulder to carrying it as her arms tolerated. With the quiet sameness of trees going by came the realization that she'd spent the past night sprawled out in the open, so exhausted she'd passed out without a single thought about the Tree Walkers. That they hadn't taken her last night despite her being so defenseless had only one explanation.

Mother protected her.

At a growl in her stomach, she began looking around for edibles, but the stretch of forest she'd wandered into bloomed with all plants she regarded as either not-food or dangerous. Mushrooms gave her hope, but she leapt away from them when she noticed a broken veil around the stem.

"White death… or white angels or something." She grumbled at herself for not remembering. "Whatever it's called, I'm not eating it."

Dad's description of feeling like she'd swallowed a whole colony of live ants that would eat her from the inside out before she slid into the Other Place had left a mark. Any mushroom with a broken membrane around the stem she avoided as if it would fly up out of the ground and try to bite her. She scurried away near a jog until she could no longer see any mushrooms.

The day ground onward, with little sign of anything to eat. Hunting for food distracted her from listening to Mother's pull, and she wound up veering back and forth. Around early evening, a terrifying sight emerged from the forest in the distance: a standing wall of vegetation.

Wisp stifled a yelp and jumped behind a tree, shaking and whimpering, begging Mother to watch over her. Once she realized no great roar of cracking twigs and snapping vines came charging forward, her trembling lessened. Perhaps a minute later, she'd stopped shaking entirely, and risked peering around the tree with one eye. Bark dappled with white lichen blurred as she shifted her focus from the tree in front of her face to the distance.

A wall of greens and browns blocked off the forest. It looked like the rolling wave of vegetation from her nightmare, only it didn't move at all… and had a suspiciously flat top. Clinging to her tree, she observed the bizarre thing for a few minutes, but it neither moved, nor roared, nor extended any vines in her direction.

Hoping it might not be a sleeping mass of Tree Walkers, she risked emerging from her hiding place enough to raise the rifle against her shoulder. In the scope's magnification, it became obvious she'd found a crisscross of metal wires suspended between posts, with strips of cloth tied all over it to create the illusion of leaves and shrubs. It reminded her of the Jeep place, the fake plants Dad referred to as camouflage.

Metal posts with wires between them did not look like something that would've grown there, so people had to have made it. Her jaw opened at the wonder of humans who had the kind of magic necessary to shape metal, but maybe it had come from the ancient ones, before the dragons.

Nervous and excited in equal measure, Wisp stood out from behind the tree and advanced, holding the rifle sideways again while stepping around roots and rocks. A few paces away from her hiding spot, she noticed a thin wire a few inches off the ground. Curious, she squatted in front of it and looked left and right along the length.

On the left, it had been tied around a tree trunk. On the right, it passed through a tiny metal loop stuck into another tree and went up into the branches where a cluster of old coffee cans hung. She rested her fingers on the wire by the ground, picking at it.

The cans reacted with a wobble. She looked back and forth from the wire to the cans a few times before it clicked.

This is a noisemaker!

She stood and stepped over the wire, creeping onward, twice as alert for where she placed her feet. While crossing the woods between the first noisemaker and the fence, she avoided four more wires, all connected to jumbles of cans. Dad taught her about 'traps' like snares or covered pits. Once, he'd even made a wire like this, but it pulled a stick away from another stick when triggered, causing a giant log to come falling out of a tree. These cans wouldn't hurt anyone, so she entertained the idea that whoever lived on the other side of that fence might not be mean.

Still, she couldn't risk contact. Best to avoid a fight if possible.

Wisp scurried over to the wall and peered past the metal mesh into a big open field that held several rows of strange, tall plants. A good distance past them stood a cabin at least three times the size of hers. Beyond that, more cabins of different shapes and sizes gathered around an open space. People appeared to be moving around there, but the distance made them too tiny to recognize any details.

Wow… this is a city!

She clung to the metal grid wall, face close enough for the cloth strips to tickle her cheeks. The barrier continued in both directions before curving inward, evidently going around the whole city. A trill of random notes came from the right. She dropped into a crouch and huddled against the strange wall, frozen in place.

A man approached along the inside of the barrier. He whistled to himself while walking at a relaxed pace, like he had nowhere really to go. His boots resembled Dad's, but his pants couldn't decide what color to be. Blobs of green, black, and brown mottled the baggy garment. A white cloth shirt with thin straps exposed his shoulders, which had taken on a reddish hue while the rest of his arms had a tan a few shades lighter than Dad. The front of his neck and insides of his arms were almost as pale as her skin. He also wore an enormous knife on his belt in a sheath, the point only inches off the ground. The man didn't have any guns or even a bow.

Wisp stayed motionless as he went right on past her, not noticing her behind all the hanging strips on the barrier. When the whistling faded to the point she could barely hear it, she twisted around to look. The man continued marching along the barrier, like he intended to walk completely around the city.

That's strange. Where is he going? This place is weird.

She stood and headed to the right, away from him, intending to ignore the city and continue going east as soon as she reached the end of the wall in her way. Within a few minutes, the wind carried a new smell across her face. Before she could identify it, a strand of drool ran down her chin. It would be dark fairly soon, and she hadn't eaten much more than a couple handfuls of raspberries after an incomplete dinner the previous night. The fragrance in the air had to be meat cooking, but no kind of meat she'd ever encountered before.

The wonderful aroma drew her to a stop soon after. Wisp leaned up to the barrier and peered in again at another cabin, also much larger than hers. This one had a small covered area behind it, which confused her as to why someone would build a roof over dirt. The door sat at the middle of the wall at the back of the roofed area, between a pair of metal chairs.

A short distance closer to her, away from the cabin, smoke wafted up from a round stack of bricks. Though no flames peeked up over the top of the tiny chimney, it had to contain fire. A brownish lump on a stick hung over it, right in the smoke's path. The meat had the same coloration as a nicely roasted grub, but whatever creature it had been was *much* bigger than a grub.

Wisp bit her lip, pondering her next move. She could get up and over the barrier pretty easily, given the holes in the lattice made for excellent footholds. That left a swath of maybe eighty yards of open dirt filled with even rows of short green plants, another type she didn't recognize. Also, strange animals roamed in the open. Some had four legs and almost resembled half-sized deer, only they had horns rather than antlers. On the left, a group of weird, fat birds waddled around. Most were white, though a handful had a brownish coloration. All had the heads and beaks of birds, however, their bodies looked in no way capable of flying. Not to mention, she'd never imagined birds could get that big. A few of them had to be larger than Dad's head. They clucked, wandered about, and pecked at the ground.

Her stomach growled at the scent of the cooking meat. Hunger won her over, and she decided the food would be hers.

I am a raccoon.

She backed away into the woods far enough to find a hiding place. There, she stashed the rifle and backpack, her two heaviest items. Her plan involved climbing the camouflage wall, running over to grab the meat, and going straight back out before anyone saw her.

Confident, Wisp approached the wall again and watched.

A cluster of men walked by in front of the cabin, far enough away not to be a concern. They too carried huge knives, but no guns. Even if they saw her, they couldn't hurt her without getting close—and if they meant to hurt her, the handgun wouldn't let them.

She grabbed on to the wall, raised her leg, and stuck her foot in one of the gaps. It hurt a little, but not enough to change her mind. The whole barrier rattled when she pulled her weight onto it, so she jumped down.

That's a noisemaker, too.

Wisp glared hungrily at the roasting meat. Going over the barrier would make so much clattering, even those people far away would probably hear her. Desperate with hunger, she roamed along the wall, hunting for a way in.

Salvation showed itself thirty feet later, where a small section of the barrier had broken apart from one of the metal poles, creating a gap big enough for her to squeeze past. Even better, it didn't look like a grownup would be able to fit. She got down on her chest and dragged herself into a nice little hiding place behind a long wooden object close to the wall. She shifted onto her knees and peered up over the top, clutching the edge. Much to her surprise, what she thought to be a short fence contained water.

Wisp peered down at a pale, delicate face with clouds gliding by in the background. Dirt smudged the girl's cheek and chin, and her eyes, huge and blue, gave off sorrow. She felt bad for the water spirit, wondering what had made her so sad. Wisp started to look to the left, and the other girl mimicked her. She grinned, and the other girl did as well. Amused, Wisp played the game, trying to move in an unexpected way that the other girl would mess up. Nothing she did, from wagging her head to sticking out her tongue, worked. Every move she made, the water spirit copied perfectly. She wanted to giggle at her strange, new friend, but did not want to be caught by the men who lived here. Wisp tried to touch the other girl, but her finger sent ripples over the water, breaking up the image. At that moment, she realized she'd been staring at her own reflection in the largest pool of still water she'd ever seen. Over the years, she'd caught glimpses of herself in drinking cups or spoons, but never before had she gotten such a perfect view. A big box of water like this must work like the mirrors she had read about. The sadness in the girl before her had been hers.

I have to find Dad. Wisp stared at herself until sorrow became determination.

A loud snort sprayed water on her from the right, and broke the reflection apart. She lifted her gaze off the water and came nose-to-nose with the largest creature she'd ever seen. Ears flapped at her on a head bigger than her chest. This creature, too, somewhat resembled a deer, but many times bigger with a shorter neck and broad head, no horns, and big eyes. Blotchy black spots dotted its otherwise white fur.

Wisp swallowed, and backed away before the creature got angry.

The animal dipped its nose in the water to drink.

She leapt to her feet and ran to the left, heading toward the prize. When she reached the rows of evenly spaced plants, one of the smaller four-legged horned critters came barreling out of the greenery at her. Wisp squealed in alarm and ran faster away from the pursuing creature, but it galloped after, seemingly intent on crashing headfirst into her. It chased her straight into the cluster of large birds, which erupted into a panicky spray of feathers as they scrambled to run in all directions. They squawked and clucked, flapping their useless wings while zipping around in circles, making far, far too much noise.

The mini-deer caught up and rammed its head into her butt, throwing her off her feet. She flew into a patch of strong-scented plants, landing flat on her chest.

"Oof," she muttered. "Ow."

With a snort of victory, the black-furred creature that had head-butted her trotted off into the field. Wisp pushed herself up with one arm and reached back to rub her rear end.

Stupid animal. Is it trying to stop me from taking that meat?

"What's all the fuss?" called an unusual high-pitched voice. Not as high as hers, but way higher than Dad's

The door at the back of the roofed area opened, and a strange-looking man stepped out. Long, blonde hair framed a narrow, rounded face, and hung past his belt. Most odd, he seemed to have stuffed something down the front of his shirt that created a pair of lumps in the blue fabric. He didn't look anywhere near as strong as Dad, with much rounder shoulders and narrow, almost delicate, arms. Like Wisp, this strange man didn't wear any shoes, but had the same green-brown-black blotchy pants as the man she'd seen walking by the outer wall.

Wisp flattened herself out on the ground, hands against the dirt on either side of her chin. She held her body stock still, staring at the unusual man with the high voice and towels stuffed down his front.

"Oh, you ladies." The man folded his arms beneath the odd pillowy masses in his shirt and shook his head at the birds. "What's got you all running about?"

A pair of the plump birds wandered over to Wisp and stuck their heads into the plants to get a closer look at her. She flicked her fingers to shoo them, but they ignored her.

The Forest Beyond the Earth

The animal responsible for launching Wisp into the shrubbery shook its head and emitted a scream startlingly close to that of a frightened human. The shrill noise set the birds into another frenzy of running around.

"Are the goats bothering you again?" The strange man approached the small chimney and spent a few minutes rotating and poking at the meat before walking back inside the cabin.

Eager to get out of this city before anyone spotted her, Wisp crawled out of the bushes, some of which smelled quite a bit like the taste powders. Crouched low, she scurried across a patch of bare dirt littered with big seeds and huge pieces of bird *ngh*. The flightless things continued to cluck and scurry, mostly avoiding her.

She stopped and took a knee by the tiny brick chimney, which indeed contained fire. Once she got close to the meat, she realized it had probably been one of those strange birds before the city person killed and plucked it. The fragrance overpowered her. She couldn't help but rip off one of the legs and chomp down. Despite it being hot, she savaged it, moaning in delight at the flavor while gasping at the heat between bites.

The goat screamed again.

"Kaya?" yelled the strange man.

Wisp snapped her head up, locking stares with the city-person who had one foot out the door.

"Kaya?" repeated the strange, small man, eyes wide.

Eep!

Wisp grabbed the wooden rod impaling the bird and jumped into a sprint for the wall.

"Kaya! Wait!" yelled the strange man.

She ran straight to the wall, the odd high-voiced city-person repeating that nonsense word over and over behind her. Wisp leapt onto the barrier, too intent on escape to care if it rattled. She'd already been seen, so no sense being quiet. Climbing with one hand and both feet, she hauled herself up to the top. The strange man's fingers grazed at her ankle, but she jumped fast enough avoid the grabbing hand, fell ten feet back to the ground, and tumbled on landing. Fortunately, she managed not to get too much dirt on the cooked bird.

Deeper voices rose up in shouts behind the wall, but Wisp didn't slow down or look back until she reached the place in the woods where she'd stashed her things. Even there, she paused only long enough to get the backpack on and sling the rifle before running into the woods, as directly away from the wall as possible. Dad's warnings replayed in her mind about how people would try to hurt her.

She hit one of the noisemakers, which nearly tripped her, but the cacophony of clattering cans only made her run faster, clutching the bird-stick tight. Once the fire in her legs and chest made it impossible to continue running, she slowed to a jog, not caring where she went as long she kept going away from those people. Their distant shouts had grown quieter. No longer able to resist the wonderful smell, she bit a piece off the bird. Jogging gave way to walking soon after as her protesting legs threatened to quit entirely and dump her on the ground. Wisp forced herself to walk onward, taking another bite every few paces.

Within an hour, darkness spread throughout the woods. The sky off to her left lit up with a shimmering dark red-orange sunset. She whined past a mouthful of bird meat, annoyed at herself for having gone south instead of east. How long had she spent heading in the wrong direction? Mother wanted her to go *east* to find Dad. She shouldn't have ever seen the city behind the green wall. Only because she'd spent at least a whole day going *south* did she find it. South. The wrong direction.

South led toward the Tree Walkers.

Angry tears fell from her eyes, but she kept on walking and eating. In addition to wasting so much time, she'd kicked a hornet nest. Not only would the Tree Walkers be after her, the people in that city would probably chase her too. She only hoped 'Kaya' wasn't a dark magic spell intended to hurt her. Why that weird man kept yelling it, she couldn't understand.

Maybe it's a different language. A few of the books have funny words, too. Dad called it Spanish. Maybe 'kaya' means thief. Or maybe that's what they call these birds. She got heartsick all over again remembering when he'd told her what the 'Spanish' words meant. His voice echoed in her thoughts even as the shadows thickened around her.

I'm bad. I did bad. I should have camped by now. It's too dark… but at least I have food.

Out of energy, she staggered along at a forced walk, unable to will herself to move fast at all. She looked around, searching for a place to hide since she couldn't run far enough (especially in the dark) to feel safe. She followed the terrain down a modest hill, trying to put earth between her and any pursuers. A short way down, a massive fallen tree lay half-buried in the hillside next to a great bundle of exposed roots. She headed closer, almost cheering when she discovered a large, hollowed-out space beneath it.

Wisp crawled into the tangle of roots, tucking herself into the deepest spot she could find. Out of breath, but hopeful nothing could find her in there, she finally allowed herself to breathe. Once her heart slowed from slamming to pounding, she pulled the rifle off her shoulder to rest across her legs and shrugged her arms out from the backpack. She hunkered down and feasted on the still-warm bird, savoring smaller bites she could taste while trying to catch her breath. Her exhausted legs ached, and her head swam from fatigue and worry.

Despite the wonderful food, scared, angry tears kept flowing. Her wrong turn may have given her a once-in-a-lifetime meal, but it had not helped her find Dad. She could be lost for all she knew, having wasted so much time going the wrong way. It might be too late for her to find him at all. What if the monster had already devoured him as she continued to devour this bird?

"Did I do bad?" she whispered. Unable to resist the magnificent feast she'd stolen, she snarled and sank her teeth into the bird flesh again, tearing away a huge chunk. While struggling to chew such a mouthful, she listened for the voice she dreaded so much.

Mother didn't say a word.

Gradually, Wisp relaxed. Hope returned. Mother had not given up on her. She could still find Dad.

And she had a... whatever this bird was called.

A broad grin spread across Wisp's face.

The Forest Comes Alive
~14~

Wisp popped awake and found herself inside her Haven. Though safe, it appeared much roomier than she remembered, almost big enough for her to stand up in. Confused, she looked down at her dingy, threadbare dress, then peered out at the cabin. It, too, had grown in size, vast and dark. She grasped one of the bars on the door and pushed. At finding it locked, she slumped with a sigh of relief.

The second she realized she had to be dreaming since she had not been six years old in a long time, a powerful wind swirled up around her. Books flew from shelves; Dad's workbench fell over, and her Haven shuddered. She clung to the bars, shouting pleas to Mother, asking her to stop the storm. With a loud *pank*, the lock snapped; the gale yanked the Haven's door open and swept her out of her safe place. Wisp landed on her chest, sliding across the room faster than she could run. Screaming, she raised her arms to shield her face from the wall rushing toward her.

The Forest Beyond the Earth

Her body crashed into the wood, but it gave way as easily as if she'd flown into a cobweb. The cabin vanished, leaving her tumbling over the forest floor, down a long hill of leaves and vines. She skidded to a stop, face down in a thick patch of underbrush. Dizzy, she lifted her head from the dirt, spat a mouthful of plant matter aside, and pulled herself up to kneel. The old dress remained, as did her six-year-old self.

This is a dream.

She got to her feet and looked around at the huge trees.

A ghostly version of her own voice echoed. "What was it like before the dragons?"

"The Earth is gone," said Dad from everywhere at once.

"How can the Earth be gone? We are still here. It's a plammit, right?"

"Planet," said Dad. "And yes, the stone and dirt remain, but the Earth that once was is no more. For many years, even longer than I've been alive, it smoldered like the ashes in the fireplace." A soft, repetitive crunching surrounded her; she imagined him jabbing a stick at the embers back home, filling the blackness of the flue with a thousand-thousand flying sparks. "But life has a way. Mother Nature decided to try again, and breathed upon the Earth, creating the Endless Forest."

"Dad?" asked Wisp, in her twelve-year-old voice, turning in place. Her voice echoed over and over in the forest. "Where are you?"

"The Endless Forest. That's where we live." Six-year-old Wisp's ghostly voice seemed to come from everywhere.

"Very good," said Dad.

The pride in his words pulled at her heart. He loved whenever she learned things. How would he react to her failure now? When she finally *had* to use everything he'd taught her, she couldn't find him.

Wisp covered her face in her hands, and bawled like the tiny child she dreamed herself to be.

"To your Haven!" whisper-shouted Dad.

Her sobs cut off to silence. She whipped her head up and spun around, searching the moonlit woods. Snaps and crunches closed in on her from one side, but her Haven was too far away to save her. Wisp ran, as she always did whenever this nightmare happened. At first, the memory of a happy moment had confused her, but the truth of the dream had finally shown itself. The Tree Walkers would not let her sleep easy that night.

Little Wisp darted back from the writhing patches of vines and leaves swelling up from the forest floor, growing toward her. Roots emerged from the earth and knotted together into the shapes of bodies. Monsters of leaf and bark, with glowing eyes of emerald green, rose from the mulch behind her. Reaching arms and grasping vines nipped at her trailing hair.

Unable to help herself, she peeked back over her shoulder. A rolling wall of vegetation with many eyes and arms, taller than her cabin, thundered across the forest coming for her. She screamed, leaning into her stride, heedless of sharp rocks or hard roots at her feet. Time lost meaning as she focused only on getting away from the Tree Walkers. Fallen logs, standing pines, a small creek, and the rotting hulks of old machines abandoned to the forest streaked by in the night.

Eventually, as always happened in this nightmare, a thin root shot up from the ground and wrapped around her ankle, tripping her flat on her chest. Her fingers clawed into the dirt, a desperate, but pointless struggle to get away. She didn't even feel the thorns biting her skin and coating her foot in blood. Wisp sat up, reaching for the root that had caught her, but before she could touch it, the great tidal wave of angry forest fell upon her.

She crossed her arms over her face and shrieked.

Wisp snapped awake, breathing hard and covered in sweat.

Usually, whenever that dream tormented her, she'd scream until Dad came to check on her, but a tiny slice of her mind understood she lay out in the open woods without her Haven, and resisted the urge to cry out. Stunned, she huddled in a shivering ball, cowering away from the darkness and wavering blurs surrounding her. Wisp floated within a fog of confusion from her abrupt return to consciousness mixed with the deathly fear of the nightmare. For a while, she couldn't tell real apart from dream, and trembled in silence.

Her fingers curled, brushing her bare stomach. The touch broke the spell, snapping her out of the haze. She looked down at herself, curled up against a wall of rotting wood, her feet half-buried in soil. The dress hadn't been real. She brushed a hand down the chest of her pink shirt. Grains of dirt dusted her legs, dark against the skin showing through the seams in her leather skirt. She gazed at her pale legs, hearing Dad's voice in her mind explain how he'd made it in separate panels so it wouldn't hamper her stride. Had he stitched all the tough leather armor scraps into a solid skirt, she'd barely have been able to walk—and forget running.

The bird remained on its stick beside her, where she'd jammed one end into the dirt. She'd managed to eat about a third of it. It would last her at least another whole day, more if she could control herself and not gorge until her belly hurt. Looking at it brought her mind back to the here and now. She had to find Dad. Mother trusted her with this task, gave her permission to leave the cabin.

Wisp did not want to disappoint Mother.

Snap.

The breath stalled in her throat.

Another faint *snap* came from farther away, along with the rustle of leaves.

She leaned her weight forward onto her left hand, edging her head closer to the shell of roots that fell like a curtain over the hollow she'd crawled into. Wisp stretched forward, shifting onto all fours, and peered out into the forest. The stars gave off enough light to make out the shapes of nearby trees. In a few places where the canopy opened up, the Moon created brighter spots like giant versions of Dad's light-maker shining down from the sky. Tiny yellow lights winked in and out among the trees from a scattering of firebugs. The forest around her had grown thick with shadows, all too dark to see into, and all of them moved.

Crunch.

Wisp shifted her eyes to the right, keeping her head motionless. At the edge of the darkness perhaps twenty feet away, a mound of plant matter glided out from behind a pine trunk, at least as tall as Dad, probably bigger. The creature pivoted toward her, revealing a black nothingness where a person's face would be, a hollow void with two huge, blank round eyes that gleamed in the moonlight.

Tree Walker!

The bad water almost shot straight out of her.

Such fear crashed into her that her mind shut down. Unable to think or move, she dangled by her grip on the roots, barely breathing. Several more mounds moved in the distance, brief gleams flashing from their mound-shaped bodies whenever a leaf caught the moon. The nearest Tree Walker flowed along the ground making little noise, like a liquid mass of vegetation. Wisp caught signs of motion, spotting other mounds creeping forward in a line, keeping even with each other. The creatures advanced in a wave, only for some reason, they didn't swell up to ten feet tall and join together to form an inescapable barrier.

They didn't see me. She shuddered, figuring these small mounds were like the forest's eyes, peeking over the blanket, trying to stay hidden until it spotted a child to take. Then, they would rise and swell into the thunderous wall of roots and vines her nightmare had tormented her with for years. This must be how they hunt, like Dad taught her—quiet and careful so the boar or deer didn't spook and run.

Wisp eased back into the shadowy space under the fallen tree. She sat and squeezed herself against the dirt wall. Bits of soil fell on her from above; roots jutted out on either side of her head. She pulled the rifle into her lap and closed her hand around the grip.

Snaps and rustling continued getting closer.

Stop shaking. Her body refused to obey that command; instead, her trembling got worse. The heavy rifle across her lap didn't offer much reassurance. Dad's voice repeated itself over and over in her head, warning her that shooting Tree Walkers wouldn't hurt them. Bullets didn't do much to bushes. The monsters appeared to be searching for something, and the more she dwelled on the fear they might find her, the angrier the bird meat in her gut became.

Wisp clamped both hands over her mouth to make sure she didn't sniffle or whimper. Her right ankle burned from imagined thorns squeezing around her leg. The nightmare always ended the same way—her being captured. By Mother's favor, she always woke up before it showed her what the Tree Walkers would do to her. As soon as the torrent of plants fell on top of her, she'd always sit up screaming, back in her Haven.

Only now, she did not find herself within a nightmare. The Tree Walkers—real, not a dream—crept within twenty feet of where she hunkered beneath a rotting log. Though the curtain of roots in front of her somewhat resembled the bars of her Haven, they hadn't been charged with Dad's magic. The Tree Walkers could send their vines right past them and get her. She missed her Haven *so* much. It could stop them.

Snaps and crunches came closer.

Sudden inspiration, likely from Mother, gave her an idea.

Wisp set the rifle down beside her, then covered it and the bird meat with her blanket. She lay sideways, as low to the ground as possible, and jammed her feet into the loose dirt up to the shins before scooping more soil on top of her legs. Last, she stuck her front half under the blanket to hide her bright pink shirt, and rested her cheek against the rifle, both arms stretched out over her head to lessen the 'person-ness' of her shape.

As much as she could, she tried to stop shaking. She had no other choice. The guns wouldn't do anything against the Tree Walkers. Running wouldn't help. The nightmare she'd had over and over for years made sure she understood what would happen if she attempted to flee. Had Mother given her that knowing?

The Forest Beyond the Earth

Without her Haven, she could only hide and hope.

Tickles up and down her legs and back made it even harder to sit still. Bugs, likely wood lice, crawled up under her shirt onto her neck, exploring this new, warm, change to their home. She kept her head down, cheek resting on the rifle, nose away from the forest. Wisp wanted so badly to look, to watch in case they spotted her, but didn't dare pull the blanket away. Besides, if they saw a human face, they'd definitely catch her. A blanket-covered lump might be mistaken for pale wood.

She closed her eyes to keep the wood lice from crawling into them, though one bug kept trying to explore her nostril. Another unfortunate one paid the price for walking over her lips, becoming a quick snack.

Slow crunching got nearer and nearer, then stopped. Dread finally managed to stall her trembles. The Tree Walker had to be close enough to stick with a spear. Strange whistles and clicks broke the stillness. Seconds later, similar noises responded in kind, quieter, farther away.

They talk, but not like people... She swallowed hard. *Mother, please protect me.*

The Tree Walker nearest her emitted a noise like an owl followed by a trilling whistle of a smaller bird. Wisp held her breath, ignoring the desperate need to scratch and swat at the wood lice creeping all over her. She cringed a little, and almost lost control when a bug tried to crawl into her ear. Another crept under her skirt, tickling the back of her thigh. Between that and the one in her ear, it took all her concentration to keep still and not swat them away.

Crunching and rustling passed overhead. Dirt rained down on her as the old tree trunk shifted. She stifled an 'eep,' not wanting to make a sound with a Tree Walker climbing on her hiding place. A soft *clonk* made her jump; probably one of the thicker branches in the creature's body banging against the dead tree.

She kept herself still and quiet, having reached a point of being too terrified to tremble.

Gradually, the rustling and snapping of the searching Tree Walkers faded to silence. The occasional whistle or owl noise continued, growing more and more distant.

Thank you, Mother!

Wisp cried silent tears of gratitude.

She waited until she could no longer hear the Tree Walkers speaking to each other before pushing herself up to sit and swatting at all the bugs, shaking her head hard to fling the one away from her ear. After scratching all the itches, she settled back down under the blanket, lying flat with her back to the dirt. To be comfortable, she'd have to curl up on her side as she did in the Haven. Stretching herself straight didn't feel natural, but it concealed her shape more against the ground. Not that she had any expectation of falling asleep again after coming so close to Tree Walkers, but she couldn't go anywhere yet.

Not until the daylight chased the monsters back underground.

Expedition
~15~

A n hour or so before midday, Wisp came to a stop, pulled a canteen from its pouch, and opened it.

She'd broken camp at the first sign of daylight, getting underway while the forest remained mostly dark. At least with the bird-on-a-stick, she didn't have to forage or cook. Walking toward the sunrise for hours had to have brought her closer to Dad, but with the sun pretty much directly overhead, she'd begun to question her sense of direction.

After drinking her fill, she recapped the canteen and stuffed it back on her belt. Deciding against a longer break, she continued onward at an unhurried pace while nibbling on the bird. Every direction looked the same. Trees, bushes, plants, moss, and here and there, rocks. An area off to the left reminded her of a place she'd walked through a day or two ago, but she questioned if her eyes played tricks. She couldn't possibly have been going around in circles since Mother guided her to Dad. It had to be a coincidence. Trees didn't look that different from each other, so it had to be a trick.

"I'm lost, aren't I?"

106

Wisp sighed in defeat. She stopped again to let out the bad water, and used the time that took to consider what she should do. Maybe she should go back to the cabin in case Dad beat the monster and went home? Maybe he'd already been eaten?

The thought of losing him set off a flood of tears. Still squatting, she folded her arms over her knees and sobbed. How could she live without him? She'd wanted so much to be big so she could go on hunts with him, yet she remained small enough that the Tree Walkers would take her if they could. Part of her wanted to run home to the cabin, crawl into her Haven and cry until she slipped into the Other Place to be with him and Mother. Another part, the one that wanted to go hunting, fought back, annoyed at the idea she remained a child.

Mother sent me to find him, said the brave part.

But, I'm scared, said the child part. *And lost. I don't know where I am.*

Child part wondered if she could find that green wall again, the settlement where she had taken the bird meat. Those people used noisemakers, not hurty-traps, so they *might* be nice to her. If Dad had been eaten by a monster, maybe she needed to find nice grown-ups.

I'm not a little girl!

No, but it's easier to have someone helping. It's harder to live all alone.

You're scared.

Wisp wiped her eyes. *I know.*

People will hurt you, said Dad in her mind. *Even if they look friendly.*

She shivered. "Okay, okay… But, I don't know where to go. I wish I had Dad's north box."

The little device he carried always pointed out north, so he never got lost. Unfortunately, since he always carried it, the north box had gone missing along with him. It had to be magic, the way the floating needle always wound up aimed the right way.

"Maybe it's Mother?"

Wisp grinned with an idea. She leapt upright and ran around hunting through the understory until she found a nice twig about six inches long. Her prize in hand, she shrugged off the backpack and sat with her legs wrapped around it, rummaging until she found the ball of twine. After cutting off a bit, she tied it around the middle of the twig and sorta-sharpened one end, more to make an arrow than a point she could stab a fish with.

That done, she put her knife away, wriggled her backpack back on, and slung the rifle once again on her shoulder. Grinning from ear to ear, she held her right arm out, letting the twig-on-twine dangle and spin.

"Mother will show me the way."

It drifted around, back and forth. She stared at the pointing end, whispering, "Mother, show me where to go," over and over.

Once the twig seemed to stabilize in a direction, she nodded, wrapped the twine around it, and stuck it in a side pocket of the backpack. Full of new confidence, she marched onward, stopping every hour or so to ask the Mother Twig to show her the way. By late afternoon, the course put the sun at her back. Hope practically glowed from her heart. Mother had guided her eastward, so she must be taking her to find Dad.

Hours later, she wandered out of the forest onto another strip of smooth black stone that warmed her feet and made her toes tingle. The road curved in a long, gentle turn to the left, heading east. On the right, it continued more or less straight to the south. A constant, gentle breeze rustled the treetops and sent strands of her long hair floating about, tickling her left arm.

Wisp pulled out the Mother Twig and let it dangle.

The sharper end went around in a circle, swung back the other way, and wavered for a little while before favoring the left.

"Mother wants me to follow the road."

She put the twig back in the side pocket and headed eastward toward the curve, amusing herself for a little while by trying to keep her feet on the faded yellow line, stepping heel-to-toe with her arms out to the sides for balance.

Can Tree Walkers cross roads? There's no dirt here.

The notion that the paving might protect her from the monsters, since they couldn't grow through it, offered a mild sense of security. Did they constantly have roots going into the ground or could they detach from the soil and roam around? If so, the road wouldn't bother them.

Eyes downcast, she plodded onward, stopping only once to make *ngh*. Soon after the sun began to weaken, a huge boxy shape came into view on the road up ahead, slumped to the side. Wisp froze in place, staring. It didn't move at all over the minute or so she remained still, so she pulled the rifle up to check it out with the scope.

The crosshairs landed on the back end of a machine with shiny red spots on either side and a rectangular plate like Dad's leg armor in the middle along the bottom. This one also had the word 'Colorado' on it, beneath an unpronounceable word in bigger letters. The machine had four deflated tires, bigger than a car's, but not as large as the ones she'd seen on the Jeep. Between rust patches and under a coating of thick grey dust, the rest of the machine had a deep maroon color. She trained the crosshairs on a group of silver letters near the left corner.

"Expo… Expa dittion." Wisp lifted her head away from the scope, eyebrows furrowed. "It's a car. The ancients were silly. Why did they name machines? You can't talk to them."

She decided to approach the long-abandoned vehicle. Maybe the ancients had magic or something that they could use to call machines by name like the dogs in her books. According to Dad, the occasional wolf they'd seen prowling about didn't act like the 'nice dogs' in the stories, and she should avoid them.

The machine turned out to be much bigger than she thought from a distance, standing quite a bit taller than her despite the tires all being flat on the bottom. The front right wheel had gone off the road onto the dirt, and the machine's front end almost touched a tree. Its windows had no cracks, though a thick layer of pale grey muck coated them, as well as most of the sides. She traced her fingers over the surface, thinking it looked a lot like the water after she washed the fireplace. Her fingertips came away with a haze of white.

"Oh…" She peered up at the sky. "This is ash, mixed with water. The machine was here when the dragons burned everything."

Again, she examined the old car, thinking back to her conversation with Dad. A limousine sounded much longer than this one, but it stood so tall it couldn't be a car.

"Essyouvee," said Wisp.

She grabbed the door handle and pulled, expecting it to be locked, but it swung free. The scrape of old metal echoing in the silent forest startled a gasp out of her. Curious, she set one foot on the single step along the side and lifted herself up enough to peer in.

The interior stank of dryness with a hint of must. No mold tainted the chairs, and bugs had apparently decided to leave this machine alone. In front of her, a strange device, like a smaller chair, perched on the bench seat.

Smiling, she crawled up inside and peered around. Nothing appeared dangerous, so she set the rifle on the floor and sat beside the little chair-on-the-chair, wide-eyed at the softness beneath her butt. She squeezed and gripped the padding, scuffing her feet back and forth on the soft floor, awestruck at how comfortable the ancients' things had been. Though the cloth nearly frayed at her touch, it didn't seem *too* brittle.

She peered into the little seat, which had a set of straps and buckles to hold someone in place. "Wow… the Tree Walkers were taking children before the dragon fire." Wisp tugged at the dry-rotted straps, picturing them snugging a small child in place so they couldn't be stolen.

The Forest Beyond the Earth

Her attention migrated to the space in front of her, where a strange circle stuck out on a post like the person in that chair should be holding onto it. She crawled between the gap and moved to the bigger chair on the left, gripping the ring in both hands while staring at a little window over a bunch of round spots with needles like Dad's north machine. These didn't say north though, they had boring numbers.

After a moment of sitting there holding on to the circle, she remembered some of her books' characters did a thing called 'driving.' The stories had spoken of people getting in cars and driving, but she had always pictured it as them disappearing from one place and appearing in another. Now, sitting inside a giant SUV and thinking about wheels, it hit her that 'driving' must have involved the whole machine rolling forward. *I bet it moved faster than people can walk.* She tried to turn the ring, but it didn't want to move. Two pedals, cool to her feet, also didn't do anything when she stepped on them.

"Gas. Brake." She pushed them down one at a time, not sure which name belonged to which pedal.

The characters always 'stomped' on the gas, so she figured maybe she didn't push it hard enough. Some even 'hammered' on the brake, but she hadn't brought Dad's hammer with her, so she couldn't test that. Mashing her foot down on them didn't work either. She gave up on the pedals and explored the buttons and whatnot in front of her. When she spotted one labeled 'engine start,' she pushed it.

And nothing happened.

"Oh… it's broken."

She gave up on trying to make it go and daydreamed about what it would've been like back when these machines worked. Wisp clutched the circle, which she figured to be 'the wheel' the books always mentioned, and gazed out at the road. In her mind, she raced forward, weaving around turns and going way faster than she could run.

When that got boring, she crawled again to the rear seat, and over it into an empty area in the far back. A spot of bright yellow caught her eye against the rear door. She pounced after it, seizing an unfamiliar, fuzzy spherical fruit. It smelled like everything else inside the machine, dry and dusty, with a hint of burned ash.

After brushing it off, she bit it, but her teeth couldn't pierce the rind. It also tasted nasty.

"Bleh!"

She threw it away and gagged. The yellow ball struck the door and bounced back to her.

"What?" Wisp picked it up and threw it at the door a second time. Again, it came right back. She squeezed it, finding it squishy and springy. "Oh… it's not a food. It's a… bouncy thing."

Amused, she spent a few minutes throwing it at the windows and catching it. Before she knew it, the forest had gone dark outside. She caught the ball, clinging to it like a squirrel with an acorn, and peered out at the night.

"Uh oh."

This machine, especially the back part, somewhat reminded her of the Haven. *Maybe I'll be safe in here to sleep?*

Since she liked the yellow ball, she put it in the backpack for later. She ate the last of the bird meat, gnawing at the bones for quite a while to claim every last scrap. Not wanting to stray too far from the shelter of the dead machine, she lowered herself to the road and crept to the front corner as the ground went downhill in that direction. There, she squatted and let out the bad water on the pavement, keeping one hand on the tire for balance above the word 'Goodyear.'

She sighed. "I don't think it was a good year, if you got burned by the dragons."

Wisp rushed the process, forcing all the bad water out as fast as possible so she could return to the safety of the SUV. Being in the open at night seemed as silly as shouting, 'Tree Walkers, take me!' as loud as she could.

As soon as she finished, she leapt back in over the driver's seat, pulled the door shut with a soft *whump,* and crawled into the open space in the back. For comfort, she decided to remove her canteen belt and arrange the blanket on the floor like the padding on the bottom of her Haven. She curled up on her side, using her left arm for a pillow, her right hand resting at her chin.

The security of metal around her, and the familiarity of a small space to sleep in, lulled her off into the realm of dreams.

TV Dinner
~16~

A few hours into her walk down the road, Wisp stopped to check direction with the Mother Twig.

It wound up pointing off the road into the woods again, not quite east. She looked back and forth from the hanging stick to the sun, confused by the disagreement.

"It's not midday yet. This isn't east, but… maybe I'm getting close to Dad!"

She followed the twig, walking off the road and scooting down a weedy embankment on the side before wading past a gathering of chest-high foliage. After about thirty feet, the understory settled back to its usual shallow depth. Not long after leaving the road, she spotted a massive green grasshopper clinging to a tree.

"Ooh!"

For about ten minutes, she scampered around the area collecting as many grasshoppers as she could find and tossing them in the deeper pot after plucking their heads off. While gently twisting the head and tugging the entrails free of the body, Dad's voice narrated her thoughts about parasites. Pulling the snotty bits out that stuck to the head protected her from getting sick, since most of the nasty stuff stayed with that part.

Once she had a respectable collection of dead grasshoppers, she left the rest of the insects in peace and hunted for a good place to make a fire. She rested her weary legs while dry frying her meal, keeping the bugs moving by shuffling the dome-shaped pan around. Dad had also warned her against eating bugs without cooking them unless she had no other choice, since that would also help prevent her from getting sick.

She missed the flavor of boar grease, but the roasted grasshoppers made for a satisfying meal nonetheless. Not wanting to waste water, she decided against rinsing the pan and simply let it cool before returning it to the backpack and kicking dirt over the fire.

Another twig check kept her going in more or less the same direction, making minor adjustments every hour or so as the device indicated. Wisp walked ahead with a bold, determined stride, grateful that Mother could help her in such a direct way.

Late in the afternoon, she emerged from a tree line of old growth to a place where much younger trees had sprouted up around abandoned cabins, joined by a network of small roads. Many of the old structures had collapsed in places, roofs falling in. Young trees and other plants had pushed up through the paving in places, shifting slabs of rock aside as they grew. A few rotten cars remained near some cabins, but nothing in this place beside the plants appeared alive.

Wisp slid the rifle off her shoulder and gripped it tight, listening to silence for a little while before advancing into the ancient settlement. Most of the cabins' doors hung wide open, some flapping in the breeze. A couple raccoons in the distance peered at her as she stepped from dirt onto a smaller light-colored path that ran alongside the dark one. The narrower paving strip appeared far too small for a car, so she assumed it a 'people road.'

A small box perched on a metal post stood beside the 'people road' in front of the nearest cabin. She tugged at the handle of a flap door on the front end, which opened to an explosion of startled chipmunks that had been nesting inside.

Wisp squealed and jumped away as the tiny brown creatures scattered in different directions. After catching her breath, she nudged the door shut again and whispered, "Sorry."

The path curved to the right, taking her past seven huge buildings, some twice as tall as hers, like a pair of cabins stacked on top of each other. Dad had built theirs after finding the metal box he used for a bedroom. He'd told her it took them almost a year to finish, with Mother helping. Wisp's jaw hung open in awe at the size of the ancients' homes.

The people who used to live in them couldn't possibly have built such things without magic, or it would've taken them most of their life to finish.

Metal squeaking made her stop and crouch, raising the rifle.

She listened, but the noise continued at an even back-and-forth tempo, matching the changes in the air. *It's something blowing in the wind.* Her rifle still at the ready, she advanced toward the repetitious scraping.

Past the corner of a huge grey cabin, an open area held a number of odd machines. Three looked a bit like the 'goat' creature she'd seen at the settlement, only they didn't have four legs. Each balanced on a single leg composed of a thick coil of metal coming down from the middle of their bellies. In the center of the area stood a large, round steel table, lower to the ground than even her cooking place, with a number of looped railings. It appeared to be the source of the squeaking, as it rotated back and forth in the breeze. Beyond that, a ladder led up to a platform with a bright red plastic roof and a long metal chute leading back to the ground. Frames next to that had chains dangling from an elevated cross bar with no apparent purpose. Rectangular wooden boards sat on the ground beneath them, as wide as the space between chains. She guessed at one point the boards had been hung from the chains, but couldn't imagine why.

Wisp approached the statue goats, examining a pair of pegs jutting out the sides of its head that looked like handles. Clearly not a real animal, it appeared to be a strange sort of seat, intended for a child due to its size. She patted the middle, finding it as hard as stone, and scrunched up her face at it. A strong gust sent the wheel thing spinning fast and made the goat-chairs wobble. At that, she pushed on it, and it wobbled harder, side to side, the spring creaking.

Curious, she threw a leg over and sat, feeling a hair too big for it. As soon as she lifted her toes from the ground, the goat-chair tilted back. Another set of pegs, low on either side, appeared to be steps, so she rested her feet on them. Soon, she figured out if she shifted her weight, the machine would rock faster and faster. Hesitation became wonder, which became giggling. She'd never seen anything like this springy goat-chair before. Bouncing back and forth got her laughing and cheering, until she raised both hands up over her head—at which point the goat-chair threw her to the ground.

Still laughing, she lay there watching the fake animal wobble slower and slower until it stopped.

After dusting herself off and collecting the rifle, she approached the large metal table. Figuring out that the goat-thing had been made for fun, she assumed all the machines in this place similar. This one appeared to be a spinning game. She stepped on the platform, pushing at the ground with her other foot until the whole thing whirled about fast enough to be scary. Careening around and around, she clung to the railing until the platform slowed, then jumped back to solid ground.

Okay, not that… I don't like that one.

She went up the ladder and down the slide a few times, until the third step snapped when she tried to climb the ladder again. *Oops. These things are old. I could get hurt if they break.* Past the slide, she found a weird hut made from two huge metal bowls. The upper one had a clear bubble at the top and a bunch of smaller bubbles of colored plastic, like windows, around the sloped sides. Two-foot tall bars, fatter than her Haven's, separated the open ends of the two bowls, forming an enclosure. Alas, it had no door, so she couldn't lock herself in. Still curious, she climbed in. The smooth steel floor had collected years' worth of windblown sand. Wisp stood in the middle, tall enough that her head wound up neatly within the bubble window. This machine didn't move or do anything but sit there and have windows, so she crawled out the other side and walked away from the play machines, following the nearest road.

"Hey," whispered a man. "What's that?"

Wisp froze.

"Looks like a kid," whispered another.

"It's a girl!" whispered a third voice, with barely-contained excitement. "Let's get her."

She tightened her grip on the rifle and pivoted toward the voices.

Three men in tattered clothing, ripped shirts, jeans, and crumbling shoes, shuffled toward her along the black car-road. They stood so close to each other their shoulders touched. The one in the middle kept trying to hold the others' hands, but they swatted at him. All had long beards and unkempt hair, and looked a few years late for their next bath. Wild eyes, twitching lips, and yellowed teeth gave her a distinctly bad feeling about them. They looked at her almost the way she probably had looked at that bird meat cooking.

"Hey," said the one on the left. "C'mere."

The middle one reached his arms toward her, which would've been terrifying if he hadn't been thirty feet away still. "Hi pretty. Come here. You shouldn't be all alone."

"We won't hurt you," said the third man, kneading his hands.

"I have to go." She pointed the rifle at them. "Dad is waiting for me."

Middle shuffled closer, no reaction whatsoever to having a rifle aimed at him. "It's all right, pretty girl. You're too small to be all alone."

"Come to us," said the guy on the left.

She backed up, lowering the rifle. *Always try to run.* "No."

Wisp ran away, feet clapping on the people-road. The men sprang after her, calling out at her to stop or lying that they wouldn't hurt her. Her backpack clattered, wobbling with her sprint. The pistol bounced and tugged heavy on her belt. Their rapid stomping footsteps scuffed closer and closer. Perhaps without all her stuff, she could've outrun them, but they had longer legs and the same desperation in their eyes that had taken her when she stole the bird meat.

Not wanting to wind up impaled on a stick and roasted over a fire, she snarled and forced herself to run faster. The men chased her across the fun machine park and around a cabin. She zoomed past three more cabins on the left before one of the men got too close. Right as he tried to grab her backpack, she ducked left in an abrupt turn off the people-road into waist-high grass. The man overextended his grab, lost his balance, and tumbled past her into the greenery. She struggled to fight her way across the tall foliage, frightened at being slowed down so much as the other two men came running up behind her.

She plowed through the grass, heading past the corner of a cabin beyond the tiny meadow, but her hopes for escape shattered at the sight of a huge wooden fence blocking off the entire gap between two cabins. Perhaps she could climb it, but not fast enough to avoid being grabbed. With nowhere to go, she whirled to face the men and again, raised the rifle.

"Stop!" she shouted. "Go away or I'll shoot you."

Neither man slowed down, and the one who'd tripped hurried to catch up.

Wisp's finger slid off the rifle's frame onto the trigger. "Stop!"

They didn't.

At a range of perhaps ten feet, she didn't even need to look through the scope.

Boom!

The butt mushed into her shoulder, knocking her two steps back, ears ringing.

Middle guy lurched to a halt, a small hole at the center of a growing red stain over his green shirt. He glanced down at himself with a vacant expression and open mouth, and fell flat on his face. The other man, who'd been a little behind him, had a spray of blood all over his front. He stopped short, staring at her.

Wisp shifted to aim at him. "Go away!"

The man who'd fallen in the grass skidded to a halt, gawking at the one she'd sent to the Other Place. He screamed, which made the other remaining man scream, and the pair of them whirled around and ran away. She stood still, keeping the rifle generally pointed toward where they'd gone, nothing other than her eyelids moving until the distant wails of terrified men got too far away to hear.

She moved her finger away from the trigger, pressing it against the frame.

"Dad, you're right. People want to hurt me."

Wisp stared past the tip of the barrel at the man. The bullet had opened a hole in his back quite a bit bigger than the little one in front. For eleven years, she hadn't seen another person aside from Dad and Mother, but being a shrine, Mother didn't really count as another person—she'd become far greater. But now, in mere days, she'd seen many people, and all of them had been scary. With shaggy, long hair, beard, and ripped-up clothes, this creature she'd shot seemed more a monster than a person. Some of her books described monsters that looked like people, zombies or ghouls, or some such thing. They *had* been people once, but weren't anymore. That had to be what happened here. Just a monster in a people suit.

I didn't hurt a person. This only looked like a man.

She crept closer to the body and poked the rifle into his head twice. He didn't move. With her rifle barrel, she picked at his clothing, searching for anything useful. A big knife had hit the ground by his right hand, an empty sheath on his belt. When she spotted it, a chill ran down her back. He'd been hiding the blade against his arm. Surely, had he caught up to her, he would've stabbed her. Any shred of guilt at sending someone to the Other Place faded. This had not been a person at all, only a monster.

Aside from the knife, she found nothing on him but a stinky shirt covered in blood, and even smellier pants loaded with *ngh*. She used the knife to cut his rope belt open, freeing the sheath.

"I tried to run. You wouldn't leave me alone. I told you to go away. You didn't." Wisp pointed at the large exit wound on his back. "That's what happens when you're bad."

She took her backpack off long enough to stuff the new knife inside, then rubbed her shoulder. The rifle had still kicked like heck, but two years had passed since it flung her to the ground. Her twelve-year-old body handled it better. Though even if firing it had thrown her on her butt, it probably wouldn't have mattered since the other two monsters ran away.

"They didn't know what a bullet is until I showed them." She stood, stepped over the man, and continued walking.

The Forest Beyond the Earth

The road led her away from the monster, past many old cabins. She kept her gaze alert for the other two returning, or any other dangerous creature coming to check out the noise of a gunshot. Roads, waist-high grass, more roads, and another dirt lot offered little of interest before she reached a wide one-story cabin that didn't look as destroyed as the rest. Car hoods and trunk panels covered some of the windows, as though someone had made an effort to repair the place. A rusting wreck of car rotted upon a short section of road leading right up to the cabin, by a huge door. She edged past the broken machine, creeping along a thin strip of people road toward where two steps connected to a raised surface under an overhanging roof.

Wisp pushed the front door aside and stepped into a dimly lit room bigger than her entire cabin. A subtle stink of mildew pervaded the place, mixed with the same odor that followed whenever Dad's butt made noise. An archway on the right led to another chamber with a counter covered in cans and a whole mess of cabinets. Out the back end of the cabinet room, a hallway led deeper into the massive cabin. To her left, an enormous black rectangle hung on the wall in front of a big, soft chair wide enough for three or four people. The odd wall hanging confused her for a few seconds until she thought of something she'd read, and decided it must be a television. She approached and touched it, running her fingers along the bottom until she found small buttons at the corner. Pushing them didn't do anything.

"You won't work, will you? Nothing from Old Earth still works. But you used to show stories like pictures."

In the far left corner, beyond the television, sat a haven with much thinner bars than hers. She walked over and squatted beside it, scrunching her face up at the flimsy metal, barely as thick as the skewers she used for grubs. Tree Walkers could probably bend these bars. Heck, even Dad might be able to bend them. A small tag on the left side had the words, "Deluxe Kennel Crate."

"This will never keep out the Tree Walkers."

Blood stained the carpet around her feet, and the faint smell of bad water hung in the air. Metal caught her eye inside the crummy haven, which didn't even have its own lock—an open padlock dangled from the latch. She pulled the door open and plucked the object from a stained, stinky blanket inside. Two rings connected by a short length of chain dangled from her grip, all coated in a thick shell of dried blood. She turned it back and forth, thinking it an unusual piece of jewelry.

"Oh... wait..."

Some of the books told stories about 'cops,' who used handcuffs on the people who did bad stuff. Since the Earth didn't have cops anymore, she didn't see any purpose to keeping handcuffs. The world still had plenty of bad people though, but it seemed much easier to shoot them than make them wear these. She tossed the useless thing aside and stood. This haven stank too bad to sleep inside it, not to mention she didn't have an opener for the padlock and… all that blood. The narrow bars also didn't look like they'd be able to protect her anyway.

Wisp wandered away from the useless haven, exploring a long set of windows covered by gauzy fabric that reminded her of the sacred tiny dress from Mother's lap. Someone had covered the glass panels with metal sheets on the outside, blocking any view. From there, she wandered down a hallway leading out from the big room to the first doorway on the left, and gasped at the sight of an outhouse *inside* the cabin. An eye-watering ammonia smell scorched the breath out of her throat. Hand over her mouth, she crept up to a fancy seat with a fluffy, black cushion and peered in, but this outhouse confused her. It didn't have a hole into the ground, only a small opening containing a lot of nasty, yellow water. Standing close, the fuzzy cushion looked more like a rampant growth of black mold.

"Eeeep." She backed away, holding her breath.

She stumbled into the hallway, coughing and spitting to the side. Once she caught her breath, she wandered deeper into the cabin, finding a couple of rooms containing broken furniture and moldy beds, one of which stank the same as the bowl of yellow water. Giving up on the cabin's small rooms, she returned to the space beyond the archway with all the cabinets. Curiosity pulled her over to the countertop covered in cans. She sifted among them, grinning broadly at the prospect of food. She located a promising one without any dents, set it aside, and hunted around the cabinets and drawers until she found an opener machine like the one at home, though she hadn't needed it in a long time. The last time Dad brought cans back from a hunting trip, she'd been nine. She clamped the device over the can's edge and squeezed the handles together until it punched a hole. Inch by inch, she twisted the knob on the side, working the opener around all the way until the metal disk popped free.

The can contained pale pillow-shaped pods in red goop. It smelled okay, so she plucked one out and nibbled on it. Nothing alarmed her about the flavor, albeit a touch on the mushy/bland side, so she carried the can with her back into the big room and sat on the wide chair facing the television set. Its cushions reminded her of the soft seats in the old SUV, only smellier.

Wisp set the rifle on the seat beside her, shrugged out of her backpack, and reclined, scooping pillows from the can with her fingers and stuffing them in her mouth while staring at the TV. Though the dead screen displayed only blackness, it filled with her daydreams of what it once might have shown.

For as long as it took to finish her meal, she pretended to be an ancient from one of her books, relaxing and 'watching television.'

The Ancients' World
~17~

Her meal done and her right hand coated in a stubborn orange stain, Wisp collected the remainder of the intact food cans—five of them—and packed the opener as well. Her pack rattled a little louder as she left the ancients' massive cabin behind and resumed her journey. The Mother Twig guided her into the forest beyond the other side of the abandoned settlement.

Fearing those monsters would return, she kept the rifle in her hands despite her arms protesting the weight. Every now and then, she thought *twenty*, the number of shots left in the weapon. The magazine held twenty, but Dad always kept a bullet inside the barrel, so she'd started with twenty-one shots. Hopefully, she'd be able to give the rifle back to him still with twenty left.

Leaves and mulch crinkled under her feet as she reentered the forest. She paused for a few seconds, gazing back at the giant cabins the ancients used to live in. The small city looked as though it once held quite a few people, and she tried to imagine what it must've been like, having others nearby you could talk to who wouldn't try to hurt each other as soon as say hello. If Dad was here, they probably would've have spent a few days searching everywhere for useful stuff.

With a sigh, she bowed her head and trudged onward into the woods.

A few hours away from the settlement, she found a tiny creek where she stopped to rest and refill the canteens. After drinking a few handfuls, she stretched out on her back, letting her feet dangle in the water while staring up at the sky. Sleep tempted her, but late afternoon was too early to settle down for the night. A battle of urgency and tiredness took a few minutes before she managed to drag herself upright. Determination to find Dad and go home added speed to her step, but she didn't break into a jog. Running wasted energy and would wear her out faster. Over the course of a day, she could cover more ground at a constant walk despite moving slower, because she wouldn't need to stop and rest as much.

She stepped out of the tress into a light breeze blowing along a broken strip of road, decomposed to little more than gravel and dirt cutting through the forest across her path. For good measure, she checked the Mother Twig again. It spun back and forth for a little while before lining up with the road to the right, so she went that way. Before long, her feet had turned pale grey from a coating of dust. Many pointy rocks kept her grimacing and grumbling. Each time she stepped on ouch and stumbled, she promised herself that after the next one, she'd move off the road... but never wound up doing it.

She walked until a mesh barrier came into view up ahead on the left by a slight bend in the road. It reminded her of the green wall around the place where she'd taken the bird meat, but this one didn't have colored cloth strips tied to it. A big car, a bit like the SUV but more boxy, had evidently crashed into the middle part, bending the wire mesh and mushing up its nose end. Hundreds of tiny holes dotted the vehicle's side.

Drawn by curiosity of the ancients, she pulled the rifle around into a ready position and approached the strange box on wheels, searching the area for any sign of danger.

This fence stood twice as tall as the one she'd seen around the settlement. Not only did it lack the camouflage strips, it had a large spiral of wire along the top studded with triangular blades. *Ouch!* She cringed, deciding not to climb it, and walked around the back end of the boxy car, noting silver letters E250 near the bottom of one of its two rear doors beneath a blue oval containing the word 'Ford.'

Dozens of skeletons lay along the road nearby, some still with their bony fingers clutching the wire mesh. Counting skulls got her to twenty-three before she lost track of which ones she'd tallied. The back doors of the wheeled box hung open, revealing a big open space with only two seats up front. Unlike the SUV, it only had windows up front. The rest of the inside contained a handful more skeletons collapsed on top of each other. Thin shafts of sunlight crisscrossed the dusty interior from all the little holes in the walls. Old, dried blood spattered everywhere. Another skeleton lay slumped over the wheel up front, most of the skull broken away.

"Is this a shrine? Do you want me to go away?"

She waited for a ten count, and decided it safe to keep exploring since no one said a word. After making her way around the boxy vehicle, she approached the fence. A short distance past it, the tiniest cabin she'd ever seen perched beside the road with a long yellow and black pole extended out as if to block cars. A white sign on the front of the cabin bore bright red letters:

Restricted Area: US Department of Defense. Trespassers will be shot.

"Restricted…" She tilted her head, thinking. "Department of de fence… is this the place that made walls?"

Wisp ducked and slipped into a gap in the metal mesh where the crash had broken it apart, crawling among a scattering of empty bullet casings all over the road. She pulled herself free of the twisted mesh, stood, and glanced back at the pile of skeletons, then to the brass littered around her feet, thinking that people standing inside must have shot the 'trespassers' outside.

Huh. Trespasser bones look like people bones.

"Trespassers must be really bad if people shoot them." She tried to think of what kind of monster could be so dangerous that it had to be killed right away like that. Could that shaggy human-like monster she had to send to the Other Place have been a trespasser? Here, they couldn't get past the wire mesh, so why did they have to be shot? Maybe they had mind-control powers like the Tree Walkers who could make her hand over the opener to her Haven. She approached the fence near the pile of bones leaning on the other side and squatted.

"What happened? Why did they shoot you? Are you dangerous? If you're monsters, why do you look so much like people bones?" She spent a few minutes waiting and asking the trespassers more questions, but none of them replied from the Other Place.

Confused, she stopped trying to understand and approached the tiny cabin. A broken window peered in on a single chair in front of a shelf holding a small TV screen and a board full of letters on buttons. She tried to read the first line, but *'qwertyuiop'* made no sense.

"Maybe it's Spanish," she muttered, thinking about those other odd words from the books that Dad explained to her.

A small white box on the wall marked with a red cross intrigued her, so she grasped the doorknob. She couldn't turn it at all, no matter how hard she twisted or grunted. The knob only rattled side to side a tiny bit. The middle of the knob had a key slit that reminded her of her Haven's door. Since she didn't have the opener, and she didn't want to cut herself to shreds on the fringe of glass teeth around the window, she gave up on the miniature cabin. *It's silly to make a cabin so tiny it's got no room to lay down inside.* Even her Haven had more room… at least sideways.

"Oh, that must be a haven, not a cabin… so small and it's locked." She shied away from the broken glass around the window frame. "Stupid. Tree Walkers can break glass. This is a bad haven."

She shrugged and walked away from the fence, heading around a long left turn. Three-story tall rock face flanked the road on both sides where it cut through a hill. Wisp gazed up at roots and vines jutting out from fissures. Empty brass casings from rifle bullets jingled as her feet sent them dancing over the pavement. Some fifty steps later, the road curved rightward again before opening into a large clearing surrounded by rocky walls. A white, rectangular cabin stood alongside the road up ahead, which continued past it to an enormous metal door embedded in a cliff. She couldn't think of any possible way to open such a thing, so she headed for the cabin instead.

Four metal steps led up to a small, elevated platform in front of the door, which hung ajar. She grasped the edge with one hand and tugged. The door only opened another two inches before sticking. A squeak came from a thin metal strut overhead that appeared to have broken away from a little box at the top of the doorjamb.

Wisp shouldered her rifle on the strap and grabbed the door in both hands, grunting from the effort to drag it open inch by inch. Once she dragged it far enough open to slip past the edge, she leaned her shoulder against and shoved it aside with her whole body. The door scraped over the metal platform, leaving a curved scratch. Wisp leaned against the door for a moment to catch her breath, then stepped inside. A wet, mildew stink saturated everything. Large spiders scurried around near the ceiling, but she disregarded them since she didn't feel hungry. Metal desks, chairs, and more of those small TV screens and letter-buttons filled the room. She meandered around, gazing and touching everything.

Holes dotted the walls, similar to the ones in the boxy car outside. Four more skeletons lay on the floor here and there, the tattered remains of clothing too far rotted to be of any use clung to their bones. She approached the wall on her left and stuck a finger in one of the holes.

"Bullet." She looked down at one of the skeletons. "People shot guns in here."

She went from desk to desk, pulling open drawers, but found nothing that interested her—only papers with boring writing. One desk had a picture frame showing a smiling man in a fancy pale blue shirt with shiny metal bits clipped to it. Next to it, a thick stack of square papers sat mounted on a plastic frame. The topmost page read, 'Friday - March 22, 2019.' She opened the drawers, but found only more papers and a few small plastic tubes. She picked one up, testing the pointy end with her finger, but it didn't feel sharp enough to be a weapon. Disinterested, she tossed it back in the drawer and kept exploring.

Near the inner wall, another skeleton lay flat on its back with a giant knife sticking up out of the chest. The end of the handle almost stood as tall as her chin.

"Ooo!"

Wisp ran over and grabbed the weapon in both hands, yanking it away from the bones, which broke apart. Grunting, she struggled to hold it up. The blade weighed almost as much as the rifle, and pulled her around as she waved it back and forth. Whenever she put any real effort into a swing, the blade dragged her stumbling after it. She widened her stance in an effort to hold her ground, and tried to chop the air again, but the huge knife flew out of her hands and stuck into the side of a desk with a deafening *boom*. She gasped in awe at finding a magic blade that could cut metal, but as soon as she ran over to pull it out, her elation died. The side of the desk looked so thin, even her little knife would probably punch a hole in it.

For some time, she played with the giant blade, slicing into the backs of chairs, stabbing a big plastic bottle on a pedestal, or trying not to fall over whenever she swung at empty air. Part of her wanted to keep it, but its weight made it impractical for anything other than being awesome to have. Reluctantly, she tossed it to the floor with a loud *clank*. Had she intended (and knew how) to go straight back to the cabin, she might've kept it as a curiosity or in hopes of using it later once she'd grown up, but she already carried a lot of weight and had no idea when she'd go home.

She started to wonder *if* she would ever find Dad's cabin again, but refused to think about that. She had every reason to believe that Mother would bring her to Dad, and he would be able to lead them home.

Another desk held a white paper box labeled 'powdered donettes.' Inside, a few dusty green rings gave off a sweet smell. She picked one up, but decided against biting it. Nothing meant to be eaten could possibly be *that* hard—or that furry. Not to mention, she caught a whiff of mold beneath the sweet. Wisp held the small ring up to the picture on the box. The one pinched between her fingers had a dull green hue, the drawing on the box looked white.

"These are bad." She dropped it, and continued walking.

A crinkle underfoot made her pause a few steps later and look down at a piece of paper she'd stepped on. Curious, she crouched and picked it up. Her dirty footprint smeared over writing like in one of her books.

```
United States Strategic Operations Command
TOP SECRET
22MAR19
```

```
Update:  Factions  allied  with  General
Falstaff  have  been  declared  enemies  of  the
state. We have confirmation that POTUS has been
assassinated by members of his security detail.
The  traitors  have  not  breached  any  critical
command  systems.  Do  not  be  alarmed  at  rumors
that the president's order was illegitimate. We
are preparing to execute the POTUS' last lawful
order  if  no  contradictory  command  originates
from EAGLES NEST in the next four minutes.
```

A small white space separated another bit of writing.

```
Update - 19:14 hours. We have followed the
directive issued by the President of the United
States. All configured weapons are in flight to
their  designated  targets.  NORAD  confirms
multiple inbound response vehicles. May God
have mercy on all of us.
```

Wisp stood and dropped the paper, which fluttered gracefully back to the floor, half covering her left foot. Something about it made her sad, but she couldn't quite place why. Perhaps it came from reading the words of a person she knew had gone to the Other Place. But, hadn't the books been the same way? They'd been written so long ago that the ones who came up with those stories *had* to be in the Other Place by now, but simply reading those hadn't made her feel like she'd watched someone die.

"Those are made up stories." She nudged the paper away with her foot. "That's real."

The paper sounded as if it spoke of the Fire Dragons, but it called them 'weapons.' Dad referred to the rifle and pistol as weapons. He also said that the Fire Dragons were gone because people made them, and after they killed all the people, no one could make more Fire Dragons.

It occurred to her that she didn't feel sad over what the paper meant, but rather because she questioned Dad. He had told her the Fire Dragons became angry, but this paper made it sound like the people *told* them to fly. But Dad wouldn't tell her false, would he?

No. He didn't. This must be something else. Some other weapons. The Fire Dragons got mad at the people for using these weapons. She nodded. That's what happened. "Mr. POTUS was stupid. He shouldn't have made the Fire Dragons angry."

Wisp sighed out the last of her sorrow and resumed exploring the building. Down a hallway, she discovered a large outhouse with four seats separated by thin walls and doors. Like the one in that big cabin, these also didn't have holes down into pits. However, no thick covering of black mold grew on them, nor did they contain nasty, so she decided to use one. A spindle of paper hung on the wall nearby worked much better than leaves. Unfortunately, the *ngh* just sat there in the bowl, stinking. In her books, the ancients did something called 'flushing,' but she had no idea what that meant. It had to have been magic of some kind that people forgot. She tried pushing the handle on the side of the seat, but aside from hollow clattering, nothing happened.

"Oops. It's broken, I guess."

She found a large cup on one of the desks and ran outside with it to collect dirt. Several back and forth trips finally buried the *ngh* so it didn't smell as bad. She backed up, dusting off her hands, and wandered again into the outer room full of desks. A sense that she wasted time came over her. Since this place offered no food or anything useful, she left. Wisp paused for a moment on the road at the base of the metal stairs, glancing at the massive door in the rock wall. She decided to walk over and give it a few minutes of examination, but could find no handles, knobs, levers, or any way to open it. A small metal box with a circular patch of tiny holes on its face above one button didn't do anything, so she gave up.

The Forest Beyond the Earth

Wisp jogged back down the road to the stupid little haven by all the empty bullet casings, heading for the gap in the fence by the crashed vehicle.

Her backpack snagged on the wire mesh when she tried to squeeze through. Grumbling, she twisted and squirmed until it popped free, and dragged herself forward until her legs slid clear of the mangled wire mesh. She jumped upright and frowned at the pale grey dust covering her hands, knees, and feet.

Clapping and swatting knocked puffs of silt into a strong breeze, which carried it off toward the forest beside the road. Next, she pulled out the Mother Twig and let it spin. The pointing device wavered back and forth for a second or two before it oriented toward the trees, the same way the dust had gone.

She closed her eyes, listening to the soft rustle of the wind in the leaves, and thanked Mother for her help.

Rifle held ready, Wisp marched off the road into the woods.

Escape
~18~

F rustration, fear, and worry crashed together, churning her breakfast of purslane and yellowgreens. Wisp had been following Mother's guidance for three days, and had gone through all of the canned food. Yet, despite walking so long, she had not yet found Dad, or any other sign of the great monster's passage. She had suffered another restless night, barely able to close her eyes without her Haven around her, and now roamed among the trees, the forest reduced to meaningless blurs by tears that refused to stop. The Mother Twig pointed her ever onward, but she still seemed to be getting nowhere.

Going home or finding Dad both became impossible goals in her mind. The first three hours of walking, she wept and sniffled, trying to keep as quiet as possible. Near midday, she found a patch of Oregon grapes, which she stuffed in her mouth by the handful despite the bitterness—in fact, she chewed slower because they tasted so strong. Girls who couldn't find their Dads when they needed help didn't deserve tasty food. Dad had only ever punished her by withholding story time.

He loved her too much to hit or force her to eat bitter food. Once, he'd threatened *not* to put her in the Haven at night, but fortunately, he'd only said it to scare her. Scarfing down the pungent berries seemed appropriate enough as a bit of self-punishment. Not that she had actively done bad, but not being smart enough to find him had to count as being a *little* bad.

The endless walking turned minutes into hours, though by late afternoon, she'd stopped crying and resigned herself to a somber sense of being a failure. At least Mother hadn't scolded her yet, the only reason she kept trying.

By early evening, she caught the sound of moving water on the wind and tried to head toward it. At least her ears didn't fail her like her sense of navigation did. Within minutes, she located a rushing stream rolling down the side of a hill. If not for Mother showing her the way, she'd surely never go anywhere at all.

Wisp followed the water to a place where it leveled off and the current slowed. There, she foraged around until locating a long, straight-ish branch. After carrying it back to the water, she sat on the bank and sliced away the smaller offshoots until she had a pole a few feet taller than her height. She started crying again while she worked, thinking of Dad teaching her how to make a fishing spear. The whole time she split the end into four prongs, wedged another hunk of wood between them to force them apart, and tied it all with twine, tears splattered on her thighs.

By the time she finished the spear, she missed Dad so much she couldn't do anything but curl up and sob. Grief lessened after a while, at least enough for her to latch onto the idea he would not want her to give up. She coughed a few times, wiped her eyes, and got to her feet.

Within five minutes of perching by the creek bank, she spotted a plump, silvery fish, and hit it on her first attempt. Her catch wound up on the small side, not quite half the size of the other fish she took, but it would be perfect for one meal. After building a fire, she scaled and gutted the fish, throwing the head and guts back in the water. Once the fish dangled over the flames on a stick, her mood alternated from sad to bored to feeling like the biggest failure in the whole forest.

A tingle spread over her left shoulder. She turned her head, but nothing appeared to have touched her. Mother must've put a hand on her for comfort.

You're right. I'm not a big failure. I'm still alive. "Did I do bad?"

She waited a few minutes, but Mother said nothing.

Relieved, she kept turning the fish around in the fire until it cooked all the way. The skin came out crunchy, the way she liked it. Wisp sat with her feet apart, elbows balanced on her knees, and nibbled at the fish until it cooled enough to take full bites.

When she finished eating, she kicked dirt on the fire, flung the stick/fish skeleton into the brush, and took out the Mother Twig.

"Mother... please help me. I've been walking for days. I know you're trying to guide me to Dad, but it... I'm sorry. It feels like I'm walking over the same ground again and again. *Please* help."

The twig took longer than usual to stop wobbling around, though she figured the constant breeze probably made it difficult for Mother to reach into the forest from the Other Side and turn the stick to point the right way. Eventually, the twig aligned with the stream, so she put it away and trudged along the bank, dragging her spear behind in a lazy three-fingered grip.

Her mind blanked out as she followed the water, ducking branches and the occasional dragonfly. Having the obvious path of a stream to follow made it easy to avoid wandering in circles, and she had a reasonable certainty of heading east. After an hour or so, a glimmering sheen up ahead beyond the trees stalled her. Jaw hanging open, she stared at the fiery glow upon the ground with an increasing sense of awe. Gradually, Wisp crept forward, pulled by curiosity and wonder. The closer she got, the more it looked as though the sun had spilled onto the ground. With an arm up to shade her eyes, she kept going, but remained wary, ready to jump back if the fire ahead became too hot. A thick mass of bushes scratched at her arms and legs, but she forced her way past the tangle and stepped out into an area of relatively short grass with open patches of dirt. The blinding glare upon the ground faded into the largest collection of water she had ever seen in one place. Stunned, she stood motionless, mesmerized by the glimmering ripples gliding across the surface.

The stream she'd been following ran down a stepped stone terrace on its way to pour into a colossal puddle. She looked from one side to the other, figuring it would take her more than an hour to walk all the way around the edge. The occasional tree and dead log broke the surface here and there, but the calm water had no visible current. A pronounced sense of serenity hung in the air.

Once the shock wore off, she climbed down the short hill alongside the stream and approached the water's edge. More of those 'goat' creatures gathered in a cluster off to the right, far enough away that they didn't react to her. Near the water, the greenery had been plucked mostly clean to dirt, likely by those animals.

She thought about the bathtub at the cabin, and remembered enjoying the water, but she'd never imagined finding a 'tub' so huge. Her last bath had been well over a month ago. Even if this giant bathtub didn't have a fire under it to make the water warm, the temptation to jump in grew strong.

A short ways past the goats, she spotted a giant elongated bowl with one pointy end and one flat end laying tilted but mostly upside down. Figuring it a decent hiding place for her stuff, she trotted over. The goats regarded her with mild disinterest, but did wander off to keep their distance. Wisp crouched beside the strange machine and peered underneath, surprised to find chairs, and a 'wheel' like inside the SUV. Wisp straightened and examined the smooth outer shell. It didn't have any tires, but a metal pinwheel stuck out of the flat end. Based on the chairs and wheel, she figured this odd contraption had rolled upside down.

The bizarre machine that kinda looked like a car but didn't have wheels defied her understanding. Still, whatever it was, it had to be as dead as everything else from the old Earth. It might not do what the ancients made it for any longer, but it would work perfectly as a hiding place.

Wisp set the rifle leaning against the steering wheel, then removed her backpack and put it next to the rifle. She unclipped the canteen belt and lay it nearby, then peeled off her shirt, exposing skin noticeably cleaner and paler than her arms and stomach. Last, she undid the one leather belt buckle and one nylon clip fastener that kept her skirt on, and let it fall to the ground, taking the knife sheath with it.

Standing nude beside the lake, she examined herself for injuries or hitchhikers.

It had been weeks since she'd taken the skirt off, and it left a dark black line across her stomach where the belts rested. She frowned at the grime, all the small scratches and dirt smears covering her, as well as a handful of grey dots: ticks. As soon as she saw them, she thought of the tall grass by where she had to shoot the monster.

"I hate these things. They're stupid. I'm supposed to eat the bugs; they're not supposed to eat me!"

Her dip in the lake delayed, she built a fire out of small twigs and branches, then sat on the ground beside it while heating the blade of her knife. One by one, she pressed the tip of the heated knife against the swollen tick bodies until the nasty things let go and backed out of her skin. She plucked them off and tossed them in the fire. Two on her right leg, three on her left—one even had the temerity to have crawled up under her skirt and lodge itself in her hip.

132

She found another on her left side. Fortunately, a few minutes of feeling around her back didn't find any suspicious protrusions, so she got lucky: no ticks on her back or anywhere she couldn't reach. She picked at her scalp for a few minutes and found one more. After burning it off with the knife, she stabbed that one so it popped, then held it on knifepoint in the flames until it caught fire.

Finally tick free, she doused the flames, stashed her knife with the rest of her stuff, and marched across the dirt to the water's edge. With Dad only warming the tub once every two or three months, she liked to go outside to have a 'rain bath' whenever the weather offered one. He didn't like getting wet, but he'd hover in the cabin door and let her enjoy the water, as long as she didn't get too far away.

She crept up to the edge and stuck her toes in, squealing at the cold. Bit by bit, she forced her way past the initial shock. Some of the streams she'd waded into over the years made this giant bathtub feel warm by comparison, so she advanced, feet disappearing into the mud at the bottom. Ooze squishing between her toes got her cringing and laughing. She eased herself deeper, inch by inch, until finally deciding to get it over with and jump headfirst.

Wisp hit the water with a soft splash and glided forward for a few seconds. Standing in a downpour had been one thing, but this enormous puddle beat it. She had—sort of—gone swimming before, but in a slow-moving creek that didn't get any deeper than her hips. Dad made it a point to teach her in case she ever needed to know, since he felt it stupid to fill her head with knowledge on how to survive and omit something so basic as swimming.

The cold water stung at the tick bites, but she savored the minor pain as a sign of cleaning. If any of the spots still bled when she got out of the water, she'd press some yarrow powder in. *That* stuff burned, but it would stop the bleeding.

She surfaced for air and dove down again, awestruck at being in water over her head. It continued to get deeper toward the middle, which reaffirmed her idea that she'd found the world's biggest puddle. For a little while, she stayed close to the shore where the water remained shallow enough for her to stand. There, she focused on washing, wiping away the past few months of dirt with her hands, since she hadn't brought along the soapwort powder from Dad's shelf.

When she could no longer find any smudges, she dove again, paddling for the deeper reaches. Fish came by to check her out, darting side to side. The tiny ones moved like little bullets, mere flashes of silver in the murk. She played with them, trying to swim along with their schools, pretending to be another fish, albeit one that had to surface for air every minute or so. Eventually, she approached the middle of the pond, and a metallic glint flashed from the depths.

Wisp popped her head above the surface, took a huge breath, and paddled downward toward the glimmer until the shape of a large machine came into view. A tall fin at the rightmost end caught the sunlight filtering through the lake, gleaming where paint had been scraped off. The opposite end had a narrow point, behind which perched an oval glass bubble. Small plants clung to its outer surface, while fish darted in and out from large holes. Behind the glass dome, the edges tapered wider, becoming flat sections in a somewhat triangular shape. One had the letters *USAF* on it. *Oh, that's a flying machine. A war bird. Why is it at the bottom of a puddle?* She kept swimming down until she hovered next to the bubble by the pointy end.

A thick layer of algae had grown all over the outside. After swiping a clear spot in the green muck on the side of the glass bubble, she peered in at a seat with a person. He had a funny ball-shaped hat on, a flap over his face attached to a hose. It covered everything but the eyes of the skull inside it. A small fish had tucked itself inside one of the eye sockets.

Wisp waved at the shrine. *Hello. I can't visit too long because I need to breathe. I hope you are happy in the Other Place. Did you see the Fire Dragons? Did you try to stop them? Is that why you fell out of the sky?* She waited a few seconds, but he said nothing. Her need for air soon became impossible to delay. *Tell Mother I love her, please.*

She pulled her legs up, planted her feet on the side of the machine, and kicked off, launching herself straight up. Her first gasp of breath made her lightheaded and filled her vision with dancing spots. *I stayed under too long.* She stretched her legs and arms out, letting her body float along the surface, gliding wherever the breeze or the water wanted to take her. The wind, which had been warm before, brushed her skin with chill. Weightless, she drifted, enjoying the tranquility. If not for the fear of slipping under and drowning, she'd have tried to sleep.

Her thoughts eventually went back to the somber message she'd found on the paper. *I wonder if the Fire Dragons lived in the Eagle's Nest.* Somewhere below her lay the shrine of a man who had been alive when they burned the world. Dad had once spoken of soldiers, a type of person who had something to do with shooting people and the world burning, but she couldn't remember exactly what. She daydreamed of a great flaming dragon surrounded by a cloud of war birds, raking its giant claws and sending one of the metal flying machines hurtling down into the puddle. While floating like a bit of driftwood, she tried to remember if any of her books had a name for such a place as this.

"Lake," said Wisp. "A giant puddle is called a lake."

A moment of guilt at wasting time nibbled on her heart.

"Mother? Am I wasting time? Am I being bad?"

Only the watery *gloop* lapping at her ears replied. Mother remained silent as ever.

I'm not bad!

Smiling, she stretched out and allowed herself to enjoy a swim.

The Boy
~19~

Tiny fish came up to nip at her from below, like a thousand tickling fingers. Wisp giggled and squirmed until she couldn't take any more. She twisted over and dove under again, exploring the lake bottom. Chased by the tiny nipping fish, she glided over old furniture, a car or two, and even an ancient porcelain bathtub covered in brown slime. The freedom of swimming melted away her worries and offered a reprieve from the persistent summer heat.

Wisp spent a little more than two hours playing in the lake before deciding to float on her back again and rest. Diving down to explore the bottom and rushing up for air over and over again had been tiring. As best she could guess, the day held four more hours of light, so she should probably get going again. It would take her a little while to dry off before she could get dressed, so she ought to leave the water soon. An argument went back and forth in her head. Part of her didn't want to get out of the water yet, while most of her wanted to find Dad.

A distant, high-pitched cry came out of the woods.

Startled, Wisp rolled over to tread water and stared into the trees from whence the sound had come. Nothing appeared obvious, but since she had no weapons on her, she did *not* want any monsters to see her. She swam fast toward the closest hiding place, a cluster of large rocks with a tree jutting up out of the water not far from the bank. Unfortunately, she'd gone most of the way across the lake, so she wound up nowhere near her stuff.

The cry repeated, along with the shouts of men's voices, all angry.

She glided up behind the tiny island on the side that concealed her from the bank, and clung to the rocks. Slimy underwater leaves coiled around her legs and brushed at her back. Soon after she ducked down, a child burst out of the trees with two men chasing. The other child wore a tiny, dark skirt and nothing else. Light brown hair, puffier than hers but not as long, trailed like flag in the air. The two chasing men both had the leather armor of marauders, and did not appear friendly.

Unarmed and naked, Wisp tucked herself tighter against the rocks and held absolutely still. She wanted to help the other child, but she had no means to do so. If the marauders noticed her now, she'd only get taken away too.

The men gained on the other child, whose head came up shorter than their shoulders. She guessed the other girl to be about her age or perhaps a year older. The lead marauder flung himself into a dive, tackling the girl to the ground.

The brown-haired child let off an ear-piercing scream, but the tone of it conveyed anger more than fear.

Alas, despite her struggling, she couldn't push herself off the ground with the marauder on top of her. The second man skidded to a halt nearby and tried to collect the child's flailing legs, winding rope around her ankles while the first marauder grabbed for her arms.

Wisp shivered and lowered herself deeper into the water so it came up to right below her eyes. She couldn't let the marauders see her, no matter how guilty she felt about not helping the other child. If she let herself get taken, not only would she be in big trouble, but Dad would be in trouble too, since she couldn't help him.

An enraged man's howl from the tree line made both marauders pause. The one attempting to bind the girl's legs let go of her and pivoted toward the woods at the same instant another man came sprinting into view, shirtless, muscular, and waving a huge knife around over his head. That weapon looked even bigger than the one she'd found in the ancient's place, yet this man swung it like it weighed nothing.

"Aaru!" shouted the large man.

"Da!" yelled the girl.

The marauder with the rope dropped it and pulled a big knife from a sheath on his belt, though it looked only half the size of the one coming at him. Marauder Two put a knee on top of the girl to hold her down while pulling a bow off his back. While the charging man's giant knife came down into a sparking collision with Marauder One's blade, the girl twisted up and grabbed a knife from the belt of the man on top of her. As fast as she swiped it, she jabbed it backward, stabbing his thigh.

Marauder Two screamed and pounded a fist into the child's head.

The large, bare-chested man roared and spun his whole body with another swing. Though Marauder One got his blade in the way again, the force of the strike knocked him off his feet. Ignoring the punch, the child twisted the knife, roaring in anger. Marauder Two jumped away from her, reaching for an arrow. The girl ripped the knife out of his leg, sprang to her feet, and slashed it across the man's throat. He dropped the bow and clutched at his neck, gurgling while the big, shirtless guy kicked Marauder Two in the side, rolling him over before chopping the huge blade down on the back of his head.

Wisp couldn't see much from her angle, but the wet *crunch* made her cringe.

The other girl spun in a flurry, moving almost too fast to follow. Three more slashes did little to the man's thick leather chest armor, but she finished off by jabbing the knife straight into his left eye. There, she left it and backed off, her bare chest heaving from rapid, deep breaths. The marauder didn't even reach up to grab the knife, simply falling over to the side and not moving anymore. Jaw set, the brown-haired girl glared down at the man she'd sent to the Other Place.

"Aaru?" asked the big man. "Are you hurt?"

The girl shook her head. "No, Da. No hurt. I hurt him."

"Son." The big man patted the girl on the head, grinning.

The child flung herself into an embrace, clinging to the man. Even on tiptoe, she barely stood as tall as the dark spots on his chest. "I'm okay."

"Check them," said the man.

The girl nodded. She crouched by one marauder while the man dragged the other one closer.

Wisp relaxed, uncurling herself. Still clinging to the rock, she let her body drape in the water, pulling herself up a little higher to watch as the two picked over the marauders and stripped all their possessions away. She couldn't pull her eyes off the other girl, never having seen another child before. Dad had once referred to her as 'scrawny,' but never explained what he meant.

This brown-haired girl had a thicker body, especially her upper torso and shoulders. While the other child scurried around the body picking at it, it became clear she didn't wear a skirt, but rather a small pair of pants with short legs that bared most of her thighs.

They collected the marauders' things into a pile, which the man bundled together and picked up like a sack.

"Pee," said the child, pointing almost right at Wisp.

She ducked down.

The man nodded.

Wisp slowed her breathing, trying to stay small and quiet as the other girl approached the edge of the water and hooked her thumbs into the top of her pants. When the other girl shoved them down, Wisp almost gasped out loud. Something did *not* seem right about her. She had… an eleventh finger or something sticking out between her legs. Even odder, a stream of bad water came out of it.

The other child stood at full height, throwing bad water into the lake.

Wisp peeked down at herself, and her clear lack of anything protruding out down there. *Did the Tree Walkers steal mine? Why does that girl have one?* If that had happened, it would've had to have been long ago when she'd been small, too small to remember now. She stared at the other child. Except for where the pants had covered skin as pale as Wisp's, the other child had a rich, brownish tan. Nowhere near as brown as Dad, but much darker than Wisp. She couldn't stop staring at the extra finger, wondering what the heck she was looking at.

The other child finished and snugged her pants back up.

Wisp continued gawking in confusion, unsure if she had been wounded long ago, or the brown-haired girl had a deformity. The big man put an arm around the other child. The way they looked at each other made her think that the man had to be the other girl's dad. A glimmer of hope that they might be nice got her pulling herself up out of the water. She slipped up onto the rock behind the tree, bracing her weight on one knee so she could stretch taller and wave, but couldn't manage to make a sound. Fear rushed in out of nowhere, chasing her back into the water out of sight. *No…* she couldn't risk contact with other people until she at least had a knife, or better yet, a gun.

Those people appeared friendly with each other, but they might not be nice to someone they didn't know, and Dad always told her people would want to hurt her. She could only trust him.

The man hefted the bundle over his shoulder while the child took the pouch of arrows and the bow. He ruffled the child's hair, chuckling, and the pair walked back into the woods together.

The Forest Beyond the Earth

She again stared down at herself. *It doesn't look like a scar. I gotta ask Dad about it when I find him. Dad…* When they'd gone to the Jeep place, he had let out bad water, and, just like that other child, stood tall the whole time. If he had one of those little tube things, that would explain how he let the bad water out without messing his jeans. What if that other child had already started becoming a dad? Wisp had always expected she'd become a dad, too, but not until she'd gotten much taller, like seventeen years or so old. The other girl couldn't have been too far from her age, so how had they started to turn into a dad already?

After waiting a few minutes to make sure the people didn't come back to the shore, she pushed off the rock and swam out toward the middle of the lake, heading for the spot on the other side where she'd stashed her things. On the way, she thought about that other child, replaying her memories of every motion and gesture. From experience, she knew people came in two types: men and girls. She understood that Dad had once been a child, but she had never seen anyone near her age before, only other men. Stranger still, despite Mother being a grownup, Dad always referred to her as a 'she.' That perplexed her since 'she' meant girl, which meant child. While swimming faster for shore, she tried to make sense of what she'd read in her books.

Dad had never once mentioned anything about how that stuff worked, how girls became men or where children came from. Well, how children became men didn't take a lot of thought to figure out: time passed. But at what point did a child decide if they were going to be a mother or a dad? Or did they decide? Would she eventually sprout an eleventh finger before becoming a dad? And why did that other child have one already?

She put her feet down in mud as soon as the water became shallow enough, and trudged out onto the shore, shivering from the crosswind. Wisp examined her body for a while, studying her overall shape. Her arms and legs were thinner than the other child's, her shoulders rounder. The most obvious differences included her not having a tube thing and a narrower chest.

All the chaos of the past few days missing Dad and running around the woods fogged her thoughts. She sat in the grass by the upside-down machine, letting the wind dry her off. One tick bite on her shin kept bleeding, so she dug out the little bottle of yarrow powder and whined at it. It took a bit of convincing to get herself to open it, take a pinch, and press it into the bite.

Wisp clenched her jaw to hold back the scream. The yarrow powder burned, but within a few seconds, the bleeding had stopped. She lay back in the grass to dry off, and let her brain wander, thinking of her many books and trying to make sense of words that she had no reference for. There had to be a word for it, a girl who turns into a man. She felt certain she'd read it often. Quite a few of her books had kids in them, but the ones Dad let her read never explained the eleventh finger (or lack thereof) thing. She'd always thought all children looked like her. She swung her feet back and forth, making faces at the clouds.

Eventually, the word 'boy' came to mind from a story about a child going to a house in the forest where magical creatures started attacking them. He had an older sister who carried a sword and...

Wisp biffed herself in the forehead. "Sword. They're *swords*, not big knives. And that was a *boy!*"

She ran her fingers through her hair, trying to help it dry faster while contemplating the idea that children weren't all girls. Boys must get older and become dads, but maybe girls like her stayed small and needed dads to protect them. A proud smile bared her teeth. She'd been alone a week and protected *herself*. Maybe she didn't *need* Dad hovering inches away all the time, but she still missed him.

While the wind lifted the water from her skin, she replayed the fight she witnessed in her head. It gave her confidence watching a child her size send a marauder to the Other Place with a knife. Marauders looked like men trying to be Tree Walkers, taking other people. They seemed way weaker than real Tree Walkers, and would probably run away like those other monsters did as soon as she shot one. Better still, marauders didn't have any magic and couldn't melt into the weeds to disappear.

Still, much better *not* to get seen—by marauders or Tree Walkers or anyone else—until she found Dad. Since Mother had yet to scold her for being bad, she knew she'd find him. Refreshed from her long swim, she lay stretched out in the grass and gazed at the clouds, wishing the wind would hurry up and dry her off.

She spotted some blueberries growing in a cluster of bushes not far from the upside-down no-wheeled car. Near to drooling at the prospect of yummy berries, she took the deeper pot from her backpack and hurried over to the bushes. Once she'd nearly filled the pot, she returned to her little campsite and ate as many as she could.

After reaching the point she couldn't force down even one more blueberry, she repacked the pot (and a nice stash of extra berries). By then, she'd dried off enough to get dressed. After one more check for bugs, she stepped into her skirt. The sun had warmed the leather painfully hot, but she wriggled it into place, gasping the whole time, and secured both belts. She snapped her shirt a few times in case of bugs before putting it on, then added the rest of her stuff one by one.

The Forest Beyond the Earth

"Ugh." She sighed under the weight of the backpack. All this stuff felt so heavy compared to floating in the lake. Still, she had at least two hours of daylight left and didn't want to sleep by the water. Especially not since marauders might come back. "Which way, Mother?"

The twig-on-twine unfurled from her hand, dangling on one finger. It spun back and forth, tossing in the breeze until she rotated herself to block the wind with her body. A few seconds later, it went still, pointing at the trees.

She nodded, stuffed the twig in the backpack's side pocket, and picked up the rifle.

sUpplies
~20~

The woods had not offered much in the way of shelter that night. She had to make do by concealing herself in a thick patch of underbrush with only delicate plants between her and Tree Walkers.

Tired from a poor sleep, Wisp trudged along for hours. The twig pointed her in an uphill direction, which she found odd since she'd been going downhill more often than not lately. Still, she trusted Mother, so she obliged, despite thinking she might be going northwest. Perhaps the beast that had taken Dad kept carrying him around, and she'd been following a moving target.

Her expression remained stoic, though silent tears drew wet lines from the corners of her eyes, pushed backward by the wind in her face. Having gone days without talking to anyone, she began trying to have a conversation with Mother.

"I miss him. I hope Dad's okay. Do you think he's okay? That's good. I do, too. I'm sorry it's taking me so long to find him. I won't give up."

She walked on for a few minutes, imagining Mother telling her she did a good job and everything would be okay. Random thoughts of home, her Haven, Dad's smile, the smell of crickets in boar grease with yellowgreens—all of it hit her and kept the tears flowing.

"Stop crying. I'm wasting water." She came to a halt, taking deep breaths to let her grief settle down.

A couple hits off her canteen and a twig check later, she resumed walking, making a slight course correction to the left. She made a brief stop around midday to munch on blueberries, and choked down a couple handfuls of yellowgreens without cooking them. At the first signs of sunset, she crested the top of a hill and came to a stop at a cliff ridge. There, she beheld an impossible sight:

The end of the Endless Forest.

Land, a vast expanse of barren dirt, stretched as far as she could see out in front of her.

"Umm…" She peered down what had to be a seven-or-eight story drop, near vertical. Windblown whorls of dust, some bigger than her cabin, glided back and forth across the ground far below. "Mother? I don't think I *can* go this way."

This cliff stood at the line of separation between life and death, with the lush forest behind her, and a desiccated wasteland in front.

She stepped back from the edge before the soil could crumble out from under her, and sighed at the distance. The red-orange sun sank behind the mountains at her back, sending streamers of fire across the clouds. A collection of dark shapes way off in the wastes resembled a 'city' she had seen on the cover of a book. She pulled the rifle off her shoulder and used the scope to zoom in on the spot. A group of what she thought were called 'skyscrapers' stood in the midst of a vast field of brown-beige rubble. All tilted at the same rightward angle, as if some great force and crashed over them from the left. Their upper ends had broken open, blooming into twisted tangles of metal spars and dangling concrete hunks.

"Whoa," she whispered. "Is that the Other Place?"

She panned the scope over smashed windows, examining fluttering curtains, chairs, and other objects she didn't recognize. The ancient buildings all had missing sections where gaping holes in the sides spanned several floors. Nothing moved in that place without the wind's help. The skeletal high-rises contained only death.

Wisp shivered, emitting an uneasy mutter. A place that looked that scary *had* to be where spirits went. But what would happen to a living person if they walked to the Other Place? Would they be stuck there or could they leave again because they hadn't lost their life?

I could visit Mother! She bounced on her toes with anticipation. Of all the stories in her books, one thing upset her more than anything: reading about young characters who had mothers. She'd always been jealous of them, since her mother had to go to the Other Place before she got old enough to remember her. Wisp took an instant dislike to any character in a book whose mother remained alive, and even more so if they acted mean to her.

But…

She remembered something a character in one of her thicker books said, and tried to mimic a man's voice.

"One does not simply *walk* into the Other Place."

Modifying the line made her want to laugh and cry at the same time.

The ruin looked so far away, she expected even a bullet from her rifle would fall to the ground before reaching it.

"It's not really here. This hill lets people see it, but we can't go there."

Skiff.

Wisp spun to the rear at the sound of a shoe in the dirt. She didn't even have the time to yelp before a marauder grabbed her in a painfully tight bear hug and hauled her into the air. Her legs pedaled at nothing; he flipped her over right as she began to scream, and threw her down, chest-first. Her body striking the dirt changed her scream to an "Oof!"

The marauder fell on top of her, grabbing at her arms. "Git her legs!"

She kicked harder, struggling to pull her arm away from the vicelike grip on her right wrist. "Let go!"

Another marauder rushed over and seized her legs. Wisp kept kicking and struggling, even with hard fingers crushing around both ankles. The second marauder overpowered her, gradually fighting her legs together and pinning her feet to the soil. Her backpack got in the way of the man trying to pull her arms around behind her. He released her left arm and grabbed the strap, trying to yank it off her shoulder. The rifle crushed into her hip, pinned to the dirt beneath her.

A brush of coarse rope at her ankle set her off like a primer to a bullet.

Wisp roared and flung herself up, smashing the back of her head into the mouth of the man on top of her. He let off a pained whimper, released her arms, and fell to the side, clutching his face. She rolled to the right, yanked the pistol from its holster, and pointed it at the man trying to tie her ankles together. He started to glance toward the gun less than two feet away from his face, but she fired before they made eye contact.

The back of his head blew out in a spray of red. He slumped over sideways and landed with his butt in the air.

"Gah!" shouted the other marauder, scooting away from her.

She twisted to aim at him. Blood streamed out of his nose over his teeth.

"Black magic," said the marauder.

Wisp pulled the trigger. The marauder's head rocked back and he collapsed to the ground, still. She lay there pointing the gun at him for a moment more, heart racing, breath rushing loud in her ears. Eventually, she calmed enough to reach forward with her left hand and pull the loose rope away from her legs, her gun still trained on the man. Another six or so minutes passed before her heartbeat slowed back to normal, or she moved.

Without a word, she popped the magazine from the pistol and counted fourteen shots left, thirteen in the mag, one in the chamber. She slid the magazine back into place and let her arms drop into her lap.

"Monsters. They're just monsters."

She closed her eyes and told herself over and over that they hadn't been people. *People* don't grab children.

Six minutes after shooting two monsters, she slid the pistol back in the holster. Still, she sat there, staring past her feet at the marauder with his butt in the air. That big man and the boy had gathered *everything* from the ones they sent to the Other Place, but she didn't want to take their clothes. Not to mention, she couldn't really carry their bows, since she already had so much stuff it made walking a chore. One had a pouch with jerky in it, which she helped herself to. The other guy had a couple pieces of bread, which she also swiped. She took a test nibble from a piece of jerky, and determined it to be deer.

After eating the dried meat and one of the small breads, she picked up the two empty casings her pistol had spat into the dirt. Dad would want her to so he could put more magic fire dust in them later.

Both marauders had canteens, and the water smelled okay, so she drank.

Water and food. She looked back and forth between them. *Could I hunt monsters for supplies instead of foraging?* She sighed. *No. I should save bullets for emergencies. Always run first. I can't run when the monsters are holding me down.*

She pulled her feet close, shifted her weight forward, and jumped upright.

"And I should get out of here. Guns are loud."

Wisp stooped to pick up her rifle, dusted it off, and jogged down the hill heading back the way she'd come.

Ʒen

~21~

At the bottom of the hill, Wisp pulled out the Mother Twig and let it spin.

It guided her left to a section of road she hadn't seen before with another rocky wall straight in front of her, leaving her no choice other than following the paving to the right or left. This time, the twig pointed right, putting the sun at her back.

"East again… That's good. Thank you, Mother."

She wound the twine around the twig, stuffed it again in the side pocket on the backpack, and proceeded to follow the road. Still on edge from the marauders trying to grab her, she carried the rifle. The thicker leather flap in the middle of her skirt slapped against her legs as she walked, creating a regular *pat-pat-pat*. She thought back to the boy slicing at the marauder with his knife, but not cutting his chest.

At least if someone tried to stab her in the skirt, she'd be protected. She didn't *want* to get into knife fights, but she decided it would probably be a good idea to ask Dad to make her some chest armor. So far, she'd sent three monsters to the Other Place all on her own, so she had to be 'ready' to go on trips with him. No more hiding in the Haven for Wisp. Nope. Once she found Dad, she would follow his third rule perfectly: never again would she be more than three steps away. Even if he made *ngh*, she'd stay close.

She grimaced at the memory of how bad it could smell sometimes. What about Dad made it so powerful? Was that a Dad thing or a man thing? Heck, Dad's *ngh* stank so bad it could probably keep marauders away. Maybe even Tree Walkers.

"We'll make an *ngh* thrower. He'll destroy all the monsters."

Wisp laughed.

The road passed into a section with high rock walls on both sides, too sheer to climb. Strange fuzzy paint writing covered the left side, but she couldn't make out what any of it said, aside from recognizing one or two individual letters. Since the canyon limited her choice of direction, she kept going along the road, which increasingly took on a steeper downhill grade.

By midday, she'd finished the water in the marauders' canteens and put the empties in her backpack, which had about reached the limit of what it could hold. Walking on road for so long made her feet hurt, so she stuck to a narrow strip of dirt by the wall. The road swerved around a sweeping left after another hour, where the tops of the walls shrank lower and lower. Two hours past midday, the incline walls on either side of the road flattened out from vertical to steep hills she might be able to climb. Another bend curved to the right, and when she peeked around the corner, she stopped short.

The paved strip became a pin-straight line heading out into flat dirt—no trees anywhere in sight. A few small green bushes sprouted here and there, as well as bizarre tall plants she'd never seen anywhere but in pictures before with thick stems covered in spines. She would've turned around and gone back up into the woods if not for spotting a settlement beside the road in the distance.

It didn't seem possible to survive in such a dead place, without bugs or edible plants or any animals. But a cluster of buildings visible past the heat blur suggested that some people *did* manage it. Mother had to know what she was doing bringing her here. Maybe *this* is the place she will find Dad. Even if it turned out to be empty, she couldn't exactly get lost anymore, not in wide-open nothingness. No landmark more obvious than the mountains behind her existed. She'd only have to follow this road back to her forest.

Wisp decided to proceed. Within minutes, sweat ran down her body in trails, dripping from her nose onto the rifle. At least a reasonably cool breeze cut across the land, making the heat bearable. As she got closer to the settlement, signs of life became apparent. The occasional voice broke the silence, and she spotted a few goats as well as some of those fat non-flying birds. One cabin even had a rectangular arrangement of green plants growing behind it.

A giant box lay on its side across the road close to the edge of the settlement. Huge tires, mounted in four pairs of two, stuck out from the left side. These tires would've stood as tall as her chest if the box had been upright, far bigger than any she'd ever seen before. In fact, the box looked about twice as long as her cabin. *This thing isn't supposed to be on that side. The tires should touch the ground. Something knocked this giant thing over, but what?* She gawked at the sheer size of it.

That machine's days of driving long ago came to an end. Metal and wood creaked as the box deformed with the wind, swaying back and forth. She crept up and hid behind it to observe the settlement, not quite ready to let other people see her.

She watched for a while, counting seven individuals, some in fabric skirts, some in jeans, and a few wearing armor like marauders, but black instead of brown, and none had face-coverings. The men with armor didn't act aggressively toward anyone, so she entertained the hope that they might not be marauders. Dad wore leather armor on his chest and he was certainly not a marauder. His *did* look a lot like theirs, but he probably sent one to the Other Place and took the armor.

"What do you think, Mother? Should I go in?"

Kneeling in the road safely in the shadow of the huge box, she pulled out the twig and let it spin. It swayed back and forth for a little while before winding up pointing (mostly) at the settlement.

"All right. I know you will protect me."

Wisp stood, took a breath, and stepped out past the enormous tires. The twig told her to go that way, and she trusted Mother. Head held high, she walked straight into the settlement along the road. People looked at her with curious expressions. One man seemed worried, but none approached or spoke. The urge to scream at being around so many people at the same time welled up inside her, but after a full minute of no one trying to convince her to come closer or running over to grab her, she relaxed.

The Forest Beyond the Earth

Another strange man with long hair, a slender build, and an unusual puffy pillow in his shirt, stared at her. He appeared to teeter on the verge of walking over, but remained in place. Wisp stared at him, wondering how he'd managed to shave his beard so well that no sign of any hair remained on his face.

The smell of food in the wind triggered a sharp growl from her stomach. She faced the breeze and looked around for the source, walking in that direction. Her nose led her to a huge one-story cabin with a round white and black sign over the door. It had no words, but a basic drawing of two curved raindrops spinning into each other. The black one had a white spot in it, and the white one had a black spot.

A small staircase led up to an elevated porch as wide as the whole face of the cabin, with an assortment of chairs and a few tiny tables, though no one sat at them. She padded up onto the warm wood, leaving a trail of footprints in the dust on her way to the entrance. Instead of a door, a curtain of hanging beads separated the inside from outside.

Wisp poked the rifle barrel into the beads and pushed half of them aside with a soft rustling clatter. The room beyond could've held four of her cabin and then some. Many round tables and chairs occupied the middle, a fair number with people having dinner. More, square tables and bench seats lined the left wall. At the far side of the room opposite the door, a man with black-and-white hair stood behind a tall counter.

She took one breath and almost drooled on herself, not even knowing what she smelled other than it being food. Licking her lips, she ducked past the bead curtain and crossed the room. People sitting at the tables glanced at her casually, except for one man who looked terrified. She glanced over at him and noticed he'd put a hand on a pistol under his left arm. Of all the people in here, only he appeared to understand the threat her rifle posed, and he seemed alarmed at how she held it ready to fire.

The armed man stared at her, but his expression radiated more worry than anything.

Wisp locked stares with him, but made an apologetic face like she did whenever Dad caught her getting too far away from him. He jumped when she let go with her right hand and the rifle swung to hang from her left. Once she'd slung it over her shoulder on the strap, the man relaxed and offered a sheepish smile.

She disregarded him and approached the older man in the white robe behind the counter.

"Why hello there, little one," said the man.

Wisp looked up. This person had an odd shape to his eyes, slightly flat across the top. Though, far stranger than his appearance was the concept of talking to someone other than Dad—or Mother... but she never expected Mother would answer her. At least she *hoped* not. If Mother spoke, it would mean she'd been bad.

"Are you all right?" asked the man. "Can you hear?"

"Yes," said Wisp. "Can you help me?"

"What's wrong?" He leaned on the counter to get a little closer.

"I'm trying to find Dad. I saw these lines on the ground, like footprints but one long big line. I think a big monster took him. Have you seen Dad or do did you see any monster tracks? I tried following them, but they stopped when the ground got hard. I haven't been able to find them again."

He appeared lost in thought for a few seconds, fingers tapping on the counter. "Perhaps. What is your name, little one?"

"Wisp."

He reached a hand toward her. "I am Zen."

She glanced at his hand, tilted her head, blinked, and straightened her head.

"You must not be used to people."

She shook her head. "No."

"Ahh." He nodded, smiling. "This is a common greeting. Please, hold out your hand."

Nothing about his body language put her on edge, so she raised her right arm toward him.

"When two people meet, they usually do this." He clasped her hand gently, and bobbed it up and down for a few seconds before letting go. "It's called shaking hands."

"Shaking hands," muttered Wisp, staring at her palm. "Why?"

Zen laughed, patting his belly. "Oh, I don't know. People have always done that. As long as there have been people. Well, now that we've been introduced, I shall try to help you."

"Introduced?" She leaned back. "That sounds like it would hurt."

He laughed again, tinged with a grimace. "Oh, child... Introduced means we have met each other and exchanged names. Tell me again what you are looking for?"

"A big monster took Dad away." She explained about the buzzing sound, Dad going outside, and being gone the next day. "I followed this trail but it stopped. I've been looking for it but I can't find it again. I don't think the monster flied."

"What did this trail look like?"

"It had two lines." She held her hands as far apart as her shoulders. "Each one was this wide, deeper in the middle, and it had all these little holes. An' I found people footprints, too. I think men sneaked Dad."

Zen rubbed his chin, shifting his eyes around. "Hmm. I believe you might have found an ancient dirt road. Those ruts had been worn into the earth long ago... but the fresh holes are probably tire tracks."

"Tire tracks? Tires don't make tracks. Cars don't work. An' the monster footprints are fatter than tires."

A few people behind her muffled whispers.

"Do you know what a buggy is?"

That made her itch. Wisp squirmed and scratched at her leg with her foot. "The little things that fly around and bite?"

Zen chuckled, as did a few people in the room.

She peered back at them for a moment before gazing up at Zen, confused. "What is funny?"

His smile only broadened. "Not an insect. A buggy is, well... You know how the ancients made all these cars, and none of them work anymore?"

Wisp nodded.

"Some people have figured out how to take parts off old cars, fiddle with them, and build something like a car that runs. They're a lot smaller, and they don't always hold together too well. They wouldn't have chewed up the forest to dig those ruts, which is why it didn't leave a track once it passed the end of that old path."

"So a monster didn't take Dad? It was a car?"

"A buggy." Zen smiled. "Marauders sometimes use them. You said you saw footprints, too? Sounds like they got him."

"Giant bugs?"

Zen sighed. "No. They're vehicles."

"A SUV?"

"I don't know what that is, but it's not a buggy. They're—"

"Limousine?" yelled Wisp.

Zen scratched his head. "I'm sorry, but I've never heard of that either."

"A limousine is like a SUV but it's longer and shorter. SUVs are tall and big." She smiled.

"Those sound like things from the old Earth."

Wisp stared down at her feet. "Yeah. They don't work anymore."

"No, buggies are much smaller, and they run on alcohol. Not whatever the ancients used. It's starting to sound like marauders took your dad."

Wisp's eyes bulged. She leapt forward, grabbing the counter's edge. "I saw marauders! We saw one right before the giant bug… uhh, buggy came. And Dad is gone."

Zen walked out from behind the counter, approached her, and rested his hands on her shoulders. "I'm sorry, child. It sure sounds like they took him. You'd best forget about him. He's as good as dead."

She tilted her head. "Dead?"

"More than likely. That's what happens to everyone when marauders take them. They wind up dead." He brushed a hand over her head, nudging her hair away from her eyes. "I'm sorry. It is fortunate that they did not find you, too."

"What does dead mean?"

"Have you heard of the Other Place?" asked Zen.

She nodded. "Yes. Mother is there. But I don't think Dad is, because Mother is leading me to him. She brought me here so I can find him."

The room got quiet.

"Your… mom is in the Other Place, but she brought you here?"

"Uh huh!" She nodded, grinning. "I've got a magic pointer, like Dad's north box. She tells me where to go." Wisp pulled out the Mother Twig and let it dangle. "See? When it stops spinning, that's where she wants me to go."

One man whistled. A few people shook their heads. About half the room gave her sad stares. The man with the pistol held a finger up to the side of his head and twirled it around while staring at Zen.

She turned back to face him and made the same hand twirl gesture. "What does this mean?"

"It, umm… means that… umm…" Zen pursed his lips. "You're very smart. He thinks you're a brave little girl to go looking for your dad like that."

The armed man made a sputtering noise.

"Poor kid," muttered a high-voiced man with chest pillows and a perfectly shaved face.

"Can you help me find the, uhh, tire marks?" asked Wisp.

"I'm afraid I cannot. I wouldn't know where to look, plus I wouldn't feel right bringing a young girl *to* marauders."

She shook her head. "It's okay. Mother is protecting me. I'm not scared of marauders. I already sent two of them to the Other Place."

For the second time that day, the whole room fell silent.

Work

~22~

Wisp twisted around to look at everyone staring at her. The people seemed relatively nice, though appeared confused at what to make of her. A few whispered phrases like "poor thing" or "she's nuts" or "someone ought'a do something," though no one moved.

She turned back to Zen. "Can I have some food?"

"Of course. Do you have anything to trade, or any coins?"

"Coins?" asked Wisp.

"Small round pieces of money?" Zen held up a tiny silver disk.

"I've never seen money, but I've read about it. How does it work?" asked Wisp. Characters in her books often wanted, stole, or spent 'money,' but she had no idea what it looked like, or how it worked.

"Forget it. Do you have anything to trade?"

"Umm." She looked over her possessions, not wanting to part with anything. "I can't trade this stuff. It's all Dad's, so I can't give it away. None of it is really mine except for my clothes."

"Hmm." Zen rubbed his chin.

"I could trade my clothes for food."

He waved her off. "No... no... you keep them."

She bit her lip. "Yeah, I guess I'll need them when it gets cold again." She sighed at the floor. Right before she gave up and walked out, she lifted her gaze to meet his. "Zen? Since I'm only twelve, would you maybe just give me food because it's nice?"

He tapped a finger to his chin. "How about you trade a little work instead?"

"Work?"

He closed his eyes and pinched the bridge of his nose. "You don't get out much, do you?"

"Out?"

"In the world." He waved his arm across in a sweeping gesture. "Traveling, meeting people."

"No. I stay at the cabin with Dad and sleep in my Haven so the Tree Walkers don't take me."

He pursed his lips, silent for a long moment. "Umm. Right. Well. Work is when you do something that you don't really like doing, but you have to do."

"Like making *ngh*?"

"I'm sorry. What is—" He emitted a sharp grunt.

"*Ngh* is what comes out your butt."

The room erupted in laughter.

"Where..." Zen leaned on the counter while laughing himself to tears. Once he got his breath back under control, he looked at her and tried to speak, but cracked up again. Eventually, he calmed down enough to ask, "Where did you come up with calling it—" He grunted again.

"It's what Dad always yells when he makes it. Isn't that what it's called?" She glanced back as another wave of heavy laughter rolled over the room. One man fell off his chair.

It took Zen a moment to collect himself. "Oh, child, you are a breath of fresh air. It is so rare to have such a moment of purity. I needed that. We have a couple words for it, but the only one I'm going to share with you is poop."

"Poop?" She blinked.

"Yes. That's what someone your age should call it."

She mentally rolled her eyes. *Ngh* was *ngh*. She didn't need a new word for something like that. "So, what work do you want me to trade you?"

"Come..." He extended an arm to the side.

She grabbed his hand and shook it.

"We're past the handshake." He grinned. "I mean for you to follow me."

"Okay."

He walked through a door behind the counter into a room with metal tables on each side and a big metal box full of burning wood at the far end. A small man with long black hair and a purplish-pink garment stood by a giant plastic bowl, kneading the contents with both hands. He only had an inch or two of height on Wisp and an equally slender body, though darker skin—but not as brown as Dad.

"Lijuan?" asked Zen.

The man turned, revealing a small set of chest pillows beneath the floral print garment. The long shirt hung down to his knees, almost like a dress.

"This is my daughter, Lijuan," said Zen. "She's seventeen."

"Daughter?" asked Wisp.

"She is my child, like you are to your dad."

"Oh." *An older girl.*

Lijuan held up her hands, coated in a mixture of something pale. "Sorry. I'm making dumplings. Hello! What's your name?"

"I'm Wisp."

Zen patted Wisp on the backpack. "Please work with my daughter for a little while. Perhaps you can peel or do whatever she asks. In return, we will feed you and give you a room for the night."

"Okay," said Wisp.

"Let me know if you need any help." Zen smiled and went back out to the front.

"One moment, kid," said Lijuan. She grabbed a cloth and wiped her hands clear before walking over and folding her arms, looking Wisp up and down. "Not much to you. Lot of stuff you're carrying. You might as well put it down."

"Where can I put it?"

"There in the corner." Lijuan pointed.

Wisp walked to the indicated spot, leaned the rifle against the wall, then took off the backpack and canteen belt, but kept the pistol and knife.

"Over here," said Lijuan. "Since you're so small, I think my father only wants you to do a little just so he feels like you're helping." She winked. "He'd have fed you if you begged harder, or were littler."

Wisp grinned.

"Do you know how to peel?"

"No. I've never done that before."

The older girl picked up a strange bulbous object and a small knife. "Watch me."

Wisp observed as the girl held the knife at a shallow angle against the lumpy plant and turned it so the outer layer of skin sliced off in thin pieces.

"You'll need to cut off all the skin like this." She held up the naked vegetable. "Got it?"

"Yes. I can do that."

While Lijuan resumed mushing the contents of the big bowl with her hands, Wisp sat on a nearby chair, grabbed one of the lumpy things, and proceeded to peel it. The first few didn't go so well, but by the fifth one, the process got easier.

"What are these plants?" asked Wisp after number ten.

Lijuan looked over at her. "Potatoes. What, you've never seen them before?"

"No. Nothing like this grows where I live."

"What do you eat?" asked Lijuan.

She grabbed another potato and put the knife to it. "Yellowgreens—Dad calls them dandelions, but he lets me use my name for them 'cause it makes him smile. Umm, Clovers, purslane, asparagus, wood sorrel sometimes. Oregon grapes, blueberries, raspberries, grubs, crickets, grasshoppers..." She proceeded to list off every edible plant or mushroom she could think of plus a bevy of insects.

Lijuan gurgled. "Ugh. Please, no more."

"What?"

"A lot of those are bugs."

"Yes. They're good." She started to describe the process of skewering a giant grub and fire-roasting it, but Lijuan gagged. "Umm. Where do potatoes come from?"

"The ground." The older girl took a few breaths while fanning herself. "We have a farm. My father made some pipes to bring water from the creek. We have carrots and turnips and corn, too. My father trades for flour with a settlement a few hours away, so we can make dumplings."

"I don't know those plants."

"They all grow out back. People plant them for food. They're much better than the stuff you usually eat. Trust me."

Wisp shrugged, tossed a peeled potato into the bin, and grabbed a new one. "Okay."

A while later, Lijuan finished whatever she'd been doing in the bowl and dragged a beat-up metal chair over to sit nearby. The older girl began peeling another vegetable, bright orange and pointy. Wisp watched her for a few minutes until her curiosity grew too great to resist. She peered over at the older girl, considered a moment, then poked a finger into her chest pillow. "Why do you have stuff under your shirt?"

The older girl grabbed the spot and gasped. "Stuff?" She laughed.

"Yes. What is under your shirt that it's sticking out?"

Lijuan's face darkened with blush, but she erupted in giggles. "They're breasts."

Wisp tilted her head. "What?"

"You'll have them too someday, and from the look of you, fairly soon. Maybe a year or two. You're a girl right?"

"Umm. I think so. How do I tell?"

Lijuan blinked. "You don't know? How could you not?"

"Dad calls me a girl, but I don't really know. I saw this other girl that I thought was a girl but when she let out the bad water, there was this thing I don't have. At first, I thought maybe the Tree Walkers took mine when I was really small."

"Thing?" asked Lijuan.

"It looked like a finger." Wisp put her hand against her skirt and stuck one finger out.

Lijuan cackled. "Oh, you are adorable!"

Her eyebrows scrunched together. "I'm not stupid. I remembered a book said 'boy.'"

"No, you're not stupid. Just... sheltered. Someone who's got one of those 'things' is a boy. If you don't have one, you're a girl. We don't have those. That's normal. No one took anything from you."

"Oh. I'm a girl." Wisp poked her in the breast again. "Why do you have those?"

"Because I'm a girl."

"Mother doesn't have them."

Lijuan raised an eyebrow. "Your mother doesn't have them? Well, not everyone's are the same size. Some girls aren't that big up there."

She tossed another peeled potato into the bin and took the next. "Do they pop when a girl goes to the Other Place?"

"Pop? Wait, what do you mean? She's in the Other Place?" Lijuan's eyes widened.

"Yes." She dragged the knife around the potato, unfurling a thin spool of skin. "Mother went to the Other Place when I was tiny. I visit her in the shrine, but she doesn't have those." Wisp puffed out her flat chest. "She looks like me."

Lijuan fidgeted. "Your mother is dead, but you still visit her? Umm. Okay. That's... wow. She's not buried?"

The sense of alarmed disgust radiating from the older girl made Wisp fidget in discomfort. How could someone not understand how much she and Dad loved Mother? "No. She's in the shrine, watching over us. I bring her flowers sometimes and tell her about what I learned."

"Does... she talk back?" Lijuan grimaced.

Wisp shook her head. "No. She never talks, but that's good. Dad said she'd only talk if I was a bad girl. So... I guess Mother doesn't have them because she's been in the Other Place so long."

"Yes... that's probably right." The girl shivered. "You poor child."

"Am I going to have breasts, or am I going to turn into a Dad when I'm grown up?"

Lijuan's eyes widened. "Wow, kid. Didn't your dad explain this to you?"

"No." Wisp shook her head and took a new potato.

"Well... boys grow up to be men and girls grow up to be women."

"Women?" asked Wisp.

Lijuan stared at the vegetable in her hands. "You know how boys and girls are different?"

Wisp figured it had to do with the eleventh finger. "Yeah."

"Well, the difference between women and men is basically the same."

"Oh. So not all kids grow up to be men?"

"No." Lijuan chuckled. "They don't."

"Am I going to have chest pillows?"

Giggling, Lijuan put an arm around her and hugged her. "You are too cute. Yes. Another year or two and you'll see. But, you're kinda skinny, so you might not notice for a while longer."

Wisp stuck out her tongue.

She worked her way through the bin of potatoes, and moved on to the long orange plants Lijuan called carrots. Those required a slightly different technique, more scraping the edge than slicing, as they had much thinner skin. By the time it got dark outside, she'd finished peeling both containers' worth of vegetables. Lijuan led her back to the outside room and set her up at a table with a big glass of water and a plate.

Wisp looked at the offering, two white puffy things and a pile of greenery. "It smells good. What is it?"

"Those are dumplings, and that's vegetables." Lijuan smiled. "When you are done eating, come back to the kitchen to get your things and I'll bring you to a room where you can sleep tonight."

"Thank you."

Wisp attacked her food, famished from most of a day's walking. Both dumplings contained a meaty filling under a dense bread-like layer as thick as her finger. She huddled over the plate, watching the handful of people remaining in the room, but none of the grownups paid her much attention. She wound up staring at one with 'breasts,' now understanding her to be a woman, not a skinny man. Feet swinging back and forth, she devoured the dumplings and veggies, which settled in her stomach to a nice warm fullness.

Once she finished, she carried the plate into the kitchen and left it on the table. "I'm done."

Lijuan looked up from a chair where she'd been wrapping meatballs in dough. "All right. Grab your things."

She collected her stuff from the corner and followed the girl out into the main room again, across it, and down a side hallway full of small doors. She stopped at one marked '18,' and stuck a key in the door.

"When will you let me out?" asked Wisp.

Lijuan's head twitched. "*Let* you out?"

"You will lock the door once I'm inside, like the Haven, right?"

"No. I'm going to give you the key."

Wisp nodded. "Okay."

Lijuan stared at her with an odd expression for a moment before handing her the key. "If you need to use the bathroom, go out the front door, walk around the building to the left, and there's an outhouse."

"Okay. Thank you."

"Good night." Lijuan smiled and walked off down the hall, muttering, "That poor kid."

Wisp shrugged, and stepped past the door into a room about half the size of the Mother Shrine. A narrow bed sat against the left wall with only a single wooden chair for company in the corner. A hole in the back wall formed a window too small even for Wisp to squeeze through.

"Perfect."

She pushed the door closed behind her, locked it, and set the key on the chair seat. This little room reminded her enough of the Haven that she figured she could sleep quite well. Perhaps even better since instead of bars, it had solid walls. Tree Walkers couldn't force her to give them the key if they couldn't see her, right?

Item by item, she stashed her stuff on the ground, removing everything except her shirt and skirt. The pistol, however, she took to bed, keeping it under the pillow for easy reach. Despite the relative sense of safety here, she stared at the ceiling for a while, unable to sleep because her brain got stuck on a quandary.

Could Tree Walkers follow her out into a dead land that had no trees?

City of Ghosts
~23~

The next morning, Wisp stumbled out of her room and locked the door to protect her stuff for a few minutes. She'd put on the pistol holster, but left her other things in the room. Eyes half-closed, she trudged down the hall to the main room, went outside, and plodded over to a pair of outhouses. One door refused to open, but the other one almost hit her in the face when she reached for the handle.

"Sorry," said a man, brushing past her on his way out of the tiny building.

She yawned while stepping inside. After pulling the door shut, she turned around and pulled her skirt up before sitting—and falling butt first into the hole, jamming to a stop when her arms hit the sides and her calves caught on the front edge. She dangled, armpit-deep in the hole over a pit of *ngh*. Her foggy brain didn't even think to scream for almost ten seconds.

"Ngh!" she yelled, kicking her feet back and forth. She gasped, struggling with her knees mashed against her shoulders.

She grabbed at the bench, but her fingers couldn't get a grip on anything. Pushing down with her arms lifted her a little, but not with enough strength to escape the hole.

"Are you okay?" asked a higher-pitched voice, but too full to belong to a child.

She tried to push herself out again, but had no leverage. "I'm stuck!"

A person with thick shoulder-length black hair, dark brown skin, and chest pillows opened the door and stared at her. *"Ay Dios!"*

Wisp stopped struggling. Stuck in the outhouse hole, she gazed up at a person she understood to be a woman, who resembled Dad a bit in terms of her complexion and thickness of hair. She held up a hand, offering a shake.

"Oh, you poor thing!" The woman reached in and took her by the hand. Wisp started to return the shake, but the woman hauled her up and out of the hole. The pistol began to slip from the sheath, but Wisp slapped her left hand over it, holding it in place as the woman dragged her up to stand.

"Stupid Pedro. I tell him all the time to put the seat down, but he doesn't! My sister's son fell in two weeks ago."

"Eww…" Wisp shivered in disgust. "Umm. Is he okay?"

"Aye. We got him out, but he was covered in crap."

"Crap?"

"The nasty stuff."

"Poop?" asked Wisp.

"Same thing."

"Oh." Wisp glanced back at the seat. "I need to let out the bad water."

The woman grinned. "Aww."

Wisp felt somehow insulted by that smile, but since this person had saved her from taking a bath in *ngh*, she kept quiet. Before she could go into the outhouse again, the woman leaned in and folded down a plastic seat ring over the hole.

"There. Now be careful."

"Thank you."

After the woman closed the door, Wisp eased herself down—and didn't fall in.

When she returned to the building, Zen set a plate of mashed potatoes and chicken on the counter, offering breakfast without asking her to work or trade for them. She hopped up on one of the stools in front of his counter.

"Thank you!" She grinned at him and attacked the food.

He asked a bunch of questions about where she came from and about Mother while she ate. Wisp told him of the forest and their cabin, and about how she'd been walking so long she'd lost count of the days. At her explanation that Mother occupied the back room of the cabin in a chair where they'd made a shrine for her, he emitted a strange gurgling noise. When she told him of how she followed Mother's guidance here, completely confident in the spirit's protection, he got quiet.

"I think your Dad has gone to the Other Place, and your mother is already there. Did your parents have brothers or sisters? Do you have any brothers or sisters?"

"No. It's only my Dad and me, and Mother. But she's in the Other Place, so she only watches us."

"Wisp, you're alone now. Your Dad isn't coming back."

"He is!" She pounded her fist on the counter. "I gotta find him. He's not in the Other Place, or Mother wouldn't have sent me to find him."

"If the marauders took him, there's not a lot of hope."

"I'm gonna find him," yelled Wisp.

Zen raised both hands in a placating gesture. "Consider this. Go and look. But when you finally accept that you chase something you cannot catch, return here. You are welcome to stay with my family while you are too young to be alone."

She stabbed her fork into the mound of potatoes, and mumbled, "I'm gonna find him."

"You should not be so focused that you walk yourself into harm. Your father would not want you to be hurt, even for the sake of his own life. Return here when you are ready, and we will welcome you."

He patted her on the arm as another man approached the counter.

"Morning," said Zen.

The new man nodded. "Whatcha' got's good?"

"Potatoes and chicken. Goat steak. Vegetables. Dumplings."

The man eyed Wisp. "Same as her."

"Coin or trade?" asked Zen.

Wisp glanced sideways as the man handed over two small metal discs.

"That 'nuff?"

Zen nodded. "Yep. Two is good. Have a seat. Food'll be ready soon."

She scarfed down the last of her meal and slid off the stool.

"You sure about going out there?" asked Zen.

"Yes. If Mother leads me back here, then I'll stay. You and Lijuan are nice, and I do not want to be alone." Her throat tightened, knowing that if Mother brought her here again, it would mean that Dad had gone to the Other Place and she could no longer help him.

He shook his head. "All right. If you were any younger, I'd not let you run off at all, but I suppose if you've made it all the way out here, you're not exactly helpless."

"Thank you for the food and letting me sleep here. If I don't come back, that means I found Dad."

"All right." He shook his head, grumbling to himself.

Wisp walked down the hall to her room to collect her things, then returned to Zen to give him the key.

He sighed. "I hope that mother of yours is really watching out. You ought to think about staying here where it's safe. Are you sure I cannot convince you to?"

"I *am* thinking about it." She smiled. "But Dad needs me."

Lijuan darted out of the kitchen and handed her a bundle. "Here… I packed you some food."

"Thank you." Wisp took it and made the finger-twirl gesture beside her head while grinning. "It's okay if you think I'm nuts."

Zen bit his lip.

"I will be careful." She took off the backpack long enough to wedge the wrapped dumplings into the pan, which still had a few blueberries left. "I will ask Mother to bring me back here if she thinks it is best for me."

Zen and Lijuan nodded in stunned silence.

She smiled, waved, and walked across the room to the exit. On the porch, she took the Mother Twig out and let it dangle until the stick stopped spinning. It pointed ahead and right, away from Zen's cabin, in the same direction distant whorls of sand danced across the scrubland. A mixed sense of relief and sorrow hit her. These people had been nice, if not a little odd, and staying here probably *would* be a lot safer than running after Dad. But Mother told her he still needed her, and she did not want to be a bad girl.

She couldn't simply forget Dad. After all he'd done for her, she *had* to find him.

Before leaving, Wisp had filled all four canteens from the well behind Zen's place. Hours into her trek across scrubland, she held the second one high, head tilted back, letting droplets fall into her gaping mouth.

Only her trust for Mother kept her going, despite growing concern that she should've brought far more water along than she had. Dad knew a lot of things because he was a grownup. Perhaps Zen too knew a lot of things, for not only had he grown up, he had a daughter. That made him a dad.

She lowered her arm and screwed the cap back on the canteen while smacking her lips. An unpleasant gumminess in her mouth made her want to drink more water. Both canteens on her belt remained full, but despite her thirst, she had to make it last. She put the empty plastic canteen in the backpack and marched onward.

Soon after the sun climbed to its apex, she reached a road spanning the scrubland. A quick check of the Mother Twig seemed to agree with the direction the road led. She stepped one foot on the paving, screamed, and jumped away, hopping on her other leg.

"Ow!"

Luckily, no blisters formed from the brief contact with the hot blacktop. She walked beside the road in the sand, grumbling to herself about Dad ignoring her whenever she asked him about having something to wear on her feet like his boots. Sometimes, he'd say she didn't need shoes because she didn't have to go anywhere. Other times he'd claim that he'd make her something as soon as he found material to work with. Yet other times, he'd say not having anything on her feet made it easier for her to wade into streams to catch fish. It didn't seem likely he ever expected her to walk across the hot sands where no plants or trees existed, but still… *he* had boots. Why would he keep avoiding making her some shoes? She could run much faster through the forest if she didn't have to always watch where she stepped.

That thought slid back and forth in her head for an hour or more. Not having the materials could explain it. His claim he didn't want to waste materials on something she'd grow out of didn't sound right anymore. Lijuan's feet weren't *that* much bigger than hers despite a five-year age gap. Surely, he could make something she'd be able to wear for five years. Of course, that girl didn't have shoes either, but neither did Zen. Maybe they had them, but didn't wear them inside their cabin? Even Dad seldom wore his boots inside.

She hated the hot sand, and hated the hotter road even more. Every step farther away from the forest (or Zen's cabin) increased the doubt weighing on her shoulders. Wisp clamped her eyes closed and balled her hands into fists.

"No. I trust Mother. I won't turn around."

Eyes downcast, she kept watching the sand to make sure she didn't step on any bugs like the giant black one she'd seen within half an hour of leaving Zen's. She had no name for it, having never before encountered anything with big pincers and a tail stinger. Still, that creature had been almost as big as her foot and the tiny wasp she'd stepped on as a small girl hurt *so* much. Her brain refused to even think about how bad the sting from such a massive insect would be.

Wisp shaded her eyes with a hand to check the position of the sun every so often as she walked. Despite following the twig's direction, she couldn't shake the thought she had made a mistake going farther into the desert. Upon finding a shaded spot under the wing of a crashed thunderbird, she caved in and opened one of her two remaining canteens, slugging down several huge gulps before forcing herself to stop.

After resting for a little while, she got up and walked along the length of the old flying machine to the end, then went around it, continuing in the same direction she'd been walking. Less than an hour later, she crested a hill and about fainted at the sight in front of her...

Skeletal high-rises clawed at the cloudless late-afternoon sky.

A span of open ground stretched out in front of her, covered in pulverized concrete with scraps of metal poles jutting up here and there. Machine parts of various sizes littered the area, but none of the junk—nor any of the rubble—appeared bigger than a potato.

Wind howled through the cavernous shells of the old buildings, punctuated with the echoing clatter of falling rocks and shifting metal. Standing in the shadow of such ancient monoliths made her shiver at her smallness, especially since they tilted so much to the side. The great towers looked ready to collapse at any moment.

"Dad?" she asked, not really expecting an answer. "Dad, are you here?"

The wind continued to moan. A distant *clank* preceded the *crack* of a big rock striking pavement.

"At least there's shade..."

She pulled the rifle off her shoulder and gripped it tight. No sense of spiritual power emanated from the area, so she abandoned her worry about this being the Other Place. She'd always thought of it as something live people couldn't go to, sitting on top of the normal world, like the other side of a book's page. All the words on one side existed in the same physical space as the words on the other side, but they would never meet.

Ahead, the road sat in the shade of the old skyscrapers, still warm but not enough to burn her soles. The nearer to the towers she got, the larger the rubble hunks became. By the time she reached the first building, she crept around huge chunks of stone, some as big as cars. Many had bent bars sticking out of them that reminded her of the Haven, since they had the same thickness and crisscross pattern. She touched a finger to one of the rods and smiled at how much Dad loved her. He had made the Haven for her to keep her safe. Had he come all the way here to find them? And how had he gotten them to stick together into one solid piece of metal?

She clutched the rods the way she used to grab the bars of her Haven, and closed her eyes. A wish formed in her mind, a wish that she would open her eyes and find herself back home, holding the door of the Haven and waiting for Dad to wake up and let her out.

Wisp took a deep breath and sent her wish into the nowhere.

Her eyes opened, revealing the same broken hunk of concrete and road full of debris.

"I'm too old to believe I can just magic myself home."

Continuing down the road, she spent as much time looking down to avoid stepping on dangerous things as she did peering up at the broken skyscrapers, still a staggering height into the air. Here and there, motion attracted her eyes to bits falling, some small, others large enough to send a person straight to the Other Place if they landed on them. The bigger ones made such loud crashes when they hit the ground that she jumped every time.

"I should not stay here long."

The mournful moan of the wind got the hairs on the back of her neck standing up and gave her goosebumps. It sounded too much like the cry of sorrowful spirits she'd expect to hear in the Other Place. With all the broken buildings, this ruin offered so many places to hide, marauders could attack her from any angle with little warning. Her best advantage seemed to be not having shoes, since her feet made no noise at all on the ground. Then again, since she had yet to see one marauder with a gun, perhaps the rifle offered far more of an advantage than her lack of footwear. The two who tried to grab her didn't understand guns… one even called it magic. Wary, nervous, and at the verge of shivering from fear, she continually pivoted about so no marauders could sneak up on her again.

The roads in this strange slice of the ancients' world formed a grid. At almost every point where two intersected, she found a pile of mashed-up cars. Some even looked like SUVs. A few had flipped, others had hit each other with so much force she couldn't tell where one car ended and the next one started.

"How dumb... Why did they make the roads cross like that? Everyone drove into each other."

The Fire Dragons had been here, of that she had no doubt. Only creatures that powerful could have smashed these enormous structures like flimsy twigs. No one knew how to build such things anymore, to shape the stone to their will, or wrap it around metal. Everywhere she turned, she couldn't help but wonder what the place had been like in the before-Earth. There had to be *so* many people here in a city like this, too many for her mind to imagine. She understood numbers to a point, but the nine or ten people in the same room with her at Zen's represented the most other humans she'd ever been around. Trying to comprehend in terms of thousands or multiple thousands resulted in blankness. Still, she couldn't help but feel like eyes followed her every step. Though their remains had been vaporized, this broken city was a shrine to an amount of people she could not fathom.

And her skin prickled as though they *all* followed her.

Ghosts she could deal with. They wouldn't do much to her but perhaps speak if they became really angry. Marauders, on the other hand, presented a much more significant problem. Zen believed they had taken Dad, so that made them all monsters. He'd told her she should always try to run from danger, but that had been before they took Dad.

If she saw a marauder, she'd send him to the Other Place sooner than talk.

Few people understand how to use these weapons, said Dad in her mind, words he'd spoken to her nine-year-old self. *Most don't even know something like this is possible. But, they won't last forever. Someday, I will run out of powder, and they'll stop working.*

She squeezed and relaxed her grip on the rifle. Twenty shots left. Forty more in the backpack. More than enough to help Dad. Even if she had to use up every last one, she'd do it. *We can survive without guns that work. I can't survive without Dad.*

Except... she had, for a little more than a week.

"Shut up," she said to herself. "That's a bad thought."

The Forest Beyond the Earth

Bright red and green attracted her to a door beneath a sign reading 7-Eleven. Huge openings on either side of the entrance had rings of glass teeth embedded in metal frames. At one point, they had most likely been enormous windows, but had smashed so long ago, not a single trace of broken glass remained on the street in front of the place.

She ducked through the bottom portion of the door into a smallish area full of metal row shelves. A counter on the left stood in front of a wall full of little cubbies. The ceiling had collapsed inward, crushing some of the shelves on the right side and blocking off a good portion of the space inside. One small gap near the floor appeared wide enough for her to fit, if she dumped the backpack. Curious, she slipped out of the pack, set it aside, and got down on her belly to stick her head into the opening. The collapse had walled off one corner of the old room. The area behind it held a lot of rubble, as well as a few white paper boxes. She shimmied into the hole, getting stuck when her canteens hit concrete.

"Ngh!" She grunted, reaching forward, trying to get her fingertips on one of the boxes.

The papery substance broke on contact, crumbling at her touch.

Grumbling, she unclipped the canteen belt and pulled herself in deeper.

Her hand tore the box like a cobweb, revealing ten bright yellow objects with a shiny, transparent outer layer. She picked one up and turned it so the printed lettering faced upright.

"Twinkies. Snack cakes." She squeezed her fingers a little, compressing the spongy thing.

Characters in the books often ate cake, but it hadn't been described as little oblongs like these... more a giant wheel that got cut into triangles. Still, she knew 'snack' as a small meal, and cake as something to be eaten, so she shrugged and chomped down on it.

The clear outer layer crinkled, and tasted horrible. A hint of sweet leaked past it, but she still spat.

"Bleh."

She cocked her arm back to throw the nasty thing, but hesitated when she looked at the top of another box. The cake there didn't have the shiny clear skin around it.

Maybe I'm supposed to take that off first? Like peeling the potatoes.

She fussed with her knife, but scraping it across the Twinkie didn't do much but make the outer layer crinkle. The blade couldn't seem to get a grip on the slippery skin. On a whim, she bit into the clear part, but used her teeth only to get a grip, then pulled. The membrane broke open, exposing a sweet-smelling, sticky bread-like substance. She sniffed it, liked what her nose thought of it, and jammed it in her mouth.

"Ooh."

Five Twinkies later, she couldn't bear to think of eating another. However, she did gather all four boxes and push them out the hole. After getting her canteen and backpack on again, she roamed the place, hunting for something to help carry all the loose Twinkies in, since the pack had zero space left and those old boxes fell apart at the slightest touch. She eventually located a plastic bag behind the counter, in which she packed the amazing food bars. No way would Dad ever believe anything like them existed unless she brought him one.

He could have some.

Or one.

Maybe.

If any remained by the time she found him.

Wisp left the 7-Eleven after tying the plastic bag on one of the canteens so it hung at her side, freeing both hands for the rifle. She checked the Mother Twig again, which pointed toward another intersection. The street became increasingly dense with debris. She slowed to a careful creeping gait to avoid ramming her toes into concrete chunks or stepping on ouch. She climbed up on one of the dead cars to bypass a wash of broken glass in the road, and walked over it to the trunk end. From there, she jumped a small gap to the next old car, stepped over its missing rear window, and crossed the roof to the front. Wisp navigated another four cars in a series of leaps and hops before her safe path ran out of vehicles. She perched on the last hood and gingerly extended a leg to a clear patch of street.

Fortunately, the minefield of sharp debris thinned out two blocks later where the skyscrapers on the right side gave way to a giant open lot full of dead cars parked in neat rows. If they hadn't all been partially melted and mostly flattened, it would've been an amazing sight. Beyond them stood a gigantic cabin, wider even than any of the high-rises, though it only had one story. She padded across the street into the lot, weaving among the cars in search of any 'buggies' or anything that might lead her to Dad.

A flurry of barking startled her rigid. Once her heart resumed beating, she swiveled to the right, raising the rifle at a group of six animals all standing around an old man who sat on the ground by the huge cabin's doors, gazing off into the sky. Giant lettering in the window read, "Weekend Special – All Deli 50% off."

"Hello?" asked Wisp.

"Oh, calm down you lot," said the old man. "It's a child. It's all right, little one. These mutts won't hurt you."

Mutts... dogs? Those are dogs? The smallest didn't look much bigger than a rabbit, while the largest could probably carry her around if she sat on its back. The rest ranged between them in size. While the tiniest one kept barking and yapping at her, the others appeared to understand the guy and settled down, but kept staring at her. One or two whined.

"Have you seen any buggies?" asked Wisp.

"I'm afraid I haven't seen much of anything, child," said the man. "My eyes don't work so good."

She crept closer, holding her rifle sideways, pointed down. "You're blind?"

"That's a word I haven't heard in a while. Yep. They crapped out on me a couple years ago. Guess I shouldn't have drunk that gasoline." He cackled, slapping his knee.

"There's no gasoline anymore," said Wisp. "And it's for cars."

"Oh, you know quite a bit little one. How'd someone your age ever hear of that stuff?"

"Books," said Wisp.

The man chuckled. "Well, since you're a smarty, it's not gasoline. It's alcohol. Them buggies run on high-test booze."

"So you've seen... umm. You know where I can find the buggies?"

The tiny dog finally stopped barking and contented itself with growling at her. Two of the medium-sized ones approached, sniffing at her legs.

"You prob-lee don't wanna do that. Them 'rauders ain't gonna be to kind to a li'l one." He patted the curb beside him. "Sit; do an old man a favor and talk a bit?"

Wisp let out a startled squeal and jumped forward when a cold dog nose went up the back of her skirt and touched her rear end. "I'm trying to find my Dad, but I'll talk to you for a little while." She hurried over and sat beside him, but a little farther away than where he indicated.

"How's a little girl come ta be out here on her own? What is your name?"

"I'm Wisp. If you can't see, how did you know I'm a girl?"

He grinned, flashing his three remaining teeth. "When the eyes stop workin', the ears get better. Sound o' yer voice. If a boy sound like you, voice wouldn't be comin' from as tall. You like my city?"

"It's scary, and there's dangerous rocks falling all the time." She shifted her weight from leg to leg, unsettled by the way this man kept staring into the sky, not even turning his head toward her. "What is your name?"

He smiled. "I am Pablo. That crap don't fall here."

She scrunched up her face. "It's not crap falling, it's big rocks. Not poop."

He cackled, startling the dogs.

A shaggy one wandered over and licked her foot. She cringed, resisting the urge to giggle. More slimy tongues attacked her face. Wisp petted them, doing her best to divide her two hands over four dogs.

"There's plenty o' poop 'round here thanks ta my friends."

"Were the ancients stupid? All these roads run into each other, and there's cars crashed everywhere."

"Oh, they been there forever. I think when the fire came, everyone panicked and tried to get out the city as fast as possible. But there wadn't no time. If I'd been around back then, I'd have just sat back and waited. Only difference bein' if ya die scared or at peace. Dead either way. Can't outrun the fireball. So, my turn. Why are you here alone?"

She kept skritching the dogs enough to come close while explaining about Dad and trying to find him. A smallish dog with short hair rolled on its back in front of her. Wisp grinned at it and rubbed its belly. Upside down, the dog stretched its head to lick her leg above her ankle. *Oh. This dog must be a boy.*

"Hmm. I'm sorry you've had such a bad time of it, Wisp. You know you're too young to be alone. If you'd like to stay here, my friends and I will look after you."

He can't see. How can he even look after himself? "Thank you, but I have to find my Dad. Can I help you at all? How do you eat? There's no plants here."

"Oh, my friends here take care of that. There are so many rats beneath us. They hunt and bring me enough to keep going."

"Rats... small. Furry..." She scratched her head. "I think. I've never seen one for real. Only in stories."

Pablo grinned, again showing off his three teeth. "Can you read, or did that father of yours read to you?"

She smiled. "I read. The window behind you says weekend deal, deli fifty... not sure what that letter means, off."

"Which letter?"

"It's two little circles with a line between them."

"Humm." He scratched his head. "Not sure either. Ain't common to run into people who can read."

She bowed her head, sensing the tears before they started. "Dad taught me how to read." Eyes closed, she took a deep breath to control her sorrow, then stood tall. "I need to find him."

"I can't rightly stop you, seein' as how I can't see... but a young girl ought not to be anywhere near marauders if ya know what's good for you."

The dogs groaned when she stopped petting them. She gave in to the pleading stares and squatted to skritch them a little while longer.

"Thank you for being nice, but you wouldn't be able to protect me from marauders either. I won't let them catch me."

He sighed and waved dismissively. "All right. No one ever listens to old Pablo anyway. No one 'cep my friends."

The biggest dog made a soft, labored moan and rested its head in the man's lap. He smiled, vacant stare still on the sky, and patted the animal's head.

"I should go. It will be dark soon and Mother might get upset with me for being wasteful with time."

"Be wary, child. Marauders are not to be trusted."

She stood, hefting the rifle. "Yes. I don't trust them. And I won't try to talk to them."

Leaving the old man to his dogs, she stepped around the smaller animals and crossed the field of cars again. All had been so flattened by the Fire Dragon's wrath that she couldn't even tell if any of them had become shrines.

The word 'dead' circled her thoughts. Zen had used that term, but she'd never thought of Mother in that sense. Dead implied nothingness, an end... like what had happened to this city. *People* went to the Other Place when their bodies stopped working. *Monsters* died.

Wisp navigated the streets of the ruin, checking the twig once again to ensure she traveled in the right direction. Daylight waned in a gradual march toward darkness. Soon, she walked into a breeze, the air cooler than the road beneath her feet. This mess of concrete and warped metal had few plants she could eat. Aside from the occasional yellowgreen growing in a crack, she found inedible weeds or grass. At least she still had Lijuan's dumplings and some Twinkies.

Worse, she hadn't seen any more water. With one and a half canteens left, she debated going back to Zen if she couldn't find any water within a few hours of sunrise. Soon after she began to search for a sheltered place to spend the night, a yellow sign marked 'Petco' caught her eye. Padding around scrap metal and concrete shards, she made her way across the street, climbing a huge crumpled car to get to the 'people road' in front of it.

The glass wall had long since disappeared, allowing her in. On her right, a row of cube-shaped hollows ran along the wall, each with a barred door.

"Havens!" She gazed at them in wonder, as well as a more distant room with even smaller ones, probably for babies. "The ancients must have feared Tree Walkers, too."

Wisp ran to one of the larger havens. She set down the rifle and wriggled out of the backpack before crawling into the space. The cramped interior forced her to curl up with her knees mushed into her face and her feet twisted inward. Canteens dug into her back most uncomfortably.

"Hmm." She grasped the barred door, noting a plastic sleeve containing yellowed paper hanging on it. "I can't sleep like this… and I don't have the opener."

A momentary thought of how she'd felt back home, *trapped* inside the Haven before she got the opener, made her shiver. Closing that door would be a bad idea. Grunting, she grabbed at the edges and pulled herself out of the cramped space, crawling onto the floor before sitting back on her heels. The sign on the bars read, 'Labrador, 8 mo.' The haven to the left had a similar sign marked, 'Dachshund 6 mo.'

"Huh…"

She whined at not being able to get into the havens, and stood, deciding to search the rest of the room. One part had shelves full of glass boxes, each containing a layer of brightly colored pebbles. Some had tiny fish skeletons in them. Past that, she found four huge havens, big enough for her to stand up inside, but their doors didn't appear capable of locking and the bars felt flimsy. They all contained the skeletons of huge birds.

"Parrot?" asked Wisp, reading the sign.

The smaller havens had signs like 'calico,' 'Siamese,' and 'domestic short hair.' She bypassed them since she couldn't possibly fit inside, and those, too, didn't appear to be able to lock with a key, only a sliding bar anyone could open.

"Oh, this isn't fair! Why are these havens so small?!"

Toward the rear of the room, she wandered between tall aisles full of ruptured bags. A heavy stink of not-quite-food permeated the air, and the ground came alive with thousands of black-and-tan beetles, some reaching four inches in length.

"Roaches!" Wisp squealed in glee.

She ran back to the first room to grab her rifle, and used it to break apart a big wood-framed enclosure filled with small skeletons. The sign called them 'guinea pigs,' but they looked nothing like boars. The wood, plus some kindling from her pack, made for a reasonable fire a little while later. She'd found a huge metal bowl on a shelf that she used for a fire pit, and grabbed a smaller one to contain a bunch of cockroaches.

Since she couldn't really tell where the roaches' heads began, she decided to cook them extra well instead of decapitating them and pulling the guts out.

They scrambled about the bowl-turned-pot, hissing and jumping when she put them over the flame, but eventually, they stopped moving and became dinner along with one of the dumplings. The roasted roach tasted somewhat like the bird meat, though greasier.

None of the havens in this place reassured her, but she missed being locked in at night so much she almost suffered the discomfort of cramming herself back in the one marked 'Labrador.' Those havens not having locks made her decision to look elsewhere for a bed possible, since the Tree Walkers could simply open it and grab her.

Wisp sat by her fire bowl until the flames died off. She stood, gathered all her stuff back into place, and sighed at the darkness, afraid of going outside at night. Still worried about the lack of a functional haven, she retreated deeper into the room, toward where the roaches scurried around the aisles. She placed her feet between them, careful not to crush any as they rushed about. A few ran over her toes or climbed her leg, though she brushed them away while approaching a wooden door labeled 'employees only.'

Only a little moonlight came in from the broken ceiling, illuminating enough to make out a short corridor lined with empty shelves. A weak sigh of disappointment leaked from her nose at not finding a haven. She felt her way along to a room with a table, four chairs, and some big metal cabinets. Those got her hopes up. She bumped into a cable dangling from the ceiling, and grabbed it. A white foam square broke in half when it fell on her head. She cringed and peered up past a metal grid that had a few more tiles clinging to it. Dust particles glimmered in crisscrossing shafts of moonlight overhead. A network of massive broken holes allowed her to see straight up for at least twelve floors.

Wisp crept up to the closer steel cabinet, big enough for Dad to stand inside of, and grabbed the door handles. Her smile died when she couldn't figure out how to make the handles lock, and also that the cabinets contained shelves. *Not havens... just places to keep stuff.* She wandered deeper into the room, grabbing at more hanging cables and wires. The soft *click* of falling stones reawakened her worry that the whole place might fall down on her even though it had remained standing for so many years already. Besides, Mother would protect her.

She shuffled across the space, pushing wires and dangling foam tiles out of her way, eventually reaching a cushioned sofa. The material gave when she pressed down on it, appearing comfortable despite a thick layer of dust. Being exposed, however, it would offer no protection against anything trying to take her in the night.

I slept out in the open, and the Tree Walkers didn't find me. And it's dark in here.

Wisp unburdened herself of everything but her shirt, skirt, and handgun, stacking it all on the floor by where she would sleep. She curled up on the soft cushions, covered completely with the blanket, and hoped danger wouldn't be able to see her.

The Many Havens
~24~

Wisp finished the second dumpling and two Twinkies for breakfast, then spent a while roasting up a bunch of roaches to bring with her. The Mother Twig led her to the edge of the ruined city not long after she resumed walking, where broken skyscrapers gave way once more to a debris field that went on for a mile or so. The ghosts of paved roads, half-buried chunks of broken blacktop, traced a bit deeper into the scrubland before disappearing beneath the shifting sand.

The sunbaked sand almost burned her feet, though she much preferred it to the scorching patches of blacktop. Each step made her miss the moist earth around her home more. She trudged for a few minutes with her eyes closed, trying to remember the cool breeze of the forest. A few sips of water got her thinking about Zen's place again. The canteen in her left belt pouch probably had about a quarter of its capacity left, leaving her one full. Ahead, the scrublands stretched on until they touched the sky.

As much as she wanted to find Dad, she had to admit that continuing into such nothingness with only one full canteen was something only a stupid person would do. Dad would not want her to wind up going to the Other Place in such a silly, avoidable manner.

She let out a long sigh and sank to a squat, grabbing her head in both hands. She wanted to cry, but held it in. Tears could wait until she had plenty of water to spare. "I'm sorry, Dad. I don't know what to do now. Mother, please help me. I don't know where to go."

For a few minutes, she listened to the gentle lament of the wind, straining to hear Mother's reply. Light scratching directed her gaze to the barrel of the rifle, low enough to the ground that one of those pincer bugs had attacked it. She stood with a gasp, scrambling away from the tiny horror. The creature dangled from the weapon by one claw, refusing to let go. It whacked at the barrel with its tail a few times before she swung the rifle to the side hard enough to fling the bug back to the dirt. It flipped onto its legs and charged straight at her.

Wisp let off a clipped high-pitched scream and ran until it gave up chasing her.

Did Mother send that bug? She blinked and stared down at the rifle.

In one last, desperate attempt to resist defeat, Wisp raised the weapon to her shoulder and sighted through the scope, panning back and forth across the distance. A flash of white led her to hone in on a small adobe cabin with a covered well nearby. She lowered the rifle and squinted at the haze of heat blur, but couldn't see the cabin. Again, she checked the scope, and the cabin returned. It looked far enough away to be a gamble. If the well turned out to be dry, she might be in trouble. Unable to decide, she twisted back and forth, staring at the ruined city behind her, then the desert before her. Well beyond the city to the rear, the shadow of mountains, and the Endless Forest, beckoned with a painful pang of homesickness. She stared at her far-distant home for a moment while the breeze tossed her hair around.

"I guess it's not really endless, is it?"

Mother wanted me look through the rifle. I have to try. I won't drink until I know if the well has water.

She sent one last longing gaze back at the forest before marching toward the little cabin out amid the wavering heat. Dust caked on her legs and the taste of sand coated her lips. Her target solidified out of the shimmering blur about fifteen minutes later, still painfully far away. Here and there, she thought she saw patches of water, but they always disappeared before she got close.

"I wish it would rain."

The Forest Beyond the Earth

A daydream of being home again, dancing about in the rain, made the journey pass faster than she expected. Out in the middle of nowhere, stood a pale adobe building, roughly equal in size to three of her cabins next to each other. Ignoring it for the time being, she bee-lined to the well. Rather than a bucket on a rope, it had a pipe going down the inside of a shaft connected to a mechanical hand pump with a crank.

She found a metal pail on the ground on the far side of the well. Sand poured out when she picked it up, so she tapped the bottom to chase the last few granules away. The pump had a hook upon which she hung the pail before grabbing the crank in both hands.

"Please work."

At first, the ease with which the crank spun made her worry it wouldn't do anything, but she kept working it around and around. Soon, sputtering noises belched from the opening. Hopeful, she cranked faster, rising up onto her toes each time the handle went around the top of the wheel. Huffing and gasping, like a person about to throw up, got louder.

A blast of water erupted from the opening into the pail.

Wisp cheered and continued spinning the crank around. Another burst of water came forth, followed by a steady pour. She stopped cranking when the pail had filled, but water kept coming up, dribbling over the sides of the bucket. With an "Eep," she fumbled her almost-empty canteen from its pouch, uncapped it, and held it in the stream until it trickled off to nothing, the canteen half-full.

After a brief cheer, she tilted it back and drank the whole thing. The cold water gave her a mild headache, but she didn't care. She stood there, dripping and trying to catch her breath for a little while before leaning over the pail and slurping up more water so it stopped spilling over the side.

Soon, she'd refilled her canteens and devoured another pair of Twinkies. Unloading everything from her backpack allowed her to rearrange her stuff to make better use of the space, and she managed to get the two extra canteens she'd taken from the marauders in as well as the remaining Twinkies, so she no longer had a plastic bag bumping into her leg.

A faint buzzing arose in the distance. Wisp ignored the insect until the noise got louder and closer.

That's a buggy!

She hurried the backpack on, grabbed the rifle, and ran from the well to the cabin. The doorway had no door in it, only a brick-red cloth curtain. She barged past it into a one-room space with a small bed, table, chairs, fireplace, and a bunch of shelves full of random junk. A body lay half on the bed, legs draped on the floor, lifeless eyes gazing at the ceiling. He appeared in much the same condition as Mother, with dry, grey skin and talons for fingernails. Only, this man didn't have a nose, and a large swath of missing cheek exposed the skull.

The buzzing grew louder, coming from a small window along the back wall.

Wisp dashed across the room and climbed onto one of the chairs to get her head up to the window. A long trail of dust in the distance billowed out from behind a black dagger-shaped machine with fat wheels in back and smaller ones in front. It veered left, turning to face the cabin. She held her breath, eyes widening with a mixture of fear and hope. If she could follow that buggy, it would take her to Dad. Mother had been right to send her here!

A marauder's head and shoulders poked up from the middle of the buggy, the rest of him sunken within a hollow. Panels of random, rusting scrap metal flapped and clattered on its sides. Buzzing fell to a low rumbling as the buggy lost speed. She ran from the chair, jumping up to stand on the bed by the wall to her right. As her feet hit the mattress, the dead man bounced up and slid to the floor, exposing a dark stain beneath where he'd been. Wisp peered out a smaller window on the side of the cabin, watching the buggy roll by not much faster than a person could walk. Once it drove out of sight past the end of the cabin, she rushed to the curtained doorway, crouching on one knee and peering out at the buggy, which came to a stop by the well.

Its back end held a tall leather tent, tied to a triangular frame of metal tubes as tall as a man. A mess of plastic gallon bottles hung on both angled sides, affixed by twine to hooks on the pipes. The driver occupied a sunken chamber in the middle of the buggy, only his shoulders and head visible over the side. A few seconds after the buzzing stopped, he grabbed the sides and pushed himself up and out of the single seat. She cringed back, hiding in the doorjamb behind the tattered curtain, only peeking with one eye. Fortunately, the marauder didn't notice her.

He walked around to the rear end and undid a buckled strap holding the tent closed. Two large leather flaps opened to reveal a small storage space, from which he grabbed a metal funnel. He untied all the plastic bottles, eight in total, and carried them over to the well.

"Huh what?" The marauder looked at the water on the ground. "Someone here?"

Wisp didn't move.

"Dern. Gonna haveta put a guard here. Someone dumb 'nuff take our water." Shaking his head, the man removed the bucket from the hook and dropped it.

He mounted the funnel below the pump and proceeded to fill the old plastic bottles, carrying each one to the buggy and rehanging it. While he worked to pump water into the eighth bottle, Wisp pushed the scope into its retracted position, and lifted the rifle until the iron sights lined up with the marauder's head.

I'm not even going to talk to them.

She moved her finger to the trigger, listening to the repetitive squeaking of the pump crank. In the distance beyond the man, dusty sand blew in clouds across the desert. *Wait.* She let off the trigger. *The tire tracks disappear in the wind... I should follow him. The trail he made coming here might already be gone.*

Slow and quiet, Wisp lowered the rifle and leaned back into hiding behind the doorjamb. Her plan came with a serious issue, however. That buggy appeared to be going much faster than she could run. Maybe she should shoot him and take the buggy? *I don't know how to work it and I don't know where to go.* She stuck her tongue out at herself.

For obvious reasons, she couldn't walk out there and simply allow the man to take her like they took Dad. Maybe if she started running right away, she would be able to follow the trail before it blew away? But he'd probably see her chasing him, since open sand didn't offer any cover to hide behind.

The marauder finished filling the last bottle and re-hung it on the triangular pipe frame. He tossed the funnel in the back, secured the leather flaps, and walked around the side. She tensed, preparing to jump up and run, but the man kept going past where he'd get into the machine, and came to a halt about ten paces farther away.

He fussed with the front of his pants, and a few seconds later, a stream of bad water came out of him.

She stared at the buggy, shaking with anticipation. *Come on. Come on...* Her eyes widened when another idea hit her. *Wait... That's so scary, but...* As quiet as she could make herself be, Wisp stood, slung the rifle over her shoulder, and snuck up behind the buggy. Shaking from nerves, she slipped under the leather flap and crammed herself into the storage space. It took a little finesse to get the rifle in there, but she managed it.

A metal plate separated the storage area from a complicated-looking machine she figured to be the engine. Above it, an open space crisscrossed with thin metal bars let her peek out at the driver's seat and the desert beyond the buggy's nose. Hopefully, the relative darkness of the back would prevent the man from seeing her.

She leaned up to check out the tiny steering wheel and a pair of pedals that reminded her of the SUV, but they didn't have rubber pads. She ducked down when the marauder spun around, tucking herself as far to the left as the metal frame allowed.

The buggy rocked a few seconds later from the marauder climbing up, and bounced when he dropped into the seat. She peered out the hole again, and watched over his shoulder as he pushed a little black button next to the steering wheel. The engine, inches from her face, roared to life with a deafening rumble. Wisp let out a yelp of shock, but she couldn't even hear herself over the noise. Fingers jammed in her ears, she cringed, wondering if her 'great idea' had really been a stupid one.

Hard acceleration flung her into the leather flaps. She braced her foot against one of the metal spars to hold herself steady, refusing to pull her fingers out of her ears. Her little chamber jostled about, sometimes tossing her up and dropping her hard on her butt whenever the buggy caught a few inches of air. Fortunately, the engine masked the rattling in her backpack, the rifle banging on the metal, or her occasional gasp of pain.

Wisp twisted forward, coughing on stinky air blowing out of the engine, and peeked up to watch the man. Turning the tiny wheel made the buggy veer left or right. His foot on the rightmost pedal made it go faster. He didn't touch the other pedal, but she guessed that one would slow them down. She tried not to breathe the hot blast washing over her face, turning her head to put her mouth by the opening in the flaps whenever she had to take a breath.

Roughly twenty minutes of head-pounding noise later, another section of ruined city came into view ahead. This one didn't have skyscrapers, though the buildings were still massive, some six or seven stories tall. The marauder steered onto a road, which lessened the bouncing and shaking considerably. Within the ruin, he also slowed down quite a bit from the speed he'd been going out on the sand.

Sudden fear gripped her. This man might take her straight into a settlement full of marauders or something, and she'd either wind up trapped in the back end of the buggy with nowhere to go, or get caught. The marauders that tried to grab her wanted to tie her with ropes. She'd barely escaped from *two* of them, and there had to be lots of them up ahead. Her mind raced to come up with a way out, until her vacant stare sharpened onto the engine in front of her. Hoses and wires threaded up from below, wrapped over metal frame bars, and plugged in to various places. One plastic tube carried clear liquid, though she doubted it was water. *Zen said they use alcohol.* Four black hoses ended with clamps connected to little metal posts. No fluid passed through them, so they had to be wires.

She remembered one of the book characters 'unplugging' something called an alarm clock to make it stop working. If she could make this engine stop working before this guy took her into the settlement full of marauders, she would have a much better chance. Maybe if she unplugged it...

Grimacing at the noise, she removed her fingers from her ears and grabbed one of the wires, twisting the cap end back and forth. In a few seconds, it came free with a bright blue spark that zapped her fingertips. She stifled the yelp of pain, cradling her hand to her chest. As soon as the wire detached, the engine sputtered and wobbled side to side with enough strength to make the whole buggy shudder. Before the sting in her fingers faded, the deafening roar went silent with a fluttering gasp.

"Huh? What?" asked the marauder. "Aww, dammit."

The wheels squeaked like an army of tiny songbirds furious at the world. She rocked to her left when he stepped on the brake and brought the buggy to a stop. Her mind leapt from 'run like hell right now' to 'wait and see what he does' to panic. Boots crunching on the pavement outside snapped her out of her indecision. She gazed up at the leather, her jaw clenching in determination at the shadow of a man falling on it from outside.

At the clatter of a buckle, she drew the pistol off her hip and flicked the safety off.

He opened the flaps and found himself staring at a gun. "Ooh. I got me a sweet little girl! Where'd you come from?"

Bang!

The brass flew from the side of the pistol, bounced off a metal spar, and glanced off her shoulder. Her shot snapped the man's head back, a thin stream of blood spurting from where the bullet struck an inch above his left eye. His arms flailed out to the side as he careened over backward. He collapsed to the pavement and didn't move.

Wisp ducked out the triangular opening and stepped over the marauder's body to the road beyond, leaving two distinct footprints in dust on his chest armor. She nodded in satisfaction and recovered her rifle from the buggy.

Without further ceremony, she ran into the nearest alley in search of a hiding spot. More marauders might come to investigate the gunshot, though this one's utter lack of reaction to having a gun in his face made her wonder if they might blame thunder for the noise. Maybe they would have no idea what the sound was? Her head hurt from the engine roar, and breathing the fumes left her woozy.

Even if she didn't have to hide from curious marauders, she wanted to sit down and not move for a while anyway. A few alleys away, she found a nice sheltered spot behind a big metal box covered in fallen chunks of skyscraper. After crawling into the shadowed space, she lay on her side and focused on breathing and not wanting to feel so spinny-headed.

Her head cleared some time later, without any angry shouts from the street. Deciding herself safe for the moment, she emerged from the little cave and spent a few minutes walking around to stretch her legs before heading back to the alley mouth.

This ruin, other than having much shorter buildings, looked quite similar to the other one. Cracked walls, missing windows, cars flat like giants had stepped on them, and debris lay strewn everywhere. The marauder had been driving down a relatively clear road with fewer obstructions than other paths in sight.

Rifle up and ready, Wisp huddled near the buildings on the right side of the street and advanced in a series of dashes and pauses. She hid behind small stairways or big trashcans, peering around in search of danger before springing up and running twenty or thirty feet to another hiding place. Three cross-streets deep, the road ahead lay clogged with the smashed remnants of buses and trucks, as well as the upper four floors of a mini skyscraper that had come apart in the middle. The blockage in the road stood taller than some of the intact buildings elsewhere in the ruin.

Well, I'm not going that way.

She ran left across the street, pressed herself against the wall of a red brick building, and peered around the corner. Two blocks away, marauders walked back and forth across the top of a wall made from corrugated steel plates, car hoods, and random squiggles of barbwire. Their barricade covered the span of a four-lane road, meeting flush to a squarish six-story building that suffered less damage than the surroundings and had a fortress-like appearance. Spray-painted skulls and words like 'death,' 'glory,' and 'party' adorned the wall. Several other writings existed, but the exaggerated letters made them unreadable.

Emerging from that corner and trying to walk down the street would surely get her seen, since the marauders pacing around atop the wall had a clear view. She considered shooting them from where she crouched, but she had no idea how many marauders might be inside. Even if they didn't understand guns, monsters dropping dead off the wall would be obvious. Better to find Dad and ask him what to do.

Wisp backed away from the corner and retreated to the nearest cross street. Far too much debris packed it to allow a buggy to go by, but maybe the marauders didn't watch it because of that. She shouldered the rifle to free her hands, then climbed up to squat atop a chunk of former building, surveying the spread of ruin in front of her. Once a path formed in her mind, she stretched one leg across a gap to the trunk of a flattened car. As soon as her toes touched metal, she leapt across, waving her arms for balance. At the other end of the car, she scaled another concrete waterfall, grabbing bits of metal bar for support and trying to step on either flat spaces or soft dust. The long hill of rubble brought her to the broken-out windows of a bus.

Wisp grabbed on to the metal above the opening and slipped her legs through first, sitting on the bottom edge with her feet on a soft, padded chair coated in sand. She lowered herself inside, moving from standing on the double-seat to the aisle, and encountered the unusual sensation of having a rubber mat underfoot. It distracted her for a few seconds of shifting her weight back and forth, exploring the sponginess. Careful not to step on any of the human bones littering the floor, she advanced toward where a large section of the floor had fallen out. Inches from the edge, she stopped and peered down a giant hole that yawned into a cavern deep enough to be below street level. All sorts of pipes jutted from the walls at various angles, but nothing flowed from them. A huge gap in the roof rimmed with shredded, buckled metal gave her a clear view of the sky and ruined high-rises. She imagined a huge chunk of broken building falling onto this giant car-box like a bullet hitting a marauder—in one side, out the other, and smashing all the way down into the chamber below the street.

After looking around at seats, overhead rails, and the still-intact front end of the huge vehicle, she climbed up on a seat and grabbed a small black strap. With half her weight hanging by her arms, toes struggling for purchase on seats or metal railings, she swung herself strap-by-strap across the hole, until she clung to the back of the big seat behind the steering wheel. Only a short ledge of intact floor separated her from the drop-off into the cavern, and it wobbled from even her slight weight.

A faint whine of fear leaked from her nose as she tiptoed around the seat and climbed out the broken front window. Cracks and other small holes riddled the street ahead, all opening to the same underground space. Numerous 'islands' of paving that could fall into the earth at any time looked like the wrong way to go. She cringed, peering back at the bus, not really wanting to go that way either. Dead cars and large chunks of concrete lay scattered about the smashed roadway, so she hoped her little self wouldn't be the last little bit of weight that made any of the slabs fall in.

"Mother, please protect me," mumbled Wisp.

She eased herself forward, testing the ground with her toes as though she tried to walk on the brittle surface of a frozen pond. The hunk of pavement shifted under her. Cringing, she crept to the end and stepped over a four-inch wide gap to the next 'island.' That one didn't move at all, which let her breathe again. Slab by slab, she made her way along until she'd left the cracked stretch behind.

"Whew."

Men's laughter came from her right.

She gasped and spun, fumbling to pull the rifle from her shoulders, but found herself staring at a tall barricade covered in spray paint. The echo of the marauders had to have come from behind it, and they hadn't been laughing at her. She eased the rifle back on the strap, and approached the wall. Haphazard construction resulted in plenty of spots to grab or put her feet, though she avoided anything too rusty on her climb up to the top.

Inches from the edge, she stepped sideways onto a slightly higher foothold, but crouched to keep her face hidden. Since none of the marauders inside sounded anywhere nearby, she eased herself up and peeked over the top at a narrow walkway of corrugated plates under her nose. Patches of metal grating filled in here and there, but the elevated path appeared to go all the way around the inside of the wall. Marauders *could* come wandering along right in front of her, but at the moment, none stood anywhere close enough to spot her face sticking up past the edge. She glanced to her right at the front gate she decided not to approach. Three men in brown leather armor continued pacing back and forth above the huge metal doors. Had she stayed hidden in the buggy, it would've come in there—straight into a big mess for her.

The marauders had walled off an intersection between two four-lane roads, plus about thirty yards down one of the streets. Several small cabins made of scrap metal occupied the end farthest from the intersection. Where the two streets crossed, they'd built a square barrier of metal fencing covered in spikes, but only about as tall as a man's belt. Blood had splattered all over the road inside the square, suggesting a lot of fighting happened inside it.

Based on where the sun hung overhead, she figured the main gate lay on the east face of the marauder's camp, and the extension full of metal cabins occupied the road leading north away from the intersection. She perched on the south wall.

Close to the 'dying square,' a rack held a large assortment of swords, big hammers, clubs, and axes. The rest of the space around the arena contained a half-dozen buggies, five more frames for buggies that had either fallen apart or hadn't been finished yet, and an array of tires, bottles, hoses, and giant blue plastic cans. Below her to the right along the south wall lay a swath of worktables where three men and two women in marauder armor worked with tools. They seemed to be fiddling with small engines like the one that gave her a headache.

She fixated on the biggest freestanding cabin all the way in the back of the extension down the road, annoyingly enough, directly opposite her current position. Something about it seemed important, but a large man also stood guard by a concrete staircase leading into one of the old-city buildings on the left side of that area.

The buzzing wail of a buggy came out of the distance, growing louder. Feeling somewhat safe, she decided to hold still and watch. Marauders ran to the wall on the right, dragging the two giant doors open a moment or two before a buggy appeared at the corner in the distance and rolled down the street into the compound. One man drove, another marauder stood on the back, holding on to the top of the triangular frame around the storage area. The buggy circled the death square once and parked by the line of other buggies.

As soon as the engine cut out, the screams of a woman became clear.

The marauder on the back hopped off. A coiled chain hanging from his hip with a fist-sized spiked metal ball jangled as he twisted side to side, stretching. The driver got out and walked around to him, and they opened the leather flaps. Inside, a dark-haired woman in tattered rags curled in a ball, her hands behind her back and her ankles tied.

Their captive shrieked and screamed, writhing and struggling at the ropes while begging them to let her go. The men hauled her out of the buggy and swung her around, showing her off to the rest of the marauders. Some cheered, including one of the armored women. The bigger man with the spiked-ball chain tossed her over his shoulder the way Dad carried deer home from the hunt. He crossed to the other side of the compound and went up the concrete stairs. The *slam* of a heavy door cut off her screams.

Wisp lost all interest in the big metal cabin, and glared at where they took that woman.

That's where Dad is... If he's here, he'll be in that place.

She examined the building, an unassuming grey five-story without any writing on the walls or any signs. After noting it as the third building from the corner on the far side of the intersection, she climbed back down to the street and flexed her hands to ease the cramping from clinging to scrap metal for so long.

A relatively debris-free road led from where she stood to the next cross street. She hurried to the corner, circling around the outside of the compound at a light jog. Ducking fallen light posts and crawling through a maze of stacked cars, she made her way along in the shadow of the scrap metal barricade. When she reached the four-lane road outside the compound's west wall, she ducked into a dark gap beneath a crashed car that had run up on top of another vehicle. From that hiding place, she peered out, glancing to her right at the wall of rusty, mismatched panels, and left at a long swath of debris packing the road. Ancient lampposts had melted; as far as she could see, pale shadows of people adorned the walls of old buildings—ghosts frozen in time at the instant of a Fire Dragon's wrath. Voices inside the compound discussed if the 'new capture' would go to the farm or be given to one of the men as a pet. Others complained about something called a 'still' not working, which resulted in them running low on moonshine.

Wisp peered up at the late-afternoon sky. *How can they run out of moon shine?*

A throaty, scratchy female voice said, "Still works just fine. Piston drinks it all 'stead of feedin' it to the buggies."

Marauders erupted in laughter.

After making sure no one lurked atop the wall that could see her, she zipped out from her hiding place and sprinted across the four-lane road into the shadows of the next block. Three buildings in from the corner, she stopped and peered up at a wall covered in regular, small windows. Some had curtains, boards blocked off others, and none had any glass left. Spiked metal plates covered every window on the first floor. Wisp stood in the shelter of ancient buildings, hearing but not feeling the wind, and let all the air out of her lungs. She couldn't remember ever being outdoors in a place with no breeze at all, and it made this ruin all the eerier.

This is where Dad is.

She pulled out the Mother Twig, but didn't release it to dangle. What would she do if it didn't point at this building in front of her? She'd *seen* them carry a captive into it. This *had* to be where they took him. Why didn't she trust that the twig would point her here?

I know this is the place.

Shivering, she relaxed her fingers and let the twig drop. It barely rotated at all, still pointing straight forward as she'd been holding it.

Yes!

She packed the Mother Twig back in the side pocket and zippered it closed.

Okay… now how do I get inside? I can't use the front door.

A small chain-link fence blocked off a channel between the building and its neighbor. That didn't look promising, as it would take her right into the compound by the scrap metal cabins. She started to get angry, but caught herself.

Stay calm. Think.

Metal porches jutted out of the building inside that alley, one at each story, connected by narrow staircases. A ladder at the lower one appeared broken, as it didn't go anywhere near enough to the ground to reach. She looked from it to the fence, to the wall of stone blocks. Inch-deep channels separated the huge, rectangular stones, gaps big enough for a girl's fingers and toes.

Got it.

As she did at the settlement with the green strips tied to the fence, she stuck her feet in the holes of the chain link, grabbed on, and pulled herself up. Rather than go over it, she clung to the edge of the building for balance and pivoted so she could stand on the pipe running along the top of the fence. Gingerly, she slid the toes of her left foot into a gap between stones and tested putting her weight on them before committing to the climb. Once sure she could hold on to the wall, she clung like a spider to the side of the building and scaled up to the second story, then shimmied to her left until she got a hand on the metal porch hanging from the side. Not allowing even a second for thought, (so she didn't chicken out) Wisp shoved off the wall and threw herself at the railing. She caught on, got a leg up, and swung herself over to stand on the grating. The whole porch clattered under her weight, evidently not too secure in its attachment to the building.

"What was that?"

A man's voice echoed in the gap between buildings, probably the marauder guarding the door by the little concrete stairway. Wisp jumped in the nearest unblocked window before he could peek down the alley and spot her. She landed in a dim room with moldy walls and the decaying remains of a carpet. She slung the rifle off her shoulder into a ready grip, gazing around at old furniture, a bookshelf, and a TV about half the size of the one she 'watched' before. Despite plenty of shadows, no Tree Walkers came out of the darkness for her. Still, she trembled. If any marauders spotted her, she'd have to send them to the Other Place before they could cry out. A gunshot, these monsters might not recognize. A marauder yelling would attract more. After swallowing hard, she forced herself to creep forward, constantly gazing left and right in case something tried to jump out at her.

This must have been someone's cabin.

Of two ways out of this room, one door and one hallway, she chose the door.

It opened without protest, letting her into a narrow corridor with multiple, identical doors on both sides. Undisturbed dust covered the dark hardwood floor.

They don't go up this high… She left a trail of footprints as she walked, pausing to stick her head into one door after the next at old, empty dwellings. This building confused her. As best she could tell, the ancients had built a whole bunch of small cabins and stacked them on top of each other. How many people had all tried to live in the same city for them to have done that?

A muted woman's scream came from below, loudest near a wooden railing all the way at the end of the hall. Wisp hurried forward, peering over the banister down a staircase, also coated in dust. The first floor looked dark, most likely because all the ground level windows had metal plates over them.

She made her way down the creaky stairs, following the screaming. Sudden heavy footsteps coming from a side corridor sent her racing into a room on the right. She pushed the door closed, fighting her urge to slam it. A *clink* came from the pan in her pack when she leaned back against the door as if to hold it closed, toes clutching at the floor. She gasped for breath, making as little noise as possible while gazing out at the room in front of her. Twenty or more crude mattresses lay scattered about a room with no other furniture except metal pails here and there, and a rickety table with cans of various sizes.

A man walked by out in the hall, chuckling to himself, his steps heavy enough to make the floor shake.

Wisp pushed off the door and speed-creeped across the room, cringing at the pungent stink of days-old bad water sitting in the buckets. Marauders who slept in here must be too lazy to go to an outhouse. Fearing someone would walk in and catch her at any second, she jogged past the crude beds to an interior door on the left that led to a room about half the size with stacks of boxes and random junk. A thick layer of dust on the floor reassured her that the marauders probably never came in here, so it felt like a good hiding place. She shut the door behind her and tried to calm down enough to think.

Her gaze roamed the assorted junk, mostly broken lamps, small tables, and cardboard boxes, until the woman's scream happened again, quite loud. Drawn by the cry, Wisp crept around a wall of stacked cartons, and discovered the room to be much bigger than she'd thought. In the far corner, a six-foot hole in the floor gave off flickering firelight, as well as an awful smell. Her eyes watered at the mixture of bad water, *ngh*, rotting meat, and sweat. She shifted her rifle to the side and buried her mouth and nose against the inside of her left elbow.

Eww.

"Don't do this!" yelled a woman, so loud she had to be down in that hole.

A man laughed. Footsteps scuffed over stone, and a door slammed. Metal rattled along with feminine grunting.

Wisp's eyebrows knit together. The sound reminded her of when she shook the door of her Haven, trying to get Dad's attention. She squatted low and crept to the edge, peering down at a tall shelf cabinet and dark cinder block walls flickering in the light of numerous small fires. She scooted around the hole closer to the shelf, which appeared tall enough to serve as a ladder. Flat on her stomach, she scooted forward and stuck her head into the opening, careful to keep her butt-length hair from draping and giving her away.

Multiple havens occupied the chamber below. Some, tall and narrow, hung from chains on the ceiling. Others on the floor had a rectangular boxy shape like hers. Men and women, mostly wearing tattered rags or mismatched clothing, occupied a few of them. The biggest havens she'd ever seen, four of them, lined the wall on the right, each a little bigger than the Mother Shrine room. They all had cinder block walls on three sides and barred doors facing the chamber that looked like the same type of bars Dad had made her Haven out of, stuck together in a poor attempt to be straight lines.

A word from one of her books leapt out at her: jail.

Best of all, no marauders were down there. Only a single door led out of the chamber, and it didn't have any windows. No monster would ambush her while she climbed and couldn't protect herself. She pushed herself up, sat on the edge, and stretched her legs out to get her feet on the nearby shelf. The sturdy wooden cabinet let her climb down to a cold, concrete floor.

Rifle held sideways, she strolled with confidence out of the shadowy corner into the light of several coffee-can lamps hung on the walls. Fat wicks burned like giant candles, lending an odd chemical smell to the stink of everything else in here.

The people gasped and stared at her.

Rattling came from a hanging haven where the dark-haired woman the men carried in only minutes ago shook and fought the door, trying to batter it open. The swinging enclosure had so little room inside, the woman had no choice but to hang her legs through the bars and sit on the bottom.

A child smaller than Wisp with wild black hair perched cross-legged inside another hanging haven on the left wall, peering at her with huge blue eyes. A belt around the child's waist held up a somewhat-skirt of tattered rags, but didn't cover much skin. Pale and covered with grimy smears, the younger child shivered and tried reaching toward her past the bars.

A second woman in a hanging haven, one empty between her and the child, gazed down at Wisp with a pleading, desperate look. She had a similar pale complexion, with light brown hair and piercing hazel eyes.

Wisp couldn't look away from her. "Are you afraid of the Tree Walkers, too? Do they come here even though it's all dead outside?"

"What?" asked a man in a floor haven. "Tree Walkers?"

"Please," said the hazel-eyed woman. "Help my son escape."

"No, Mama." The black-haired child tried—quite futilely—to reach her. "I don't wanna leave without you."

"What are Tree Walkers?" asked another man in a ground haven, also with a fair complexion. He almost looked as old as Dad.

Wisp shivered. "Monsters who take children away into the forest. That's why we have havens. You must be afraid of them because you're inside havens."

"Havens?" asked the boy's mother.

She walked closer, her head about even with the bottom of the swaying metal enclosure. "This." She patted the bars. "It's a haven so the Tree Walkers don't steal you."

"Nah, kid," said the dark-haired woman. "These are *cages*, not havens. We've been abducted. The marauders took us as slaves."

Wisp looked around at perhaps a dozen adults and the boy. "Slaves?"

"Stupid tribal," muttered a distant man.

The mother hissed at him before giving Wisp an imploring smile. "The men outside are marauders."

"I know that." Wisp glanced over at the huge room-sized havens. Two had figures under blankets, likely asleep.

"A slave is when marauders grab people who don't want to go with them and keep them locked in cages. They make us work on their farm, or when they get tired of us, fight each other to the death. Please! You must take Kit and get out of here."

"No, Mama!" yelled the boy.

About half the adults shushed him.

"Quiet, boy," snapped a blond-haired man much younger looking than Dad. "You'll make them come in here and they'll grab this girl before she can find the key."

"Please let us out," whispered Kit, rattling the door of his haven. "I want to go home."

His mother burst into tears.

"Be quiet, Noma," moaned a man in a floor haven on the right. "They will hear you. This girl is simple."

"I'm not simple." Wisp marched across the room to glare at a man with dark brown hair and brown eyes. "I'm Wisp."

He chuckled. "And I am Daz, but we are still locked in cages."

"Havens," said Wisp.

"Whatever you want to call them, please let us *out*." Noma tried again to reach for her son, but couldn't even touch her fingers to the empty haven between them.

She scratched her head. "Why are you sad to be safe in your havens? The Tree Walkers can't get you?"

"I don't have a clue what the heck a Tree Walker is, kid, but this ain't no haven. It's a cage." Daz reached out between the bars and grabbed a fistful of Wisp's pink shirt. He tugged her closer, nose to nose between the bars. The man smelled like he hadn't had a bath since he'd been her age. "You can call it anything you like, but please get us out of here."

Wisp frowned at his hand, but tolerated his grip for the moment since he seemed more pleading than threatening. "I've come to find my Dad."

"Unbelievable," said a man sitting a floor haven closer to the big cells. His dark brown hair hung all the way to the floor. "Come here, kid."

Daz let go of her shirt and whispered, "If this kid is sneaky enough to get in here, she can get the key. Some of those tribals are scary good at hunting, even this young. Big guy right outside has it. All ya gotta do is sneak in there like ya snuck in here, and grab the keys."

"Kid, get outta here before you get caught," said a younger man with blond hair.

"Stuff it, Olim," rasped Daz, spittle flying from his lip. "She's our only chance!"

She padded over to the man beckoning her, but stayed far enough away to avoid another grab. "What?"

"I'm Tavin." The longhaired man pointed a thumb to his right. "Poor guy in that cell kept talking about having a daughter. It's why he put up such a fight. Damn marauders beat him something fierce. Doesn't seem possible that some little kid could find this place all the way from the Rockies. That guy said the marauders had gone way up into the hills."

"He killed a couple of them with his bare hands," said Noma. "Almost escaped."

"Rockies?" asked Wisp.

"Endless forest or something?" Tavin scratched his head. "People up there are pretty isolated."

A shudder ran down her body at the words 'Endless Forest.' *Dad?* She ignored Tavin and darted over to the big cell. A man lay on the floor, half propped against the wall, partially covered with a blanket. Bruises, stab wounds, and welts covered his bare chest. Puffy dark spots distorted his face; cracked lips exposed a mouth missing a few teeth. Blood had seeped over his chin, dripping onto blotchy green pants with all-too-familiar metal plates protecting the shins.

"D-Dad," whimpered Wisp.

She rammed herself into a gap between the bars, reaching, but her backpack got caught, trapping her. Snarling, she wriggled out of the straps, dropped it, and shimmied into the cell, sliding to a stop on her knees beside him, grabbing his shoulders and shaking.

His skin held no warmth.

"Dad!" yelled Wisp, gathering his left hand in both of hers, but his arm wouldn't bend, stiff as a tree branch. All four knuckles had thick scabs, and a snipped-off arrow shaft protruded from his bicep.

She grabbed his shoulders again and shook him harder, then pawed at his frizzy black-and-grey beard. When he showed no sign of moving, she collapsed over his chest. No heartbeat sound came from within. Wisp stared at the wall, unable to breathe or even blink. Her cheek peeled away from his chest, tacky with semidry blood. She turned her head to stare into his eyes, but they gazed off, unfocused. The once rich brown of his face had taken on a slight pallor.

"D-Dad?" she blubbed, tears streaming down her face. "No, Dad. Don't go to the Other Place. I need you here. Dad! You can't go to the Other Place. You just can't!"

She hovered the back of her hand by his nose and mouth, feeling for breath, but no air moved.

"I brought your rifle. See? It's right outside. I've got your stuff with me too. Want me to get it?"

Your Dad's already gone, said Zen's voice in the back of her mind.

Wisp pictured the Mother Twig pointing her at this building, but why would it have done so if she'd been too late? She patted his cheek, pushing his eyes open wider with her thumbs. He didn't react, nor did his eyes focus on her. She grabbed his head and tried to shake it, but his neck had the rigidity of a boulder.

Dad had gone to the Other Place.

She flung herself on him, wrapping her arms around and snuggling her face against his shoulder. Great, heaving sobs burst out of her. Every memory of Dad flashing in her head brought harder and harder tears. With each thought of him protecting her, smiling whenever she learned something he'd taught her, or quizzing her on plants, she lapsed deeper and deeper into grief.

Nothing mattered anymore. She had found him, even if he had gone to the Other Place.

Wisp couldn't survive without Dad.

She didn't want to.

So, she'd stay right here with him.

The Purpose of Bars
~25~

Wisp cried herself to silence, clinging to Dad. She knelt in his lap, arms still wrapped around him, face still buried against his shoulder. She had no desire to do anything but hold on to him until she, too, slipped into the Other Place.

The other people talked in whispers, mostly about possible ideas to escape, except for Kit, who upon witnessing her crying about Dad, had begun wailing for his mother. Juliana, the recently captured woman, shared her name with the others, and told of her abduction. The marauders had driven their buggy right onto the farm where she lived, chasing the fleeing people like a wolf barreling into a herd of deer. A man on the back grabbed her while she ran. They'd never even stopped driving, until they'd gone too far away for anyone to help her.

Minutes passed in relative calm before a random thought that Dad *couldn't* be upset with her for leaving the cabin triggered another wave of heavy crying. Time and reality blurred. Wisp glided in and out of waking dreams, seeing her happiest moments. Dad smiling; Dad carrying her on his shoulders across the snow to the outhouse; hours spent sitting safe in her Haven reading; Dad standing a few feet away with his back turned while she bathed, making sure nothing would hurt her. These silly people had nice havens and didn't even want to be in them. Well, maybe not quite as nice as hers. None of them had soft bedding, merely cold bars and colder stone, and the hanging ones looked uncomfortably small. Being forced to sleep sitting up sounded awful.

Eventually, a sense of numbness came over her. She sat back and neatened Dad's hair. Without the emotional crash of finding him dead engulfing her mind, all his wounds became glaringly obvious. He'd been stabbed with knives, hit with clubs, and shot with arrows, but no single injury looked fatal. Likely, he'd lost too much blood. Or maybe something inside broke.

Or perhaps Mother had told him that Wisp had learned enough from him to survive, and, being unable to get away from the marauders, he had gone to be with her.

"I'm not ready. I don't wanna be alone," she whispered, tugging on his stone-stiff arm. "Please don't go away."

The constant murmuring of voices outside the cell needled at her brain. She scowled at them for disturbing Dad's shrine. Eyes closed, she mentally commanded everyone to be quiet, to respect Dad's journey to the Other Side. When they didn't shut up, she sprang to her feet, intent on screaming at them, but lost the energy to do so after walking up to the cell bars.

"Hey," said Kit. "Please let us out. I don't wanna be in a cage anymore. I want my mom!"

She looked at him. "It's dark out. The Tree Walkers will get you if you're not safe. You're too little to be out of a haven at night."

"No..." Kit shook his head. "These 're cages, not havens. They's not to protect us. They's so we can't escape. I *hate* being in here!"

Wisp grabbed the bars and leaned her head out between them. Being in such a huge haven that let her stand up dragged a hint of a memory from somewhere long ago to the surface. She hadn't wanted to be in the Haven, but she'd been so small... It made no sense that she'd dislike being in her safe place, so she figured it a scrap of nightmare. "You're little. You need to be inside a haven so the Tree Walkers don't get you."

"Marauders killed my dad, too." Kit sniffled into tears. "He tried ta stop 'em from takin' me an' Mom, but they killed him." The boy lost the ability to speak as grief brought him to sobbing.

Noma strained to reach him, but could only get her fingertips on the empty haven between them.

Once he noticed his mother trying, Kit also stuck his arms out past the bars. He kicked his feet back and forth, swinging his cage, but couldn't get to his mother.

A lump formed in Wisp's throat. That boy had a barrier of steel and open space between him and being able to touch his mother. She had a barrier of spirits and magic. Mother had been gone for so long, she couldn't remember ever seeing her alive.

"Please, child," said Noma, tears in her eyes. "Please help us get out of these cages."

"You can do it," said Juliana. "There's a man right outside with the keys. You got inside here without anyone seeing you. You can get the keys and let us out."

"She's only a little girl." Olim shook his head. "Kid, get out of here. Those men will do unspeakable things to you."

"Shut up," whisper-shouted Daz over his shoulder at the other caged man. He grinned at Wisp. "You can do it, kiddo. Find the key. Be quiet, take the key and bring it back to us."

"But the Walkers," muttered Wisp. "We need to be in havens at night." She pulled her head back inside the cell, wondering if it would even protect her. The spacing of the bars would let her slip right through, but only because she hadn't grown up yet.

"Where did you get that tree walking nonsense from?" asked Tavin. "Who told you that?"

"Dad," muttered Wisp. "Where we live, there are monsters who take children. I have to hide in my Haven when it gets dark, or when Dad's not there to protect me."

"This…" Daz patted the bars of his cage. "Is what you call a haven?"

"Yes." She nodded.

"Uhh, I hate to break it to you, kid, but your Dad lied to you. I, uhh, not sure I wanna know why he put you in a cage, but that ain't normal." Daz shook his head. "And I ain't never heard of a Tree Walker."

"They're real!" shouted Wisp. "I've seen them! They almost got me, but I'm good at hiding and they didn't find me! Take back what you said about Dad! He's not a liar! He didn't put me in a *cage*. It's a Haven!" She wiped tears from her cheeks, her body shaking from erratic cry-breathing.

The other people all stared at her, except for Kit and Noma, still trying to stretch far enough to touch hands, despite it being impossible.

Wisp turned away from the bars and walked over to kneel by Dad. "Are you in the Other Place?"

Dad didn't reply.

She bowed her head. Tears splattered on her thighs, running down over her knees. "I will bring you home to be with Mother."

The not-quite-as-old-as-Dad man stifled a chuckle. "No offense, girl, but you don't look anywhere near strong enough to carry that guy. Let me out of here, and I'll carry him wherever the heck you want."

Wisp pushed herself up to stand and grabbed Dad's arm. She struggled to lift him off the floor, but her feet slid on the stone. The harder she pulled, the more she slid, but Dad didn't go far at all.

"You gotta get us outta here," whisper-shouted Kit. "If the 'rauders see you, they'll lock you up too! Please help before you're caught!"

"The heck is all that noise?" shouted a man from behind the room's only door.

Wisp gasped.

She scrambled to the bars and dragged the backpack inside before grabbing the rifle and scurrying deep into the cell, her back against the wall next to Dad. Footsteps echoed from behind the outside door, drawing nearer.

"Dammit," whispered Daz. "Oh well. Your own fault, kid. You shoulda moved faster. Now, you're caught."

She set the rifle flat on the floor and slid it into the space behind Dad. A heavy wooden door creaked open. Wisp pulled the blanket up to cover herself, curling her body tight against Dad, left knee across his lap, her other leg straight beside his. She tucked her head under his left arm and threaded her right arm around his back, squeezing herself into him.

Hard boots clomped on the stone floor of the outer chamber.

"What's all the damn yellin' goin on?" bellowed a man. "Someone askin' for a good attitude adjustment?"

Dad... please protect me.

Negotiations

~26~

Dad's cold skin offered little comfort.

Her fingers kept slipping over his back, unable to get a good grip on the sweaty, bloody mess coating him. The outer room fell silent save for the squeaking of chains and Kit's muffled sniffles. Wisp's breathing echoed in the stony space between her face and the wall. She squeezed herself into Dad.

Something inside him murmured.

"Was it you?" bellowed the man outside.

"No," whimpered Kit.

"Sounded like a kid yelling," said the marauder.

Another unsettling noise churned within Dad.

"I didn't yell," whispered Kit.

"You know what we do to slaves when they don't do what they're told…"

A sharp metal-on-metal *clang* broke the quiet, startling Wisp into squeezing Dad tight.

"I didn't. I didn't!" shouted Kit.

The Forest Beyond the Earth

The high-pitched whine that started coming out of Dad grew into a breathy, fluttering gasp… only it hadn't come out his mouth. Wisp, her head stuffed under his arm, face trapped in the hollow between his back and the wall, bore the full brunt of his gaseous disaster. She had once compared his *ngh* to a weapon, but a fart from the Other Side made everything else he'd ever done in the outhouse smell like flowers.

She convulsed, fighting the urge to throw up. Bile leaked out of her mouth, but she kept her jaw clenched, her whole body shuddering from the effort. If she puked, the marauder would definitely catch her. *He's*—she gagged—*trying to protect*—she retched. *Me.* Not even a Tree Walker would want to be anywhere near that smell. It could wither plants brown in seconds.

The marauder laughed. "Good one. Hope it stinks so you can stew in it." He waited a few seconds. "What's wrong, mate? Nothin' ta say back ta me now? Heh. 'Bout time you learned ta keep your yap shut."

"And you…" said the Marauder. "You're awful pretty."

Noma's voice shook. "I'll do whatever you want me to if you let me be in the same cage with my son. Please…"

Wisp tried to hold her breath.

"You'll do whatever we want you to, because we tell you to." The loud *clank* happened again. "You're meat now, you got that, slave? You don't get to make requests."

Silence came at an inconvenient moment. Wisp needed air *now*. Of course, the cloud floating around her didn't exactly qualify as air, but she couldn't hold her breath any longer. Whatever went on in the outer room didn't involve words, so she forced herself to let her lungs empty as quietly as possible out her nose before breathing back in her mouth. Still, she gagged, and nearly threw up.

"No!" shouted Kit. "Stay away from my mother!"

"What are you gonna do about it, termite?" asked the marauder.

Metal clanked against metal again and again, though not as hard as before.

Unable to bear the smell in the confined space anymore, Wisp pulled her head back and risked a peek out from under the blanket. A tall, fat marauder stood by Kit's haven, banging on it with a metal-capped club. He appeared to be trying to hit the boy through the bars, but the kid jerked his hands away or shifted his legs fast enough to avoid contact.

Wisp eased herself off Dad and lay flat on the floor beside him, still clinging. She stretched her legs out together and gathered the blanket off to the side on top of herself, hoping to look like a rolled up lump of cloth beside Dad that *didn't* have a skinny girl hiding in it.

She pulled the stinky fabric up to her eyes, glaring at the man tormenting a little boy while Noma pleaded and begged him to stop.

Maybe these people are right. Those aren't havens… Dad made the Haven with love, to keep me safe. Marauders are mean. She narrowed her eyes. *That's the difference between a cage and a haven: love.*

Kit dodged the club for another minute or so before he burst into tears. At that, the marauder stopped and laughed, taunting him for being a little girl. Noma glared at him. The marauder thrust his arm into her cage, grabbed a fistful of her tattered shirt, and pulled her face against the bars. He forced his lips to touch hers, held her there for a short while, and let go.

"Later, I gonna have somethin' for you ta do." The marauder laughed again, bonked Kit's cage with the club one last time—making the boy flinch—and walked out.

Too angry to remember to duck, Wisp watched him go by. When the door slammed, she threw the blanket off and looked at Dad. She couldn't leave him here with these monsters. He had to be with Mother again. That one marauder had taunted Dad, so at least some of his bruises had to come from that monster's club. She blinked away the bleariness of the stink, crawled over to the corner, and puked up a few mouthfuls of bile. Once she regained her composure, she grabbed her rifle and walked to the cell door.

Daz made a soft whistle. "Wow, kid. I thought you were in trouble there. Guess it's darker in here than I thought."

Her sadness had gone so deep it had become something else. Not truly anger, but not exactly resolve. The future would hold a great many tears, but not until she had the safety to set them free. She gazed down at her hands and arms, smeared with Dad's blood, and flicked a tiny beetle off her stomach.

"I will bring you home, Dad."

Kit curled in a ball sniveling while Noma tried to comfort him from a distance.

Juliana and Tavin whispered at her, asking for help.

Wisp squeezed past the bars, ignoring them all while pulling her backpack on. She padded up to Daz's cage and peered down at him, rifle held sideways, her finger braced on the frame above the trigger. "You were wrong. The monster didn't catch me." She turned on her heel and walked over to the hanging cage containing the man who'd offered to carry Dad. "You said you would help me bring Dad home if I let you out."

The man extended his arm out, hand open. "Yes. Name's Falo."

She stared at his hand, thinking of that greeting Zen taught her, but didn't quite trust he wouldn't try to grab her rifle. "I'm Wisp."

"Don't know a handshake?" asked Falo.

"I don't trust being grabbed by a person in a hav—cage who doesn't want to be in one." She shivered at a fleeting memory of waking up trapped in her Haven. Without Dad to let her out, it *had* kind of felt more like a cage than a sanctuary. She refused to think what might've happened to her if she didn't know where he kept the opener.

"Fair enough." Falo lowered his arm. "I won't hold that against ya. You are kinda small, so being afraid of grownups is understandable."

"How old are you?" asked Wisp.

"Thirty-one or two." He shrugged. "Don't really know. So, you'll do it?"

She glanced at the room's only door. "If you promise you will help me carry Dad. But if I let you out of there, I can't really protect you from the Tree Walkers."

"No problem. I can handle a bunch of walking trees." He smiled.

"Probably some nonsense that guy made up so she went to bed on time," muttered Daz.

"No. They're real. I've seen them. Like, all the plants and vines and roots in the forest stand up and come running after you." Wisp shifted to glare at him. "And if you say bad about Dad one more time, I will leave you here."

The man shot her a sour look, but stayed quiet.

She faced Falo again. "Say you promise."

He appeared ready to roll his eyes, but kept on smiling. "I promise I will help carry your Dad if you let me out of here."

Wisp looked at Kit. "I'm going to let him out, too. He should be with his mother. My mother went to the Other Place when I was only two."

"Please…" Noma grabbed the bars of her enclosure, pressing her head to them. "Let us go home."

Kit shifted in his hanging cage, hiding his face, still sniffling from the marauder harassing him.

"All right." She looked from Kit to Falo. "Mother is watching you. If you break your promise, you'll be bad."

He put a hand over his heart. "I would *never* dream of 'being bad.'"

"Where's the opener?" asked Wisp.

"The what?" Falo tilted his head.

She poked her finger in the keyhole. "The opener. To make the haven open."

"You mean the key?" Falo shrugged. "I don't really know. Probably with that big moron who likes to make little boys cry."

Wisp raised both eyebrows. "You don't know? How couldn't you know where the opener to your haven is?"

Falo held up a finger. "First, it's a cage, not a haven. We are captives, not… being protected. Second, we're captives. They don't want to let us leave. The entire point of these things is so we can't get away."

"I knew where Dad kept the opener for my Haven. He put it up on a high shelf under a can so the Tree Walkers couldn't find it."

"Sounds like he didn't want you to escape," said Kit.

Wisp spun to glare at the little snot. "That's not true! He wanted to protect me. I had to go in the Haven when it got dark because of the Tree Walkers. And in the day, I always had to stay near Dad so he could keep me safe. He got upset if I wandered too far away."

Noma gave her a pitying stare.

"Kid," said Daz, "The only time people put other people in cages is when they don't want them to escape. Lockin' you up in a cage wouldn't protect you from any Tree Walker things… it would make it *easier* for them to get you since you can't run away. They'll just reach in the bars and get you."

Wisp shook her head hard. "No. Dad made the Haven from love. They can't break that."

Tavin whistled. "Wow."

Noma's pitying stare grew more intense.

Daz's gruff expression fell flat, almost sad. "Whoa."

"Just get the key and we can get outta here," said Falo.

"Where is it?" asked Wisp.

"The fat pig marauder has it," hissed Julianna. She thrust her arm out, pointing at the door. "Out there."

Wisp's reply stalled in her mouth at the sight of bleeding rope marks on the woman's wrist. "All right. I'll get the opener. Maybe these *are* cages, not havens. The marauders don't want to protect anyone." She looked at Kit, who'd finally stopped sniffling. The boy seriously needed a meal soon; she could make out every rib on his sides. "I'll let you out."

"Great," said Falo.

"Remember, you promised. Mother is watching you. If you break your promise, you'll be bad."

She approached the door on the far wall.

"Oh… better not be 'bad,'" muttered Daz, with a hint of a chuckle.

"Stop it," hissed Juliana. "The girl's lost her father. Have a little respect."

Tavin groaned. "And hey, if that girl *can* help us, why make her angry?"

"You should just get lost, kid," said Olim. "You're only gonna wind up caged like us. Run, get away while you can."

"Shut up," snapped Julianna. "She's gonna help us."

"I have to bring Dad to the Mother Shrine. I can't leave him here."

"Don't be stupid, kid. Get out of here before you wind up dead." Olim cringed. "You are pretty, and young. Do you have any idea what these marauders would do to you? Run away!"

She flicked the safety off the rifle, and faced the door. "No."

Black Magic
~27~

Wisp grabbed the knob and pushed the thick wooden door out of her way. It swung out on creaky hinges, coming to a stop against a cinder block wall on the left. The captives all fell silent.

Twenty feet of corridor lined with empty, dented metal shelves led to an open doorway peering into another room aglow with firelight. She crept forward, bare feet silent on the concrete, and stopped at the end where it connected to a large, square room.

Orange glow and shadows danced across the walls from a fireplace in the wall to the right. The big marauder who'd menaced Kit reclined on a dingy sofa, feet up on a coffee table while slurping brown goo out of a bowl with a spoon. He faced the fire, which put his right shoulder toward her, but she stood far enough behind him that he hadn't yet noticed her. A scent similar to boar meat, laden with a heavy vegetable essence filled the air.

She padded into the room, swinging left to stay out of his field of view. Coarse fibers from an ancient carpet crumbled under her feet, dry and brittle. Behind the sofa, a single door on the left wall stood between two tall cabinets with the words 'Utility Room' on it in white. The left one had no doors, revealing shelves holding coils of rope and bundles of chain. Straight ahead, another passageway opposite the corridor to the haven room offered a view of stairs leading up to the first floor.

The marauder's spoon scraped the bowl in a random series of *clinks* between satisfied mumbles. She walked up behind him close enough to spot a jumble of openers hanging on his belt. His metal-capped club lay beside him on the sofa. The keys did not appear in any way vulnerable to theft.

I won't be able to steal those unless he's asleep. Or gone to the Other Place.

Wisp pulled the rifle up and set the butt tight to her shoulder, aimed at him, and moved her finger onto the trigger. "Let the people out of their havens."

The marauder coughed on his soup. He choked for a second, wiped his mouth on his arm, and twisted around to look at her. "Oh, you're cute... where'd you come from, girlie?"

She lined up the iron sights with his face. "Let the people out of their havens. Or give me the openers. They're grownups... well except one. Grownups don't belong in havens because Tree Walkers don't take grownups."

"Hah. Aren't you a strange little sprite?" He set the bowl on the coffee table. "Too damn skinny to work. Ain't got no shape to ya, but that gold hair of yours. You gonna be real pretty when you get a little older. Don't worry, honey. I'll keep ya nice and safe until ya ripen up."

"I'm not going to ask you again. I'm trying to be polite. Open the havens."

He swiped the club from the cushion and wagged it at her. "Now, I've been accused o' bein' dumb before, and maybe my ears ain't the best, but I almost thought I just heard a little girl give *me*"—he poked himself in the chest with the club—"somethin' that sounded a whole lot like an order."

"I didn't give you anything." She shifted her jaw. "Open the havens or I'm gonna send you to the Other Place."

Whispers came from the prisoners, mostly comments about how she'd been careless, gotten caught, and their chances at freedom had died. Tavin couldn't believe she spoke to the marauder like that.

He snarled. "You askin' me to give you a hard lesson, girlie."

"No." Wisp started to squeeze the trigger, but hesitated. With the stairs so close, more marauders would probably hear. She edged to her right. "I don't take lessons from monsters. Open the havens, *now*."

The man's eyes flared. He growled and loped around the couch, reaching for her with his open hand. She ducked, scurrying into the corridor to the haven room, then whirled to keep the rifle trained on him.

"Oh, you's not too smart, huh?" The marauder laughed. "That's a dead end. Ain't no way out. Or maybe you learn yer lesson. G'won back there. That's yer new home." He grinned, stalking after her. "You ain't got no meat a'tall on ya, can't rightly"—he slapped the club into his open hand—"teach ya the lesson ya need, but maybe if you're *real* sweet like, I'll change my mind 'bout your attitude needin' 'justment."

"You will open the havens or you will give me the keys." She backed up, inch by inch, into the room.

The captives all stared at her from their havens, except Dad. He continued gazing into nowhere.

"Kid, what the heck are you doing?" whispered Daz. "You keep antagonizin' him, he's gonna break your neck."

The marauder slammed the door behind him and walked closer, pointing his club at her. "Pick one and I'll open it for ya. Pick good; yer gonna be there a while."

"No. You will open them all." She continued retreating, leading him as deep into the room as possible. The farther she got from the stairs, the less likely anyone would hear the shot. Even better, he'd closed the door. With inches left between her back and cinder blocks, she widened her stance, sliding her right foot back to brace herself.

"You ain't bein' sweet. You mine now, and you gonna do what you is told." He stormed toward her, raising his club. "Now I gotta teach ya some respect. You gonna learn, girlie."

Bang!

The rifle kicked her back, but she held her ground. A small hole appeared in the marauder's chest; a wide spray of blood painted the floor behind him. His charge lurched to a halt, the club flying from his hand to smack the wall beside her with a metallic clatter. He wheezed, teetered on his feet for a second, and careened over, hitting the floor with a meaty *slap*.

Gasps came from all the captives, even Daz.

"What was that noise?" whispered Olim. "I can't hear anything."

"Black magic," said Juliana. "She killed him with a stare."

A woman in a ground haven who had not yet spoken snickered. Straight light brown hair hung down over a black cloth shirt. More loose, black fabric covered her legs all the way to her boots. She peered at Wisp past the bars, shaking her head with an eye roll as if calling the other captives idiots.

Noma spat at the marauder, snarling, evidently *quite* happy to see him dead. Kit covered his eyes.

"Crap... That thunder. I've never heard anything so loud." Falo stuck a finger in his ear and wiggled it.

Wisp waited for the ringing in her ears to fade. *Maybe using a rifle in a room with stone walls is a bad idea.* She swallowed a few times until sound returned to normal with a popping sensation. Her mouth opened, but before she could deny having magic and explain bullets, she changed her mind. If these people understood what really happened, they might steal Dad's gun. *That* would leave her pretty much helpless, so she let them continue believing in magic.

"Get the keys," rasped Juliana.

Keeping the rifle pointed at the door, Wisp hurried over to the dead marauder and squatted beside him. Not wanting to waste the time untying the cord, she one-handed the rifle while pulling her knife and cutting keys loose from his belt. After sheathing the blade, she picked up the keyring and walked over to crouch in front of Falo's cage.

"You're right. I have black magic. You promised to carry Dad to the Mother Shrine. If you lied, I'll do the magic on you."

High GroUnd
~28~

Wisp stared at Falo with no emotion on her face. She sent monsters to the Other Place. If this man betrayed Dad, she wouldn't feel bad about doing the same to him.

"Right. No problem kid." He smiled. "A deal's a deal."

She fumbled the keyring past four keys too large for the haven. The other fifteen all looked more or less the same. "Which one is it?"

"Try them all," said Falo.

Wisp checked them one after the next until the cage opened. Falo scrambled out, wrapped her in a huge hug, and kissed her on top of the head. Once he put her down, she cut the twine holding that key to the ring and left it in the door so she didn't waste time trying a known key on the other cages. Falo grabbed the side of his former cage and pulled himself upright, stretching and moaning.

"So good to stand up again. Ugh…"

She went to Noma next, but couldn't reach the keyhole, since the bottom of the hanging cage wound up even with her eyes.

"Come on… hurry up before more of them find us," said Juliana, bouncing and making the haven sway.

Noma reached for the keys. "Give me the keyring."

"I got it," said Falo. "You keep your magic ready in case more of them marauders show up."

She didn't hand him the keyring, but didn't put up much resistance when he took it from her.

Falo tried the first key on Noma's cage. "Easier to do from outside. And you're shaking."

The third key worked, and he helped the woman climb down to stand on the floor. She rushed over to Kit's cage and grabbed him through the bars. He burst into tears again, clinging to his mother's arms. Falo unlocked the door, and the boy leapt out into Noma's embrace, still sobbing. Noma fell to pieces as well, sinking to her knees and crying all over him.

Wisp got sad for a little while before a nasty spike of jealousy welled up. She whirled away so they couldn't see her scowling. That boy had a mother who hadn't gone to the Other Place. He got to hug a warm body instead of a crusty, dry shrine. She hadn't known what a woman's voice sounded like until a week ago. She hadn't even known what a woman really *looked* like until then either. And Noma had rather large chest pillows.

Wisp padded over to stand by Dad's cell, wallowing in jealousy and anger. Why had Mother been taken to the Other Place? At least she had *some* time with Dad. Mother, she'd never even met. Falo went around trying keys in cages. The groans of metal hinges and weary people filled in the room behind her. She refused to cry, but couldn't feel happy. The louder Kit sobbed or yelled "Mama," the more she wanted to go far away from them. Watching the marauder terrify the boy had made her furious, but as much pity as she'd had for him then, now that he had his mother back, she only found jealousy—toxic jealousy that made her want to lash out, but she couldn't blame that boy for what happened to her mother. She had to get away from them so the tiny voice ceased mocking her for not having a mother.

Wisp sank to kneel by the cell, her head pressed against the bars. She stared at Dad, no longer sure what to do with herself.

Eleven men and women, plus one small boy, eventually gathered around her.

"You have my thanks," said Daz. "I'm sorry if I was a little testy before."

"Thank you." Julianna bowed.

Noma tried to say something, but wound up crying more than forming words. Despite the blubbing, she looked quite happy.

Kit grinned at her. "Thanks for helping Mama."

"And one more to go." Falo walked up beside Wisp and stuck one of the big keys into the cell door, which worked on the first try. "Heh. Second cell, second key. At least that one was easy."

Wisp leaned away so he could pull the barred door open. The metal cried out with a harsh scrape that made everyone cringe.

Falo wrapped Dad in the blanket, and picked him up over his shoulder. "Okay, where's this guy gotta go?"

"To the Mother Shrine," said Wisp.

"Great. Umm. Need a little more detail."

She looked up at him, but cringed away, hating the sight of Dad being carried like a dead tree. "It's in our cabin."

"You know how to get there?" asked Falo.

"Yes… and I have Mother to help."

"Oh yeah," yelled Daz from the fireplace room. "Everyone, check this out!"

The other captives filed down the corridor one by one, Noma still carrying her son.

Wisp went last, right behind Falo. She kept staring at the floor so she didn't have to look at Dad's rigid body.

Daz held up a pair of big swords, cheering. "This room's full of weapons. I suggest everyone arm themselves. We may be outta the cages, but we're not free yet. The marauders ain't gonna let us walk out."

Murmurs of agreement came from everyone except Noma, who trembled. Juliana and the quiet woman with the black shirt both pushed past Daz, eager to grab a weapon.

"Not you." Daz put a hand on Noma's shoulder. "You watch the kids."

"Better idea," said Falo. "Instead of just fighting our way out, we get the hell rid of them. Wipe out *all* the marauders. There aren't that many of 'em. If we sneak away or kill only enough to get out the gate, the rest'll only wind up taking us all over again… or grabbin' other people."

The silent woman emerged from the back room with two swords, one long, one short. Her shirt and baggy black pants looked in far better shape than the rags the other captives wore. She swatted the longer blade against her boots, a similar style to Dad's, knocking crud off the blade. "The marauders will be mostly in their beds at this hour. I will go first and take as many as I can while they sleep."

"That's suicide, hon," said Daz. "Don't go alone."

"My name is Alina, not 'hon,' and I have spent twenty years learning the art of silence."

"You ain't that old." Olim scratched his head. "I'm twenty."

Alina smiled. "I started when I was seven."

"Girl looks good for near thirty." Daz chuckled.

"Alina," said Wisp. "There is a hole behind us. I walked through a room with many beds. They may be in there."

"Take that one with you. She's sneaky, too." Tavin patted Wisp on the head. "Made it in here alone."

"Her"—Alina glanced at the rifle—"*magic* is not quiet."

Other captives emerged from the door in the fireplace room carrying bows, axes, and swords. A few had even put on thick leather vests.

Wisp looked up at Alina. *She knows what a gun is, but she didn't try to take it.* "I can go with you, but I will stay quiet unless I have no choice."

"All right." Alina looked back toward the cage room. "Where's that hole?"

"Well I suppose you're down to watching *one* kid." Daz nudged Noma toward the couch. "Stay here with the boy."

Falo put Dad on the floor behind the sofa. "Sorry, pops. You gotta wait here, too. Can't carry you *and* fight."

Wisp scowled at him, but he had a point. "The way up is back where the havens are."

"That guy already pulled his share," said Olim. "Last count, he sent five of 'em to the next world."

Quiet tears ran down Wisp's face at the thought of how hard Dad must've fought to get back to her.

"I wanna fight," said Kit.

"No." Noma squeezed him until he gurgled. "You're only nine. Children do not fight."

"Everyone should stay down here and be quiet until you hear signs of alarm… or this girl's magic. If you alert the marauders before I'm ready, you threaten my life."

She's creepy. Wisp stood still, turning her head to watch Alina walk by. The woman showed no emotion at all, and spoke with a toneless voice that reminded her of a story she'd read about robots.

"Be careful." Falo patted her on the head, then went into the doorway in search of a weapon.

Wisp trailed after Alina into the room of cages. The woman walked straight to the hole, and gripped the shelf as if preparing to climb.

"That's it," said Wisp.

"Follow me, but be quiet. Show me where that room is, and then wait outside. Don't fire unless I am overwhelmed." Alina looked her in the eye, her face still blank. "Do you understand?"

Wisp gulped, more unsettled by this woman than any of the marauders. "Yes."

Alina gathered her light brown hair up into a knot at the back of her head, then climbed without another word.

She's halfway to the Other Place. Wisp shouldered the rifle, and climbed the shelf to the room full of junk. Alina seized her wrist when she put her hand on the upper floor, hauling her up and out of the hole with one arm like she weighed nothing. Wisp froze in panic, expecting an attack, but the woman merely set her on her feet.

They stared at each other in silence.

Wisp opened her mouth to speak, but closed it when a soft snarling noise came from the hallway outside. Instead, she whispered, "They sound like Dad when they sleep."

Alina stooped close, her lips almost touching Wisp's ear. "Some of them sleep now. Others are awake outside. Do not make any sound."

She nodded.

The woman slid her longer sword into a sheath she'd also taken from the room and gripped the smaller blade in her right hand. Wisp nodded toward the stack of boxes and led the way around it. She pointed at the door connecting to the room with the mattresses and stinky buckets.

Alina grasped the backpack and tugged her away from the door. Wisp readied her rifle, but kept it pointed down to the side. The woman approached the door, listened for a moment, and eased it open enough to peek. A few seconds of tense quiet passed before she pushed the door in the rest of the way. Snores and wheezy breaths got louder. Alina disappeared into the room. Alone, Wisp didn't know what to do with herself. She stood there fidgeting for a ten count before deciding to creep up to the door and look.

Only four marauders occupied the room, despite there being about twenty rotten mattresses. Alina snuck up to the nearest man, hovered by him for a second or two, then grabbed his mouth and nose with her left hand and raised the blade at his neck. Wisp looked away, cringing at the *squish* of a sword meeting flesh. The noise repeated a few times before the gentle creak of floorboards told her Alina moved to the next sleeping person.

Wisp huddled against the doorjamb, not wanting to watch. At least moonlight didn't offer much detail except the silhouette of a woman moving from bed to bed. Two of the men died without any noticeable reaction. Two murmured and flailed, but didn't make enough noise to draw attention from the outside.

"Kid," whispered Alina, walking back over. Finally, a hint of emotion showed on her face—concern. "Wow. Wasn't expecting you to be so squeamish."

"What is squeamish?"

"You didn't watch. I thought a kid who could shoot a man without flinching wouldn't mind a little blood."

"Umm." She glanced down at the moonlight glinting off the rifle. "It's different. He was about to hurt me. They're sleeping."

"Ahh, one of those." Alina poked her in the forehead. "You're little yet. Sometimes people need to do… uncomfortable things for a good reason. Any of those men would've killed us."

"I know. It doesn't bother me that you sent monsters to the Other Place. I just didn't want to watch."

"So." Alina folded her arms, bloody shortsword gleaming. "Where'd you get a FAL?"

"I'm sorry. What?"

"The rifle."

"Oh." Wisp's lip quivered, hearing Dad's voice in her head. "Fabric national three-oh-eight. It's Dad's."

Alina stifled a laugh. "Close enough." She patted Wisp's cheek twice. "It's yours now, kiddo. Your dad doesn't own anything anymore."

Had this woman not been so unsettling, Wisp would've glared. Instead, she stared down at the floor, worried and sad.

"Okay, kid. Since you've got a cannon, I want you to get up on that big ol' hut outside."

"Huh?"

Alina put an arm around her back and guided her to the other side of the room where a window looked out over the cluster of scrap metal huts. "See the big one in the back?"

"Yes. I was looking at it before. I thought Dad might have been in there because it's the biggest."

Alina sighed. "It's the best spot for you. All the way in back out of sight, and the highest place except up on the wall… but the wall's too obvious. A sniper wants high ground. Get up on the roof with that rifle, lay on your belly, and wait for all hell to break loose. Then shoot as many of them as you can… just try not to hit any friendlies."

"Sniper?"

"Someone with a rifle who shoots from far away." She pushed Wisp closer to the window. "Come on. I'm gonna go door to door."

Alina jumped out the window.

"Hey," said a man to her left.

She pulled the longer sword off her belt and spun into a flurry. Metal clanked against metal. A man let out a roar of anger, which turned to pain. Wisp leaned out the window right as Alina swiped her longer blade across the throat of the man who had been guarding the concrete stairs. He collapsed over backward, gurgling.

Other marauders in the distance, and on the wall, started walking closer. A few shouted.

"Now!" said Alina. "Go!"

Wisp leapt out of the window and ran to the left down the sidewalk in front of the buildings until she hit a dead end by the compound's outer wall, then darted to the right into a narrow space passing behind the big metal cabin. An old bathtub and a pushcart piled together with a mess of other junk beside the structure made climbing easy. As Alina suggested, she flattened herself out on her belly and crawled to the edge of the roof.

Evidently, Daz and the others heard the ruckus, as they came spilling out of the door by the concrete stairs. Wisp flicked the scope into position, but couldn't see much with it in the dark. The marauders had several barrel fires going in the compound, but the Moon gave off more light. Alina ducked into a nearby hut. A man's muffled gurgle followed soon after.

Marauders charged at the former captives, shouting and roaring war cries.

Wisp pushed the scope aside and took aim at a marauder with a huge sword running in. She tracked him until he stopped moving sideways, and squeezed the trigger a second after he nearly took Tavin's head clean off. The rifle jolted her, but she only slid a few inches down the angled roof.

The marauders all froze at the loud rifle blast. A spurt of blood flew from the man's left shoulder. He slumped over, clutching the wound. Tavin finished him off with a sword before the man could recover. Wisp scooted back to the roof edge and surveyed the line of confused Marauders. One man wore a bulky black armored vest as thick as her thighs and a helmet like a cage for his face. She thought of that boy slicing at the marauder's leather armor and not hurting him. Hoping her bullets would work better on the armor than the captives' swords, she aimed at him and fired. Puffs of white foam exploded from his chest. He flailed and dropped motionless.

That's not armor… it's a… pillow.

At the second thunderous *bang*, the marauders snapped out of their daze and resumed charging at the captives. Another large man advanced on Juliana, swinging a giant piece of engine on a chain around over his head. Wisp aimed and fired too fast to be accurate, nailing him in the hip. He hit the ground screaming while his engine-on-a-chain sailed into the air and came down on top of one of the male captives, smashing his leg. The man crumpled in place, holding his shin and howling in agony. Juliana raised her axe and swung for the shrieking marauder's head. Wisp looked aside before it hit.

Daz ran into the fray, spinning and swinging a sword at any marauder who got too close. Alina ambushed another man emerging from a cabin in front of Wisp, thrusting her blades into his back as he tried to charge forward toward the former captives.

Wisp tried to find another target, but the marauders had mingled into the people she'd freed, and everyone swarmed around too much to get a clear shot at the monsters without hitting a person. A deep bellow came from inside the large cabin, vibrating the corrugated metal beneath her. Alina spun to face her with a worried expression that fell a hair shy of fear.

"Oh, that's not good," said Alina, backing away.

At the repetitious clanking of metal, Wisp grasped the edge of the roof and pulled herself forward a few inches so she could peek down. She stared at the top of a man's helmet: round, black, and shiny, with a picture of a bird above the words 'Harley Davidson.' Metal plates covered his chest, back, arms, and legs, all of different colors, turning him into a walking, clanging, scrap heap. The word 'stop' in a red patch hung at the center of his back, and his right forearm read 'one way.' He carried a metal pipe taller than Alina with two enormous axe blades on one end. A slow, steady noise came from him, part laugh, part growl.

In one of her books with magic and dragons, a 'barbarian' carried a great axe infused with magic that, according to the bard, could cut a mountain in half. She hadn't pictured that weapon anywhere as big as this monster's axe, and shivered in fear of how much power it might have.

He could beat everyone in one big swing!

Alina pointed her swords at him. "The thunder magic is going to ki… uhh, send you to the Other Place."

The man growled deeper, stomping toward her.

"The thunder magic is going to take you!" yelled Alina.

She wants me to shoot him. Wisp locked eyes with her and nodded.

"Come on, big boy," shouted Alina, backing up and clanking her blades together.

The marauder chief leaned into his stride, walking faster.

Wisp waited for him to get far enough away from the cabin that she could aim the long rifle properly at him, and lined up his helmet in the iron sights. Alina, noting the angle, stepped to the side and waved 'goodbye' to the man. As soon as the woman moved out of the bullet's path, Wisp squeezed the trigger.

Bang!

The recoil pushed her a few inches back.

Her bullet punched through the helmet, shattering the outer shell and leaving a fist-sized white spot of exposed foam with a small black dot in the middle. The huge guy's roar cut off to silence, and he crashed face down into the street. Alina dove away from the giant axe, which rang like a bell when it bounced on the blacktop. After a quick nod to Wisp, she ran after another marauder who'd come out of a hut three rows closer to the courtyard, and attacked one of the male captives with a wooden bat.

Wisp again tried to draw a bead on the fray; her gunsights landed on one of the female marauders who'd been at the worktable before, right as she rammed her knife into Olim's gut. Wisp clicked the trigger, putting a slug into the woman's chest. The marauder fell in a heap, Olim landing on top of her. Neither one of them tried to get back up.

The roof wobbled under her. She twisted to look back, surprising a skinny male marauder covered head to toe in brown leather armor. The man had climbed up onto the roof behind her, and managed to sneak almost close enough to grab her. When they made eye contact, he pulled a large hatchet from a back sheath, his intention seeming to change from kidnap to kill.

Wisp flung herself to the side, abandoning the rifle and rolling onto her back as the axe blade sparked on the metal where her head had been a half-second before. The man lunged, grabbing for her throat with his left hand. She raised both legs. Her feet hit his chest the same instant his hand closed around the front of her neck. Grunting, she tried to shove him away with her legs while clutching his wrist in both hands. Fingernails dug at her skin; warm sandy metal scuffed at her back. He held her down by the throat, raising the axe high over his head, but couldn't quite line up his aim while she kept shoving her feet into his shoulders, trying to push him away.

Wild eyes behind a leather armor mask widened. "It's dyin' time, slave! Go on and beg, eh? Maybe I change my mind again."

"Ngh!" gurgled Wisp, twisting her head side to side in a futile effort to get away from the axe.

An instant before he brought the blade down into her forehead, she stomped him in the face. The kick faltered his balance, making him flail his arms to avoid tumbling backward down the angled roof. She gave up trying to pull his grip away from her throat and grabbed the pistol from her hip, raising it in two hands.

"Die!" shouted the marauder, raising his axe for a killing stroke.

The barrel of her pistol hovered inches away from his chest between her feet. She fired three times as fast as she could click the trigger.

His arm fell limp; the axe banged against the roof and slid off to the rear of the cabin. All his weight crumpled down on her feet. A long, labored moan came out of his mouth as the focus in his eyes faded.

Behind her, the continuous shouting and clanging of weapons continued.

She shoved her legs out, tossing the marauder away. He flopped, bounced, and slid off the end of the cabin out of sight.

Wisp lay still on her back for a moment, heart racing, breath rushing in and out. Dad couldn't protect her from monsters anymore. He couldn't make bullets anymore either. The ammo she carried could very well be the last ammo in the world. A gun let a twig of a girl like her send monsters to the Other Place no matter how big they were. Without them, what could she possibly do? That boy at the lake got one with a knife, but he fought with speed and fury like nothing Dad had ever showed her. *Maybe* she could take on a monster with a knife, but the idea of it frightened her. And the boy had been visibly bigger in the shoulders and chest, so he had to be stronger than her.

She rolled onto her belly and peered over the roof edge at the battle. People and monsters tangled together to the point she didn't want to fire into the crowd. Besides, the bullets she had left, she needed to save for her own defense, not use up on monsters other people could send to the Other Place.

Always try to run, said Dad in her mind.

Wisp put the pistol back in the holster and took hold of the rifle. She watched the fight over the iron sights, deciding that she would only use up bullets if a monster was about to kill someone, only if her *not* doing so meant a person would die. Alina and Daz fought the hardest, or perhaps the most skilled, the two of them taking out more monsters than all the other former captives combined. A few minutes later, the shouting and clanging of weapons wound down to a stop, without Wisp having fired another shot.

Dead marauders lay strewn about the intersection. Some had arrows sticking out of them, most bled from sword or axe wounds. A few had died to gunshots, but she didn't bother trying to figure out how many she'd sent to the Other Place. When it became clear the battle had ended, Wisp rolled around to sit up, and scooted down the roof to the low end. The monster who'd tried to kill her lay flat on his back in the narrow section of street between the cabin and the compound wall.

She ignored him, climbing down the pile of junk on the side. Head bowed, she crept out toward the remaining people, careful to avoid stepping in any blood.

Eight of the fourteen captives remained alive. Olim had perished, and Tavin lay wounded but alive. Five men had paid for the freedom of the others with their lives. Alina limped over, an arrow sticking out of her left thigh, but she smiled. Juliana bled from her mouth and nose, but kept cheering and whooping.

"Nice work, kid." Alina ruffled Wisp's hair. "Where'd you get hardware like that?"

She slung her rifle over her shoulder, clinging to it defensively. "Dad. Here, sit. I have yarrow powder."

Alina cringed. "Damn shame, that. Sorry, kid. These rubes have no idea what kind of, umm… magic you've got. So, don't tell 'em. Your secret's safe with me. I prefer blades. Quiet and they don't run out of ammo." The woman took a seat on the concrete steps and grabbed the broken arrow shaft.

Wisp stared blankly at her.

"You okay? Never killed a man before?"

"I didn't kill any men. I sent monsters to the Other Place. They were bad." She glanced at the door. "I am sad because Dad has gone to the Other Place."

"Yeah. You got somewhere to go, kid?" asked Alina.

She thought of Zen and his daughter, Lijuan. "Yes. But, I need to bring Dad to the shrine first. Mother wants me to."

"All right then. If you got a place to get to, good luck. Do me a favor first—let me have a bit of that yarrow?"

Wisp pulled her backpack off, knelt, and fished out the jar of yarrow powder. It stung almost as bad as the wasp she once stepped on, but it made bleeding stop. Alina clenched her jaw and pulled the arrow out; fortunately, the poorly sharpened head hadn't gone too deep. A hint of pain flickered across the woman's otherwise stoic expression. She held up a wad of cloth to use as a bandage. When Alina nodded, Wisp popped the jar open and sprinkled some of the dust into the wound.

The woman grunted and gasped, clamped her hands over the bandage, and pressed down. "Damn, that hurts."

"Means it's working," said Wisp in a lifeless tone, quoting Dad.

Falo walked by, waving at her. "One sec, kid. Be right with ya."

Alina kept pressing on the bandage, managing a little smile. "You're still small. If you get into a scrap, take advantage of that. Being quiet is your best chance. That's how I lived this long."

"Always run if you can," said Wisp, her voice faint. "Dad told me that."

"Good plan." Alina clapped her on the back, forced herself upright, and limped over to the row of buggies.

Falo strolled by again, having put on most of a marauder's leather armor, and went up the steps into the building. Daz led a raid on the marauders' food stores, which turned into a feast among the remaining people. Noma and Kit hurried down the steps a minute or so after Falo went inside. Wisp turned away from the sight of the boy holding his mother's hand. She sulked, staring at the ground and teasing a pebble around with her big toe. Not only had she never known the touch of a mother's warm embrace, or heard the brightness in her voice, she had lost Dad.

All those days spent journeying at Mother's behest, and for what?

Had she stayed home, nothing would've changed. Dad would still be in the Other Place, but perhaps she would be safer. At least there, she had the Haven, and could find food and water fairly easily. Though, she had never hunted before and they always weathered the winter months subsisting on boar, deer, or fish—sometimes even bear. Wisp sank into a squat, feeling afraid and exposed without bars around her. Bars that Dad had made with all his love to keep her protected.

These people told her havens were cages, and only monsters put people in cages. *Stupid liars! They don't know about Tree Walkers. They're gonna be sorry.* She peered through a curtain of her hair at Kit, sitting beside his mother while devouring soup. He looked so innocent, so small... so happy. Wisp's eyes narrowed. *His mother won't put him in a haven... she'll be sad when they take him.*

"Okay, kid. Now what?" asked Falo.

She looked up and to her left. The man stood behind her with Dad over his shoulder, as promised.

"We bring him to Mother." Wisp got to her feet.

"Let's eat first. And it's dark. We should wait until morning. It's pretty safe inside this compound now that all the marauders are dead."

"All right." Wisp grasped Dad's dangling arm and hugged it tight, hating that the skin against her cheek had no warmth.

War
~29~

Instead of Tree Walkers, a new monster plagued Wisp's dreams. The man who'd grabbed her by the throat, holding her down the same way Dad had butchered small boars, appeared over and over, leaping out of the trees and chasing her. She tried to run for the Haven, but he grabbed her by the leg before she could crawl inside. The instant he dragged her back from her safe place, she snapped awake.

Falo shook her left leg side to side, having gripped her around the ankle like the monster in the dream. "Hey, kid. You ready?"

The terrifying fog of a nightmare gave way to her present situation: lying on a dingy mattress inside one of the metal cabins. Falo let go and stood back up, waving her to follow him before leaving the room.

She wiped at her eyes, yawned, and wobbled upright. After collecting her things, she stumbled outside. Daz and two other men to the left let the bad water out all over the wall of a crumbling concrete building. Wisp walked to the end of their line and squatted, tugging her skirt out of the way.

All three men made startled noises and turned their backs to her before hurrying off without looking.

I guess they're afraid of my 'black magic.'

She almost passed out again, but managed to stay awake long enough to finish. Yawning, she raised a hand to shield her eyes from the sun and peered around the compound. Falo waited for her over by one of the buggies. The former captives swarmed the area, gathering all the useful supplies they could get their hands on and packing them on the other buggies. Alina and Juliana struggled to carry a rectangular box out of the fortress-like building next to the gate. Despite it not being that large, it appeared to weigh quite a bit.

Wisp tilted her head.

"Coins," said Falo. "Marauders had a stockpile. We're gonna divvy it up."

Still squinting from the glare, she padded across the hot blacktop. "Where is Dad?"

Falo gestured at the leather tent compartment. "In the back, ready to go. This is going to be a whole lot faster than walking with a dead guy on my shoulder."

She looked the buggy over from nose to end. "You can make this machine work?"

"Yeah. Ain't hard." Falo collected some gallon jugs of water, and a few red plastic ones, which he tied to hooks on the triangular frame around the back compartment. "You can either stand on the backplate"—he pointed at a metal shelf beneath the leather flaps—"sit in my lap, perch behind the seat"—he pointed to a flat part of metal between the recessed driver's seat and the triangular frame. "Or, I dunno…" He shrugged. "I could tie you to the frame so you don't fall off."

Noma approached (with Kit by her side) and handed Falo a coffee can that rattled. She offered one to Wisp next.

"Oof. This is heavy." Wisp peered down at a bunch of round, metal discs. Some had a brownish or greenish tint while others appeared silver. "Money?"

"Yes." Noma hugged her. "We're splitting up all the coins the marauders had."

The other captives continued packing stuff in buggies.

"Thank you." Wisp hefted the can. Putting it in the backpack seemed a bad idea. This can weighed almost as much as the rifle.

While Noma and Falo discussed their plans to go off to different settlements, Wisp wandered around the side and peered into the opening containing the seat. It didn't look big enough for two people, even if one was her size. Riding on top of the buggy behind the driver's chamber would probably be the most comfortable idea, since it didn't require standing the whole time. She headed around back and peeked in to make sure Dad was, in fact, where the man claimed. He'd been stuffed into the compartment standing, facing away, his body frozen in a slightly-sitting-upright position as he'd been in the cell. She poked his leg and found it quite rigid.

Wisp frowned at the can. No sense lugging it around as they had the buggy. Carrying the can down the hill from where the marauders took Dad wouldn't be too bad. She stashed it by his boot, and tied a bit of cloth over the top to keep the little metal bits from bouncing away.

"We're going home, Dad." She couldn't see his face past his thick black hair, which had a lot more new white strands than she remembered.

"You okay, kid?" asked Falo.

"No. I'm not okay, but I can't do anything about what happened." She trudged around to the side.

Falo stashed his coin can in the back, tucked the flaps closed, and hopped into the driver's seat while she climbed up to sit behind it on the metal plates. The hollow had some space on either side of the chair, so she stuck her legs in and braced her feet against the sides. She scooted back a little and reclined against the triangular compartment, clutching the rifle across her lap.

The other captives came over to thank her again and wish her good luck. Alina made a shooting gesture with her finger, and winked.

Kit leapt up onto the buggy, his bony knees thumping on the thin metal. The scrap of a child flew into a hug. "Thank you for letting me an' Mama out!"

It took all of Wisp's self-control not to fling the boy off. He didn't mean to make fun of her for not having a living mother, but seeing him so happy with Noma filled her with jealousy. Repeating *not his fault* over and over in her head, she returned a limp hug and managed a weak excuse of a smile.

"I'm so sorry about your father," said Noma.

Wisp bowed her head. "Thanks."

"Ready?" asked Falo.

She looked away from the boy and his mother, narrowing her eyes at the gate. "Yes."

He pushed the little black button. The engine roared to life, vibrating the metal under her butt. She grimaced at the sensation, having second thoughts about sitting there. Before she could say a word of protest, he stepped on the right pedal and the buggy lurched forward. She grabbed the lip of the driver's compartment between her knees, holding on tight as the buggy whirled around in a turn and headed for the now-open giant doors.

Falo followed the road she'd walked into the ruin on, passing the buggy she disabled the day before. The dead marauder remained where she'd left him, though someone had taken most of his armor.

Crumbling buildings zipped by on both sides, a good deal faster than she could run. Each time Falo swerved around a hunk of debris, she lurched to the side, too petrified of being thrown to shriek. She briefly considered telling him to tie her to the frame so she couldn't fall off, but he probably meant that as a joke since it would be a silly thing to do, especially if monsters attacked.

Not long after they left the ruined city behind and entered scrubland, the metal beneath her backside heated up like a cooking pot. Despite her heavy leather skirt, it soon became intolerable. If she'd still had her dress, the metal probably would've burned her.

"Stop!" yelled Wisp. "My butt is cooking!"

He let his foot off the pedal, and the engine dropped from loud buzzing to a soft rumble. "What?"

"My butt is cooking!" shouted Wisp.

Falo peered back over his shoulder. "Oh. You're sitting right above the motor."

"What?"

He slowed to a gradual stop. "There's enough room in here. Climb around and sit with me."

Wisp jumped up, fanning air across her backside for a moment. "Wow, it's so hot." She glowered at the shiny aluminum panel. "I think I could cook on that."

Falo laughed and scooted back in the seat.

She stepped around him and lowered herself, aiming for the front edge of the seat.

"Oof!" Falo grabbed her backpack after it hit him in the face. "Gotta put this thing in the back or we won't fit."

"All right."

She jumped to the dirt and wriggled out of her pack before trotting around to stuff it in with Dad. Wisp also decided to leave the canteen belt in the storage compartment since it would probably be uncomfortable to wear while sitting so close to Falo. After securing the buckle over the flaps again, she hurried back and climbed up. Falo guided her to sit on the front edge of the seat between his knees. She curled up in a tight ball, rifle in front of her gripped in both hands, stock on the floor between her feet, barrel pointing straight up. He reached around her shoulders to hold the wheel, and though he wasn't Dad, she tolerated the almost-hug.

The walls of the driver's compartment came up to her eye level, making her feel like she sat in a small, but deep, bathtub. She glanced down at the pedals at the front end of the compartment, not far in front of her toes. Falo again put his foot on the right-side one, and pushed it down. The engine's low idle raced up to roar like an enraged cabin-sized bitey bug. She slid backward, pressed into Falo for a few seconds, wind blasting her in the face.

Moving at such a speed, the sheer awe of it, kept her speechless. Riding up front instead of the storage compartment offered an entirely different experience—and fresh air. She prairie-dogged up to gaze around at scrub brush, cacti, and random pieces of broken machines. Falo steered toward the distant haze of the mountains without her prompting.

The awe of driving lessened after a little while, leaving her to sink into a wallow of sadness. Wisp kept her head down, teetering on the edge of tears. She wouldn't cry in front of Falo. *People will try to hurt you*, said Dad in her memory. If she appeared weak, this man might get the idea of sending her to the Other Place and taking all her stuff. Or maybe just taking all her stuff.

After a few hours, he slowed to a stop and pushed the black button, cutting the engine off to silence.

"Pee break, water, and food time."

"Pee?"

"Umm." Falo fidgeted. "You don't know what peeing is?"

She thought it over for a moment. "Maybe I do since you think I should, but I don't know that word."

"Yellow liquid comes out of you?"

"Oh. Yes. Letting out the bad water."

"Right. That. Do that. Then we drink and eat, walk around a little… rest, you know? If we spend too much time sitting in this cramped little space, our legs will hurt."

"Okay."

She climbed up out of the buggy and wandered a few steps away to let out the bad water. While she did that, Falo grabbed one of the red plastic jugs and poured about half of its contents into a pipe sticking out from the buggy's side. She stared down at the bad water soaking into the sand, and said "Pee" a few times to test the word. Maybe she'd call it that, since it took less effort to say 'pee' than 'let out the bad water.'

When she walked back to the buggy, Falo handed her a skinned, roasted rat on a stick and a cup of water from one of the gallon bottles. As she ate, he wandered off to pee. At a shift in the wind, a stink washed over her, making her cough. It reminded her of the unpleasant odor within the Mother Shrine, but much stronger and without the pinesap.

That's the smell of the Other Place. Wanting to move away from the odor seemed rude to Dad, so she forced herself to keep eating.

"Whoa…" Falo coughed. "We better hurry, huh?" He drank from one of the jugs without untying it from the frame, then grabbed another cooked rat from a cloth sack hanging on the side of the buggy. He hopped back in the driver's seat with the rat held in his teeth.

Wisp trudged over and got in again, stuffing herself down in front of him as she had been before.

Once they resumed driving, the stiff breeze chased away the foul odor. She nibbled on rat meat while watching scrubland roll by.

"So what's that thing you keep carrying around?" asked Falo, a while later.

Her hands tightened on the rifle. "It's a seeing machine. If I hold it up and look through it, I can see far away. It's Dad's. I brought it for him because he likes it."

"Aww. Man. That's rough. You know, we probably should bury him."

She jabbed her elbow into Falo's gut. "Dad is not *ngh!*"

"Oof." He wheezed. "What?"

"You bury *ngh*, not people."

"Why are you grunting?"

Wisp scowled. It took a few seconds for her anger to subside enough to remember that other word. "Poop!"

"You have to go?"

She snarled. "No! I mean… you bury poop, not people!"

Falo kept quiet for a moment. "Umm. What do you think happens to people when they die?"

Wisp swiped her fingers across her forehead, pulling hair out of her eyes. "The people who love them make shrines for them."

"Make shrines? What do you mean?"

"Like Mother. She's home, in the shrine." Wisp explained how Mother sat in a chair in the cabin's third room, surrounded by sacred substances in cans and all the flower offerings she'd gathered over the years. "She watches us and protects us."

"Wow, kid. Just wow. You grew up with a dead person in the house? That's umm…" He whistled.

She peered back at him. "What?"

"Oh, forget it." He stared at her, his eyebrows about as high up as they could possibly go. "That's… an unusual custom. I've never heard of it before. The people I know bury their dead."

"Well, that's not what we do." She faced forward again. "Dad does not treat people we love like poop."

They drove in silence for about an hour before the curiosity whirling around in her head grew too insistent to ignore.

"Why would you bury people?" asked Wisp.

"Well… it's what we always do. Dead bodies smell bad. You can also get sick if you stay around them too much. A body out in the open attracts bugs. And, in the ground, they go back to the earth and help plants and stuff grow."

Helping plants sounded nice, but all the other stuff had to be wrong. Mother had been with her as long as she could remember and she never made anyone sick, though there had been some bugs. Those, they couldn't eat since they had been charged with Mother's energy. She decided not to ask this man anything more since he obviously didn't know much.

They drove for the rest of the daylight hours, with the occasional rest stop. For most of the trip, Wisp kept quiet, gazing out at the terrain, bouncing whenever the overly springy buggy hit a bump, and sometimes shuffling her feet back and forth over the sandy aluminum floor.

At one point, she asked if she could try holding the wheel. He decided to show her how the machine worked, and even let her work the pedals. She thought about her books, and characters who drove cars. Images rearranged in her mind from the way she had previously imagined. After seeing the SUV, watching the marauder drive while hiding in the storage area, and now sitting up front holding the wheel, 'driving' turned out to be nothing like what had been in her thoughts from the books. The characters always seemed like they got in a car and vanished, reappearing wherever they wanted to go. After sitting in this seat for hours, she realized that driving took all darn day.

The Forest Beyond the Earth

Once the sun began its journey beyond the mountains up ahead, Falo steered toward a group of four small buildings. They drove off the dirt onto a scrap of old paving, rolling up to the largest, most intact of the structures. A row of three strange boxy machines stood in a line on a concrete island to the left of a big open room with a giant rolling door. Falo drove around in a circle so the back end of the buggy pointed at the opening, then killed the engine.

"Gonna be dark soon. This thing ain't got lights, so we're gonna sleep here."

She climbed up and jumped to the dirt. "Okay."

He got out as well, and pushed the buggy backward into the huge room. She trailed after him, looking around at the old cabins. Except for the cinder block one in front of them, the others had mostly collapsed. A sign on the wall inside the big room displayed, "Oil Change - $30." Another shot-up sign outside read, "Regular, Premium, Super, Diesel" over empty black spaces. A few odd machines occupied a worktable in the back, and a shelf on the right contained three white cans.

While Falo shoved the buggy into the building, she walked over and picked one of the cans up, examining the writing on the outside.

"Oil filter?" asked Wisp. "What's that?"

"Umm. Something that filters oil, I'd guess."

She squinted at him. "What does that even mean?"

He shrugged. "The ancients had things we can't even think of."

"Can we let Dad out of the buggy? It's not comfortable back there."

Falo glanced at her. He seemed to be thinking about something complicated, based on the faces he made. After a while, he nodded. "All right. You sure you don't wanna bury him? It's probably the best way to help him rest."

"I'm sure. Mother wants him home."

"You're going to set him inside your house next to her?"

"Yes." She set the oil filter back on the shelf, having no use for it.

He let out a low whistle, and walked around behind the buggy. "Ugh. Gah."

Wisp hurried over to help. They eased Dad out of the cargo compartment together and dragged him a little ways away, leaving him on the floor. His back still bent upward at a slight angle, as though he slumped against a wall. Dark patches had formed here and there on his skin, and he gave off a fairly pungent stink.

"It's hot, but at least it's dry here," said Falo.

Wisp knelt beside Dad, fussing at his hair and beard with her fingers, trying to neaten them. "It's all right, Dad. We're going home now. Are you glad those people sent all the marauders to the Other Place? Can you see Mother yet?"

Falo mumbled and walked off. He returned with a water bottle, which he put down beside her before pouring more from the red jug into the buggy. A metal pipe cap squeaked at an irritating pitch when he tightened it back in place. Whistling, he hung the red jug on the triangle frame again and unhooked the sack of food he'd taken from the marauder compound.

"Come on over here, away from that smell." Falo walked off, taking a seat on the floor by the open end of the room.

Wisp lingered by Dad until Falo began eating without her. She begrudgingly stood and padded over the sand-swept concrete, into the breeze blowing by outside. Her hair fluttered around, strands crossing her face, but she kept staring angrily at him.

He tossed her a potato, which she caught as a reflex, then held up another roasted rat.

"This feels strange." She sniffed the potato. "It's soft."

"It's been cooked." Falo waved the rat-on-a-stick at her.

"Oh." Wisp sighed, sat, and bit the potato. The mashed from Zen's tasted better, but she decided she would like this one, too. She reached out and took the rat stick.

"So where do they bury people?"

"In the ground, usually," said Falo.

She blinked. "No. I mean where do people live who they think something so rude is normal?" Dad taught her that whenever she had to make *ngh* in the woods, she should dig a hole, and then cover it afterward. Treating people like that after they'd gone to the Other Place made her sick to think about.

"Heh. You're one odd little kid." Falo chuckled. "I'm from a little village far off to the west, up in the hills where there are trees and life. None of this desert crap."

"I'm from the forest, too. Did your home have a big green wall around it? I think maybe I saw it."

"Nah. If we had a wall, the marauders wouldn't have got us." He gazed down. "They took four of us. I'm the only one still alive. Was stuck in that place for months. Ain't your fault though. Meryl, Rod, and Lew were dead before you showed up."

"Your friends are not dead. They went to the Other Place. Only *monsters* die." She bit a chunk off the rat and chewed.

"Marauders rolled in on us with their buggies, grabbed us." He shook his head. "We didn't have much warning."

"Why do they take people?"

"They forced us to work on their farm. Sometimes they would make two people fight, bet coins on who'd win… sometimes they'd drag the women… never mind. I ain't going to talk to you about that."

She hesitated with her teeth around the potato, pulled back, and asked, "Drag the women?" before biting it.

"They did bad stuff to them."

Wisp hurried to chew the mouthful of potato and swallow. "Like what? Why won't you talk to me about it?"

"Because it's bad stuff and I ain't talkin' to you about it. You're too little."

Grumbling, she made a sour face and turned her gaze out at the sand outside, aglow in the moonlight. Dad had never refused to answer her questions about anything. When she'd asked him why they were alone, he'd told her of the Fire Dragons. When she asked why she had to sleep in the Haven, he'd told her of the Tree Walkers. When she'd asked if she could have a sister, he'd told her of the spirits, and how they'd sometimes collect a person who'd gone to the Other Place and wanted to come back, make them into a baby, and bring them to deserving people. Unfortunately, the spirits had laws, and they could not bring him another baby because Mother had gone away.

A weak smile broke through her gloom. When she got older, maybe the spirits would bring her a baby to take care of… but she'd have to find someone to be the dad, or the spirits would never answer her request.

"Mother sent me to find Dad, but she didn't tell me he'd be in the Other Place."

Falo looked at her for a long while, staring into her eyes. The weight of his gaze made her uncomfortable, but not frightened he would hurt her.

"Why are you making that face at me?" She tossed the rat skeleton aside.

"What makes you think that man is your father?"

Wisp's jaw hung open. *How dumb is this guy?* "He's Dad!"

"Are you sure?"

"Of course! He's been Dad my whole life. Why are you asking such stupid things?"

"Well… he looks like one of the Neva Da tribe. They live quite far away from here, and, according to some of the stories I've heard, have many things—machines—from before the war."

Jeeps. Guns? Magic? She thought about her Haven, and how Dad had gotten the metal rods to stick together so well, like they'd been one solid piece. Then again, the Marauders had done the same with their… cages, but those looked sloppy by comparison. Dad also had given her lots of books, which she hadn't seen even *one* of since leaving home. Perhaps he *had* come from some tribe off in the distance. He'd told her that he and Mother had traveled for a long time before finding the trailer, which he'd built into their cabin.

Falo leaned over and grasped her hand. "Look at yourself. You're white as a ghost and have yellow hair… blue eyes. That man's dark, black hair and brown eyes. If that man's your father, I'm half goat."

She ripped her hand away from him, leapt to her feet, and shouted, "Take that back! You take that back or I'll magic you!" Wisp grabbed her pistol, but didn't pull it out.

"Whoa!" Falo raised both hands. "Okay. Okay. Fine. He's your father."

Wisp glared at him. She'd never been so furious with anyone before, except for the marauder who sent Dad to the Other Place, but she had no idea which one of them had done it. Her knuckles whitened on the pistol grip. How dare he say such mean things!

Falo's eyes widened. "Calm down, kid. I'm sorry. He's your father."

She thought of the Fire Dragons.

Anger will only destroy you, said Dad's voice in her memory.

She let her hand slip off the pistol, arm limp at her side. Fury drained out of her, becoming defeat. "I won't magic you. It's bad to get angry." *I need to apologize.* She walked over to the buggy, where the smell of decay hung heavy. Despite feeling rude to Dad, she held her breath while rummaging her backpack out of the storage compartment, then returned to sit by Falo. "I'm sorry."

"Don't worry about it." He leaned back, uneasy.

"Here." She pulled a Twinkie out and offered it. "You can have this."

He gingerly reached over and grasped the cake. "What is this?"

"It's cake. For eating. It tastes like happiness."

Falo examined the Twinkie for a few seconds before raising its end to his mouth.

"Wait," said Wisp. "You should peel the skin off first. The see-through part, you don't eat."

Crinkling plastic filled the silence as he unwrapped the treat. Both his eyes shot open when he bit off a piece.

"See?" asked Wisp.

"Yeah." He nodded. "This is… wow. I've never had anything like this before. How did you make it?"

"I didn't make it. I found it."

He eyed the half-Twinkie. "This is from… before the war?"

"War?" asked Wisp.

"It's from before the war." He stared at it for a few more seconds, shrugged, and took another bite. "Still good."

"What is war?" She took the pot out of her backpack. "I still have some roaches. They're not going to last much longer. Want one?"

"Nah, you need the food more than I do." Falo smiled, and tossed the last bit of Twinkie in his mouth.

She plucked the legs from one of the roaches and bit the end off, testing the flavor. Still a bit like a greasy version of the bird meat. Not spoiled yet.

"War is what happened to the planet. Used to be lots and lots of people, but they lived in different tribes. And those tribes didn't all like each other. They had powerful weapons the likes of which we can't even imagine. One day, they used them, and—boom—end of the world."

"They weren't weapons." She pointed at the sword hanging from his belt. "That's a weapon. Dad said Fire Dragons burned everything."

"Fire Dragons?"

"Great dragons of glowing orange fire slept in hidden caves. The people made them because they were big and powerful, and the people loved having lots and lots of dragons. Each tribe of ancients kept trying to have more Fire Dragons than other tribes. The people did something bad, and the Fire Dragons got angry. So angry, they flew out of their caves and turned the sky orange." She held her hands up and made 'fire breathing' noises. "From the sky, they spat burning down on everyone, sending almost all the humans to the Other Place. Because the people made the Fire Dragons, they destroyed themselves by getting rid of all the people. That's why it's bad to be angry."

Falo dusted his hands of crumbs. "I think your dad was telling you the same thing, just saying 'fire dragon' instead of missile."

She narrowed her eyes. "What is a missile?"

"I don't know exactly, but my grandfather used to tell stories about them. Sounded like huge arrows, like you'd shoot from a bow. Only these sat in 'silos,' underground… and they flew way up to the stars, and came back down before blowing up and destroying entire cities."

"Sounds silly." Wisp shook her head. "People couldn't have destroyed the whole world. They don't have as powerful magic as *dragons*. Dragons are still kinda like animals, so they don't think. People wouldn't be that stupid to burn everything."

He opened his mouth, closed it, then smiled. "Yeah. You're right. Stupid fire dragons."

She smiled, but something didn't sit right. His smile felt like a lie. Dragons lived in caves, but these 'missiles' also sounded like they sat in caves. Could Dad have learned wrong? Again she thought of the people stuck in havens and wanting to get out, how they told her *cages* keep people from escaping. No… she couldn't accept that Dad had been 'keeping her from escaping.' Why would he? And why did this man think he wasn't really her Dad? Simply because he didn't look like her? How stupid! Falo didn't know her. Didn't know Dad. Didn't know Mother.

Dad loved her. He'd always loved her. He loved her so much he'd get upset if she walked too far away from him. She stared down at her hands, pale, but not quite as pale as she'd been most of her life. Over the past few days, she'd seemed to have gotten some color. But, she couldn't argue that Dad was a lot more brown.

That didn't mean anything. She'd gone from almost snow-white to kind of a dark beige. Apparently, she could change color. Maybe Dad just did a lot of changing.

"You're wrong." Wisp held up her hand. "I'm darker."

"What?" asked Falo, flinching.

"At home, I was lighter than I am now. I got darker. Dad got darker darker darker."

"You've been in the sun a lot. You're from the deep woods, right?"

"Yeah."

"Spend most of your time inside?"

She shrugged. "Yeah."

"Not much sun gets through the trees, and even less inside your house. You've been out here in the scrub a while. Nothing between you and the sun. That's normal." He glanced back at Dad, sighed, and smiled at her again as if he'd caught himself doing something silly. "But maybe he just spent way more time in the sun."

She wiped at her left ankle and shin, clearing away a spritz of blood from the monster that tried to hit her with the axe. This man said mean things. All the people she had helped said mean things. Havens were *good*. Dad made it to protect her. He loved her. They even saw how much he loved her because he fought so hard to get away from the marauders—who had put him in a cage so he couldn't get away.

Tears brimmed at the corners of her eyes. It made no sense at all to suggest that Dad had locked her up so she didn't 'escape.' She couldn't 'escape' her home because she wanted to be there. And the lies calling Fire Dragons missiles, and the horrible burying people like poop! She needed Dad to explain everything to her, but he couldn't talk to her anymore.

She gasped, tears stalled cold. *Will Dad only speak to me if I'm bad?*

Overcome by guilt and confusion, she scrambled over to Dad and sat beside him. Despite being barely able to breathe with the smell, Wisp snuggled up to his arm and rested her head against his shoulder. His skin squished a little strangely, and his stomach had gotten bigger.

"Aww, man, kid. What are you doing?" Falo cringed, covering his mouth. "Get away from there. You're gonna make yourself sick."

"I need Dad!" she yelled, her voice teary.

Falo let out a low whistle. "Okay then. You do your hugging the dead guy thing. I'm gonna sleep over here."

Not that he could see in the dark, she stuck her tongue out at him and whispered, "Don't listen to him. He's only saying stuff to trick me."

Dad didn't smell like Dad anymore. Truth be told, the stink alone brought tears.

Wisp closed her eyes and snuggled tighter to the rigid arm, pretending that he only fell asleep and hadn't really gone to the Other Place. She had her protector back, and soon, she would finally be home again.

Abandoned
~30~

Nausea dragged Wisp out of sleep.

Her eyes opened to dusty, grey painted concrete. She'd slumped over sideways with her back to Dad, curled up with one arm under her head for a pillow. Half a breath triggered a convulsion in her gut. She scrambled up onto all fours, gagged, and threw up a puddle of sickly yellow liquid. Not until she'd vomited three times did her brain process the awful foulness in the wretched, hot air.

Still choking and retching, she crawled forward, her body demanding to breathe. She didn't stop going until her fingers dug into sand. There, she stayed for a few minutes, taking deep breaths until the storm in her gut fell back from imminent eruption to an angry bees' nest.

She wiped a tendril of yellow drool from her lip and sat back on her heels, listening to the distant howl of the wind. Dust clouds blew around in whorls, rising and falling here and there out across the landscape.

"Sorry," she muttered. "You were right... I got sick."

A moment later, when Falo didn't say anything, she looked back.

He—and the buggy—were gone.

Two one-gallon bottles of water remained by her backpack and rifle. She turned her head, staring at the ground along the path the buggy would've rolled out on, at tire marks in the dirt. He must've pushed it out so the engine noise didn't wake her up. He left her here—and kept her can of coins.

He lied.

He never intended to help her carry Dad all the way home.

"You... you... bad person!" Wisp pounded both fists into the dirt. "I'm gonna shoot him!"

She jumped up and stormed around in random path, kicking sprays of sand into the air while fuming. "I'm gonna shoot him in his stupid face. He lied to me! He lied to Dad! Ooh! Mother is gonna get him!"

Out came the pistol.

She aimed at the desert. "I'm not even going to talk first." Wisp let her arm drop at her side and yelled, "He left me here!"

Her voice echoed twice over the desert.

"How could he just leave me here alone? I told him I wasn't gonna shoot him." She jammed the gun back in the holster. "Dragons... don't be angry."

She closed her eyes and took deep breath after deep breath, trying to let furious thoughts go away. Shooting Falo wouldn't help her. She'd only waste a bullet she might need to protect herself from a threat. Clenched fists relaxed to open hands. She walked back and forth, thinking about how stupid the Fire Dragons had been for lashing out with their anger.

Dad wouldn't want me to destroy myself.

Wisp looked over at him. His stomach appeared even larger, and more of his skin had purpled. Overnight, an army of flies had come out of nowhere, settling on him. A few even checked out what she threw up.

She cringed away. "I have to bring him home."

After a minute (or six) to build up the determination, she held her breath and walked over to Dad. His skin squished under her fingers as she grabbed his wrist in both hands and tried to pull him up.

No matter how hard she struggled, she couldn't lift him off the floor. She adjusted her stance and tried again, but his skin began to slide off like a glove. She shrieked and spun away, refusing to look at that. Shivering with disgust, she fast-walked back out into fresh air, near to puking again.

Once the second wave of nausea faded, hopelessness set in. She'd been a complete and total failure. She couldn't find Dad fast enough to save his life, and she couldn't even bring him home to the shrine.

She crossed her legs and hung her head in both hands, elbows against her knees. Sniffles grew to sobs, and she wept all over again as though she'd found him lifeless for the first time all over again.

"Dad, please tell me what to do?" She sniffled and sobbed harder. "I don't know what to do without you. Please?"

Dad didn't say anything.

"*Pleeeease!*" she wailed. "Dad, I need you!"

He didn't reply.

Eventually, she quieted to fits of erratic breathing and sniffles. Amid the grief swimming around in her head, the thought emerged that Dad hadn't been in the Other Place long enough to figure out how to help people still here in the people world.

"Mother? What should I do?"

She listened to the wind.

"I need help," said Wisp. "Where should—?"

Wisp ran to the backpack and pulled out the Mother Twig.

She let it dangle, but it kept pointing straight out in front of her as she had been holding it. Wisp rotated her body left a half turn, but the stick turned with her, still pointing straight out in front. *No! It can't be broken.* She started to gear up for an explosion of tears, but a loud gust of wind off in the hills gave her an idea. *Maybe this old building is in the way? Or maybe I'm too close to Dad? The stick's trying to listen to him and he can't move it.*

"Coming, Mother!" She ran outside. "Where should I go?"

Her hair fluttered in the constant breeze, and the twig drifted around in a continuous circle. She frowned at it. "It's only blowing in the wind."

For a fleeting instant, she wondered if the twig had ever really worked, or if it had always been the wind or random chance. *No! It led me right to Dad!* She clenched her eyes shut to hold back tears. *Mother's been watching me for my whole life!* Kit's joyful cry when he first got to hold his mother after she'd let them out of their havens replayed in her mind.

She hated him for having a living mother.

An upwelling of rage made her tremble.

No… She took a deep breath.

She hated not having a living mother, not some innocent boy who still had his.

It's not his fault.

The twig kept spinning, the same twig that had brought her to Dad refused to work. But had it? She'd stumbled across that buggy completely by chance. If a marauder hadn't gone to the well at that moment, she'd never have found Dad. *She* hadn't found him—the marauder drove her there. If he had taken ten minutes longer to arrive at the well, she would have given up and walked back to Zen's.

Had the Mother Twig been a lie? A lie she told herself?

She frowned at the stick.

Either Mother had abandoned her too, or she'd never been there to begin with.

Wisp collapsed to her knees and cried into her hands. Both of those options stank. Even having a mother watching over her from the Other Side beat having *nothing*. People didn't die, did they? Zen tried to tell her *dead* people don't watch over anyone. She wouldn't believe it.

No. Mother is real.

She wiped her tears on the back of her arm. "She loved Dad so much she had the strength to reach out from the Other Place and guide me to him. She made a wish, and it's over. I found him. Now, I'm too far away for her to talk to."

While she had no way to bring Dad home on her own, she *could* ask for help. Wisp got up and walked to the door, looking out over the scrubland. The tiny bushes didn't appear edible, but perhaps the giant plants with spikes on them would be. Dad's book had pictures that came close to the tall, green stalks.

"Prickly pear cactus," said Wisp. "Yes, you can eat it."

She squinted off to the left, back east. Nothingness covered the world as far as she could see. Zen's place could be anywhere out there. Without Mother guiding her, she'd go in circles and wind up in the Other Place when the water ran out. To her right, the forest appeared much closer. She wouldn't run out of water there, though even with the two big bottles Falo left her, it would be close. Of course, the forest and the mountains it grew on, were impossible to miss. She simply could not get lost going that way. If not her cabin, she would *definitely* be able to find the forest where she knew how to survive.

Once she reached the forest, Mother should be able to guide her home.

"I'll go home and ask Mother what to do. She'll want to talk to me even if I'm not bad, because she needs to tell me how to help Dad. And making a twig spin won't do that."

She turned on her heel and marched over to Dad. The flies all over him burst into a cloud, but settled back in seconds. "I have to go talk to Mother to find out what to do. I know you understand that I'm not strong enough to carry you. I'm sorry that man lied to us. I was foolish for trusting him." She fidgeted, almost-but-not-quite thinking she'd lied to Dad. "Maybe… maybe he would've helped us but I scared him, so he ran away. I shouldn't have threatened to shoot him. I'll find a way to bring you back to Mother, so you can be with her."

Wisp backed up a few steps so she could breathe easy for a moment, then hurried over to kneel beside him and kissed him on the forehead. "I love you, Dad. Thank you for everything you have taught me, and for protecting me."

A few tears fell on him before she forced herself up and gathered her things. With the rifle slung over her shoulder, pack on her back, and a gallon bottle of water in each hand, Wisp walked out into the scrub desert, heading west.

Food could wait.

She had absolutely no appetite.

BUggy
~31~

To spare her feet the scorch of sunbaked blacktop, Wisp kept to the sand along the edge of the road. For hours, she walked westward with the sun at her back, heading toward the looming shadow of the great forest. Eyes downcast, she spared little thought to where she went, using only the haze of pavement gliding along the edge of her vision to steer.

Every so often, a bush, rock, or car part broke the sameness of the ground, forcing her to go around or step over. While she hoped Mother would be able to give her an answer once she returned home, guilt at leaving Dad behind weighed heavy on her heart. He had always told her how dangerous anger could be, but she'd lost control. Falo had said something mean about Dad, mere words, but she screamed and threatened to shoot him. Maybe if she'd stayed calm, she wouldn't have had to abandon Dad.

Though, she hadn't trusted that man much. Something about his false smile made her suspect he would've ditched her anyway, ever since his reaction to her not wanting to bury him. Dad *did* smell far worse than the Mother Shrine. Even Wisp couldn't help the urge to keep back and avoid the stink. Falo probably didn't want to touch Dad again. Why would a man she'd only known for a few hours put up with that smell once she'd already done what he wanted? She'd let them all out of their havens, so they didn't need her anymore.

"Cages," said Wisp, while punting a dirty plastic bottle that happened to be close.

It hit the pavement, bounced, and rolled to a halt, spraying sand onto the road. She stopped walking and looked around at the desert, enjoying a momentary breeze. At her best guess, midday had passed less than an hour ago, yet only now had any trace of feeling hungry started.

When she happened upon a giant, rectangular box beside the road, she took advantage of the shade and sat cross-legged near its wheels, drinking warm plastic-flavored water from one of the gallon bottles and feasting on three Twinkies plus her last two roasted cockroaches. This wheeled box hadn't flipped. A huge car with an open, flat back end had run off the road into a ditch on the left side. A skeletal arm dangled from the driver's side window above the words 'Swift Trucking.'

Wisp stared at the bones, wondering how long ago the person had gone to the Other Place. It had to have been before Mother, since her fingers still looked more or less like fingers, only dark grey and dry. She opened and closed her hands, picturing the bones inside. At the thought Dad would never again hold her hand while walking her to the outhouse (or any other time), she let her arms drop into her lap and sighed.

"I can't stay out here long. There's nowhere to hide from monsters." In the forest, she knew how to stay out of sight from anything bad—except Tree Walkers, but if she went home, she'd have the Haven. She stretched her legs out straight, rolling her feet around to chase away the soreness. "But I can rest a little."

Eventually, she resumed walking. Hope that Mother would help, plus the welcome idea of being home again in a place she wouldn't roast alive or run out of water, elevated her mood. While she remained far from smiling, she no longer stared at the ground.

Hours later, with the sun creeping behind the distant mountains, she crested the top of a long, shallow hill. Off to the right lay the crushed remains of an ancients' settlement, little more than squarish outlines of rubble, and one stalwart stop sign. Closer to the road, a tiny cabin near the paving somehow managed to remain upright. The minuscule dwelling had a brown metal frame with clear panels, but the wall nearest the road had gone missing. On the narrower wall, a fading picture of a woman's face half hid behind her hand, displaying inch-long fingernails in a bright shade of purple.

Wisp walked up to the odd cabin, stopping in front of the picture. She stared at the woman, unable to imagine what could possibly turn someone's nails that color. A picture of a bottle occupied the lower right corner of the image, labeled 'Revlon.' Dad sometimes used a brush to take a liquid from a can and spread it on the outside walls of their cabin, and this made her think of someone doing the same to their fingernails. Why people had made such a thing, or put a picture of it on the side of a tiny cabin baffled her.

"The ancients were weird."

She stepped onto the road to check inside the structure, and found a bench seat made from the same brown metal. It appeared to be less a dwelling and more a covered place to sit, but it offered at least *some* protection from the wind, and an elevated platform upon which she could sleep to avoid bugs. Despite having some daylight left, she decided to stop for the night so as not to wind up stranded out in the open once it got dark.

Not far from the roadside shack, she found a cluster of prickly pear cactus. Though the orange blobs were (according to Dad's book) edible, they had nasty hairy stickers all over them. She used the butt of her rifle to break a few of the more reddish ones off and stabbed them with her knife to carry them back to her sleeping spot one at a time. After shaving the spines and cutting the pods in half, she munched on the fruit, annoyed at having to constantly spit out dozens of seeds. The pods tasted pretty good, but took so long to eat that it had gotten dark before she finished.

Wisp curled up under her blanket on the bench, using the backpack as a pillow, and closed her eyes.

Next morning, Wisp's first attempt to hunt failed in a grandiose way. Upon spotting another pincer-bug with a sting tail, she'd shot it with her rifle, but couldn't find anything more than a splat on the sand. The insect appeared to have simply exploded. With that potential meal wasted, she settled for a tedious breakfast of more prickly pear fruit, then continued following the road toward the forest.

The sky remained cloudless, though a stiff, constant breeze blew in off the mountains. Her walk fell to a trudge by midday, both water bottles dangling on fingers tired of carrying them. Growls from her stomach went unheeded as she had run out of food and the land offered nothing even remotely tempting.

The bottle in her left hand kept pulling her over sideways, so she stopped to rest and transfer water from the full bottle into the one she'd been drinking out of until they both contained the same amount, each a little more than halfway full. Her dry throat scratched, but she wanted to be careful with water. Those bottles had to last until she reached the woods.

"I'm getting closer, Dad. I should be back in the forest in two days… if I can find food. What should I look for out here?"

A faint voice replied, "Anything you can eat."

"Dad?!" Wisp perked up and looked around at the heat blur. No one, not Dad, not marauder, not total stranger had appeared. "Is that you?"

She listened to the wind for a few minutes. When no more voices spoke in her head, she worried she'd imagined hearing someone that didn't exist and decided to chug water until she couldn't make herself swallow another mouthful. Dad once mentioned how people who spend too much time alone, especially if they aren't eating or drinking enough, could start 'hearing voices.'

After recapping the bottle, she continued walking.

"I hope you'll help me find the cabin, Mother."

Wisp stared down at her feet eating up the terrain. No matter how much she walked, the mountains didn't seem to be getting much closer.

"Am I going the right way, Dad?"

Minutes later, she sighed at the lack of reply.

"I'm trying. I'm sorry for making that man angry. I hope you're not upset with me for leaving you there, but I'm not strong enough to carry you… and I didn't want to pull your hand off."

An odd rattling noise like someone shaking a bag of small rocks came from the ditch on the opposite side of the road. She glanced that way, but nothing in plain sight seemed responsible for it.

"I'm going home to ask Mother what to do. She's not moving the twig anymore. I think she made herself tired leading me to you."

Sensing something dangerous about the rattle, she kept her eyes on the ground. The noise repeated a few times, but whatever made it didn't follow her. She decided against investigating, and walked a little faster to get away.

Wisp chatted on and off with Mother for a while, alternating between telling her about the desert and begging for help.

A faint buzz arose in the distance behind her.

Wisp squatted, both gallon bottles hitting the ground at the same time, and spun around. Far off behind her, a long plume of smoky dust billowed across the desert, the narrow tip heading her way. She let go of the bottles and swung her rifle off her shoulder, bringing it up to peer through the scope.

Her crosshairs homed in on a buggy driving along the road. For a second, she started to cheer with relief that Falo had changed his mind, but the man driving it wore a black leather jacket and a ball-shaped, blue helmet with a clear visor. The man who ditched her and Dad in the middle of nowhere had a shredded T-shirt and jeans, although he did put on a marauder's armored vest. However, this man's shoulders appeared much wider.

That's not Falo!

Heeding Dad's advice, she decided to save the bullet since the man didn't present an immediate threat to her life. Besides, she'd never tried to hit a target so far away before. After throwing the rifle over her shoulder, she grabbed the bottles and ran. Water sloshed; the pan and pot in her backpack rattled, and the rifle kept clonking against a canteen. She knew she couldn't outrun a buggy, but he *had* been far away. If only she could find somewhere to hide…

Open desert lay in all directions, but the nearest potential hiding spot (a dead car crashed into some cactuses) sat well off to the left over so much open ground the buggy driver would easily see her before she could disappear.

Engine roar grew alarmingly loud behind her.

She slowed to a jog, preparing herself for the likelihood that she would wind up sending yet another monster to the Other Place, even if she didn't want to use up a bullet. Before she could drop the bottles and pull a weapon, a shadow running over the dirt up ahead caught her eye. She kept going forward, skidding to a stop at the edge of a shallow creek that cut sideways across the road's path. Only an inch or two of muddy water trickled along the bottom, but went into a corrugated steel tunnel that passed under the street.

She jumped down into the trench, landing ankle-deep in mud, and duck-walked into the pipe. Up above, the screaming engine fell to a lazy idle for a few seconds before cutting off to silence. Metal and springs creaked. Boots clomped on paving, drawing close.

Poop!

Wisp crawled deeper into the pipe, trying to get far enough in that the man couldn't reach her. She peered between her legs at the opening behind her while crawling as fast as she could go. A male grunt preceded a heavy *thump* as two booted legs fell into view, sending up a splash of muddy water.

The helmeted face of a marauder filled the opening five feet away. "Hey, there. Why you runnin'?"

She huddled in the pipe, peering back at him. The rifle over her shoulder couldn't turn around in the narrow space, and between it and the backpack, she could barely shift her position. If she wanted to shoot him, she'd have to use the pistol. Ahead, another opening led back outside…

And that gave her an idea.

Wisp faked a whimper. "Go away."

"I can't do that, girl. Leave you all alone out here. Come on. You can trust me."

She couldn't see his eyes behind dark sun goggles, but she didn't trust his smile. This man gave off much less creepiness than the marauder with the keys, but Falo had been honest looking, too. She grunted and wobbled, pretending to be stuck.

"How'd you end up out here?" The man squatted by the opening. "You gonna make me crawl on in there after ya, aren't 'cha?"

Again, she pressed herself against the side of the pipe so it appeared she tried to flee deeper into the tunnel, but couldn't.

The man leaned his head in and crawled closer.

As soon as he crawled waist-deep into the pipe, Wisp lifted her head to face forward and scrambled toward the opposite end of the tunnel. The two one-gallon bottles slowed her down, but she didn't want to give up precious water out here. Still, in seconds, it became clear she couldn't get away from him while lugging so much stuff. Gambling on her idea, she abandoned the jugs to crawl faster.

"Hey, git back here," yelled the man.

She scrambled on all fours to the end of the pipe, leapt to her feet outside, and hurled herself at the dry, crumbling wall, grabbing clusters of dead roots. Clods of dirt broke away from the side of the culvert as she climbed. Full panic launched her into a sprint for the buggy as soon as she got out of the ditch.

"Hey, wait!" yelled the man, his voice coming out of the pipe opening.

She pulled the rifle off her shoulder while dashing across the dirt to the road. Eager to spare her feet from the scorching blacktop, she vaulted into the driver's chamber and shoved the rifle down beside her. Her hand slapped the starter button before her butt hit the seat.

When the buggy engine roared to life, the man started screaming a whole mess of strange words she'd never heard before. She mashed her foot down on the gas pedal the same instant his helmet rose into view from the ditch. Whatever he yelled, she couldn't make out over the engine's ear piercing shrill. Acceleration crushed her into the seatback.

The buggy shot forward with such force that the two front wheels left the ground. She let out a shriek of fright, which faded to a breathless wheeze when the buggy's backward tilt came to a hard stop and her butt left the seat for two seconds. If not for her death grip on the steering wheel, she'd have been flung backward out of the chair. Metal scraped the road behind her for a few seconds until the engine fell to idle, her foot no longer pushing the pedal. The front end crashed down, banging her face first into the steering wheel. Seeing stars, she swooned around until the distant yelling of the man snapped her back to reality.

Wisp looked down the length of her leg at the pedal under her toes. *Not all the way down!*

Pressing the pedal halfway to the floor kicked the buggy into motion, and kept the front wheels in contact with the ground. She sent a quick look back at the man fading into the distance, and cheered, thrusting both fists in the air.

"Hah! You aren't gonna catch me!"

Wisp laughed at outmaneuvering him with the tunnel. Though she'd lost quite a bit of water in the process, she hoped having a buggy would more than make up for it by getting her back to the forest faster. She also felt a little less bad about stranding him there. Marauder or not, shooting him would've been kinder than leaving him with nothing to drink.

She couldn't see much over the side of the pit, but decided to keep her head down in case the man had a bow. No cactuses or objects tall enough to be dangerous appeared to be anywhere in front of her, so she held the wheel as straight as possible in an attempt to follow the road. Within seconds, the buggy went off paving onto dirt, bouncing her up and down. She cranked the wheel to the right, but the hard maneuver threw the cart into a flat spin, the rear end sliding out to the left, tires spitting sand. Wisp's body rammed against the side of the driver compartment as the world went in circles.

Screaming, she mashed both feet into the brake. The buggy spun around twice more before skidding to a stop in a cloud of dust.

She kept pushing down on the brake as hard as she could, her hands locked around the wheel in a death grip. Hard breathing lasted only until she got a mouthful of dust and lapsed into choking. *He's gonna catch me!* Gasping for air with tears streaming out of her eyes, she forced herself to let off the brake and hit the gas again.

A gentler touch on the pedal nudged the buggy forward. She swerved back onto the road, stretching tall in the seat so she could see. The walls around the driver's chair were taller than the other buggy she'd been in with Falo. This one had more room as well, as the whole machine appeared larger. It also had four fat, knobby wheels all the same size instead of giant rear tires and narrow front ones—probably why her spinout had been a spinout and not a flip.

On paving, the knobby tires created a droning buzz and made the whole frame vibrate. This buggy's steering had a stronger reaction than the other one, turning harder for less twist of the wheel. She tested by veering side to side until she got the feel of the handling. Eventually, her death grip on the steering wheel loosened. With confidence in her ability to drive, she relaxed her posture and allowed herself to enjoy the wind. It made sense to her now why the man had lenses over his eyes; the fast-moving air hitting her face made it difficult to see, especially when it also carried sand particles. Since she had nothing to shield her face, she drove only as fast as she could before the wind forced her eyes closed. While she didn't use even half of the buggy's power, driving still covered ground much faster than she could walk—and travel by buggy didn't make her tired.

The momentary escape offered by her enjoyment of driving faded after an hour or so to the idea that she'd run away from one of the monsters who had sent Dad to the Other Place. She scowled at nothing in particular, angry at herself for eluding him and stealing the buggy rather than getting revenge. She perked up tall and looked back to the left, at the road rushing away behind her.

It hadn't been *that* long. She could spin around and go after him.

Wisp clenched her hands around the wheel.

I'm gonna get him for you, Dad.

She lifted her foot off the gas, letting the buggy coast slower before attempting a turn.

Dad…

Her rage dissipated. Dad wouldn't want her to go to the Other Place. Not yet. Not at twelve years old. What if that man was hiding somewhere and jumped on the buggy before she could get a gun out? She'd watched the adults go after each other with swords and axes at the marauder camp. No way would she have a chance in a fight like that, especially if he caught her trapped inside the buggy. However unlikely the idea, what if he had a gun too? Alina recognized them, as did that man at Zen's, so other people out there must know about them, too. Sure, only *two* people out of everyone she'd run into knew guns, but how many people existed? Up until a week ago, she thought the Endless Forest covered the entire world. This... sandy nothingness appeared equally as vast, and who knew what lay beyond it? Her forest turned out not to be endless, so it made sense the desert didn't go on forever either. And that Neva Da tribe Falo mentioned, where he thought Dad came from—they all had guns, so maybe they traded them sometimes.

I'm not a stupid Fire Dragon. She closed her eyes for the length of a meditative exhale. *I'm not going to get angry. I got away. Going back to shoot him is stupid. I could get hurt.* With calm came the thought that the man might not have been a marauder at all. The former captives all took buggies. Having one of these things didn't make someone a marauder. *She* drove one now, and that didn't make *her* a marauder. Had she turned around to shoot that man, she might've sent a nice person to the Other Place for no reason other than anger. Maybe that man had been trying to help her after all? He didn't say the same kinds of things they had. He hadn't called her 'girlie' or claimed she belonged to him now.

Wisp shivered. Surely, that would've made Mother say something. If she'd shot a nice man, she definitely would've done bad.

She debated turning around again, only this time out of guilt for possibly taking a friendly person's buggy. Of course, that could end badly, too. If he wound up being a marauder, she could get hurt, or taken and put in a cage. Even if he had been intending to help her, he'd probably be angry with her for taking the buggy, and wouldn't be so nice anymore.

"Bleh," she muttered... and decided to keep on going.

For hours, she drove toward the mountains, holding a moderate speed while following the road, except for wherever she had to go onto dirt to avoid the ruins of ancient cars or collapsed poles. As she drove, she tried to make sense of what Falo had said about him. Dad *did* once tell her about his journey, how he and Mother had traveled from a faraway place because those who lived there did not approve of the two of them being together. Mother had been promised to another man she had no feelings for, but she had fallen in love with Dad.

He'd told her the other people would have killed him for breaking the custom, so they had snuck away in the night.

When the sun started to set, the mountains (and forest) had gotten noticeably closer. She stopped only once it had become too dark to see. After pushing the button to make the engine go silent, she climbed out for a stretch, relieved herself, and finished off the canteen she'd been sipping on all day.

Hoping to find food, she went around back, but this buggy didn't have the same tall, triangular storage tent as the others. Four metal boxes with leather straps holding lids closed hung two per side in front of the rear wheels. The first one had tools, the second a bunch of machine parts she didn't recognize. In the third bin, she found four canteens, two of which were full. The last box contained kindling, and a bunch of empty plastic bottles of various sizes.

She sighed at the lack of food.

With nothing else to do, she closed the bin and curled up in the driver's pit under her blanket, shivering more from fear than at the chilly desert night.

The growls of an empty stomach sang her to sleep.

For€st Wisp
~32~

Soon after she resumed driving the next morning, the terrain became hilly. Within an hour, tall rock walls rose up on either side of the road. The air cooled with each passing minute, losing the dryness she'd never quite gotten used to.

The buggy engine groaned and labored on a steep grade. A few turns later, trees came into view, a dense spread of greenery up ahead. Wisp cheered and let go of the wheel to thrust both hands into the air. Eager to get home, she pushed the gas down more, picking up speed and grinning at the hope of being with Mother again.

She hit a rightward turn a bit fast, screeching tires as the buggy started to slide out of the curve. Wisp stomped on the brake too hard; the wheels locked, and her buggy went into a spin. She screamed and tried to push the brake even harder in an effort to stop sliding, but it didn't help.

The buggy skidded off the road, bouncing up onto a mulch-covered incline, covering her with leaves and vines. It took her a few seconds to process that she'd stopped moving, and the buggy faced back the way she'd come from.

Wisp stared platter-eyed at the road, breathing hard. The hammering noise of her heart in her ears drowned out the idling engine. She did *not* like how it felt to be in a buggy spinning around and around like that.

"This thing is scary."

A few minutes of silence later, she peered down at her feet, still curled over the brake pedal, both legs pushing with all her strength. She exhaled and relaxed enough to release the brake pedal, then cranked the wheel all the way to the left before gingerly poking the gas with one toe. A gunshot like *bang* went off behind her, but the buggy rolled around in a turn, went across the road, and up the hill on the other side, tilting sideways at a worrisome angle. She stomped the brake, spun the wheel the other way, and eased the buggy back onto the road.

"Phew… I don't really like driving. Traveling somewhere isn't supposed to be dangerous!"

The road kept a mild incline for almost an hour before she once again found herself surrounded by trees. Small at first, they increased in size and number over the next few minutes. By the time she could no longer see any sign of desert behind her, she once again felt like she'd returned to the Endless Forest.

Wisp kept her speed down much slower than she'd been going before, since the road here curved back and forth in a meandering route that barely let her go straight for a full minute before another turn came up.

With a sputter from the engine, the buggy shook.

"What was that?"

Seconds later, the engine sputtered again—and conked out.

The buggy lurched as if she'd stepped on the brake, a labored, mechanical groan coming from the engine. It didn't take long before she'd rolled to a halt.

"It broke?" She pushed the start button.

Clicking and a belabored *rurr-rurr-rurr* noise emanated from somewhere behind her for as long as she held the button down, but it didn't start.

"What's wrong?" She ducked her head to examine the front panel. Other than plain steel, and the hole through which the steering wheel post came, she didn't find anything else to push or twist.

The same labored whirring rose up again behind her, coming from the engine.

She perked up and looked over her shoulder at the metal shell of the buggy, mostly flat to the back end except for a pair of pipes sticking out. "Why is it making that noise?"

Whirring increased in pitch.

A tree branch went by.

She snapped her head around to face forward and stared at the road, which moved *away* from her.

"I'm going backward! It's not supposed to do that! These things don't have a backward!"

A bank of trees came up fast behind her. Wisp stomped on the brake and flew back against the chair. All four wheels squeaked, but the buggy stopped.

"Whew…" She slouched with relief.

After allowing a moment to calm down, she started to climb out of the apparently useless buggy, but it resumed rolling backward as soon as she let off the brake.

"Eep!"

She mashed her foot on the brake again.

I'm stuck! If I get up, it'll crash…

Wisp looked over her shoulder at the tree-filled ditch behind her, forward at the uphill, and once again at the trees before staring at her toes curled over the brake pedal. *I can't sit here forever.* She considered her situation. *It's like a pinecone rolling down a hill. But, pinecones don't have steering wheels.*

She tried to turn the wheel, but it didn't want to move. Grunting, she twisted harder, and it eased a bit to the left with a noticeable crunch coming from both front tires. *This is hard when it's not driving! Oh. I'm being stupid again.*

After easing the brake up a little, she again tried to spin the wheel. Once the buggy began rolling, the wheel turned easily, and she steered around in a curve. As soon as the buggy pointed straight across the road, she jammed on the brake again.

"Okay. I should be able to get out now."

She eased off the brake. The buggy more or less stayed in place, since she'd parked it sideways on the hill. Happy to be free of it, Wisp climbed out and grabbed her rifle. If the buggy should decide to go rolling off without her, she didn't care. As long as she wasn't sitting in it when it flipped into a ditch, she'd be happy.

Once more on foot, she continued climbing the hill. Within ten minutes, she located a spread of pennycress. That plant had a habit of drinking up anything bad in the area, so she checked around to make sure nothing smelled like chemicals. Confident the plant hadn't absorbed anything poisonous, and having not eaten anything for a full day, she dropped on her knees and stuffed handful after handful of pennycress into her mouth. In the midst of her feasting, she caught sight of a huge burdock plant a short ways off in the woods.

To celebrate being back in her forest, she took a long break from travel. After removing her backpack and canteen belt for comfort, she set up a fire pit then stacked rocks to hold the pot from her pack. Next, she hunted up some usable wood, and filled the pot with the canteen water from the buggy's storage compartment. She scraped the ferro rod across the file, raining sparks over the kindling. For a minute or so, she puffed and fanned the smoldering, until it grew into a proper cooking flame. Kneeling by the fire as she so often did at home, Wisp boiled burdock leaves mixed with a handful of yellowgreens and a few crickets of opportunity.

Once she'd finished eating, she lay flat on her back, legs slightly apart, hands on her stomach, and stared up past the treetops at the scraps of blue sky. Her happiness at being in the Endless Forest set off a bad thought: she didn't want to return to the desert. Not even to collect Dad. She couldn't move him anyway, and without the buggy, she really had no way at all to transport him here.

Wisp closed her eyes. *I have to bring him home. I have to go back.* She exhaled out her nose. *Mother will show me what to do.*

An unexpected nap drained a few hours from the day. She collected some wide, inedible leaves and dug a hole to make *ngh*. To ensure the fire went out completely, she dumped the boiled leaf-water on it. For the first time in days, she felt confident—out of the heat, with seven canteens of water and plenty of creeks and streams around, plus access to food. In no particular rush, she resumed walking down the road.

Now, of course, she faced two problems, one new and one old. The new problem being that she had no idea how to get to her cabin. The old problem being Tree Walkers. Having returned to the forest also put her once again within their reach.

Wisp clutched her rifle, despite knowing it couldn't hurt them. At least she had some daylight left before she *really* had to worry. Shivering from dread, she pressed on, but kept looking around for a place to take shelter despite it only being late afternoon.

In a moment of clarity, she stopped and pulled out the Mother Twig.

"Which way should I go to get home?"

The twig spun a little to the left, came back to the right, swayed left a little less, glided right, and stopped.

A second before Wisp put it away, a light breeze arose, making the twig spin around and around counterclockwise. She stood there for a while watching it sway back and forth, slower and slower. Before it could stop, another breeze set it swaying again.

"It's the wind…" Her lip quivered. *Has it always been the wind?* "Mother? If you're listening, please show me it's really you. Make it point at me."

Wisp stood statue still, the twine dangling from her finger, the stick continuing to sway back and forth—away from her.

"Mother," said Wisp in a teary voice. "Please make it point at me. Show me you're listening."

Another strong breeze set it spinning around and around, but it swayed back to point away from her.

She stared at the sharpened tip of the twig wagging back and forth. Tears welled in her eyes, not knowing why Mother had become upset with her. Before she burst into sobs, she caught herself and took a deep, calming breath.

"Mother is still tired from bringing me to Dad. She's not upset at me." She wound the twine around the twig and put it away. "I've got to find a place to hide before the Tree Walkers come out."

Canteens and pots jostled around in her backpack as she jogged. She slowed after only a moment, worrying about making so much noise, and walked the road around curve after curve.

What are the Tree Walkers going to do to me if they take me? Dad never answered that beyond saying it's too horrible to talk about. She shivered and forced the idea out of her head. No, Mother might be too tired to move the twig anymore, but she would still protect her from the Tree Walkers. She might not be warm and alive, able to hug her like Noma hugged Kit, but she *was* Mother, and she would protect her daughter no matter the cost.

A familiar red wreck came into view along the side of the road.

"The SUV!"

She ran over and placed her hands on it, grinning. Finding something she had already seen had to be a good sign. She'd at least arrived somewhere close to home. Her grin faded. She had been walking for days before finding this old thing. But… Dad taught her to use the sun to find direction if she didn't have a north box.

How would he have felt about her Mother Twig? A simple stick and twine she hoped Mother would aim for her that had possibly never reacted to anything but the breeze?

Accepting that Mother didn't move the twig would be painful, but it would also mean that she may well have spent days roaming in circles before finding the end of the woods to the desert. If that's what happened, she might not be days away from home—*if* she could somehow now manage a straight line. Of course, that would also mean that Mother either chose not to help or *couldn't* help. Or maybe she *had* helped, but in ways more magical than a stupid stick on a piece of twine?

She looked at the woods where she remembered emerging the first time she found the Expedition on the side of the road. From there, she looked up at the tallest pines in the area, memorizing them as a reference point. The sun hung overhead behind her and to the left. Considering it had to be a few hours or two until twilight, the sun would be in the west. By that, she figured the direction she had originally come from to this place would've been northwest. Going northwest now would bring her deeper into the woods *away* from the desert, so it sounded like a good direction.

After one final look around to get her bearings—she chickened out and climbed into the SUV.

Wasting three hours of daylight might be stupid, but if I've got a twelve-hour walk ahead of me, getting caught by Tree Walkers would be stupider.

She drank from one of her canteens before heading back into the woods in search of dinner. Wild asparagus made for a surprising treat, since she adored it so much. She gathered enough for dinner and carried it back to the SUV, to eat raw.

Once the light weakened, she prepared to settle in for the night, hoping to fool the Tree Walkers again by hiding inside an ancient machine. The tiny seat with all the straps tempted her, but even if the ancients had made the device to protect their small children from Tree Walkers, it wouldn't do her any good. For one thing, she couldn't fit into it, and also, it would be uncomfortable.

As she had last time, Wisp curled up in the rearmost part of the SUV, completely hidden under her blanket.

A Home of Silence

~33~

W isp awoke in the middle of the night, biting her arm to keep from screaming. Her usual nightmare had happened again. Every time she fell asleep scared, she dreamt of being chased by Tree Walkers.

She hunkered down and tried to return to sleep, but the bad water wanted out. Drinking an entire canteen right before bed had been dumb. Hoping that Tree Walker's vine-like fingers couldn't operate the SUV's handles, she climbed up front to the driver's position. Hanging herself out the door so she could leap inside at the first sign of moving plants, she let the bad water fall to the road as fast as she could be rid of it.

For the next few hours, she huddled under the blanket, but didn't get close to sleeping.

At the first sign of daylight, she gathered her things and climbed down out of the SUV. The early morning air carried a chill despite the summer month. Cold paving under her feet served as another reminder of *not* being in the desert, and made her smile. A quick spin around to check landmarks reaffirmed her confidence, and she hurried off into the woods.

Once she left road behind and her toes sank into soft soil with each step, she widened her stride, taking advantage of the less punishing terrain. Instinct took over and she stepped around roots with nary a conscious thought, too focused on keeping track of direction. Along the way, she swiped the occasional handful of creeping Oregon grapes or wild strawberries, munching without stopping.

Several hours later when she began to doubt her heading, she halted by a tree, shrugged off the rifle and backpack, and climbed for an elevated look around. After going up three stories off the ground, she spotted a cliff ridge studded with rocks. Instant recognition hit her.

That's where I lost the tracks!

She made her way back to the ground, gathered her things, and jogged in that direction. Within minutes, she emerged in a clearing and scaled a steep hillside up to the ridge where the marauder buggy's tire marks had disappeared due to the hard soil. She squatted at the edge, thinking about how Zen thought the buggy hadn't dug these ruts from driving there once. They'd been worn into the earth from many long-ago cars using this stretch as a road. Still, losing that trail had been such a painful moment, it all came flooding back to her in a wave of images and sorrow, but she did not cry.

Her jaw clenched in determination.

The buggy had followed a path through the forest wide enough for it to navigate among the trees. She put the early morning sun high and to her back, and headed off due west, following the dirt ruts that had originally led her away from home. Elation came with full body shaking. She jumped up and down out of pure joy at knowing where she was. When she had first followed this trail, she'd walked all day, spent the night under a tree, and reached the end a couple hours into the next morning. Tomorrow, she would be home. Then again, she had been hesitant and somewhat slow on the initial journey, as leaving home had been terrifying.

Wisp leaned into her stride, hurrying along at the edge between walking and jogging. She followed the swerving trail for hours, refusing to stop. She allowed a short break when she found a creek, enjoying fresh, cold water. There, she dumped out all her canteens and refilled four of them with the clean water that hadn't been sitting in plastic for days.

Not far from the creek, she stumbled upon a huge patch of chanterelles growing around a dead tree, which played host to a sizable grub colony. The hunger that had been gnawing at her all day proved too insistent to ignore. She built a fire and cooked up a batch of grub-on-a-stick with pan-fried mushrooms, making enough to have a dinner portion later.

Perhaps she ate a little too much. Her stomach hurt soon after she resumed walking, but she didn't care. It had been a while since she could eat herself full. Dad might've scolded her for being wasteful, but she had a week of barely eating to make up for.

Her hopes of completing the trip in a single day died hours later when twilight arrived and she still faced a long swath of trail.

"Poop." She sighed. "It's all right. I'll be home early tomorrow. I'd better get out of sight before the Tree Walkers wake up."

She set her backpack by the base of a tree and used her knife to dig out a shallow area in which she could lay down and not be so far above ground level her 'person shape' would be obvious. After arranging the blanket over that, she dusted it with handfuls of duff so it blended in with the forest floor. Satisfied at her camouflage, she covered her backpack and rifle with more leaves, vines, and pine needle castoffs, and lay down. Careful not to displace her camouflage, she eased herself under the blanket and pulled it up over her head.

Despite feeling invisible, Wisp barely slept a wink. Especially when the snaps and cracks of things moving around the woods at night began.

Mother protect me. Please, Mother, protect me.

She lay awake, too frightened to sleep for what felt like hours. Her eyes snapped open when the crunching of a creature drawing close became loud. In the dark, with a leaf-covered blanket over her face, she couldn't see a thing, but pictured a monster walking within ten feet of her. Crackling and shuffling, like a mass of leaves dragging along the ground, edged by at an agonizing pace. She stopped breathing, playing dead. An owl cooed in the distance, answered seconds later by another bird she didn't recognize, then a series of whistles and clicks from a different direction. It *had* to be Tree Walkers—people didn't rustle like that. Another *coo-aww* broke the silence; some giant bird must've been perched in the tree almost right above her, but something told her the Tree Walkers made those sounds. They didn't talk like humans.

She nearly lost control of her bad water.

Mother. Dad. Please help me.

A nearby *crunch* accompanied the blanket tightening across her feet. Something put weight down on the far corner. Wisp vomited a little in the back of her throat, but refused to cough. She refused to breathe.

At a more distant owl hoot, the Tree Walker nearest her moved away, and the tension on the blanket let up. Wisp swallowed the bile in her throat and stifled a grub-flavored belch. The crunching, dragging mass of Tree Walkers grew quieter and quieter, until the susurrus of the forest filled in behind them.

She listened to the insects and birds, too petrified to move, managing to breathe in and out her nose without making a sound.

Mother was with me. She swallowed hard. *She had to have been.*

Wisp startled awake. Sunlight filtered through the fibers of the blanket covering her face. She didn't remember falling asleep, only staring at darkness, too frightened to move. Exhaustion had eventually pulled her under.

"Ugh."

She started to close her eyes again, drained from a restless night, but changed her mind and sat up. The blanket slid off her face and gathered in her lap amid a rainfall of forest debris. Confident she had made much better time yesterday, she expected to arrive home in only an hour or two. Sleep could wait until she had her Haven around her once again. That hope gave her the energy to shake off the weariness of getting so little rest. She shook the dirt and duff off the blanket, folded it, and packed it before finding a spot to let out the bad water. Her eagerness to get home allowed her to skip breakfast, and she drank from one of the canteens while walking.

Within an hour, she reached familiar ground. Again, she shivered with joy.

"Mother!" shouted Wisp. "I'm here!"

Mother, I'm here, echoed back to her twice from the trees.

Giddy, she cupped her hands around her mouth and shouted, "Mother!" again, as loud as she could, and listened to herself echo back three times.

Wisp broke into a sprint, covering the last hundred or so yards of dirt road before skidding to a stop at the place where they ended. From here, a bit of her cabin's roof peeked out of the trees to her left, a hundred yards or so away down a modest hill. She spared a moment of sorrow and anger at the place where the marauders had attacked Dad.

"Mother!" shouted Wisp, her voice echoing again.

I'll bring you home, Dad. I just have to find a way.

She hurried down the hill, waving her arms for balance and nearly tripping in her haste. An unusual sight met her when she reached the bottom of the hill: a shallow dirt mound about six feet long and three feet wide that hadn't been there before. Momentarily taken by the oddity of it, she crouched nearby and poked it with a finger.

"Some kind of giant mole monster made this?" She tilted her head in confusion, tracing her fingers back and forth over the dirt. "Or a marauder?" *Dad has a shovel, but why would someone steal our shovel, dig a big hole, and fill it back up?*

She swung the rifle off her shoulder and brought it to bear on the cabin. If someone tried to steal her home, she'd… try not to shoot them. *Only if they're going to hurt me.*

Wisp stalked around the corner of the cabin, aiming, but found no one. Aside from the strange mound, and the front door being wide open, everything else looked the same as she remembered.

Drat! I forgot the opener for the cabin door. It's with Dad. She sighed. *At least I can still lock it when I'm inside.*

She leaned in the doorway, rifle raised, but found no one in the cabin's main room. Step by step, she eased her feet down on the floorboards to stay as silent as possible. Still, one or two creaked, making her cringe. Wisp reached out and grasped the handle of Dad's door, part of the old trailer he and Mother had first found here before they built the rest of the cabin. She pulled the door aside and re-grasped the front of the rifle.

Still unwilling to disobey Dad about going into his space, she only peeked in enough to check that no one had stolen his bed. Relieved at the room's emptiness, she closed the door again and padded over to the Mother Shrine. The scent of pinesap wafting from the door filled her with warmth and comfort.

Worried that someone might be lurking in there, she kept quiet and nudged the door aside. She started raising the rifle to aim in case of an intruder, but emitted a startled squeak at a horrifying sight: the sacred chair was empty—Mother had vanished.

"Mother!" she shouted, refilled her lungs and belted out, "Mooootheerrrr!"

No one answered.

Wisp screamed. Her voice rose to a high note of surprise and fell into anguished sobs.

She ran to the chair, dropped the rifle on the floor, and collapsed over the seat, resting her head upon her folded arms. The wood still gave off the unpleasant odor that had always pervaded this room, similar to what she'd smelled from Dad, but nowhere near as potent.

She bawled like a five-year-old until she couldn't cry any more. All her hopes, her plan to come back and ask for help, evaporated. How would she ever bring Dad home now? And, even if she *did* manage to do that, he still wouldn't be with her.

Sniffling, she sat back on her heels and wiped her eyes. "Mother? Did you come back from the Other Place to protect me last night? The Tree Walkers almost got me. One even stepped on me."

She pictured Mother sensing her peril and the dried-out body springing from the chair, rushing out the door, and falling upon the Tree Walkers in a flurry of power. But… she hadn't heard anything like that at all last night. No fighting, only bird noises and leaves crunching about.

So what had happened to Mother?

"Did you go away because Dad's with you now in the Other Place?" She sniffled. "What about me? I'm too little to be all on my own. I take it back. I'm not big enough to go on hunting trips. I want you or Dad to watch me. Why did you leave?" *The Twig stopped working… how long has Mother been away?* Again, she lapsed into sobs, burying her face in her hands.

I'm truly alone. I don't want to go back to the desert. Even if Zen was nice. I want to be here.

Her tears dried up in a little while, and she sprawled on the floor staring blankly at an empty chair stained with dark blotches.

"I've been alone for weeks, and I'm still okay." She wiped her tears on her arm. "I'll be okay. Dad taught me enough to live. I have water and food. Maybe I can harvest enough bugs and plants to get by the snow times. And I can still talk to Mother. Dad might be upset with me, but I don't know how to bring him home."

She put a hand on the chair seat.

"I will still keep your shrine, waiting for you if you come home, Mother."

An owl call broke the stillness outside.

Wisp gasped. *No… it's daylight. That has to be a real owl, not a Tree Walker.*

She leaned over and grasped the rifle from the floor, swung it around into a firing posture, and rose to her feet. *I should lock the front door.* Clutching the rifle so hard it shook, she crept to the shrine room door all of four feet away from the chair. The cabin seemed *so* still and quiet, no Dad to talk to, not even the trailer springs creaking from his moving around in his room at night. Even the sense that Mother had been here with them had gone away. The overwhelming emptiness made her feel truly alone.

It's like I don't even know this place anymore. It feels so different.

The Forest Beyond the Earth

She gazed around at the worktable, Dad's door, the bullet press, the high shelf, the fireplace, and her Haven. *It does kinda look like a marauder cage. No!* Wisp clenched her jaw. *Dad made it with love! The marauders are evil!*

Another owl hoot broke the quiet outside, far too close for comfort. *Door!*

She spun toward the front door, but before she could take a step closer, it swung open.

A mound of leaves, vines, and branches hovered at the cabin entrance. Where a face should be, the creature had only a black spot with two huge, round eyes. Behind it, the air had come alive with a standing wall of vegetation blocking off the forest.

The Tree Walkers had found her.

Wisp screamed.

Tℏe Tree Walkers
~34~

"Go away!" shouted Wisp, pointing her rifle at them.

The Tree Walker squeezed its mound-shaped body through the door, branches scraping the walls.

Stupid! Guns don't hurt them!

With a high-pitched shriek, she spun on her heel and sprinted for the Haven, tossing the rifle on the floor before scrambling on all fours past the small opening in the side. She twisted around and pulled the door shut with a loud *clank,* holding it closed with her hands a moment before remembering it had to be locked to make the magic work.

The Tree Walker approached, gliding straight at her. Four more filed in behind it, one at a time, gazing around at the room. Wisp thrust her hand under the pillow and snagged the key. Gasping for breath, tears streaming from her eyes, she fumbled to reach outside the Haven and get the key in the socket. She had only to lock the door and be safe, but such a small task had become impossible. Her hands outside the bars became vulnerable. Her key kept sliding around the metal face, not finding the keyhole.

She looked up at the approaching Tree Walker, so close she could almost feel the longing radiating from the creature's great, round eyes. Oddly, it appeared to be clutching a bow in its vines. Two of the others had spears caught up in their branches.

The key finally slid in place. She twisted it locked not a full second before the closest walker's vines reached for the bars.

She recoiled back against the innermost bars, clutching the key to her chin. "You can't get me in here! My Haven is magic! Tree Walkers can't touch it!"

The nearest Tree Walker stared at her in silence, almost stunned.

Her Haven surrounded her with the safety of Dad's love made into steel bars. Once again within her safe place, the sense of solace that came with it broke the fangs of her panic. Nothing could hurt her in there, not even *these* creatures. She shivered, staring over her knees at the group of Tree Walkers shambling closer. No longer terrified beyond the ability to think, she found herself unable to look away from the manifestation of her greatest fear. Indeed, the sight of Tree Walkers so close fascinated her.

Each creature appeared to move upon two distinct legs made of leaves, similar in shape to those of a person, hidden somewhere within their leafy mound bodies. She gasped at the sight of boots poking out from beneath the curtain of leaves and branches outside her Haven. A horrible thought formed in her head: this creature had once been a person before the vines grew into their body.

"D-did you used to be p-people before the trees took you? Is t-that what happens when the Tree Walkers take someone?"

The closest creature shrank down to about half its height, rustling and crackling, then leaned closer to the Haven. Wisp flinched away from the inhuman black face drifting toward her with its soulless silvery eyes. A pod of vines unwrapped from the bow, which it placed on the floor. Paralyzed, Wisp gazed in horror as the same extension of roots wrapped itself around the barred door. She twisted her feet in, trying to get even one more inch away from the monster.

Metal rattled as the Tree Walker tested the Haven's door.

Wisp shivered, but as she stared at the roots encircling the bars, her brain latched onto the shape of a five-fingered dark grey hand beneath them. It almost appeared made of… fabric.

The Tree Walker released the bars and reached up toward its black, featureless face.

"Don't!" yelled Wisp, raising her arms crossed in front of her. "I don't wanna be a Tree Walker! Please don't take me!"

The creature's root hand closed around the side and pulled, peeling its face down and away from the rest of its body. Too stunned by watching a creature rip its own skin off, Wisp couldn't do anything but gawk. The torn-off piece of Tree Walker lowered away from the upper part of the mound, revealing the face of a pale human woman, staring at her with red-ringed eyes of bright blue. Tears streamed down her cheeks; she looked too grief-stricken to speak.

"Were you a person before the monsters took you?" asked Wisp in a small voice.

The creature kept staring at her.

After a moment, it spoke in a halting half-whisper, "Kaya?"

Mirror
~35~

Wisp huddled tighter into herself, trying to hide behind her knees.

"Kaya," said the Tree Walker, in a voice eerily close to human.

"Hello... I'm Wisp. Please don't take me away."

"What do you mean?" asked the woman-thing.

Wisp clamped her hands together tight around the key, squishing them into her chin. "Dad told me you would take me away forever, but you can't get me in here. This is the Haven. It stops Tree Walkers with magic."

The woman-thing covered her mouth with one hand. Silent tears leaked from her eyes.

Another somewhat larger creature—one of the spear carriers—advanced up behind the half-woman that had ripped its face off. It also shrank in height, and extended an arm-shaped collection of leaves to grip the first one's... shoulder.

"Amazing," said a muffled, male voice from the spear-carrier.

Wisp glanced back and forth between the beautiful human face and the blank, black nothing of the second monster. *They can talk?* Her voice leaked out, barely over a whisper. "Does it hurt?"

"Does what hurt?" asked the woman-thing.

Wisp pressed herself against the bars at her back, but couldn't get any deeper into the Haven. "Being a Tree Walker."

"I'm a person. Like you." The woman-thing grasped the barred door again. "We're all people. I heard you calling for me, and we came running as fast as we could."

One by one, the other Tree Walkers peeled away their black faces with the enormous eyes. The one next to the woman had short black hair and the visage of a human man. Two men, one pale, one with skin as dark as the forest floor, and a woman stood behind them, all with sad expressions. Wisp's fear gave way to confusion, then curiosity at the sight of the dark skinned man.

"This is Navas," said the nearest woman, indicating the man beside her. "The others are Ionna, Lanos, and Marr."

At the word 'Marr,' the dark man nodded in greeting.

Wisp shifted her gaze back to the yellow-haired woman.

"My name is Eden." She reached up and pulled back a hood covered in leaves, exposing blonde hair. "Kaya, I'm your mother."

What! No! The Tree Walkers are trying to trick me. Anger sprang up inside her, devouring fear. She kicked at the bars. "No! Mother's gone! She was in the shrine, and she's not there anymore. She watched over us…"

"The woman who was in that room has been dead for a long time. She was not your mother." Eden reached in past the bars, offering her hand.

Wisp screamed; her feet slipped over the bedding in a futile effort to push her away while her back already squished against the bars. "No! Don't take me! Dad said you can't get me in the Haven. The magic is supposed to keep Tree Walkers out."

"Kaya," said Eden in a soothing tone. "If the magic can keep Tree Walkers out, and it does not stop my hand, what does that mean to you?"

Wisp stopped scrambling and sat motionless, staring at the hand reaching toward her.

"It is a glove, Kaya. A glove with camouflage so we can hide in the forest." The woman retracted her arm from the Haven. Another vine-covered limb emerged from under the mound of leaves and tugged at the roots on the first projection. Vegetation and fabric slipped away, exposing a pale human hand. She held her palm up, fingers splayed. "See. I'm a person like you, wearing something that helps me hide."

"This poor child," said Ionna. "What she must have been put through."

"That man kept her in a *cage*," said Marr. "Death magic or not, I say we show him justice."

The other two men nodded.

Wisp stared down at her feet, half hidden in the rumpled folds of her plush red sleep bag. Her voice sounded far away and quiet, as if it came from someone else. "It's not a cage. It's a Haven."

Navas squeezed Eden's shoulder. "He's trained her to feel safe in there. Probably so she wouldn't run away in the night when he wasn't watching her, and come home."

"She doesn't know any home but this." Lanos, a man much younger than Dad, with long, brown hair, sighed. "She was so small when he took her."

"Took me?" asked Wisp.

"Kaya." Eden reached her arm in again. "Days ago, you took a chicken from a place behind a green wall. Do you remember that?"

She bit her lip and nodded. "Yes." A second later, her eyes shot open wide. "You were there!"

"I was. We tried to find you, but… I'm sorry. I'm *so, so* sorry for not being able to find you and bring you home."

"This is my home." Wisp's voice faltered. *Isn't it?*

The woman reached into the Haven again. "Kaya, you are my daughter."

Her eyebrows knit together. "Why do you keep calling me 'Kaya?' My name is Wisp."

"Are you sure this is her?" asked Lanos. "It has been nine years. What are the odds she's still even alive?"

Eden bowed her head. "I *know* this is my daughter. I can feel it."

"*Look* at her, man." Navas gestured at Wisp.

"I…" Wisp stared into Eden's deep blue eyes. The woman's face looked as pale as Eden had been before her trip to the desert. She thought of Falo accusing Dad of not really being her father because he looked so different from her. What did looks have to do with being Dad? Kit's joyful wail as he leapt into his mother's arms replayed in her mind, along with the nasty thoughts she'd had about him for still having a *living* mother. A fat tear dripped from her cheek and ran down her shin. Dare she hope this creature told the truth? Would Mother be angry with her for doubting? "How… do I know you're not trying to trick me?"

Seeing Wisp so close to tears got Eden crying. "Please come out of there. I promise we will never hurt you."

Wisp stared at the outstretched hand invading her Haven. How happy would it make her if this woman told the truth, if she still had a real mother? But that would mean *Dad* (and not Tree Walkers) had tricked her. Hope at this chance crashed into guilt at betraying Mother and heartsickness at the idea so much might have been lies. She reached up, but hesitated.

"Come on, sweetie," said Navas. "Children don't belong inside cages."

The words of the people she'd freed from the marauders haunted her. Only bad people put other people in cages. Havens *were* cages. Did she have a mother who wasn't a dried-out body?

Wisp's hand trembled. She had seen this same woman at the settlement, without all the leaves. Could it be that Tree Walkers didn't really exist? Or maybe these people dressed up like them to be scary. Even if this woman lied, Dad wouldn't want her to be alone. Not at twelve.

One final moment of hesitation passed, and Wisp took hold of the woman's hand, the key to the Haven pressed between their palms.

Eden's fingers clamped around hers; tears ran free. "I've missed you so much. I never gave up trying to find you."

She started crying as well. "Are... are you really my mother?"

Navas nudged Even. "Get her out of there."

Wisp didn't protest as Eden pulled her hand back with the key. The tiny bit of metal snapped into the lock with a *click*, and the faint *creak* of the door swinging open became the loudest sound in the world. Her worst nightmare unfolded before her eyes. Tree Walkers inside the cabin, and her Haven breached.

No...

My cage open.

Sniveling, Wisp crawled forward. Eden grabbed her into a desperate, tight embrace, sitting on the floor and sobbing. She gingerly reached up and wrapped her arms around the woman's leafy body. Beneath layers of vines, branches, and fabric, radiated the warmth of a living person.

Numb, Wisp stared into nowhere, unsure if she should allow herself to believe.

"Hey, kid," said Navas. "You look confused."

Wisp peered up at him.

"There's no doubt in my mind," said Marr. "Use a signal mirror."

"Good idea." Navas's vine-covered body shifted about, and a hand popped out holding a bright silver rectangle. "Hon, turn around. Put your faces together."

Eden shifted her about, seated in her lap, and rested her chin on Wisp's shoulder, so their cheeks touched. Navas held the device up in front of them.

In a little two-by-three inch space, a pair of faces stared back at Wisp. One small, one large, both with bright blonde hair and blue eyes. They had the same nose, and their lips had the same shape. Except for some faint lines around Eden's eyes, they appeared to be the same person in two different sizes.

"What is that?" Wisp pointed at the device. "Who are those people?"

"That's a mirror," said Navas. "Do you know what that means?"

Wisp's breath caught in her throat. "Yeah" emerged as a teary whine. She'd read about mirrors in her books; characters who stared at one always did so in order to see themselves. In that instant, she understood she gazed upon her own face for the first time... and the woman looked *just* like her.

The smaller face, her face, also looked like the reflection she'd seen in the water she mistook for a water spirit. Falo told her a child was supposed to resemble their mother or father. If this... little mirror showed the truth, her dearest wish had come true.

She reached up and touched one finger to the glass over Eden's face, whispering, "Mother."

"Yes. I'm here, baby." Eden sniffled and squeezed her.

My mother is alive!

Overwhelmed, Wisp lost the ability to speak. Like Kit, she'd crawled out of a cage into her *living* mother's arms. After a moment of mute staring, she whirled around to bury her face in Eden's shoulder.

Wisp clung to her mother tight, unable to stop bawling.

Head Sickness

~36~

E motions stormed across Wisp's heart. Joy, dread, anger, confusion, and sorrow.

Once they ceased crying on each other, Eden leaned back to look at her. "Are you really here? Am I really not dreaming this?"

"We're here, E." Marr patted her on the shoulder. "This is real."

A somber silence settled over the cabin for a few minutes.

Wisp broke the quiet with a weak voice. "Sorry for taking your dinner."

The grownups burst into laughter. Except for her mother, they split up and searched all the cabinets and shelves, with Ionna going into Dad's room. Wisp opened her mouth to yell at her for breaking the rule, but… maybe it didn't apply to a woman as it applied to a child.

"It's all right, Kaya." Eden squeezed her again.

"Why do you keep calling me that?"

Eden brushed a hand over Wisp's head, fussing with her hair. "That's the name I gave you when you were born. The man who brought you to this cabin stole you from us when you were only two years old."

"Dad told me Mother wanted a daughter more than anything in the whole world, but right after she had me, she went to the Other Place."

"We saw them when they first came to this area, almost eleven years ago," said Eden. "Our scouts made contact, and we thought them friendly. The man would come and trade with us sometimes. One day, he told us his wife had fallen ill. He wanted to buy a 'medicine,' but we do not know of such a thing. We think the woman died not long after. You were out in the yard playing with the chickens when I heard you scream." She hesitated, choking up. "I went inside for just a moment..."

"I don't remember," said Wisp, bowing her head.

Eden rocked her side to side for a little while before she regained the ability to speak. "I ran outside as fast as I could, but it wasn't fast enough. I watched that man carry my child over our fence and run into the woods."

"Some believed he took you as revenge for not providing this 'medicine' he had asked for," said Navas. "A search party went into the forest after him, but the man's horrible magic struck our people dead from afar in a flash of thunder."

"We lost five, including your father. I don't understand why, but the man you called Dad did not use his magic on me. He tied me to a tree and disappeared into the forest. The last words he ever spoke to me were, 'I shall raise her as my own and protect her, but do not follow or my magic shall be the end of your entire village.' The others who had been hurt but survived heard him say this, and when we returned home, the elders forbade us to keep looking for you, fearing that he would kill everyone."

"She didn't give up," said Marr. "Three times a week, she'd lead a team out into the woods, hunting for you. I was only twelve when you disappeared, but once I became old enough, I went with her every time."

Wisp blinked. She couldn't imagine Dad being so cruel, leaving a mother tied to a tree and forcing her to watch him steal her child... or threaten to send a whole settlement to the Other Place. "He wouldn't... He told me bullets don't hurt Tree Walkers... but you're not Tree Walkers, you're people. Bullets *would* hurt you."

"Bullets?" asked Eden.

"He didn't want me to send you to the Other Place." Wisp sniffled. "He knew you wouldn't stop looking for me, and he didn't want me to hurt my real mother."

Eden caressed her cheek, lifting her head so they made eye contact. "What is bullets?"

"Dad didn't have magic… he only said that to scare people who don't understand." Wisp drew the handgun from her hip. "This is a gun. It's a powerful weapon that even a child like me can use to send huge marauders to the Other Place."

All the grownups, except Lanos who'd gone into the Mother Shrine, gathered around.

She took the magazine out and pulled back on the slide to eject the round in the chamber, which landed on the floor. "These things are bullets." Wisp held the cartridge up. "Well, it's really the front end. The back part's a case. There's magic fire dust inside. It burns real fast, and it makes the bullet go flying *way* fast. Kinda like throwing a rock, but throwing it so hard it goes all the way through someone."

They gasped in awe.

"A relic of the ancients." Marr pointed at the pistol. "I have seen such a thing once before, but could not figure out what it was for or how to make it work."

"You… have used this magic?" Eden coughed. "I mean… bullets?"

"Yes. But only on monsters who tried to hurt me."

Eden clutched Wisp's hands around the gun. "You are much too young to take life, Kaya. Such a thing as this does not belong with you."

"Dad showed me how to use it to protect myself. He didn't want to lose me."

Navas scowled. "He would've had her shoot her own people, so he could keep holding her prisoner."

"No!" Wisp shook her head. "He told me bullets don't hurt Tree Walkers."

Eden bowed her head.

"The elders will want this magic for our defense," said Ionna.

Wisp pointed at the books on Dad's shelf. "Some of those books explain how it works."

Navas pulled one off the shelf and held it to his ear. "It is not speaking."

She laughed. "No… they don't talk, you read them."

"Read?" asked Eden.

The other grownups all looked at her in bewilderment.

"Wait. You can't read? But you're *grownups!*"

"How does it work?" Lanos picked a book off the shelf by her Haven.

"You look at the words and they become pictures and stuff inside your head," said Wisp.

"So you just stare at this thing and it gives you knowledge?" asked Lanos.

Wisp nodded.

Lanos held the book up and peered at it. After a minute, he glanced at her. "It's not doing anything."

"No, silly. You have to open it and read the *words*, not look at the outside." Wisp made an 'open the book' gesture.

He fumbled with it since he had the spine facing him.

"Turn it over. And it's upside down, too," said Wisp, frowning.

Lanos flipped the book over and opened it down the middle. "There are marks inside."

"Those are words."

"I'm not getting any dreams from this." Lanos closed it after a few seconds.

She stood and padded over to him, tugging on the book until he opened it. Finger tracing along the page, she read, "Robert couldn't let himself be late for work a second time in a month, or he'd be fired."

"You got that from these markings?" asked Eden.

"Yes!" said Wisp.

"What does that mean?" Navas tilted his head.

"Umm. A character named Robert was late to do his task, and he was worried his dad would light him on fire for being slow." Wisp couldn't believe these grownups didn't understand something so obvious.

"I would like you to show me how to get the dreams from these words," said Lanos.

"Me too." Marr smiled.

Wisp sighed. "Oh... That's going to take a while."

"Eden," said Lanos, from the Mother Shrine.

"What?" Eden twisted around to look.

Lanos held up the small gauzy garment that had been in Mother's lap.

As soon as he handed it to Eden, she lapsed into crying again. "You were wearing this when he took you."

Wisp leaned against her mother. "I'm sorry."

"It's not your fault." Eden kissed her on the head. "None of this is your fault. I should've searched wider and more often. Gone farther away from home. I—we... had to sneak out at night or we would be exiled for disobeying the elders. They feared this man would kill us all. We never realized how far away he had taken you. When I saw you days ago, right in the very spot he'd stolen you from nine years ago, I thought I was dreaming."

"The elders allowed us to go this time," said Navas. "She convinced them that if you were out on your own, you'd somehow gotten away from him and he was no longer a threat. We found this cabin a few days out, but no one was in it except for a dead woman."

"You found Mother? You saw her?" Wisp looked up at him.

"Yes. The man had kept her body right in the house… The dead belong resting in a grave."

Wisp blinked, remembering the dirt mound. "You buried her!"

They all nodded.

"The man had a head sickness to leave his dead wife in the next room," said Marr.

All the grownups cringed and made faces.

"For nine years." Lanos shivered. "That's horrible."

"I can't imagine how bad that smelled," said Ionna.

"And to put a little girl in a cage," said Navas, a bite to his words. "Crueler still to make her feel *safer* in there."

"Head sickness," said Wisp. "He loved Mother so much, when she went to the Other Place, he made a shrine for her so she could watch over us."

Navas squatted next to her. "That's what he told you? He must have treated the body with something. I've never seen a dead person that old still… umm… intact. If he loved her, he would have buried her so her spirit can rest."

"We had best return home before he realizes we have found her," said Marr.

Wisp peered at him. "He's gone to the Oth— I mean…" She bowed her head. "He's dead. I wasn't strong enough to carry him back here."

"Dead?" asked Eden.

"Yes." Wisp gazed at the floor and traced random lines in the dust with a finger. "Marauders were here in one of their buggies. I thought it was a giant bitey-bug, but it wasn't. He didn't come back inside, and I spent a whole day in the Haven waiting for him. But he still didn't come back. I couldn't get out because he kept the opener—I mean key—on that shelf way up there. I had to escape…" She stared along her arm, still pointing at the shelf, shocked at what she'd said, more shocked for understanding it to be true. "I had to escape…"

"Oh, Kaya, don't be afraid. You're safe now." Eden clamped her in another tight hug. "There are no such things as Tree Walkers. That man wanted you to be afraid of us, knowing we dress like this to go scouting."

"I had to escape," said Wisp, teetering on the verge of tears. "Daz was right… he did *take* me."

As if watching Dad die right before her eyes, Wisp collapsed in Eden's arms and sobbed.

Navas stroked her hair. "Shh, child. I believe in some strange way, that man *did* love you."

"But he had head sickness," mumbled Wisp.

She clung to her mother, her mind awash with thoughts. Dad's wife had desperately wanted a daughter, but died before the spirits brought them a baby. Grief-stricken, he had stolen Wisp into the woods as his child. Mother may or may not have ever watched her from the Other Place, and apparently, leaving a dead person sitting in a chair in the back room for nine years was wrong.

And for as long as she'd wanted a living mother, Wisp had come within inches of finding her…

"I'm sorry for taking the bird meat and running. I didn't know you were my mother!"

Eden hugged her again before pulling her to her feet. "Don't be sorry. If you hadn't done that, I don't know that I'd have ever found you. Wow, you're so big."

"Actually, she's kinda skinny," fake-whispered Navas.

Wisp stuck her tongue out at him.

Ionna patted Eden on the shoulder. "You'll never guess what I found in the trailer."

"What?" asked Eden.

Smiling, Ionna went back inside Dad's room. A moment later, she emerged carrying a bundle of leaves and vines that looked like a dead, deflated Tree Walker. "He took two of the ponchos. Had 'em in a trunk back there."

Wisp crouched to pick up the gun and magazine. She snapped the loose bullet into the mag and slid it back into the handle, leaving the chamber empty. With a sigh, she stuffed the pistol in her holster. "I wasn't allowed to go in there. Dad had rules. I had to stay close to him, or the Tree Walkers would get me. I wasn't allowed outside the Haven at night when Dad slept. And I wasn't allowed in his room."

Ionna shook the bundle of vegetation at her. "Yeah. If you saw this, you'd have figured out there ain't no such thing as Tree Walkers, an' caught him lying."

Wisp hated that the woman made sense. She hated it more that it now sounded so much like Dad didn't want her to *escape*. "He got really scared if I walked too far away. I don't think he lied. He didn't treat me mean like the marauders treated the people they took."

"Maybe you weren't the only person he lied to. After a couple years, the guy might've convinced himself that Tree Walkers existed." Navas set his hands on his hips and whistled.

"Man…" Lanos shook his head at the cage. "He had a powerful head sickness."

Mother

~37~

The people Wisp had believed to be Tree Walkers listened as she explained everything that had happened from the day the marauders took Dad until she returned here and found Mother buried.

"I guess that twig didn't really work, did it?" Wisp stared down at her feet.

"Old Adna thinks the dead talk to her in her dreams, but I've never heard of a ghost doing anything like that." Navas shook his head. "Most likely, the wind moved it."

Wisp thought about the stick pointing at the building where she found Dad, but there had been no wind there. In her mind, she saw the twig unfurl and dangle over and over again. It hadn't turned at all, merely continued pointing the same way she had been holding it.

A long, sad sigh leaked out her nose. "Mother was a lie, too. She wasn't watching me."

Eden knelt in front of Wisp so they wound up eye-to-eye, and grasped her shoulders. "Kaya, I have been roaming the woods for nine years hoping to find you. I never gave up believing you were still out there. I want you to come home with me, where you belong. Will you return home with me?"

"You're *asking* her?" Navas blinked. "You're *asking* a little girl *if* she wants to go home with you after all you've gone through to find her?"

"Yes." Eden kept staring into her eyes. "She has already been abducted once. Though she is my daughter, I do not wish to steal her from the place she considers home."

"This is her cage," said Lanos. "Not her home."

Wisp bit her lower lip. This cabin had been the only home she ever knew. Whatever had happened during the first two years of her life had fallen off into a void she could not see into. Maybe she had been so terrified or sad at being taken, she simply refused to remember that had ever been. Dad still lay dead in a garage off in the desert—or at least, the man she had called Dad. This woman looked like a grownup version of her. Dad, with his dark brown skin, black hair, and sharp nose…

"Do kids have to look like Dad or Mother, or can that be who loves and protects them?" asked Wisp.

Eden brushed her hand over Wisp's forehead. "I know of many children who call people father or mother and have no blood tie to them. Love means more than blood. But here, what that man did to you, was not done out of love. He may have thought so. He may have made you think so, but he *stole* you. That"—she gestured at the Haven—"horrible thing has *nothing* to do with love."

If what this woman said rang true, Dad would have to be 'bad,' yet Mother never spoke.

"He said that if I was a bad girl, Mother would speak and tell me I did bad. Is that true?"

Navas whistled.

"Wow." Marr sputtered. "That's about as 'not right' as 'not right' can get."

"Oh, Kaya…" Eden took her hand in both of hers. "I think he wanted to make you feel safe. That dead woman can't talk. No matter what you did, she would've never spoken. He wanted you to believe you were always good. And I'm sure you were."

"If my father told me a corpse'd get up and yell at me if I messed up, I'd have stayed my butt in my damn room," said Marr, shivering. "What a messed up thing to tell a kid."

Wisp raised and lowered her toes while blowing air out her nose. Whatever he had been, Dad had gone to the Other Place, leaving her alone. She'd spent so much time daydreaming about what it would be like to have a mother who could talk to her, hold her hand, laugh, smile, and hadn't... died. Her books sometimes mentioned burying the dead, but Dad had always told her the ancients had strange customs, and they didn't respect their loved ones, just put them in the ground like poop. These people thought it a head sickness to keep Mother in the house after she'd died.

Old memories slipped out of the cracks forming in her mind. As a small child, she'd been terrified of Mother. She couldn't recall the moment she'd gone from frightened of a dried-out body to talking to her like a person she adored.

Maybe I have head sickness, too.

"Dad used to make me stay in the Haven a lot. When I got older, he said it was safe for me to be out of it more, but only during the day. He said he was protecting me, but I think you're right. He wasn't afraid the Tree Walkers would take me. He didn't want me to run away."

Eden teared up, nodding.

"Are you really my mother?"

"Yes, Kaya. I feel it inside my bones."

"No doubt about it," said Navas. "The two of you look so much alike."

"No doubt." Marr clapped. "Not even a little."

"Yes." Wisp picked her gaze up off the floor and smiled at her mother. "I want to stay with you. I don't want to be alone."

Eden let out a joyous cry, and wrapped her in a hug.

"Mother?"

"Yes, baby?"

"Can head sickness get better?"

Eden leaned back to peer at her. "Why?"

"I think maybe I have it, too." She managed a weak smile. "I was talking to a dead person."

Navas raised both eyebrows. "Did the dead person ever answer you?"

Wisp shook her head.

"Then you're fine. Not sick." Navas glanced around the room. "We should pack anything of use."

While the grownups proceeded to gather her former life into piles in the middle of the room, Wisp hovered by her mother's side, staring at the Haven. Something turned over in her gut, making her lean away from the... cage.

282

The box of steel bars no longer seemed warm and inviting. She found it cold and frightening.

Wisp shied away from it and buried her face in the leaves of her mother's poncho.

Epilogue: A New Haven
~38~

t had taken them three days to make the trip back to the settlement with the giant green fence around it. They knew as much or more about the plants as she did, though none could read so much as two words. These people considered the plants and insects she had been eating almost every day of her life to be for emergency survival. Back home, they farmed different ones like corn, potatoes, carrots, beans, and a whole bunch of other vegetables she'd never heard of.

When they'd arrived at the settlement, going in the main gate, the sheer size of it kept her jaw hanging open and her voice hiding in shock. Huge farm plots and giant cabins stretched out as far as she could see to the wall, alive with people as well as animals. The elders, amazed that Eden had found her missing daughter, welcomed her with open arms. On the day following her arrival, a great crowd gathered to celebrate. More people than she had ever seen in one place approached to tell her how happy they were that she had been found alive and unhurt. She lost track after two hundred, but did count fifty-six other children.

With so many grownups all telling her the same thing—that she had been taken away from this place as a tiny child, she abandoned any lingering doubt.

The town held a great feast beginning early in the afternoon of the third day following her arrival, and continuing until dark. During the festivities, Wisp learned about dancing, as well as a few 'games' the other children insisted she play.

The adults hadn't taken the rifle or pistol away from her during their walk home, though once they arrived, her mother insisted the weapons stay in a closet—except for when the town elders requested she explain how they worked. She didn't fire them, since she did not want to waste any bullets, but taught the elders (and her mother) about guns. When she explained that she had a limited supply of ammo, and how few shots she had left, the elders became dismayed at the idea the threat to the whole town had been a lie. An argument began among the old people whether to allow her to keep them or if such powerful relics should belong to the people as a whole.

Wisp couldn't decide how she felt about that. After carrying them for weeks, and using them several times to protect herself, she didn't want to part with them. But on the other hand, they reminded her of the man who claimed to be Dad, and also of shooting people. Because of that, she wouldn't mind never seeing them again. The old people decided they would vote on it later. She would talk it over with her mother, but wouldn't really care one way or the other if the elders took the guns or let her keep them.

Surprisingly, her mother didn't get too upset with the elders once they realized they had believed a lie that Dad could wipe out the whole settlement. After seeing the sheer number of people here, the fifty or so bullets Dad kept on hand at any one time wouldn't have been near enough to do that. Once the elders left, and her mother repeated her rule that the guns had to stay in the closet, she told her about how Dad always took them apart and cleaned them with oil. Unfortunately, he had never shown her how to do that, but the knowledge had to be in one of the books he'd kept in his trailer.

She couldn't quite figure out how to feel about Dad. What had once been total adoring love melted down into an ever-shifting mixture of anger, sadness, and regret. Leaving him out in the desert didn't feel like the right thing to do, but she couldn't bring herself to even ask her real mother to march all the way out there to do something nice for the man who'd made the past nine years of her life so miserable. Perhaps things *did* happen for a reason, and his not having a proper shrine somehow became his atonement.

Wisp had her own room in a new cabin many times the size of the one in which she had spent the past nine years. The room contained a real bed, plenty of shelves for her books, a window that peered out over the farm fields behind the house, and even a closet in which she kept new clothes. Several of the villagers had given her gifts of dresses, sandals, and even fur-lined boots for later when it got cold. In this new home, she wouldn't be kept inside during the winter.

Despite her big, comfortable bed, she had trouble sleeping. Part of it came from excitement: everything about this settlement was so new, she couldn't stop thinking about what she wanted to do the next day. Also, the lack of bars around her still made her nervous at night despite her knowing the cage had been evil. The fourth time sleeping in her new bed, a nightmare woke her screaming, only this time, the Tree Walkers had Dad's face on them, trying to steal her away from her real mother.

However, something amazing happened. Her mother ran in to check on her (which, Dad had always done as well), but once she had calmed down, she slept the rest of the night in her mother's bed, free of bad dreams. With each passing day, and her *real* mother's help, she gradually stopped worrying that monsters would grab her in the dark.

Only her mother called her 'Kaya.' To everyone else, she continued to introduce herself as Wisp—especially to her new circle of friends. Being around other children had been the single strangest part of this new life. But, after settling in with a group of eight kids all around her age (give or take a year or two), she had a strong feeling her new friends would be one of the best parts.

The settlement also had something they called 'school,' but even the old wise woman who spent a few hours every day teaching the kids about farming, weather, counting, cooking, and so on didn't know how to read. Word spread from the initial group that had found her about the 'books,' and she wound up becoming the village's 'reading teacher,' despite being half the age of most of her students.

In addition to reading for fun, the elders also wanted her to 'translate the knowing' out of the boring books that explained things like how the bullet machine, motors, electricity, and other things worked. Of course, it wouldn't do them any good since they didn't have many supplies, only what they had taken from the cabin in the hills.

Navas turned out to be something of a new Dad. Her mother explained that her father by blood had been the first one killed trying to get her back. Only a few months ago, Eden had become close to Navas, having spent many years too focused on finding her to care about anything else. The two of them loved each other like Wisp imagined Dad had loved Mother—only without the head sickness.

The village became her home.

Wisp had a real, live mother, friends around her age, and a much bigger Haven.

But her new Haven didn't have any bars. It didn't have to defend her from the Tree Walkers.

The Tree Walkers now protected her.

fin

Acknowledgements

Thank you for reading The Forest Beyond the Earth! Reviews are the lifeblood of independent and small press authors. To all who take the time to leave an honest review, you have my utmost thanks and gratitude.

ADDITIONAL THANKS TO:

Merethe Najjar for proofreading.
Amalia Chitulescu for the beautiful cover.
Ricky Gunawan for the interior artwork. http://ricky-gunawan.daportfolio.com/

About the Author

Originally from South Amboy NJ, Matthew has been creating science fiction and fantasy worlds for most of his reasoning life. Since 1996, he has developed the "Divergent Fates" world, in which *Division Zero, Virtual Immortality, The Awakened Series, The Harmony Paradox, and the Daughter of Mars series* take place. Along with being an editor at Curiosity Quills press, he has worked in IT and technical support.

Matthew is an avid gamer, a recovered WoW addict, Gamemaster for two custom RPG systems, and a fan of anime, British humour, and intellectual science fiction that questions the nature of reality, life, and what happens after it.

He is also fond of cats.

Links

Please visit me on the web at:

http://www.matthewcoxbooks.com/wordpress/

Also, for news, updates, and exclusives, join my readers group on Facebook:

https://www.facebook.com/groups/137705036768984/

Find me on Twitter: @mscox_fiction

For contact or inquiries regarding this novel, please email at: mcox2112@gmail.com

Other books by Matthew S. Cox

MIDDLE GRADE

- Tales of Widowswood series (fantasy)
  - Emma and the Banderwigh
  - Emma and the Silk Thieves
  - Emma and the Silverbell Faeries
  - Emma and the Elixir of Madness (coming soon)
  - Emma and the Weeping Spirit (coming soon)
- Citadel: The Concordant Sequence (coming soon)
- The Cursed Codex (LitRPG – Fantasy/contemporary)
- The Menagerie of Jenkins Bailey (contemporary fantasy – with J.R. Rain)

YOUNG ADULT

- Caller 107 (contemporary paranormal – Note: strong language)
- The Summer the World Ended (nuclear apocalyptic/family drama/contemporary)
- Nine Candles of Deepest Black (witchcraft horror)
- The Eldritch Heart (fantasy / LGBT)
- The Forest Beyond the Earth

ADULT

- Division Zero series
  - Division Zero
  - Lex De Mortuis
  - Thrall
  - Guardian
- The Awakened series
  - Prophet of the Badlands
  - Archon's Queen
  - Grey Ronin
  - Daughter of Ash
  - Zero Rogue
  - Angel Descended (coming soon)
- Daughter of Mars series
  - The Hand of Raziel
  - Araphel
  - Ghost Black
- Virtual Immortality
- The Harmony Paradox
- Divergent Fates Anthology
- The Roadhouse Chronicles Series (post nuclear apoc/zombie)
  - One More Run

- o The Redeemed
- o Dead Man's Number (coming soon)
- Faded Skies series (post-ww3 / sci fi)
  - o Heir Ascendant
  - o Ascendant Revolution (Coming soon)
- Chiaroscuro: The Mouse and the Candle (vampire)
- Temporal Armistice Series (urban fantasy)
  - o Nascent Shadow
  - o The Shadow Collector
- Wayfarer: AV494 (sci fi horror)
- Operation: Chimera (sci fi – with Tony Healey)
- The Dysfunctional Conspiracy (nonfiction memoir – with Christopher Veltmann)
- Winter Solstice series (urban fantasy – with J.R. Rain)
  - o Convergence
  - o Containment
- Alexis Silver series (urban fantasy – with J.R. Rain)
  - o Silver Light
- Samantha Moon Origins series (urban fantasy – with J.R. Rain)
  - o New Moon Rising
  - o Moon Mourning
- Maddy Wimsey series (detective / witchcraft – with J.R. Rain)
  - o The Devil's Eye
  - o The Drifting Gloom (coming soon)
- The Far Side of Promise (anthology)
- Axillon99 (LitRPG – with J.R. Rain)

CPSIA information can be obtained
at www.ICGtesting.com
Printed in the USA
BVHW031922200120
569986BV00002B/167